Wolf Constellation

Also by Lauren Small

Choke Creek

WOLF CONSTELLATION

a novel

Lauren Small

Bridle Path
Press

Bridle Path Press, LLC
8419 Stevenson Road
Baltimore, MD 21208

www.bridlepathpress.com

Direct orders to the above address.

Printed in the United States of America.
First Edition.
ISBN: 978-1-7321630-2-7

Library of Congress Control Number: 2018906859

Book Design by Elizabeth Ryan Cole
Cover photos from Adobe Stock by Viktar Malyshchyts, Ryan, prostooleh

To Don

What then is she?

–Dr. Adolf Meyer, The Phipps Psychiatric Clinic

All men are the abode of wandering souls.

–Martin Buber on the Baal Shem

One

∴

*T*he men have captured a wolf.

It's a she-wolf. She must have just birthed a litter of pups. The agha takes note of her ragged teats. She's also starving. Her muzzle's thin and pinched, her belly shrunken, her rib bones emerging beneath mangy fur. She would have made easy prey, drawn to last night's cook fire, the stink of the sheep the men stole then butchered drifting through the air, gutted offal staining the ground.

The wolf star, the Turkish commander thinks all at once. It had been exceptionally bright last night in the late spring sky, a flickering orb of light in the retreating heavens. *Al-Dhib*, the Arabs call it. *Lupus* to the ancients. *Bozkurt* to the Turks. We went to battle with a wolf's head on our standards. So his father once said. The star is still visible in the sky, growing paler with each breath he takes. An omen? He rolls his first cigarette of the day.

The soldiers have put the wolf in a rectangular pit, four paces around, two this way, two that. This distance she travels again and again, testing, probing, sensing. She wants to escape, but the men have done their job well, and the pit is too deep. A mottled blackish tongue slips sideways between her teeth as she pants. She draws her head between her shoulders and gazes upwards, studying the men with

3

yellow eyes, an even, calculating stare. No sign of anger or fear, not even when one of the soldiers prods her with a stick smoldering from the fire. She simply dances nimbly away, her back sparking, while the others hoot with laughter, the burnt odor of singed fur invading the dawn.

Most certainly an omen, the agha thinks, lighting his cigarette. The star and the wolf, too. But for what?

At his side his adjunct appears with coffee in a porcelain cup. "Sir!"

The agha takes the cup, as smooth and delicate as newborn skin. Such a pleasure to the touch. What work the adjunct must do to maintain this little cup, to keep it and its brethren safe in this miserable place, a border outpost on the banks of the lower Danube. There are crates of wood that must be looked after, packets of sawdust, reams of paper, balls of twine. All of these the adjunct is responsible for, and all of them he resents. He thinks such occupations are beneath him. He finds them womanly. He thinks he should be plotting strategy, studying tactics, firing weapons. Such, he thinks, is the essence of warfare. The agha knows this, just as he knows how deeply the adjunct is mistaken. Of all the things he does, maintaining the porcelain cups is the most important. Without such civilizing effects, how quickly one descends to the level of the brute.

As if in agreement, the men burst again into howls of laughter. The soldier with the stick has plunged it back into the fire until the tip glows red, then returned to the pit to thrust it at the wolf. She skips nimbly backwards then suddenly lunges forward, rising on her hind legs, snapping at the stick, crushing it between her murderous jaws, catching, too, the soldier's hand. With a yelp he stumbles

4

backwards, tumbling hard on his backside, his fingers bloodied, his eyes white with fear. The men hoot and yowl, their pleasure livened by the scent of blood.

I should put an end to it, the agha thinks. I should put an end to a lot of things. He takes a sip of his coffee and grimaces. No matter how many times he shows the cook how to brew it properly, the coffee is still bitter.

Morning arrives, and the last of the wolf star fades away. The Danube is deep here, wide enough that the gulls require several breaths to wing across. As a young man the agha might have tried swimming across it. Unwisely. The current is too strong; he would have been swept away. Water is the eye of God, his father said. The beginning and end of all things. He meant Empire, or so the agha thought as a boy, but now he wonders. Maybe his father meant something else entirely, akin to the musings of the mystics, the shadow world of memory—and oblivion.

On the far side of the river the Romanian port town of Galați takes shape in the growing light, a cluster of houses and shacks huddled beneath a smudge of smoke and soot. Masts of sailing ships shift and swing in the breeze. There's commotion in the city despite the early hour. A crowd has gathered, shouldering its way to the docks, swelling then shrinking then surging through the narrow streets. At its center is a knot of people, pushed and prodded, clinging to suitcases and bundles, to babies and baskets and hats.

"They are ridding themselves of their Jews again," the adjunct says. He spits on the ground as if even the word is unclean in his mouth.

"Ah, yes, Jews." The agha looks on with interest. "They call themselves God's chosen people. Did you know that?" He allows himself a smile. He prides himself on his erudition, on knowing little things the adjunct most certainly does not. The smile vanishes as he endures the dregs of his coffee.

"They might tell the Romanians that. Sir!" With a bow and a smile of his own the adjunct takes the empty cup, leaving the agha to wonder if maybe the adjunct knew about the Jews all along and was only too politic to say so.

The crowd nears the docks. The agha can hear the Jews now, the faint sounds of their piggish, monkey voices, borne across the river by the wind, the women's wails, the men's shouts. The soldiers hear them, too, give up torturing the wolf to stare at the spectacle. The garrison is staffed by a miserable bunch of mercenaries, a score of men indistinguishable from the Bulgarians the agha has been sent here to suppress, dressed in thick felt boots, black wool caps, stinking sheepskin coats. Still, entertainment is entertainment, rare in these parts even at the best of times, and while hounding a wolf has its appeal, nothing trumps the suffering of a Jew.

The crowd has reached the river. Herded by thick-necked constables, the Jews stand alone at the top of a boat ramp, an island of evil and contagion. On either side the townspeople fan out, shoving and jostling for a better view. The agha's view is just fine, only slightly impeded by a low, marshy sandbar that runs down the middle of the river. The Jews' god has chosen a dozen of his people for special consideration today. Three are old men, bearded, dressed in tall hats and gabardines. A man holds tight to his wife and son, a young couple carries a babe in arms, a thick-necked tradesman in a blue cap accompanies a pregnant wife, an old woman carries a yellow bird in a cage. The bird is a pleasant surprise. The soldiers point at it, chattering in delight.

The agha knows about these expulsions, has heard about them before, Romanians banishing Jews—or not—from their country, depending on the bribes the Jews can afford to pay. Some of the refugees have made their way to the east, swelling the Jewish quarters near Istanbul. This is the first time he's seen the whole sorry affair unfold.

I should tell the adjunct about it, the agha thinks, lighting his second cigarette of the day. Then he remembers the adjunct's smile and thinks, Perhaps not.

The agha has no affection for Jews, a rootless, ancient race of people who as far as he can tell—despite their claims to the contrary—have long been abandoned by their god. He has heard the usual complaints against them, tales of murder, poisoned wells, bread baked with the blood of martyred children. He puts no more weight in that than he does in the other stories old wives tell, legends of dragons' teeth, gold coins, beheaded men come to life. His native Ankara has had a ghetto filled with Jews for as long as anyone can remember, silk merchants for the most part, some of them quite wealthy. They keep to themselves. At times they are useful.

The agha sighs. One learns to get along. This hysterical Christian hatred is beyond fathoming. If it's blood the Romanians are after, they might look to their own people. Didn't Vlad the Impaler, the infamous Wallachian, more than earn his name, cutting his way to the throne with his saber, massacring thousands?

The Jews, the Christians say, killed their god. Well, if that's the case, they ought to be thankful. How else could he have risen again? The thought pleases the agha. It is, he decides, quite clever. He almost shares it with the adjunct.

Meanwhile, the Jews huddle on the boat ramp, surrounded by their heaps of baggage. They are waiting for something. The soldiers grow impatient, lose interest, wander away to start their morning prayers or squat down to eat the remains of last night's stew. The soldier who prodded the wolf sucks on his mangled fingers, spitting out blood. A few head down to the river where they keep a rowboat for fishing. One man stands at the side of the pit, casting a hissing stream of urine onto the wolf. This indignity she ignores. Back and forth she paces, nosing the sides of the pit, probing, searching. Now and then she rises on her hind legs, her nostrils flaring, but there is no escape. Once again the agha thinks he ought to do something about this. Idly he thinks of her pups. He crushes the butt of his cigarette beneath his heel. Unlike his men, he takes no pleasure in the misery of others, not even a wolf.

He's about to order her release when a flash of movement on the other side of the river draws his attention. A pair of horsemen trots down to the docks, escorting a carriage. It comes to a halt, and a man steps out, dressed in the black hat and coat of town prefect. He swaggers through the crowd, the constables clearing the way. At the sight of him, the Jews shrink back. This pleases him. With an air of satisfaction he takes a document from his pocket—he has a sense of theatre, this man!—unfolds it with a flourish, and begins to read.

Caught by the wind, the prefect's words float across the water to the agha with mesmerizing incomprehensibility. Silently, surreptitiously, the adjunct has reappeared at his side. He coughs. "He says the Jews are vagrants. He says they have broken the law."

The agha looks at him with surprise. "You speak Romanian?"

"My father had a slave woman for his enjoyment." The adjunct coughs again, leaving unsaid his own enjoyment in that trade.

"They have an awful lot of baggage for vagrants," the agha observes with a philosophical shrug. So the Romanians hide their perfidy behind legal statutes. Well. They aren't the only ones to resort to masks for their cruelty. This line of thinking will only take him to places he doesn't want to go. He puts it aside.

The prefect returns the document to his pocket then stands with his thumbs in his belt, surveying the Jews with satisfaction. Cowed, they look back at him in silence. The crowd parts as he returns to his carriage, and a moment later he is gone.

In its cage the little bird hops, a flutter of yellow against the drab background of the docks. The old woman seeks in vain to soothe it. One of the constables has noticed the bird. He draws near, bends at the waist, crooks a finger, smiles. A flicker of a smile crosses the woman's face in return. A moment of reprieve? Of reconciliation? The crowd draws its breath. The agha's men sigh with disappointment. Surely it can't be over so soon? Then the constable steps back with an indifferent air, and the soldiers cheer. The spectacle will continue after all.

Now the constables set to work. One remains to guard the Jews while the second hauls a boat to the bottom of the ramp. It's small, a flat-bottomed dory, the kind used to ferry goods back and forth to the ships. It will never do to hold so many people, let alone their suitcases, bundles, and bags. The Jews know it. So do the soldiers. They watch with heightened anticipation, jostling one another, stamping their feet on the ground. As the constable steadies the boat, the Jews become excited, raising their arms, pointing, calling to one another in their gibbering tongue. One of the old men steps forward, trying to speak to the guard. The constable pulls a truncheon from his belt and makes a show of brandishing it in the Jew's face. The Jew scuttles back.

Together the constables press forward, pushing the Jews down the ramp. The woman with the bird comes first. She carries the cage in one hand, a suitcase in the other, a bundle under her arm. As she struggles to board the boat, the other Jews make a great noise, shouting at her. She turns, puts down the bundle, and as the Jews continue their animal yowls, puts down the suitcase, too. The boat dips, and the suitcase, teetering on the edge of the ramp, falls into the water with a splash. The Jews want her to give up the bird, but she refuses, sitting defiantly in the boat, clutching the cage to her chest. The couple with the baby board next. The father helps them into the dory along with his own family. The old men take their seats, clinging to a scroll in a velvet covering that they, too, refuse to relinquish. The tradesman in the blue cap hands in his pregnant wife, but the boat is already too full, listing to the side, dangerously low, water lapping over the gunwales. He will never fit in. He looks at the boat, then at the constables, then at his wife.

All at once he makes a run for it. Lowering his head like a bull, he charges the constables who, taken by surprise, fail to react in time. As he slips past them, a shout rises up in the crowd. His wife holds a hand to her mouth.

"Ah, so one has some fight in him after all," the adjunct says, a note of admiration in his voice. Jews are supposed to be as weak as they are cunning. The agha's men are similarly charmed, laughing, pointing, elbowing one another. The tradesman reaches the top of the ramp—one more step and he will be free—just as a man emerges from the crowd and with a blow of his fist, sends him reeling. The Jew stumbles, and the constables are on him, dispatching him with a series of kicks. In the boat his wife pales, her hand to her mouth. The agha's men look on with sorrow and delight—sorrow over the Jew's failure to escape tempered by the pleasure of seeing him pummeled. The tradesman rises to his feet and limps to the bottom of the ramp where he is pushed into the boat with the others. So there is room for one more after all. The constables release the rope, and the boat bobs free.

The adjunct lifts his chin, testing the wind. "They might come here."

"Indeed," the agha says.

"And what are we to do with them?"

"Perhaps nothing." The water is choppy this morning, ruffled with white-tipped waves. Hard going for any boat, let alone one so small. "Perhaps Allah will decide."

The sun is higher now, the wind stronger, the river glittering in the light. The Jews' boat bobs uncertainly in the current. Surely it will founder. But perhaps the Jews' god has other plans for his people after all. The wind catches the boat and moves it across the river. It floats towards the agha, rising and falling in the waves. The Jews cling to one other, gasping each time the boat sways. The old men are praying; the agha sees their lips move and catches the sound of their melodic chanting. As the boat rocks, water splashes over the sides. The father seizes the tradesman's cap and uses it to bail. Meanwhile the tradesman sits slumped in his seat, dazed, his hands dangling loosely in his lap. Blood trickles down his face. His wife weeps, clutching her pregnant belly. The little bird, however, is enjoying the voyage. It hops back and forth on its perch, preening itself in the sun.

The boat reaches the marshy sandbar in the middle of the river, stalls, then shudders and breaks free. Caught by the current, it changes trajectory, spins around, and floats downstream. Allah be praised. The agha sighs in relief. Yes. He nods to himself. That's it. Go away. Disappear.

All at once a shout comes from on board. The father has found an oar in the bottom of the boat. He holds it above his head. The old men smile at one another. Their prayers have been answered! The Jew begins to paddle. No matter, the agha thinks. The current is too strong. The boat will be borne away. But the man works hard at his paddling, and slowly the boat turns. It passes the sandbar and with the wind at its back comes straight towards them.

So it has come to this. Let Allah decide, the agha said, but he knows there's no Allah here but him. And what is he to do? So far these expulsions have been a trickle, but given the chance, they could well become a flood. He has no time to care for babies and birds and old men. The townspeople sense this change in the tide of the Jews' affairs. The constables, busy plundering the Jews' baggage, stop to look at the agha. So do his own men. The Jews, too, sense the change. They fall silent, staring at him with anxious eyes. Meanwhile the father increases the tempo of his paddling, hoping to reach land before the agha makes up his mind.

Only the wolf in the pit pays no heed to the Jews. She has left aside her pacing and is digging furiously in the bottom of the pit, deepening it. Dumb beast, the agha thinks. Does she really know no better than to increase her own misery? He reaches into his pouch and rolls himself a cigarette—the third of the day. He turns his back to the wind and waits while the adjunct lights it. For a moment he smokes meditatively. Then he says, "Send them away."

"Sir?" The adjunct swallows hard, averting his eyes.

Some officer. He may have distaste for Jews, but he has apparently even less taste for death. He's better off with his porcelain cups after all, his bales of straw and twine. The agha can hardly contain his anger. "Do as I say."

"Sir!" The adjunct pulls himself up with a smart salute. Then he strides to the river. "Go away," he yells at the Jews. He waves his arms above his head. "You can't land here."

His words are meaningless to them, but his intent is clear. The Jews gibber in their language, consulting. The old men point to the scroll. Furious, the father grabs it and tosses it into the river, causing the boat to rock. Water flows in, almost swamping it. The old men beat at the father with their fists. The women scream. Fending off the blows, he ignores the adjunct and paddles towards shore.

The adjunct removes the pistol from his belt and fires a warning shot, spilling the acrid smell of gunpowder into the air. The Jew stops paddling. The adjunct levels the pistol until it points at his chest. The two men stare at each other. Deliberately, his eye on the adjunct, the Jew resumes paddling, one stroke, two. His wife turns ashen. As the adjunct cocks his pistol, she seizes the paddle, wrenches it from her husband, and throws it into the river.

13

Once again the boat rocks, and water flows in. Borne on the current, the oar sails away. The boat is too heavy. This time surely it will swamp. The old men's voices rise in prayer, lamenting. The pregnant woman clutches her belly. The young mother raises her baby into the air. The old woman fumbles with the door to the cage.

The tradesman is close enough that the agha can see him clearly now. He has the face of a peasant, fleshy with broad cheekbones, muddied skin, full lips, and high, arching eyebrows. He has recovered from his daze. He's the only Jew in the boat who has yet to say a word, who is sitting entirely, utterly still. He looks at the agha and smiles.

Not a fighter. The adjunct was wrong about that. The man's crazy. His wife knows it. Her eyes wide, she stares at him, her hands cradling her pregnant belly.

Suddenly a gray shape streaks across the ground. The wolf has broken free. The dirt she dug sits in a heap at the side of the pit, high enough for her to climb onto and escape. Clever girl, the agha thinks. You have defeated us after all. She bolts through the soldiers and flings herself into the water, swimming hard for the boat. Chaos has overtaken the Jews. The old woman wrests open the cage, freeing the bird. Somehow the tradesman comes to his feet. He stands in the boat with his head tipped back, following the flight of the bird, a spot of yellow against the morning sky, captured by its beauty, its flight of freedom. On his face is a look of sublime pleasure. Then he closes his eyes and with a thrust of his boot, steps over the side.

"Lupu!" screams his wife.

Wolf. So the star was an omen after all, the agha thinks, auguring death. The shock is too great. Water, as his father once said, calls to water. With a shriek the tradesman's wife doubles over, and her womb opens, water gushing forth, flooding the bottom of the boat.

Later the agha will swear the Jew stood on the river for one breath, two, even three, as the wolf swam to him. A miracle? The Christians say their god walked on water, but the Jewish god delivers no such wonder for his people. Standing upright, as straight as the masts on the shore, the tradesman sinks into the waves. Just as he is about to go under, the wolf reaches him, and he grasps at her, pulling her into his arms. The pups, the agha thinks. What of the pups? The wolf closes her jaws around the Jew's neck, and so entwined, each embracing the other as if in a spasm of ecstasy or joy, they disappear.

Two

GUS, 1947

*I*nside the walled-in courtyard of the Phipps Psychiatric Clinic at the Johns Hopkins Hospital, a girl in a blue skirt, white blouse, and ballet flats is walking, her long legs emerging beneath the hem of her skirt like a bird's.

"Her name is Anna," Gus Thaler says. "Anna Glanz."

"Age?" Adolf Meyer asks.

"She just turned fifteen."

"Ah. So young." Meyer shakes his head. "A shame."

Gus nods his assent. He would say more, but he's hesitant to speak up. He's only a third-year resident, after all, and Dr. Meyer is far his superior, the founder of psychiatry at Johns Hopkins, famed head of the Phipps Clinic for over thirty years. Gus stands silently at Meyer's side, looking out the window of his office, waiting for the great man to speak next. Meanwhile, Anna walks the path around the courtyard, circling the pond at its center where koi hover in the depths like drowned clouds. Her hair is dark, and her eyes are dark, too—this Gus knows, although it's harder for him at the moment to see. She has tipped down her head, obscuring her face, passing beneath the trees from shadow to sunlight then back to shadow again, a white-capped nurse following at a discreet distance. She's counting steps, Gus thinks all at once, the way nervous children do: Step

16

on a crack, break your mother's back. But Anna has no fear, at least not of cracks; she steps as easily on these as on the stones.

"Symptoms?" Meyer says.

Gus considers. There are so many. "Mutism, primarily."

"And she came in—?"

"About six weeks ago." It's early in the morning, not quite ten, but already beastly hot, promising to become even more so as the day goes on. Baltimore, Gus thinks. August. No surprises there. The sky is whitish with heat. He stretches his neck, seeking escape from the strictures of his suit and tie. The open window only makes things worse, letting in thick, humid air from the pond, the overripe smell of hollyhocks and magnolias. "Her father is Lionel Glanz. An industrialist. Quite wealthy. Perhaps you've heard of him?"

"Glanz." Meyer says. A thoughtful look comes into his eyes. "Jewish, I suppose?"

"Yes." The elephant in the room. Meyer has gotten right to it. Hopkins is known for its antipathy to the people of the book. There isn't a single Jewish department head in the entire hospital, and according to many, never will be. Meyer, on the other hand, has been fair in his hiring, recognizing talent when he sees it. The psychiatric service has its share of Jewish physicians—including Gus. Leo Kanner, Gus's immediate supervisor, is brilliant, creative, the author of the nation's first textbook on child psychiatry—and a Galician-born Jew. Meyer is known in the medical world for his tolerance. Then again, it would be hard to work in psychiatry without becoming used to Jews. Freud, Adler, Ferenczi. The list goes on and on. It isn't for nothing that the field is known as the "Jewish profession."

"Glanz," Meyer says again. "You mean the New York man, the one making a bid for Senate?"

"That's right."

"He's sent her awfully far from home."

"A Manhattan doctor he consulted recommended us." Meyer is a small man while Gus is quite tall, a good head taller. It's a difference Gus finds disconcerting. Officially, Meyer retired as chief of psychiatry six years ago, but inside the clinic, nothing much has changed. The great man still holds court daily in his office with its sprawling chairs and seminar table, bookshelves reaching toward the towering ceiling, microtomes, skulls, charts, and folios littering the room. Even at the advanced age of eighty he cuts a formidable figure. His beard, neatly trimmed to a point as in the oil portrait that graces the clinic's reception room, has gone to white, as has his hair, and there is a trembling in his hand that he attempts to conceal by tucking it beneath his arm. But his eyes retain their brightness, along with their famous piercing stare, glacial, direct.

The Mind Reader. The old man's nickname. If anyone can see into your soul, Gus has heard it said more than once, it's Adolf Meyer. The thought makes him uncomfortable, although why should it? It's nonsense, of course, and even if it were true, Gus has nothing to hide. Nevertheless, he finds himself wilting beneath the older man's gaze, hunching his shoulders to minimize the contrast between them. Taller— "taller," he hears vaguely in his thoughts, the chant the children shouted at him when he was a boy, making the inevitable play on his name—Thaler—with its silent "h." It was better than their other taunt, Carrot Top, for his ginger hair.

18

"The doctor the Glanzes consulted—the Manhattan man—thought Anna might be suffering from a form of autism," Gus says. "He suggested she be brought here so that Dr. Kanner could have a look at her." Kanner was the first to diagnose "Kanner's Disease," the strange syndrome that left children oddly locked into their own minds. *Autistic*, he calls them, for the way they moved about the world as independent selves, emotionally remote, cognitively detached. Language difficulties often accompanied the disorder, sometimes the failure to speak entirely, occasionally the bizarre echolalia, in which children repeated whatever they heard. Bizarre and unnerving, as Gus has learned from his own interviews with children suffering from the disorder.

"But it isn't autism," Gus adds. "Dr. Kanner cleared her of that immediately. The mutism didn't appear until the spring. If she'd been autistic, it would have surfaced much earlier." It's the one characteristic Kanner insists on. If a child suffers from autism, he does so early on. "Anna stopped speaking after an incident in the family—the death of her brother. Before that she spoke quite normally."

"Ah." Meyer's face is shrouded in mystery. Silence descends on the room, and Gus finds his discomfort increasing. It's the oldest psychiatric trick in the book: say nothing until your patient, unable to tolerate the vacuum that silence brings to a room, blunders into speech, often revealing the very thing he is trying hardest to conceal. Is Meyer trying to pressure Gus into speaking now? What does the old man expect him to say?

Gus deals with his unease by looking out again at the courtyard, giving the appearance—he hopes—of looking meaningfully engaged in thought. Several more patients have come outside now to join Anna for their morning outings. An elderly man in a black suit has taken a seat on a bench by the wall and bats the air with fleshy hands, fending off demons that apparently torment him like gnats. Another, a young fellow in his early twenties perhaps, strides vigorously about the courtyard, his face creased in a manic smile. Beyond him a grey-smocked woman comes to a stop beneath an oak tree as if to admire it, only she isn't admiring anything at all, she has simply come to a standstill like a wind-up toy wound down. The path takes Anna to her. She stops, glances up, then continues her walk, stepping carefully around the woman the way she would an inconveniently placed piece of furniture.

"So, Dr. Thaler," Meyer says finally, breaking the silence himself. "What can I do for you?"

"Dr. Kanner asked me to consult with you. You see, we've had Anna for over six weeks now, but I'm afraid we haven't done much good for her."

"A tough case, then?"

"The mutism isn't her only problem. She suffers from night terrors. Sleepwalking. There have been problems with self-mutilation."

Meyer shakes his head. "Pity."

Pity, yes. A bird wings suddenly from the oak tree and Anna looks up at it, momentarily showing her face. Gus's heart goes out to her. The girl is in such anguish, such pain. Round and round the courtyard she goes like a penitent, like one of those medieval nuns who endlessly walked the cloisters, purging themselves of sin. She's trying to be good, he thinks suddenly, she's trying to be oh-so-very good. He shakes his head. She's such a puzzle, this girl, such a

20

mystery. Will he ever find a way to reach her?

"I don't want to say we've made no progress at all with Anna," he says. "In many ways she's improved. The nightmares have receded, and the mutilation has lessened, too."

"But?" Meyer leaves the window, taking a seat at his desk, and with some relief Gus follows, taking a seat in the chair opposite. If this is a test, he hopes he's passing it. Anyway, it's a relief to sit down. By slumping into his chair, he can almost meet the old man at eye level.

"Last week she stopped eating. Dr. Kanner thinks she will need long-term care. He recommends the Children's Home at Spring Meadow. He's spoken to Anna's father about it. They can administer tube feedings if needed. It's in New York, closer to the family's home."

"I see." Meyer nods. His eyes drift closed, and for a moment Gus fears the old man has fallen asleep. Then all at once turtle-like his eyes snap open, pinning Gus with their penetrating gaze. "You don't agree?"

"Well, sir, I mean, of course I do. I would never contradict Dr. Kanner, but—"

"Yes?"

"Well, sir, that is . . ." Gus hesitates. True, he's only a resident, still in training, but no one knows Anna better than he does. If he doesn't speak up for her, who will? He pulls himself up in his chair, for once using his height to his advantage, and looks at Meyer directly. "I think Anna Glanz may not need long-term care after all."

"Is that so?" Meyer stands and takes a book from a shelf behind his desk, making a big show of studying it. Then he closes it and puts it back—remaining, however, on his feet so that his superior position in the room has been restored. "You're one of ours, aren't you, Dr. Thaler?" He looks pointedly down at Gus.

"One of—" Gus doesn't understand, then he does. "Yes, I suppose so. I did my medical studies at Hopkins, my undergraduate work here, too."

"Your psychiatry training?"

"Here, for the most part." A voice sounds in the courtyard, a high-pitched hoo, hoo, hoo. Another bird? Gus looks, but it's only the man on the bench. He has begun calling out, communing with the air-spirits that torture his soul. Hoo, hoo, hoo. A nurse hurries to his side and manages to quiet him. "I spent two years at St. Margaret's during the war for my Public Health Service."

"And?"

"I liked it well enough. Most of my work was with war veterans."

Meyer makes a face, something between a grimace and a smile. "You weren't bitten by the Freudian bug?"

"No, sir. Well, a little." Meyer's antipathy to Freud is legend. The two men were rivals for years, Freud's psychoanalysis pitted against Meyer's psychobiology, the former emphasizing internal conflicts of the mind, the latter grounded in the organic study of the brain. Gus is well aware of this and knows what he needs to say. "I believe in a scientific approach to mental illness. Find the source and you will find the cure."

The old man smiles. The maxim is a well-known Meyerism. "Good." Mollified, he sits back down, leans back, surveys Gus with content. "So tell me about Anna."

Gus relaxes. This is a question he has been expecting.

He's well prepared, with the facts at hand. "The father, as I said, is a wealthy businessman. His parents came from Romania at the end of the last century. They were refugees of some kind. According to Mr. Glanz, his grandfather was murdered in a pogrom—drowned in the Danube. Life, as you know, has never been easy for Jews in that part of the world, even before—" He pauses, out of delicacy for Meyer's feelings. And his own. The unspeakable horrors of the war lay over all of them, Jew and non-Jew alike, and hardly needed elaborating. "The Glanzes settled in Riverport, Rhode Island. Lionel was born there. They were quite poor by all accounts when he was a child. He's made a success of himself since then."

"And Anna's mother?"

"Frieda. I'm afraid we don't know much about her. All of Dr. Kanner's communications have been with Mr. Glanz. Apparently she's been quite overcome, incapacitated with grief since the death of their son. She's an artist of some kind. Sensitive. Temperamental."

"Any other children in the family?"

"One sister. Hettie. She's eleven. No talk of any trouble there."

"And the son—the one they lost?"

"Alexander. They called him Sasha. He was only four when he died."

Meyer's smile fades, and his eyes narrow. A change has come into the room. Gus has the feeling the old man's studying him like one of the specimens on his bookshelves, the brain of a possum swimming in formaldehyde, perhaps, or the skull of a lizard. "So you disagree with Leo about Spring Meadow."

23

"Yes, sir," Gus says, not sure how to handle the direction the conversation is taking.

"You must think you've found the key to Anna's illness."

"No, sir, I wouldn't say that." To his shame, Gus feels himself coloring. Carrot Top. "But I have reason to believe—that is, Anna has begun speaking again."

"And what does Leo have to say about that?"

"I haven't told Dr. Kanner yet." Hoo, hoo, hoo. Stop, Gus thinks, please. Where is that nurse? The noise is getting on his nerves, as if the man is calling out deliberately to mock him. "I wanted to wait until I was sure of it. So far she only speaks in fits and starts. There's no pattern to it, and it isn't every day. But she has spoken to me."

"To you," Meyer says slowly. "No one else?"

"No sir."

Hoo, hoo, hoo.

"How do you explain that?"

"Well, sir." Gus braces himself, considers backing down, then decides against it. The Mind Reader. If it's true what people say, Meyer will get the truth out of him one way or another. "I've been trying a different approach."

Meyer frowns. "A different approach."

"Yes, sir." The color, he knows, is high in his face now. But there's nothing to be done about that. He lifts his chin, looks at Meyer directly, hoping to come across as knowledgeable and confident and not the way he's feeling, which is the opposite. "I think it's working."

The old man taps a finger on his desktop. "How long have you been treating Anna Glanz?"

"Ever since she came in."

"Over a month?" Meyer looks surprised. "You haven't

24

rotated off her case?"

"No, sir."

"You know that's against hospital protocols." Tap, tap goes the finger on the desk. "*My* protocols."

"Yes, sir. I asked to stay on." The old man's gaze is relentless. Gus finds the urge to look away all but irresistible. "Dr. Kanner was kind enough to grant my request."

When he ventures to look again, the old man's frown has deepened. His hand is trembling again, and he tucks it under his arm. "So what does Anna say to you when you hypnotize her, Dr. Thaler? You are hypnotizing her, are you not?"

How could he possibly know that? Gus feels the heat in his face. The Mind Reader, indeed. "Yes."

"Another technique I assume you acquired at St. Margaret's?"

"Yes, sir. A psychiatrist there—Hans van der Ploeg—found it quite useful at times with the veterans, and I, myself,—" Gus breaks off. This, he realizes from the look on Meyer's face, is the last thing he should be saying.

"Indeed. Have you tried holding any séances with your patient, too?" There's a bright hint of sarcasm in the old man's eyes.

"No, sir, of course not." Gus withers under his glare. "I can explain, if you'll only allow me—"

Meyer waves off the rest. He returns to the window, leaving Gus slumped in his chair: a little boy who has been found out. Anna is on the far side of her loop and has her back towards them. For a time Meyer watches her. "Children." His voice softens, and he sighs. "Whoever decided children should suffer so?" His body has become weighty, the anger

25

giving way to an air of sadness. "Hypnosis. There was a time when we all used it. Some believed it gave us insight not just into the mind, but into the soul." He grows silent, reflective. "Never mind." He turns back to Gus. "So, Dr. Thaler. What does Anna say when you put her in her trances?"

It's a relief, frankly, to have the secret out. At least the old man hasn't said anything about disciplinary action—not yet, anyway. At least Gus still has his job. He leans forward in his chair, glad at last to be able to talk about it. "She's tormented by wolves."

"Wolves?"

"They come to her in her dreams. She dreams she's outside, in the woods or in the fields, and they're chasing her. They swim to her in rivers. Or they're with her, inside the room." He reaches into his breast pocket, removes a square of paper that he unfolds carefully and hands to Meyer. On it is the painting of a wolf, in mottled colors, with a blood red background. The face of the animal is oversized, occupying the center of the page, staring directly at the viewer with a menacing gaze. "I gave her some watercolors. I thought it might help with her treatment."

Meyer studies the painting, his face impassive. Then he hands it back to Gus. "What do you make of these wolves?"

Gus folds the paper, returns it to his pocket. "Well sir, we know Anna spoke normally before her brother died. The mutism set in afterwards. I believe it's a reaction to the boy's death. She blames herself for it. She's conjured up these wolves as a delusion, a kind of punishment."

"Ah. The wolf constellation. Ptolemy called it Lupus." Meyer blinks at Gus as if considering whether or not to go on explaining something that ought to be immediately

26

evident to any educated man. "It stands in the sky near Centaurus. The Greeks saw it as signifying repentance, the centaur holding a wolf impaled on a spear, taking it as an offering to nearby Ara—the altar. A penitential sacrifice."

The penitential girl in the courtyard. "Only there's nothing to sacrifice," Gus says, "so Anna offers up herself."

"Precisely." To Gus's great relief Meyer smiles, and gratefully Gus smiles back. The power of a shared idea. Perhaps this meeting will go well after all. Then the expression on the old man's face changes, and his eyes narrow again. "Or perhaps your patient has some reason to feel guilty. Perhaps she had a hand in her brother's death."

"No, sir. Not at all." Gus finds the very idea shocking. That a child could be capable of murder. That *Anna* could be capable of it. She is such a sad little girl; such an innocent. And yet, if the truth be told, they had all considered it. Even Kanner. They had to. They wouldn't be worth their salt as psychiatrists if they hadn't. "Dr. Kanner made sure of it. He spoke to Mr. Glanz about it expressly. The boy died in a tragic accident, a drowning. Anna had nothing to do with it. She wasn't even there."

"So she's created this torment . . ."

"Exactly. Children often blame themselves for things they have no control over." Gus is skating dangerously close to Freud now, but he's hoping Meyer won't notice. "The divorce of their parents. A grandparent's death. They feel terrible about it, and imagine themselves somehow more powerful than they are, capable of making it happen. It's a way to disguise their dependency, how weak and powerless they are."

Meyer nods. "So what do you suggest?"

27

"We can't send her to Spring Meadow. You know what those places are like. They don't even have decent doctors on staff. It's a warehouse for lost causes. It means giving up. If she goes there, there's a good chance she'll never recover. She could be locked away for the rest of her life."

"But she can't stay here if she won't eat."

"No. Dr. Kanner is right. We're not equipped to force-feed children."

"And so?"

"Well, sir." Gus rises to his feet, drawing himself up, glad to see for once that Meyer makes no objection to the looming superiority of his height. "I believe we should send Anna home. This refusal to eat—it's her way of saying she's had enough of the hospital. She wants to be in the loving arms of her family again. It's only natural and—if I may say so—logical. She ate before she came here. If we send her home, she'll eat again."

Meyer nods, considering. "It could be risky."

"Yes, sir. That's why I've offered to go with her."

Meyer raises his eyebrows.

"Just for a day or two. To see her settled. Until she's eating again and out of danger."

"And to continue her hypnosis?"

"I don't see why not." Gus tries, without much success, to keep the defensiveness out of his voice. "I believe it's helping."

"And the Glanzes? What do they think of your plan?"

"They're quite eager to have Anna home again."

"I can imagine." Meyer gives a thin smile. "It won't do any good for a man running for Senate to have the papers reporting insanity in the family."

28

No, Gus thinks. No good at all. Although he has no reason to believe that Lionel Glanz's concern for his daughter is anything but genuine. Kanner was clear on the point. He said the man broke down when he brought his daughter in, his tears running freely, almost childlike in his anguish. "Dr. Kanner says Mr. Glanz is willing to do anything to see his daughter cured."

Meyer pulls his hand out, studies it for a moment. The trembling has stilled and he allows the hand to fall open to his side. "So Dr. Kanner has approved your plan."

"Yes, that is—well, he asked that I speak to you first. He said he would abide by your decision."

"Ah." Meyer smiles. "Now I understand why he sent you to me."

"He says you've handled cases like this before—that you've treated wealthy patients in the privacy of their homes."

"I suppose I have." Meyer drifts off, a dreamy look on his face. Gus would like to ask him more about it, but knows not to. He's heard rumors of the famous private patients Meyer tended to in his years at Phipps: movie actors, writers, business tycoons, heirs to fortunes. Psychotics, murderers, manic-depressives. One by one their families—or their families' lawyers—came to the old man, seeking help, seeking a solution, seeking a reprieve. One thing they knew they could count on: the great man's discretion. Meyer was famous for it. "It isn't easy," he says finally. "You serve two masters. There is the patient, and then there is the patient's family." He studies Gus. "How old are you, Dr. Thaler?"

"Twenty-six."

"Married?"

"No, sir."

"Girlfriend—if you don't mind my asking?"

Gus colors again. "I'm afraid my work doesn't leave much time for a personal life."

"Psychiatry has demanded much from you."

"Nothing more than I'm willing to give." The old man's gaze is unflinching, and Gus forces himself to return it. "I can help Anna. I'm sure of it."

"Are you?" Meyer says softly.

Father Confessor. It is, Gus remembers all at once, the old man's other nickname. Gus had no intention when he came to this meeting of revealing anything personal about himself, but suddenly the urge to talk is irresistible. "I had a sister once. She was Anna's age when she died." Why not tell Meyer about Rosa? He has nothing to be ashamed of. "She had leukemia. At the end her pain was—" he looks away "—intolerable. I was only nine when she died, but I vowed I would never let anyone suffer like that. Not if I could help it." He lifts his chin. "Anna Glanz is suffering. Her pain may be in her mind, but it's nonetheless crippling, and it's real. I believe I can help her. I'm asking for that chance."

Meyer sighs. He sits down, leaving Gus at the window. "Delusions can be quite dangerous, Dr. Thaler, even in children as young as Anna. Children—as you rightly say— hold themselves responsible for all kinds of things. They act as judge, jury, and sometimes—" his voice grows stern "—executioner, too. Don't think we haven't seen suicides in girls like Anna. We have."

Gus nods soberly. "Yes, sir."

"I thought once . . ." Meyer waves his hand, a tired

30

gesture. "At my age, it's better not to think too much. Go, Dr. Thaler. Take your patient home. You have my blessing. Although I suspect you don't need it. I suspect you would have found a way regardless."

"Thank you." Gus feels a surge of relief, so strong, it surprises him. "I won't disappoint you."

Meyer offers a wan smile. "I'm sorry about your sister, but you mustn't confuse one thing with another. Especially not in psychiatry. I have been, I fear, greatly misunderstood. It's one of my greatest regrets. I began my career studying the brains of reptiles." His eyes light up and take on mischievous air. "Imagine that! Lizards. Chameleons. Snakes. Over time I migrated to humans. I've never given up hope that we will find scientific sources for the illnesses that afflict us. Not just our mental disorders. Physical ailments, too." He holds out his hand unashamedly, letting Gus see the tremor at work. "But I also understand that human beings are complex animals. We are more than our brains. We are also our minds." His voice sharpens. "There's a reason I banned hypnosis at Phipps. It's a powerful tool, but not without risk. Hypnosis can bring you close to your patient—sometimes too close. I myself . . ."

A look of regret comes into the old man's face. Then he shakes his head and snaps his attention back to Gus. "I don't believe in everything your Dr. Freud has taught, but I do believe this: the mind is a powerful thing. By that I mean your mind, not just the mind of your patient. Be careful, Dr. Thaler. Do what you can for your Anna, but make sure you do it for her sake—not your own."

31

*T*hree

CLAIRE, 1996

*T*he wolf sits in the corner, bares its teeth, and grins.

"So," the detective says. "Do you want to tell me about it?"

No, Claire thinks, she most certainly does not. She shakes her head. The wolf seems to agree. It lifts a paw and delicately begins to wash it, pink tongue darting across the leathery pads, through the silvery-grey fur, along the tips of the black nails. Overhead a fluorescent light blinks and hums, threatening to bring on one of her headaches. The room they are in, deep in the bowels of the Washington, D.C., Hecht's department store, is close, airless, claustrophobic, with cinder-block walls painted a sickening green. The table they sit at—she on one side, he on the other—is made of Formica, a similar green color, with metal edges. A holdover, Claire thinks, from the fifties. The air hisses with the faint smell of moldy air conditioning. She tries not to think about it. She is trying very hard not to think about anything.

"Seventy-nine dollars." The detective turns the earrings in his fleshy fingers, scrutinizing the price tag. He's a horrid little man, greasy hair combed straight back, dressed in a cheap tweed jacket, shiny trousers. She saw him on the floor of the department store, of course, drifting by the perfume displays, fingering the bins of scarves. He'd even smiled at her in a smarmy way. Flirting, she'd thought. It had made her flesh crawl. One of those hopelessly boring married men shopping for his wife, looking for a little excitement on the side. How could she have been so stupid? She should have known. Well, wasn't that the point? Store detectives were supposed to look harmless, to blend in. "Seventy-nine dollars and ninety-nine cents to be exact." He speaks with an air of satisfaction as if he expects his precision to impress her. As if he expects her to congratulate him on a job well done. "Hardly seems worth all the trouble."

Yes, she thinks wearily, on that point she can agree. Not worth it at all. The earrings are gaudy and glittering, green glass hearts encased in gold-colored tin. Costume pieces. Not even remotely her type. That, of course, was what attracted her to them in the first place: the feeling that by possessing them she could transform herself, make herself into something she wasn't, the kind of woman who wore cheap and sentimental jewelry. Who wore her heart on her sleeve, instead of burying her feelings so deeply, most of the time she doesn't even know what they are.

"May I?" There's that smarmy smile again. He's clearly enjoying this. He puts the earrings down, lifts the strap of her purse with the crook of his finger.

She shrugs. "Go ahead." He's already been through her pockets.

Bored by the whole proceeding, the wolf slumps to the floor. She—it's a she-wolf; Claire can see her teats— exhales, drops her face to her paws. Her eyelids drift closed. Meanwhile the detective goes through her purse, emptying it methodically and carefully, placing each item in a neat

33

line on the table. Not like last time, when the guard simply turned her pocketbook over and dumped the contents out. Tissues, lipstick, calendar, pen, that broken watchband she's been meaning to get repaired for months, a brown plastic bottle of pills. This last captures his interest. He holds the vial up, capturing the light, reads the label. "Xynolith." He looks at her.

"They're legal," she says. "Prescription."

And well-deserved, she might add, although she doesn't. "Manic-depressive illness," so Grimmsley, her psychiatrist, said as he wrote out the prescription, enunciating each syllable with excruciating care as if he was afraid she wouldn't understand if he didn't. What was there to understand? It's in her genes, after all—and isn't that what they say counts nowadays?—beginning with her great-grandmother Dora who, according to family lore, was a famous kleptomaniac. And don't forget Claire's mother, Anna, who—well, the list is too long, and they really don't have time.

The detective rattles the bottle and the pink capsules dance. "Xyn-o-lith." He mulls it over. If he doesn't know what they're for, she isn't going to tell him. He knows he's not allowed to ask. He shakes his head, puts the bottle down, opens her wallet and thumbs through her cash. "Two hundred dollars." He gives out a low whistle. The wolf pricks up her ears. Even he can do the math. Why shoplift seventy-nine dollar earrings when you have two hundred dollars in your handbag? It's not just the cash, it's the way Claire looks, the dark green suit, black handbag and matching pumps, the styled red hair, dipping just below her ears, the well-kept nails, and trim figure, all of it indicating a certain comfortable station in life. A working woman—a professional—God knows the kind of woman who doesn't need to be stealing cheap costume jewelry. Who might very well consider herself above his class. He smirks at her, as if he takes pleasure in this reversal of their fortunes. "Are you sure you don't have anything to say?" He peers at her driver's license. "Miss Sadler."

"*Mrs.* Sadler. And no."

"*Mrs.* Sadler," he says, mocking her. "Mrs. Claire Glanz Sadler," he adds, reading her name out in full. The expression on his face changes, becomes distant, thoughtful. "Glanz." It's coming to him now. "Glanz. Wasn't there someone, a politician, that man, a mayor or something, the one from . . .?"

"New York. And he wasn't a mayor. He was a senator." My grandfather, she almost says, but manages to stop herself. When will she ever learn? This, above all else, is one thing she has no desire to talk about, not with anyone. Certainly not with Mr. Store Detective. "No relation," she says quickly, covering her tracks. She's a terrible liar, and only the most obtuse can't suss her out. Fortunately he fits the bill.

"Okay, Claire." He drops the pretense of respect. The fun is over. He's all business now. He sweeps up her things, deposits them back into her purse. "Fill this out." He shoves a piece of paper across the table. He jams a thumb at the bottom. "Sign here."

The wolf has fallen back asleep and is dreaming. Her legs jerk, her eyelids tremble, she lets out a low moan. The detective hasn't provided a pen. Claire pulls her bag over, taking possession of it again, digs through, finds her pen, begins to write. *That, I, Claire Glanz Sadler, admit to having taken from Hecht's Department Store one pair of*

35

earrings valued at . . . She knows the drill. *I, Claire Glanz Sadler, admit to having taken from Brown's Jewelry Store one gold necklace.* She's been through it before. *I, Claire Glanz Sadler, admit to having stolen from Woodward and Lothrop's one pair of gloves. A bottle of perfume. A silver spoon. A ring.* Mostly small things, ones she can slip into her pocket. Only once in a life of thievery has she gone seriously wrong. She was seventeen, and she stole a car. Hettie had to come to her rescue then. Claire still doesn't know how Hettie got her off. With Lionel's money, no doubt. At the thought of her aunt—arms akimbo, hair flying—marching into the precinct station, Claire smiles. It's a relief to smile after all. Then she sighs, signs, pushes the paper back.

"I want you to know we take shoplifting seriously here." The detective is going to give his little speech now. She wishes he wouldn't bother. She wishes she could sleep through it like the wolf. Claire can smell her now, a musky rank odor of urine and blood. The smell of death. The smell of the wild. Of things running amok, out of control. Not a good sign. She needs to get out of here. She needs her pills.

"Shoplifting hurts us all, we all pay for it, it's not a victimless crime . . ." Blah, blah, blah. She mouths the words as he says them. He's just finishing up when the door opens and a uniformed cop walks in. "I'll take it from here." He's a young man, sandy-haired, loaded down with a radio, handcuffs, billy club, gun. He clanks like a metal robot when he crosses the floor. Thomas. Of all people. Why did it have to be someone she knows? Claire averts her eyes, her face coloring. Will he give her away? Apparently not. His face is blank, all business. He picks up Claire's declaration, folds it in thirds, then in half, then slides it into his pocket.

36

"If you'll just come with me."

She still can't look him in the face. She stands up and shoulders her bag. She waits docilely to see if he will handcuff her. Sometimes they do, sometimes they don't. She wouldn't hold it against him if he did. Mercifully he doesn't. He takes her arm—he could be a gentleman escorting her; they could be on a date—and guides her out of the room. The store detective watches them go with a faint air of satisfaction and boredom. For a moment she almost feels sorry for him. What does he have to look forward to? Soon he'll be out on the floor again, trolling, pretending to be something he's not, looking for more women to ensnare. The earrings are still on the table. Even now, irrationally, embarrassingly, she wants them. Despite everything, she'd reach back right now and grab them if she could, shoving them into her bag. That, and nothing else, makes her want to cry.

Thomas walks her through the tunnels of the basement of the store, through cavernous, dim, evil-smelling hallways, past a janitor mopping, a stock clerk smoking on a break. She feels them eyeing her. To her great shame, she feels her face redden again. The wolf is afraid of cops; she slinks after them, keeping her distance, trying to look invisible, trying to look harmless. Thomas pushes through a grey metal door and they emerge onto the parking lot. The wolf skitters through just before the door slams shut. It's not even noon yet but already the sun is beating down, an unseasonably hot fall day, shining on oily pools of asphalt. The glare finally brings on her headache, thudding dully at the side of her temple.

Thomas leads her to his cruiser. The wolf sidles up to her,

so close, Claire can feel her bristly fur on the skin of her leg, the moist heat of her soft panting.

"Mrs. Sadler." He drops her arm.

"Hello, Thomas."

It's the first time she's seen him in months. Mostly she sees him in the courtroom, when he comes to testify in cases where he's been the arresting officer: bar fights, domestic disturbances, gun violations. And shoplifting, of course.

He looks embarrassed. "I'm sorry."

"Please don't be. It's not your fault."

He has sad eyes. He looks all of nineteen. He could be her son, if she had children. He takes the confession from his pocket, unfolds it, looks at it, then back at her. "Are you okay?"

She musters a smile. "Yes, thank you. I'm fine."

He looks miserable. She feels so sorry for him. It's the first time in this whole pathetic situation that she's felt truly sorry about anything. It's a bad sign. The wolf looks up at her with hopeful eyes.

"Are you going to do this again?"

"No, Thomas. Of course not."

He fingers the paper, his eyes averted. "You're going to get some help for this, right?"

"Yes, I will." She smiles again. "I promise."

He crumples the paper, throws it way. "Okay then." He gives her a shy grin. "Hell, it's not every day I get to arrest a D.C. prosecutor."

Her car is on the far side of the parking lot. By the time she reaches it, Thomas is gone. She gets in, opens the pill bottle and, her mouth dry, manages to gulp one down. She should go into the office, spend the rest of the afternoon catching up on paperwork, but she called in sick that morning—not far from the truth—and she might as well take advantage of it. She can trust Thomas's discretion—she thinks. She won't know for sure until the next time he shows up in the courtroom. Part of her still can't believe how stupid, how dumb, how utterly worthless it all is. She must want to get caught. That's what Grimmsley would say if she told him about this latest episode, which she most definitely will not.

She rattles the bottle. Only about thirty pills left. That means she's due to see Grimmsley again soon. She's hit by a sudden surge of anger, so strong, it takes her breath away. This is all Cassidy's fault. He never should have called her. She recognized him on the phone before he even said a word, that characteristic hesitant intake of breath as if he were unsure about what he should say even as he said it. Coward to the core. Covering for Anna. If Anna had something to ask Claire, she could call and ask herself. Except that Anna hadn't spoken to Claire in—what was it now?—over twenty years, keeping her silence. No wonder she sent her husband to do her bidding. Some things don't change.

"Home," she says to the wolf, who has somehow gotten into the car and is sitting on the seat beside her, although Claire has no recollection of letting her in. She turns on the radio, gets rock music blaring. Sometimes music drives the wolf away. Not this time. All it does is make the headache worsen, throbbing in time to the beat. The wolf looks at her expectantly. She likes car rides, even more so with the window open. She waits for Claire to roll it down, then sticks her head out and grins as they drive away.

The Journal of Baruch Zalman

PART ONE

Every word I write here, every event and every detail, is exactly as it was. This, dear Reader—if such a one there might one day be—you may believe with complete faith as if you saw it with your own eyes and heard it with your own ears, straight from the mouth of the spirit itself. So I declare as I write this account at midnight on the twelfth day of Elul, 5653 years since the Creation, known to the nations as 1893. As the prophet said: Open thy mouth for the greater glory of God.

Outside it is all darkness. The others have long gone to bed. Raisel, my wife, sleeps peacefully, her slumber untroubled for the first time in years by visions and dreams. Keiner Glanz is in the sanctuary, taking what rest he can, while Dora Aizic lies on a straw pallet in the corner of the room, her sleep deepened by the dose of valerian tea I gave her just a few hours ago. I steal a glance at her as I write these words, this girl who came so late in my life, long after I had grown to believe such a thing was no longer possible, and altered my destiny.

More than anything I, too, wish to sleep. My limbs tremble with exhaustion; I have scarce strength to wield my

40

pen. But I must make haste now and finish this account. Tomorrow when darkness comes Keiner and Dora will steal from the village and embark on their journey to the *goldene medinah*, the New World. I no longer have the heart to try and dissuade them. Their marriage contract is prepared, the glass and the wine stand ready, my signature alone as witness will suffice. In a cloth pouch, hidden inside Dora's bag, I have secured the few coins I have managed to accumulate over my lifetime; Raisel and I will have to do without. Inside that same pouch, when I have finished, I will secrete this account—a missive sent into a future I know now I will never see.

You, dear Reader, will scarce believe what I have to say. This I know. The things I witnessed this night are beyond the powers of any mortal mind to comprehend. Yet they are true, a wonder of our earthly existence and exceedingly strange. How can the soul of one who has died enter into the body of another, speak with its voice, and use all of its limbs and senses? To God alone, the Almighty, is given complete understanding of this mystery. This story is far larger than I, an insignificant, lowly man living out the end of his days in a forgotten corner of the Carpathian Mountains, could ever hope to tell. Yet I must tell it so that you, dear Reader, and others who may come after you, will acknowledge the immortality of your soul, fear the Word of the Lord, and repent of your sins. As the prophet said: The Lord is slow to anger but immense in power. In storm and whirlwind He takes his way, the clouds are the dust stirred up by His feet.

The candle gutters. A breeze flows in from the garden, bringing the scent of the cool, rushing river waters, the shuddering beeches and firs. My head is heavy, my hand trembles. I can scarce pen these words in this simple pocket ledger I acquired years ago to record the harvest from the bees, then set aside. I fear I am not up to the task. Even more so, I fear not finishing. So I begin.

My name is Baruch Zalman. You may know me, Reader, as the son of Rav Menachem Zalman, himself the son of the great Rav Isak Zalman, famous throughout the world for his commentary on *Kedoshim*, the laws of holiness: *V'kara zeh el zeh—And They Called One to the Other.* As surely as the angels call to one another in the heavens, singing the praises of the Lord, we must sing of His Glory to the multitudes of the earth. So I have always believed, and so I have always conducted my life, even to the very writing of this account.

For eighty-two years I have lived and breathed this earthly existence. I was born in the city of Iași in the land of Moldavia, a great province on the eastern edge of the Romanian nation. In those days, my father was rebbe of a powerful court of Hasidim, Jews who lived according to the laws of *Hesed*, God's loving-kindness, wanting nothing more than to realize their love for the Divine in this earthly life. My father was a learned man, as upright as the Cedars of Lebanon, and much beloved by his followers, so gentle that if a fly were to disturb him at study, he would rise to shoo it through the window rather than put it, that most insignificant of beings, to death. This I witnessed myself many times, just as I witnessed everything I relate here.

My parents named me Berel-Baruch for my mother's father, a noble rabbi in his own right. Berel, as the name says, was a bear of a man, strong in both body and spirit, and surely they hoped that by giving me his name they would impart to me a measure of his blessings. But I was a sickly child, thought for a long time not to live, and so became known simply as Baruch: *Praise.* As my father said, He who walks the face of this earth must learn to bend his knee to the Lord. So from early on I knew my lot in life: to worship and praise God, to serve only Him, to submit, and to endure. So demands our Creator, the Holy One, blessed be He.

My mother's father died before I was born, but I knew my father's father well. Isak Zalman, may his name be for a blessing, was a true *Tzaddik*, a righteous man. In his youth he was a disciple of Rabbi Israel Ben Eliezar, the Baal Shem himself, the great Master of the Name. Together they wandered and worshiped in these very mountains where I now reside. Later Rav Isak grew to rule a mighty Hasidic court in Iași, and there he spread the teachings of the Holy One, even unto the belief, much disputed, that the Master was the prophet heralding the coming of the Messiah. Did not the Baal Shem say, And if the righteous Redeemer does not come within sixty years, I will be compelled to re-enter this world? If he has not yet returned, who is to say that he will not come, or that we can do better than to live our lives each day as if he will? So we affirm each day in our daily prayers: The Lord will send our Messiah at the End of Days to redeem those waiting for His final salvation.

My grandfather was a much beloved rebbe, his rulings sought by pious Jews from near and far. His opinions, it is said, bore the weight of thirty sages, and a single word from him had the power to avert the evil decree. But when he grew old, he determined to leave Iași and return to the mountains of his youth, to live a life of study and contemplation, growing closer in spirit to the Master as he grew closer to him in death. The people wept and begged him to stay, but he would not be turned, and so took up residence in Alba-Bistriţa, the Carpathian village where I, too, now reside.

With my grandfather's departure, my father rose to take his place at court, full of fear and trembling, and with great reluctance in his heart. For although he was a learned man in his own right, he knew my grandfather had been touched by the Baal Shem, and the spirit of the Master infused everything he said and did. Each summer my father sent me to live with my grandfather in order that I, too, might take to heart the teachings of the Baal Shem, and the spirit of the Master might reside in me. As my father said: The words of the Master are like a fountain that does not run dry, and his deeds are like a stream that never exhausts itself. But in his presence are the living waters that lead to redemption.

Each year my departure for the mountains pained my mother, but Iaşi was hot and congested in the summer months, and she hoped the cool air and pure waters of Alba-Bistriţa might strengthen and restore me. So she let me go. I was sickly, as I have said, pale and thin, prone to pains in the head and falling fits where I lost awareness of myself and my soul, it seemed to me, departed my body in search of that place where it ultimately would abide. As the Baal Shem taught: In redemption the spirit shall return home from its exile.

Once in a fit I traveled as if in a dream to the Heavens where I saw the Almighty Himself enthroned in His splendor, with ranks of angels arrayed on either side. As

I stood dumbstruck in the face of such Glorious Majesty, a man took my hand and in a voice as pure and clear as crystal spoke to me, saying, I have waited for you for a long time. Then I looked up, saw the Master beside me, and was flooded with the deepest and most complete happiness I have ever known. When the fit subsided, and I found myself once again within these earthly confines, I was full of sorrow. But since that moment I have had no fear of illness nor death. Indeed I wait the day of my departure from this earthly life with impatience, knowing I will once again stand at the Master's side.

My fits, however, frightened my mother and brought her no end of worry. Many were the times that I woke on the floor of the hall where I had been studying to find her cool hand on my forehead, her tears bathing my cheek. One doctor after another she summoned to court, but none had the means to cure me. Finally in desperation she determined to take me to Chernivtsi to consult with a rabbi there who was well known for his healing powers.

Three days we traveled by wagon to the capital city, where we joined a line of petitioners at the rabbi's study. When at last we were admitted, the rabbi—a man not much bigger than a child, who had a white beard that hung to his waist and who smelled most pungently of onion and garlic—put his ear close to my mouth to listen to my breath. He told me to extend my arms wide and then, with my eyes closed, bring my fingertips together. Finally he asked me to stand first on one foot then the other. When this examination was complete, he informed my mother that a wandering spirit had taken up residence in my breast, and unless it was expelled, would wage war inside me, seeking to gain total possession of my body.

As my mother watched, he directed me to a couch and bade me lie down. He told me to close my eyes and performed a series of rituals that I was grateful not to see, for I believe they were wondrously strange. Once, when I peeked, I saw him turning in place like a top while he murmured a nonsensical series of words. But my mother was much encouraged by this display, and when he was done, gladly gave the rabbi the gold coins he demanded. Scarce three days had passed upon our return home when I fell senseless to the ground with a fit like all the others. Then she knew no mortal man, only God, had the power to alter my fate.

So as a child I spent the summers in Alba-Bistrița with my grandfather. Together we studied the ancient texts and delved deeply into the mysteries known as Kabbalah. Many were the walks we took in these mountains, climbing the forested slopes, crossing streams and rivers, passing through meadows and dells. I deemed those days, then and now, as among the happiest of my earthly life.

Three score and ten are our years, the psalmist tells us, eighty with good health. God granted my grandfather a long life, but the year I turned thirteen, his soul returned to its Maker. My father journeyed to Alba-Bistrița to bury his father and afterwards took me home with him to Iași. There I read from the Torah for the first time as a Bar Mitzvah and took my place at court. Now, under my father's direction, the burden of my studies increased as I prepared myself for the time when I would become rebbe in his place. I had a younger brother, but since I was the eldest, the succession was my duty and my right.

So short a life, and so short the years! Five years later my father died, felled by apoplexy, the blood draining from his heart and congesting in his brain. In my grief I sat on a low stool, meditating on the words: Man lasts no longer than grass, no longer than a wild flower he lives, one gust of wind and he is gone, never to be seen there again. How could I possibly ascend to my father's place? Surely I was too frail for such weighty responsibilities. When the thirty days of ritual mourning came to an end, I grew cold with terror and fled to the mountains where I prayed for guidance at the grave of my grandfather. There a delegation of elders from Iași found me, and after three days of hard argument, persuaded me to return.

Ten long years I ruled my father's court, ten grueling and arduous years. In that time I took Raisel as my wife. She was a worldly woman then, much enamored of life at the court, where all accorded her the honor due a rebbe's wife. In time she gave birth to a girl, as beautiful as she was beloved, whom we called Bathsheva, for my wife's grandmother. Bathsheva was a delightful child, full of affection and mischief; nothing pleased me more than to hear her voice calling out to me—Papa!—and to feel the embrace of her little arms, the touch of her lips to my cheek. She had a white kitten that followed her everywhere, accompanied by the tinkling of a bell that hung from a ribbon around its neck. Whenever I heard the sound of that bell, my heart leapt with joy.

Soon, however, my joy turned to grief as I realized our daughter had inherited my illness and like me was sickly, subject to fits. Night and day Raisel devoted herself to our child and, as my mother had before her, sought the advice

47

of doctors and rabbis, traveling the face of the earth in search of a cure. To no avail. Bathsheva only became sicker and sicker, until by the time she reached the age of eight, we despaired of her life.

As my daughter grew ever weaker, my discontent at court increased. With each passing day I became more and more certain I was not only unfit but also unwilling to serve as rebbe. Longing for the mountains, for the cool purity of the rivers and the solitary shade of the forests, consumed me. Finally I determined to flee again to Alba-Bistriţa, this time never to return. I feared at first my wife would refuse to accompany me, but she, too, had changed in the years since our daughter was born. Raisel had become convinced that Bathsheva's illness was punishment for deeds of arrogance she had committed at court in coveting wealth and prestige. She began to long for the simple life of the mountains where she hoped she might redeem herself— and where, perhaps, our daughter's life might be saved. So in the end she determined to accompany me, and we fled to Alba-Bistriţa.

Three months later our beloved Bathsheva died, and we buried her in the earth at my grandfather's side.

Long after the formal mourning period had passed, I grieved for my child, giving myself over to the darkness of melancholy, even though I knew it was a sin to despair. Eventually the years passed and my sorrow lightened, although I still cannot hear the sound of a bell without feeling a stab of pain to my heart. But my wife's grief has been without end. For a time I thought the Lord might grant her the blessing of another child, but such was not to be. God has given us much in this life, but He has not given us more children.

Even so we have lived a good life here, a humble life, close to the graves of my daughter and my grandfather, holding dear to our hearts the teachings of the Baal Shem. At one time our village boasted three synagogues, but now only one remains, an old wooden building where it is said the Master himself once prayed. Inside is a sanctuary with pews where over fifty men prayed; nowadays a handful of Jews struggle to maintain the *minyan*, the quorum of ten needed for our daily prayer service. The rest of the Jews in the village have gone, some to the New World, others to Palestine where they attempt to do the work of the Messiah with mortal hands. Upstairs an open balcony serves as a gallery where the women pray; at the front of the sanctuary stands the holy ark, the one remnant of the synagogue's former glory. The ark is over thirty handbreadths tall, made of richly carved cedar, fronted by a ruby-red silk curtain, and topped with the Eternal Light, an oil lamp that is never extinguished. Inside we keep our most precious possession, the Torah scrolls containing the word of God. The synagogue has no rabbi, and when called upon, I rise from my lowly position as caretaker to perform the necessary rites. I lead the daily prayers, tutor the youth who are still willing to learn, preside occasionally at weddings, and sadly far more frequently at funerals. I even perform the ritual of circumcision, although perhaps it is fortunate that the need for this service dwindles, since my hand grows less steady with age.

Meanwhile my wife and I live out the remainder of our days in these two small rooms attached to the back of the synagogue, summer and winter, winter and summer. We eat from our garden, drink water from the courtyard well, sell honey from the bees we tend, and collect our pennies to purchase oil for lamps, for cloth and candles, a bit of Sabbath wine. At night I sit by the window and admire the stars that are our daily reminder of the Creation. According to my grandfather, I am descended from the tribe of Benjamin, known for its fierceness in battle. I seek out the constellation of the wolf in the night sky and trace it with my finger, a cluster of stars with the brightest one shining for the eye. As it is written in the Torah: Benjamin is a ravening wolf. In the morning he devours his prey, and in the evening he is still dividing the spoil.

During the day I wander the mountain paths that have long become familiar to me, climbing and descending alongside the white, fast-moving waters of the river that give the village its name. I collect the herbs that brighten and assuage our daily lives: the valerian root I brew into tea for my wife, easing her each night into sleep; the rose hips I make into ruby-red wine to soothe the pains in my joints. If above the river's tumult I no longer hear the voice of my grandfather, the voice of his Master, the Baal Shem, has called to me ever more clearly, and I recall the joy I felt in my vision as I stood at his side.

I am older now than my grandfather was when he left this earth. The world I once knew has departed and it is long time I depart with it. My parents are gone, and even my brother has taken his place amongst the righteous in the heavens. Nowadays his son, my nephew Ezriel, holds court in Iași. Even there, I have heard, the foundations of the world shake. I turn aside from the mirror, not wanting to see what is in it: this old man, bent and shrunken as a twig.

My wife is like an empty coat. When I visit my grandfather's grave, the cemetery pathways are overgrown with brambles, the stones green and dripping. My daughter sleeps in earth that is thick and moist and smells of Paradise. I push aside the branches and scrape away the lichens with fingernails as thick and yellow as beeswax to read the fading letters of my grandfather's name. As he has been forgotten, so will I. So I have long wished it. My work on this earth is finished. So I believed. But it was not meant to be. Not after Dora came into my life.

Four

.·.·.

GUS

Gus steals a glance at Anna, who is sitting quietly in the car beside him as she has since they left the hospital that morning, her hands in her lap, her legs crossed demurely, her eyes focused on the passing landscape. The nurses helped her dress that morning, wanting her to look good for her homecoming, and she's wearing white gloves and patent-leather sandals, a sleeveless sundress with a flared skirt and red-rose pattern. She isn't particularly pretty—Gus has long since decided that—caught at that awkward stage all girls must go through, when they give up their childishness for a blossoming womanhood. Her features are too large for her face, her lips too full, her eyebrows high and arching. Still, there's something striking about her, and he can well imagine she will one day be the kind of woman men will find attractive.

"Almost there," he says, using the bright, cheerful voice he reserves for his patients, the one he hopes they will find reassuring, but which so often rings false in his own ears. Anna turns to him, fixing him with dark eyes. He ventures a smile but to his great disappointment it goes unanswered. Three days earlier, when he forged his plan to bring her home, Dr. Meyer had issued a grave warning about becoming too close to his patient. Too close! Gus could only wish. Ever since he met Anna, his struggle has been to get close enough to her—to get her to open up enough—to enable him to cure her. He remembers how she walked around a fellow patient in the Phipps courtyard as if the woman were an inconveniently placed piece of furniture. Sometimes, when he is with her, he has the same disturbing feeling: as much as he is there, he isn't. Even now he could be nothing more than an anonymous chauffeur, hired to take her home.

The Glanzes live on an estate in the village of Marby, just north of Rye, New York, on a spit of land that runs along the coast between the Marby River and the Long Island Sound. On the water, Gus thinks suddenly as he turns onto the shore road and the Sound comes into view. This must be it: the place where Anna's brother drowned. He hadn't thought of that. He's returning her to the source of her trauma. Is she ready for it? He finds himself feeling distinctly uneasy as he navigates the car down the narrow country road. The mind is a powerful thing, Meyer had said. Also this: Children are capable of acting as judge, jury—and executioner, too. Well, Anna couldn't stay at Phipps. That much is clear. Gus settles himself. He certainly couldn't let her go to Spring Meadow—he might as well lock her away for life. She's just a child, with her life ahead of her. He had to try something.

It's a lovely summer day, the brightness of the sky softened by the haze that comes from being so close to the water. Trees line the road, poplars and magnolias and oaks, their leaves trembling in the shore breeze. Gus allows the beauty of the area to infect his spirits, lightening them, too. Anna is eager to return home, at least so he has managed to convince himself. She hasn't actually said so herself. To his great disappointment she hasn't said anything since the day he told her he would be taking her home. The hypnosis session he conducted with her immediately afterwards ended in failure, with Anna refusing to speak a single word. The breakthrough, if it is to come, will have to come later.

Even more troublesome is the fact that ever since his announcement, Anna has reverted to sleepwalking. Twice the charge nurse found her wandering the halls of the ward and fetched Gus to return his patient to bed. He's never gotten used to these night rambles of hers, in which she gives every outward appearance of being awake—moving about with her eyes open, gesturing, even responding to his voice—while inside she remains withdrawn, deeply asleep, tangled in a dream world of her own making. The wolves must have driven her from her bed again; she looked terrified. The doctor in him wonders how she reconciles the mix of stimuli that come to her during her night walks, the images generated by her sleeping mind, with the signals flooding into her physical body. Do they blend together? Does the outside world become integrated into her inner narrative? Or do the two realms remain distinct? And what about him? What happens when he takes her arm, soothes her, brings her still asleep back to her bed? Does he take on a fictitious role in the story generated by her imagination, or is he still in her mind Dr. Thaler, himself?

He had vaguely hoped she would start eating again once she learned she was going home. Instead, over the last few days her refusal to eat has become, if anything, more entrenched. With a great deal of coaxing, the nurses have managed to get some broth to pass her lips, nothing more.

In the back seat of the car is the thermos of coffee he packed for himself along with a bottle of lemonade and extra sandwiches he brought optimistically for Anna, just in case the journey would encourage her to break her long fast. But she has touched nothing and subsequently he hasn't either. After ten hours on the road, he feels tired and parched, a bit lightheaded. It's almost five o'clock.

One might as easily say that by taking Anna home, he is making her worse instead of better. Over and over again he has watched her put brush to paper, generating paintings of her wolf visions, the faces looming large on the page, staring at the viewer with a threatening gaze. But he's also noticed a heightened awareness in her eyes, a growing alertness he interprets as a good sign. For over six weeks now she's been at Phipps, living the life of a patient, a kind of shadow existence. She's about to be thrust back into the messiness, unpredictability, and complexity of the real world. It's only natural that her symptoms might flare up again. The setback, he is sure, is only temporary, like the spike of temperature that often comes just before a fever breaks. It would be a mistake to read anything more into it. She will be better off once she is at home.

The road winds past sprawling waterfront estates, hidden behind privacy walls and copses of trees, yielding bright glimmering glimpses of the Sound. Gus has never been this far north before, never gone farther than Manhattan, and then only once by train, when he was just a child and his parents took him to a concert at Carnegie Hall. The focus of the trip was his sister Rosa, who already showed signs of being a musical prodigy; he was brought along almost as an afterthought. On the opposite side of the road modest clapboard cottages line the river. These must date from the time when Marby was nothing more than a fishing village—before the millionaires came, drawn by the beauty of the area and its proximity to the financial halls of Manhattan. Some of the villagers fish still. Boats strung with nets ply the river, traveling between the docks and the Sound. Heavy, moist sea air flows into the car through the open windows, bearing the faint tang of seaweed, of shells and rotting fish.

It's an impressive place, this stretch of shoreline, with its frank, unabashed display of privilege and wealth. Also intimidating. Gus thinks back to what he has heard about Lionel Glanz, his massive accumulation of wealth and power, his driving political aspirations. Gus is unused to money and privilege, has always felt awkward around people who have them, painfully aware of his own modest circumstances. The narrow row house he grew up in was scarcely large enough for the four of them, his parents, his sister, and himself. The piano where his mother gave afternoon lessons to the neighborhood's children took up most of the front room. Rosa and his parents had bedrooms on the second floor, but Gus slept in the attic in a small room that once must have been meant for a servant; the Thalers had no money for such luxuries. Each night at bedtime he climbed a narrow set of back stairs from the kitchen past the second floor.

His parents had come to Baltimore from their native Vienna shortly before the outbreak of the first Great War; his father had received an invitation to serve as guest conductor to the Peabody Orchestra while the maestro was on sabbatical. When the commission expired, they had simply stayed on, his father cobbling together a meager salary by serving part-time on the faculty of the conservatory, his mother teaching privately. Rosa was born as the war ended, Gus a few years later. Later when the political situation for Austrian Jews worsened and then reached catastrophic proportions, the Thalers had congratulated themselves on their foresight in leaving their homeland early. But really foresight had nothing to do with it. It was simply luck.

"A lovely day to be coming home, isn't it Anna?" he says now with the same forced cheerfulness. Once again Anna turns to face him and then after a moment, impassively turns away. But the look in her eyes lingers with him, the pain in her gaze tugging at his heart. How she is suffering, this girl! Her face is so pale, her lips dry and cracked, scabbed from the incessant picking he has yet to wean her from.

Rosa was just as pale in the months before she died. What Gus remembers most is the feeling of helplessness that came over him as he stood by his sister's bed, watching her suffer, watching his mother weep, his father grow stony and remote. They tried to spare him, sending him from the room, but that only made things worse. He felt excluded, abandoned by the family: felt acutely how small he was, how weak and worthless. The feeling of worthlessness led to anger, and the anger led to his vow to do something, to be the kind of person who would eliminate such suffering from the world. His parents always treasured musical ability, prized virtuosity above all else in the world. But through his bedroom window beneath the roof of their house, Gus could see the dome of the Johns Hopkins Hospital, sitting high across town on the hill, and from that moment on, it became his beacon.

Now he's the doctor he long dreamed of becoming, making decisions in the best interests of his patients—in the best interest of children like Anna. The truth—something he has never admitted to anyone, not even to Meyer the Mind Reader, Father Confessor—is that part of him feels like a little boy still, the one who was so helpless in the face of his sister's death. He's plagued by doubts, by the fear that he's not at all up to the task he has set for himself. Even worse are the feelings of grandeur that occasionally seize him, fantasies that he has somehow been chosen to be a healer, destined to lead a life of higher purpose and meaning. Neither extreme, he knows, reflects the truth, which is simply that he is a young doctor, reasonably skilled and trained, with much yet to learn. He worries these extremes will blind him, when what he needs most as a psychiatrist is the ability to see.

See, that is, Anna Glanz. Once again he turns to her. "Home, Anna," he says. "It will be good to be there, don't you think?"

This time she doesn't even turn at the sound of his voice.

The weeks Gus has spent hypnotizing Anna, the nights he has spent poring over her paintings—all of these things convince him she suffers from the delusion that she is responsible for her brother's death. What other possible explanation for her mutism could there be? But he's also aware that he has no real proof. What if he's wrong? What if there's something else tormenting Anna, something dark and sinister hidden behind those eyes?

The thought troubles him, and he puts it aside. He needs to concentrate on the present. He will return Anna to the bosom of her family, see her eat again, and see her safely settled. A day or two in Marby, and he will be ready to go back to Baltimore. With luck, he will see her speaking again, too. And if not? Surely in time the mutism will resolve. The girl is young, and children are remarkably resilient. All that matters is that the immediate crisis will have been averted. There will be no more talk of Spring Meadow.

For some time now they've been following a low stone wall that dips and curves with the road. All at once Anna straightens up and peers forward. They have come to an entranceway marked by stone pillars, cast-iron numbers announcing the Glanzes' address. Gus slows the car and turns onto a gravel drive that winds through lawns studded with quince trees and copper beeches. In the distance, on a rise above the water, sits a white stucco mansion, softened by thick boxwood hedges.

"Here we are," he says. Anna ignores his voice, staring straight ahead, but with a quickened intensity that reassures him he's done the right thing by bringing her home.

He pulls the car to a stop at the end of the drive. He's about to get out and open the car door for her when he sees there's no need. She's already getting out herself.

"Well, then!" he says laughing, feeling the cheerfulness genuinely this time. "It's good to be home, isn't it, Anna?"

All at once, as she slides away from him in her seat, she tugs on her dress, and it rides up, revealing a stretch of her leg, the curve of her thigh. Gus finds himself drawn to that revelation of bare skin, his eyes traveling to the thin waist above it, to the swelling of her young breasts. Heat rises in him, coloring his face.

Good God. Did she do that deliberately? What was she thinking?

"Anna, wait," he says. No use. She isn't listening. She has leapt from the car and run to the house. Just as she reaches the door, she stops and turns to him. On her lips is a knowing smile. There's a clear look of triumph in her eyes. For the first time he wonders who is in charge here. Was it his idea to bring her home—or hers?

"Anna," he says again, "I—" But what is there to say? In any case, it's too late. She has vanished into the house, leaving him in the car to think about what has just happened. Leaving him to think about her wolves.

Five

CLAIRE

By the time Claire gets home, the headache is worse, the throb giving way to an iron band that tightens across the back of her head, pinching both temples. It'll be a full-blown migraine soon; a shimmery worm of light has already begun to glimmer at the edges of her vision. At least she won't have to feel guilty for calling in sick. Migraine, she imagines herself telling Flore tomorrow morning when she comes in to the office, seeing the secretary shake her head, hearing her sympathetic tut-tut. She manages to maneuver the car into the garage—never an easy feat, even on her best days. The garage is so narrow the car barely fits, and the distortion in her vision doesn't help. Anyway she's not a good driver, she never has been. Usually she takes the bus to work. Roger always does, but then her husband doesn't get visits from the wolf.

She closes the garage door and steps outside onto the sidewalk. In the migraine's glimmering light the wolf vanishes and reappears like a staticky image on a poorly tuned TV. Claire ascends the stairs, the wolf patiently dogging her heels. She and Roger live in the second-floor apartment of a modern steel and glass duplex that sprouts from the middle of a row of stately brick townhomes like a poisonous mushroom in a meadow. This is Georgetown, where every inch of space is accounted for, fought over, and priced accordingly. Even the streets are only barely wide enough to allow for a single lane of traffic, the branches of the trees on either side reaching for one another overhead, never quite touching. Hence the witheringly small single garage, the winding, clacking metal staircase that leads to their door, lashed in the summer by wind and rain, in the winter by ice and snow.

She's not complaining. They chose the apartment for the light. They both remarked on it when they toured the place after they got married, Roger a brand-new hire in the George Washington University history department, Claire already settled in her job as a prosecutor downtown. Light on that winter day poured through the windows of the living room, streamed across the blond wooden floors, gushed through the skylight into the kitchen, cascaded into the bedroom through sliding doors that gave out to a balcony gleaming with more light. A twisting spiral staircase led to a tiny loft where Roger would have his study while Claire would curl up like a bird in a nest downstairs, would cook and read and dream in the midst of all that glass, all that glorious, life-affirming light. How she craved it. How she needed it. She could breathe here, they could be *happy* here, she told Roger as he agreed to sign the lease, giving in to her infectious optimism, even though he knew the apartment was more than they could afford.

All that light: surely, if nothing else, it would keep the wolf away. So Claire had told herself. Weren't wolves creatures of the night, denizens of the shadows, of dark thickets and dense, gloomy forests? That had been eight years ago. It had taken the wolf all of six months to make her first appearance in the apartment, curling up one morning in the middle of their sun-soaked bed, her tongue traveling delicately over a paw, making herself quite easily at home. Since then she comes and goes according to her own schedule, disappearing for months, even years at a time, then reappearing at will.

What Claire wouldn't give just now for a dark, shady copse of her own. The light cuts into her eyes, making the headache worse, intensifying the migraine's shimmer. She drops her bag on the kitchen counter, throws off her shoes, pads in her nylon stockings to the cabinet—ever since Princess Diana visited the States, shocking the world with her bare legs, Claire's younger colleagues have taken to going about with naked flesh, but not Claire—and pulls out a bottle of aspirin. Then she twists the cork out of a bottle of white wine. Two tablets, chased with a brimming glass. Not the best combination, she knows, but one that sometimes works.

The first glass gone, she walks into the bedroom and opens a drawer in her dresser. She rummages through to a box in the back, takes it out and sits on the bed. Inside is a tangle of costume jewelry—most of it stolen—a bottle of patchouli oil that is all but empty but still emits a peppery scent, a dried out mood ring, a paper star. On the bottom is a black and white photograph of a girl who looks like Claire, or what she must have looked like decades ago. The photographer has managed that most elusive trick, bringing her to life on paper, as if he'd captured more than just her appearance; he'd captured her soul. Her hair is luminous, falling to her shoulders, her eyes, wide and gleaming with a knowing look, her mouth, ripe, full, expectant. She shows the picture to the wolf, who lies on the bed agreeably beside her. "Before your time." She fingers it gently, carefully, then her hand tenses as if she will make a fist and crush it.

She jams the picture back in the box and shoves it into the dresser.

Back in the kitchen she pours a second glass of wine, takes it into the living room, then drops into the Eames chair—another purchase they couldn't afford. She'd gone out and bought it on her own, without Roger knowing. Afterwards they'd fought over it, Roger insisting she had to get her spending under control, Claire saying the apartment all but demanded it, the polished wood, the rounded contours, the tufted black leather. She sinks back with a sigh. Roger is right about the money, of course, he always is. But she was right about the chair.

She picks up the phone and dials.

"Mount Rose Hospital," says a woman at the other end of the line, her voice crisp and hollow, a heartbeat from automated.

"Dr. Levy, please. Nathan Levy. Tell him it's an emergency." Her brother Nathan is head of cardiology at one of Houston's best hospitals. He's a specialist—an electro-physio-cardio something or other—who gets called in when ordinary cardiologists can't cope. He puts people on the table in his operating room, knocks them out, stops their hearts, fixes them, then restarts them and brings them back to life. A modern-day resurrection of the dead. What happens if you make a mistake? she asked him once. What happens if you kill them and they don't revive? He smiled and said, "It hasn't happened yet."

"Dr. Levy." Nathan's voice is crisp, efficient, not a wasted word or breath.

"Do you want to tell me what's going on?" she says.

"Claire." Ten seconds into their phone call and already Nathan sounds weary, resigned.

"Cassidy called me." The window's open, letting in the ashy, autumnal scent of the trees, which have turned sanguinous, yellowed. A Japanese beetle has found its way into the apartment and beats against the screen.

"Cassidy—what?"

"Called me." Claire registers the surprise in her brother's voice. He's just as shocked as she was that Anna's husband phoned her.

"Why?"

"He wanted to know about Sasha."

"Sasha?" She hears the puzzlement in Nathan's voice. In her mind's eyes she sees him shaking his head, the thick dark hair that once fell to his shoulders reduced to stubble on his bald pate. Nathan's lucky. He takes after their father. He has Julius's tall frame and lanky limbs, whereas Claire is Anna all over again, from her thin figure to her high arching eyebrows. Only their hair differs—Claire's is red while Anna's is brown. At least it was the last time Claire saw Anna, at Olivia's bat mitzvah, which was what, three years ago? Two years after Eloise's. The color was probably from a bottle, although Anna, ever trying to look younger than her years, would never have admitted it, even if she had been talking to Claire, which she most decidedly was not. Claire was not about to subject herself to the humiliation of asking. Two thin, high-strung, nervous women stalking the floor of the ballroom Nathan and Ruth had rented for Olivia's party, eying each other from a distance, keeping carefully apart like cheetahs thrust into the same territory.

Faintly in the background the hospital's paging system sounds. *Dr. Mars, paging Dr. Mars.* Claire wonders if her phone call has pulled Nathan from a consultation or from the O.R. Is he wearing a suit or scrubs? Is he in his office? No, not his office. She wouldn't hear the pages there. One of those phones in the hospital hallway.

"Yes, Sasha. You know. Anna's brother." There's an edge of irritation in her voice. Why is Nathan asking her to explain things he knows very well himself? "The one that died."

"Sasha." She hears him mulling it over, imagines him rubbing his palm over his head the way he does when he's at a loss of what to say. The beetle wings dangerously close to the wolf, who snaps at it but misses. "He was a toddler, right? Mom was—what—a teenager?"

"Something like that. Cassidy wanted to know how he died. He said he asked Anna and she said, 'It was never explained.'"

This time the silence goes on so long she fears she has lost him. *Dr. Lowry, Dr. Yards, paging Dr. . . . .* There's a huff of breath, the sound of footsteps, a door closes, then the pages fade away. Nathan has slipped into a room, taking the phone with him, stretching the cord tight. "What did you say?"

"Nothing. What could I?" Her irritation increases. Why does he keep asking her about things he knows as well as she does? "He wanted to know if Hettie ever said anything about him."

"Did she?"

"Of course not. That was the whole point. We weren't

supposed to talk about him, remember? It was too painful. We were supposed to spare their feelings. Anna and Hettie both. Their childhood was one big train wreck. Poor little rich girls and all that. Losing their brother was just the icing on the cake." Nathan has fallen silent again, a discernible shift on the other end of the line. Something is happening, although Claire has no idea what it is. She feels the first pricklings of fear. She is like Alice in Wonderland, falling, tumbling through a rabbit hole to a new place, but where? "What's going on? Why is all this coming up now?"

The answer comes after a careful pause. "Cassidy didn't say?"

"No. I didn't give him the chance." She smiles in a grim, satisfied way. "I hung up on him."

There's no answer to that.

"Nathan?" Falling, falling, falling—landing, she fears, in a place that isn't good at all. "What is it? What's wrong?"

"Cassidy's worried about her."

"About Anna? Why?"

"She's sick."

"What do you mean, sick?"

"She has cancer." There's a knock, the sound of the door opening, Nathan's voice, sharp, gruff—"Give me a minute"—and then: "She's dying."

"Dying?" Falling, falling into the wolf's lair. "How long have you known?"

"A few weeks."

"And you didn't tell me?" Claire's voice rises in anger.

"She asked me not to. I was hoping, when you said Cassidy called—"

"Fuck, Nathan. Anna? Dying?"

"I'm sorry, Claire."

"What is it? What does she have?"

"Lung cancer."

"But she stopped smoking ages ago. You told me so yourself, after Olivia was born."

"The damage was done."

"They have treatments for these things nowadays."

"Treatments—yes. Cure—no." The knock on the door again. "I said a minute," Nathan barks out. Then, to Claire: "She has a good oncologist. The best out there. They say she'll have some time yet."

"So not now—"

"Months, Claire. Not years."

Claire feels her anger building—better that than the fear that's behind it. "Anna's dying and you thought I didn't need to know?"

"I wanted to tell you. I was going to." He hesitates. "I wasn't sure I should."

"Afraid you'd send your little sister over the edge?"

"Something like that." She hears the worry in his voice. "Have I?"

"No. Although I almost got arrested for shoplifting today." She shrugs. "I felt like going out." What choice did she have? The wolf was breathing hot on her heels, practically chasing her out of the apartment after Cassidy called.

"Claire."

"It's all right. It's fine. *I'm* fine. I got off. I knew the cop. And yes"—she recites the words like the good little schoolgirl that she most certainly is not—"I'm taking my meds." She took a pill in the car, didn't she? Her voice

68

drops. "How is she?"

"Okay for now. They're starting chemotherapy in a few weeks. Things will get harder then."

"Have you seen her?"

"We went to Midfield when we heard."

"You and the girls?"

"Yes."

"Ruth?"

"Yes."

Claire laughs, a short angry burst. "Anna must have loved that. The good daughter she never had."

"I said—" Is he talking to her or the door? "Claire, stop."

"I can't believe it. Anna, dying?" She twists the phone cord around her finger. She would pick at her lip, too, if she didn't stop herself. "I thought she'd live forever. I thought she'd be there to the end, this old crone, sitting in her rocking chair, still refusing to speak to me."

"Talk to Roger. Let him know."

"Sure, if I can get him away from his desk long enough to listen. I don't mind that he's writing a book on the Cold War. I just wish he'd stop reenacting it in our kitchen."

"What's wrong?"

"Nothing. Everything. The usual." She takes a breath. "He brought the baby up again. He thinks we should have one."

"Roger's a good guy. He just wants normal things."

"Then he shouldn't have married me."

"Claire—"

She doesn't let him finish. "It's sad, isn't it? They're gone, Nathan, they're all gone, Lionel, Frieda, too, they took their whole world with them." She can still see it: the big house

69

in Bethesda they lived in when Lionel was senator, the chauffeur, the maid, that silly cook with the frizzy hair who doted on Frieda. No one even remembered them anymore. The detective who arrested her got it all wrong. He thought Lionel was a mayor. And they were everything! They were larger than life. Lionel sponsored acts in Congress. Frieda got a medal for the arts. They knew the president. They had dinner in the White House. And Lionel, silly Lionel, who remained so devoted to his long-dead mother through it all, keeping the portrait of Dora—the kleptomaniac—hanging in the hall.

Don't blame me for shoplifting, I come by it honestly, she wants to say to Nathan but doesn't. Meanwhile the wolf has succeeded in capturing the beetle. Gulp and it's gone. Claire sighs. "I don't get it. It's been years and years. Why is Anna bringing up Sasha's death now? And why would she say it was never explained?"

Nathan falls silent. She can almost hear him biting back his words. "Claire. I'm at work. Can we talk about this later?"

"Anna made Cassidy her errand-boy, Nathan." The anger is subsiding, not a good sign. Claire feels hurt and wounded, the rawness surfacing in her voice. "She didn't even have the guts to call me herself."

"Claire, please. I can't do this now."

"What's going to happen to her?"

"She's going to die. Tell Roger. Don't keep him in the dark."

"Fuck you, Nathan. Fuck Cassidy, and Anna, too."

The line goes dead.

"Nathan?" Her voice grows wistful, small. The wolf stands beside her, looking at her fondly, her head resting companionably on her knee. "What's going to happen to me?"

Six

GUS

"Dr. Thaler. Would you like to come in?"

The woman in the doorway gives Gus a bemused look, bordering on outright amusement. She's of medium height with a full figure, the kind of woman his mother would call pleasingly plump, dressed in a dark pencil skirt and white blouse, the sleeves turned up. Her eyes peek out from under her hair which, dark and cut in a bob, falls in a long fringe across her forehead. She appears to be having some trouble keeping her mouth, which is generous and mobile, from breaking into a smile. Is she making fun of him?

Gus is still in the car, stunned by his glimpse of Anna's bare leg, even more so by the look she gave him as she entered the house: the knowing smile, the triumph in her eyes. What has just happened? What—if anything—does Anna know? And why does he feel so sure that, whatever it is, he doesn't?

He hastens to get out—never an easy task given his height and the small size of the car, the only one he could afford—managing to bump his head in the process.

Ouch. The woman mouths the word, her eyes widening.

"Mrs. Glanz." He strides towards her, ignoring the pain in his skull. He straightens his tie, attempting to restore some sense of professional gravitas as he holds his hand out

71

to his hostess. "I'm pleased to meet you."

"As she will be to meet you." The woman takes his hand in a warm, steady grip. "I'm Beatrice Chase. Mrs. Glanz's secretary." She has lost the battle with the smile, and it spreads across her face, lightening her eyes, which have tones of amber like a cat's.

He has yet to release her hand and hurries now to do so, executing a small bow. Damn that proper Viennese upbringing. This kind of thing looks so ridiculous to Americans. "Miss Chase." He could kick himself. He should have known. She's far too young to be Anna's mother, in her early twenties at most. And rich people never open their own doors, do they?

"I can't tell you how grateful we all are to you, Dr. Thaler." Her face takes on a sober cast. "We're so thankful to have Anna home again." She steps to the side, ushering him into the house. "Please, do come in."

"I—that is—" He stumbles over the words, his face reddening. Carrot Top. "The bags. I've left them in the trunk."

"Don't worry yourself about that." There's that smile again. Is he really so amusing? "We'll take care of the luggage."

Nor do rich people carry their own bags. Will he ever get anything right?

The Glanzes' mansion is broadly rectangular in the middle, flanked by projecting wings. Small balconies with scrolled railings adorn the upstairs; downstairs French doors open the house to views of the outdoors. Gus steps past Miss Chase into a small foyer, lit by a crystal chandelier, then into a grand entrance hall that easily, he notes without

72

irony, would swallow the Baltimore row house he grew up in. The feeling is one of immersion, like wading into the sea until the waters flow over his head, making it impossible to breathe. Everything is too much, the Oriental carpet—did they ever make them that big?—and polished wooden floors, the table with its vase of white lilies, the enormous gilded mirror, endlessly reflecting. The air is hushed, scented with the flowers, with undertones of rich woods and dark oils. Hallways on either side lead to more rooms; a wide staircase curves to the second floor. Straight ahead is a formal living room with silken sofas, gleaming tables, a shining grand piano. The doors are flung open to a terrace studded with boxes of blood-red geraniums. Beyond them comes a broad expanse of green grass, and there at the bottom of the hill, filling the view to the horizon, the bright blue reaches of the Sound.

The most arresting feature in the room, however, is the stone hearth, large enough for small children to stand in. Over it hangs the portrait of a woman with an Old World air, dressed in a violet velvet gown, a glorious mane of auburn hair—her best feature—cascading to her shoulders. On her lips is a secret smile; a golden chain glimmers around her neck; a silver charm on a ribbon gleams at her wrist. Only it's not a charm, Gus realizes all at once: it's a bell, the kind a cat might wear. How strange. Who would—? He doesn't have time to finish the thought.

"Mrs. Glanz has asked me to give you her apologies," Miss Chase says. She has appeared suddenly beside him, while he still stands in the middle of the hall, lost, wondering. "She's gone upstairs to be with Anna. She's hoping to speak to you later, after you're settled."

"Of course." Gus executes the bow again; he can think of nothing else to do.

The smile twitches at the corners of her mouth. "If you'll just follow me?"

She leads him up the staircase, his view of the hall rotating and changing as he climbs. High above, a clerestory of windows lets in the sun, streaming light onto the crystals of a magnificent chandelier; the one in the foyer, he sees now, was only a foretaste. At the top of the stairs he encounters a grandfather clock with a transparent face, intricate brass gears manipulating images of the sun and the moon. As Gus stares in wonderment, it chimes out the quarter-hour, startling him, reminding him to catch up with Miss Chase, who has gone—she is a fast walker—quite a distance down a long hallway without him.

Quickly he passes the opening to a nest of rooms, bedrooms, closets, dressing rooms, baths. "The master suite." Miss Chase speaks to him over her shoulder as she hurries down the hall. The suite is cast in gloomy shadow, the faint sounds of a woman's voice, speaking in low and urgent tones, emerging from the depths. Is that Mrs. Glanz, engrossed in her reunion with her daughter? He can't make out her words and has no time to stop and listen.

"Anna's room," Miss Chase is saying, farther down the hall. Anna's door is open, and he hurries to look in, getting a glimpse of the detritus that fills the rooms of young girls: book cases, shelves crammed with dolls, a table covered with glass animal figurines. There are baskets of trinkets, a red-white-and blue flag—France?—on a stick, a broken pinwheel on the dresser, heaps of sheet music. Through the window he can see the Sound. Everything is carefully clean

74

and dusted, even the phonograph and stack of records on the floor, giving the room a static, lifeless air. As if it has been converted into a museum where nothing is allowed to be touched, and where nothing is ever allowed to change.

They have been waiting, Gus thinks, with a sharp intake of breath, for their daughter to come home. Both of Anna's parents. They have never given up hope.

He realizes he's been staring, realizes also that Miss Chase is waiting for him with an impatient air. "Hettie sleeps here," she says at the room opposite Anna's. Hettie's door, too, is open, giving Gus a glimpse of a room much like Anna's, only very much lived in, with the contents strewn about as if a tornado has hit.

He catches up to Miss Chase at the next room, which like Anna's, overlooks the water. The door is ajar, giving him a view of a small bed, the mattress bare, a few empty shelves, scrubbed clean. "Who," he starts to say, meaning, Who lives here?, when all at once he sees Miss Chase stop. She draws her lower lip between her teeth—a charming gesture—but with a look of distress in her eyes. He's surprised to see it. Until now she's been perfectly self-possessed. Then he realizes. Of course. No one lives in this room. It must have belonged to Sasha—to Anna's brother. Is Miss Chase going to say something about that? No. With a quick tug, she closes the door.

She picks up the pace again, taking him to the last room on the hall, this one on Hettie's side of the house. Inside is a suitcase flung open on a bed. "Mr. Zharkov is staying here. He's one of Mr. Glanz's associates. You will meet him at dinner tonight. He and Mr. Glanz have gone into the city for the day. Mrs. Glanz told me to tell you she is sorry that their guest room is taken. You will have to sleep in the servants' quarters." Miss Chase's face is impassive as she recites these facts, her judgments kept to herself. She sweeps past him to the end of the hall, which culminates in a closed door. "If you'll just—" She turns back to make sure he is following, then opens the door and sails through to the other side.

The feeling is one of narrowing, of constriction, the light, expansive spaces of the front of the house giving way to a warren of dark rooms at the back. "Mr. Slocum lives here," Miss Chase says, ticking them off. "Mr. Slocum is Mr. Glanz's chauffeur. This is Mrs. Arturo's room, the housekeeper. This room is for the maid, her name, I believe, is Marie. She's new. Elena Sauer lives here. Mrs. Glanz's cook."

Gus laughs, a loud guffaw, a clumsy attempt to bring Miss Chase over to his side.

She turns back to him, her eyebrows raised.

"I'm sorry, it's just that *sauer* is German for *sour*. A funny name for a cook, if you see what I mean."

He falls silent as the cook, a pudgy woman with a halo of frizzy red hair, suddenly emerges from the far end of the hall, casts a dour glance at him, and vanishes into her room.

The joke, in any case, is lost on Miss Chase. Without a word, she marches to the next room. "Mrs. Glanz's studio."

The middle of this room is taken by a tall table draped in a sheet. Beyond it stands a cupboard filled with tangles of twisted wire, putty knives, rags, gobs of dried clay. More clay fills buckets on the floor, giving the room an earthy, moist scent. "Mrs. Glanz sculpts?" Gus says in surprise. He knew she was an artist, but he'd assumed, based on Anna's artwork, that she was a painter.

Miss Chase lifts her chin, once again keeping her opinions to herself. "Mrs. Glanz is well known for her sculpture."

The next room is clearly empty, with no one living in it. Gus knows better this time to ask, but to his surprise Miss Chase volunteers the information. "The children's nanny used to live here."

Used to. Ah, of course. The nanny would have been for the boy. Now that he is gone—well, the girls would be too old to need looking after. They could take care of themselves.

"And this, Dr. Thaler, is your room."

Miss Chase steps to the side, allowing him to enter before her. Gus's room is much like the others, with a bare wooden floor and plain plaster walls. There's an iron bedstead made up with pillows and sheets, a wardrobe, a desk, a sink and washstand in the corner, a vase with yellow roses set before a mirror.

"Mrs. Glanz offers her apologies." Miss Chase casts down her eyes, making it clear that she is sorry, too. "We know it's not what you were expecting."

How do any of them know what he would expect? The room is far larger than the one he grew up in, more private than the one he currently occupies in the clinic, with nurses and staff passing constantly back and forth outside, knocking at all hours on the door. "It's perfect. The view is lovely." It is. He has a direct line of sight to the water. "Thank you." He feels his face coloring again. "I'll be just fine here."

"I'm glad." Is she blushing, too? "I mean, Mr. and Mrs. Glanz will be pleased to hear it." She smooths down her skirt, drawing herself together, restoring her professional self. "There are two baths at your disposal, one by Mr. Slocum, a second near the servants' stairs." The blush deepens. "Naturally Mr. and Mrs. Glanz expect you to use the stairs at the front of the house."

Naturally. Now that she has said so. Left to himself, Gus would have likely gone up and down wherever he could. If he could find his way through this maze of a house, that is.

"Cocktails are on the terrace at six. I will have Mrs. Arturo come for you."

"Thank you."

She has thought of everything. She turns to leave, hesitates, then turns back again. "I know I have no right to ask, Doctor, but do you think . . ." She draws her lip between her teeth again in that gesture Gus finds so charming. "That is, about Anna, now that she's home, will she—"

"Anna has a long road ahead of her." Gus speaks in a solemn tone, putting on his best doctor face. "But she's taken an important step today." It's a bland, meaningless statement, and he knows it, but he can think of nothing else to say.

Miss Chase seems pleased to hear it. "Thank you. I'm so glad." She breathes out with relief, breaking unrestrained into a smile. It's grateful and warm, this smile of hers, and Gus finds himself wondering if he will have other opportunities like this to see it light up her eyes.

"And you, Miss Chase, where do you live?" He surprises himself by asking.

She, too, appears surprised by the question. "I live out." She purses her lips, and for a moment he wonders if she will say more. Then she straightens. "If there's nothing else then?"

He wishes there were. He would love to find a reason to make her stay. Just having her there makes his fears and his doubts recede. But no, he's sorry to say, he can think of nothing else. And so with a quick nod she is gone, pulling the door closed behind her.

Precisely at six, as promised, a dowdy woman, her black hair tied into a knot at the top of her head, appears at Gus's door, dogged by a mournful air. Mrs. Arturo. Silent as a phantom, her clunky flat shoes with crepe soles gliding effortlessly across the wooden floors, she guides Gus to the terrace and deposits him there, like a package, in the hands of his hostess. Mrs. Glanz. "Frieda," Mrs. Glanz says, taking Gus's hand—taking both his hands—and holding them in a warm embrace. "You must call me that. I couldn't bear it otherwise."

"And you will call me Gus."

"Oh, no," Frieda says, laughing. "I could never do that. Will Doctor do?"

"If you insist." Gus finds himself laughing, too. In one instant she has banished the last of his doubts. She looks at him with such admiration, with gratitude, and respect. She looks at him as Anna's doctor, and in that moment he finds himself becoming it. She's nothing like what he expected the wife of a man like Lionel Glanz to be. He worried so much about what he would say to her, how he would act, what she would think of him. He imagined her as some kind of cold, imperial, commanding presence. Instead he's found her to be sympathetic, infectious, warm. She's dressed modestly in plain cotton slacks, a light sweater, sandals. As far as he can tell, she's wearing no makeup, although he's not very good at telling these things. Her hair, which is long and dark, is pulled back into a simple bun at the nape of her neck. Her jewelry, too, is modest, a necklace with a small onyx pendant, a thin gold chain bracelet, a wedding band.

Mr. Glanz, she informs him with a sad smile, has unfortunately been detained. He will be home shortly but in the meantime sends his apologies. She hopes it isn't too much of an inconvenience for Gus to be entertained by his hostess, alone.

Inconvenience? Gus is horrified by the thought. He is charmed, utterly charmed, and hastens to tell her so.

"Very well." She nods her head in gracious acquiescence, just as a tall black man in a white jacket appears at her side. Mr. Slocum, Frieda explains as she introduces him, is their butler and also acts when needed as Lionel's chauffeur. And what would Gus like to drink? She will have a Manhattan and Gus, speaking quickly, requests a whiskey. He doesn't drink and doesn't know what to ask for. Whiskey, he thinks, is what distinguished men drink. He soon discovers he doesn't care for it. It burns his throat and goes right to his head.

The terrace is wide and broad, a stone patio running along the entire length of the house. Here are the red geraniums in long tin flower boxes that Gus glimpsed earlier from the grand entrance hall. In the middle of the terrace a double set of steps leads down to a grassy slope, which culminates, at the bottom of the hill, in a stone sea wall. From there a second set of steps go down to a concrete pier with a rowboat tethered at the end. Across the way stands a small piney island with the ruins of a gazebo, beyond that distant sails, freshened by the wind, dot the Sound.

"I can't thank you enough for bringing Anna home," Frieda says as she takes Gus's arm and leads him solicitously to the stone balustrade so that he might better appreciate the view. Her eyes fill with tears. "I have been beside myself ever since Lionel told me she stopped eating."

"I'm sure it's only temporary," Gus says, anxious to reassure her. "She'll do better now that she's home."

"I hope you're right." She's being brave for him, holding back the tears, giving him a smile that deepens in its sadness. "I tried to persuade her to eat this afternoon, but she would take nothing from me."

"You must be patient. She needs more time." Although time, he knows, is precisely what Anna doesn't have—unless she will eat.

She takes his hand again. "Do you think she will speak again, too?"

"I do." He pulls himself up, saying the words firmly as if that will make it so.

"I can't tell you how relieved I am to hear it." She clutches his hand briefly to her heart before letting it go, the tears falling freely now. "You'll tell me, won't you, if there's anything I can do to help?"

"Of course." He smiles at her. He would tell her, he thinks, anything.

Gus looks away to give Frieda a chance to wipe her tears, and when she's composed herself, says, "Tell me about Anna, about the girl she was before she became ill. About the girl I'm sure she'll become again." It will be good for him to hear it—good for Frieda to say it, to think back to better times.

"Ah. Anna." A wistful look comes into her eyes. "Difficult at times. I won't deny that. But passionate. Wonderful. A delightful child. Talented in so many ways." She smiles. "Of course I would say that. I'm her mother. But I assure you she was very happy." The smile fades. "We all were."

Then she is there, Anna and the girl who must be her sister, Hettie, coming around the side of the house, walking past the bottom of the terrace steps, down the grassy slope to the water.

Frieda takes a breath, touches him, a light hand on his arm. "Hettie is so pleased to have her sister home. She missed her terribly. The two girls are very close. Anna would do anything for her sister."

Close. Yes, even Gus can see that. Arm in arm the girls descend the steps to the pier, sending a clutch of roosting seagulls into raucous flight, like scraps of white paper thrown to the wind. They sit at the end of the pier, side by side, barefoot, their legs dangling over the water. Anna has changed from her sundress to a sailor's blouse and navy shorts; Hettie is dressed the same. She would always dress the same as her adored older sister, Gus thinks. Hettie has even pulled her hair back in a ponytail identical to Anna's. He can see the resemblances between the two girls, can see the differences, too. Both girls have high, arching eyebrows, broad Slavic cheekbones, olive skin. Those features must come from their father. Frieda is much paler, much more delicate, with a thin, oval face. But Anna, Gus thinks, has also inherited much from her mother: the frail, artistic sensibility, expressed in clay and bronze for the mother, in paint for the daughter.

Does Anna know he is watching her? She turns, looks

up, idly meet his eye. Casually she fiddles with the neck of her blouse, letting it fall down her shoulder so that the bra strap beneath is revealed, the curve of her collarbone, the hollow of her neck.

What is she doing? Flirting with him? Gus finds himself coloring again. He rubs a hand over his face and when he looks again, the blouse is back in place. Thankfully Frieda doesn't seem to have noticed.

"I never wanted any of this," she says with a wave of her hand. "Can you believe it?"

This, Gus understands, is everything: the house, the terrace, the great wealth that surrounds her, the magnificent fortune and estate.

"All I ever wanted is Lionel. I fell in love with him from the start. But this? Senator Glanz? Everyone says he will win, you know." She shakes her head with an air of wonder. "Lionel had absolutely nothing when I met him. He never went past the eighth grade. Can you imagine?" Her face lights up with the memory. "His family had a grocery store in Riverport. He drove a truck. He delivered coal. When we went out on our first date, he had coal dust under his fingernails."

She was the educated one, she explains to him, equally poor, but with refinement. She went to college. Her parents made sure of it. They were from Riga, Latvia, came to Providence, Rhode Island, shortly before Frieda was born. Her father loved to read, loved conversation, had a fine singing voice. In the old world the family had been booksellers. In the new world he painted houses. Her mother took in boarders to make ends meet, but every week put aside a few pennies to buy a thing of beauty to adorn their home: a picture, a flower, a piece of lace. "Food for the soul," Frieda says. "She understood beauty is nourishment, too."

Yes, Gus thinks, nourishment for the soul. That's something Frieda would understand well. In the corner of the terrace stands one of her sculptures, the life-size figure of a man striding forward, launching himself into the future. The body is knife-thin, composed of dabs of bronze adhering to a wire frame. In the center of the chest is a jagged opening: a window to the soul she is so intent on nourishing.

Nearby, on a glass-topped table, sits a gold cigarette case, a matching lighter beside it. Frieda picks up the case, offers it to Gus, and when he refuses, takes a cigarette for herself. For a moment she stands poised with the cigarette in her fingers, a vague look in her eyes, until all at once he understands and hastens, as clumsy as a schoolboy, to take the lighter and light it for her.

"For our first date, Lionel took me dancing on the rooftop of a Providence hotel," she says, exhaling smoke. The cigarette has transformed her. Gone is her air of sadness and regret. She appears confident, sure of herself, controlled. Inspiring, entrancing. Gus can't help but think the words. He's never been around an artist before—he's never been around a woman like Frieda. He can well imagine her—despite what she says—quite at ease in her role as a senator's wife.

"Lionel was a large man, compelling. When he entered a room, people noticed. He didn't have to say a word. We were on the dance floor when he picked me up and turned me upside down. Literally. I fell head over heels in love that night. I've never gotten over it."

Lucky man, Gus finds himself thinking. And lucky woman. To have found such love in their life. It sounded like a dream.

"My parents were horrified. My mother said he would never amount to anything." Frieda laughs, inviting him in on the joke. "In the end we eloped. I've never regretted it. He's been a wonderful husband, a devoted father, and son, too. I never met Dora—his mother—but by all accounts she was a remarkable woman. I'm sure you noticed her portrait in the hall when you came in."

Ah, yes, the woman with the secret smile. Anna's grandmother. Of course. How could he miss it? Dora had the same high arching eyebrows: a Glanz family trait. If Lionel's mother was a remarkable woman, Gus thinks, his wife is no less so. Beauty as simplicity, as honesty, as generosity. It's the mantra by which Frieda lives her life, borne in the modest circumstances of her upbringing, retained despite the radical rise in Lionel's fortunes. She doesn't have to tell Gus this; he can divine it for himself. She's like a composer, orchestrating everything he sees. She might even have conjured the sunset, the black stones of the terrace warmed by the last of the sun, cool dark shadows slipping over the pier where the girls still sit, streaks of red sky reflected in the waters of the Sound, captured in the crimson geraniums. He breathes in deeply, the flower-scented sea air. "It's beautiful here."

"Is it?" Frieda gives him a small smile, the sadness returning to her eyes. "I thought so once. I can't see it anymore."

Ah, yes, of course, Sasha. For the Glanzes this would

85

be a place of tragedy. Not just the loss of their son, but the suffering of their daughter. Behind the veil of cigarette smoke, Gus sees the tension in Frieda's face, the darkening of her hooded eyes, bluish shadows underneath.

"We're leaving here at the end of the summer," she says. "I've asked Lionel to sell the house. He was against it, but I've persuaded him. We're going back to Manhattan. We lived there once, years ago. We're looking for an apartment now. And if Lionel's great ambitions are realized"—her eyes soften, and he sees in them a touch of regret—"then I expect we will be moving again in the new year."

To Washington, she means. He sees how little she wants it. Beauty, simplicity, honesty: where in the halls of the nation's capital will she find those?

"All I ever wanted was to spend my life with people I loved. For the people I love to be safe. My children." The rest, unstated, is understood. All the money in the world, and it couldn't buy the Glanzes safety for their son. For Anna.

All at once there is a commotion below, two men coming around the side of the house onto the hill. The first strides quickly forward with an energy that reminds Gus of Frieda's sculpture, although there are no knife-edges to him; he is a large man, bearish, with thick limbs and a barrel chest. Behind him, coattails flying, comes a shorter man with a frantic air.

The girls scramble to their feet, come running up the steps, Anna leading the way, so that she meets the bearish man on the grass by the sea wall. Then she is in his arms, enfolded, all but disappearing. A moment later his arms open and Hettie, too, is drawn in. The other man stands

86

to the side, breathing hard, running a handkerchief across his forehead. The bearish man straightens, reaches into his pockets, withdraws two apples. The first he hands to Hettie, who bites into it. Anna takes hers, holding it in her hands, studying it as if it were some kind of exotic, foreign object. He bends down, whispers in her ear, stands back with a grin, with the air of a magician, of delights and surprises to come. Presto! Anna bites into her apple, a smile spreading on her face, juice spilling onto her chin.

"Oh." Frieda breathes out in wonder, turning to Gus with shining eyes. Her hand is on his arm again, gripping harder this time. You see this man? her expression says. You see why I love him so?

Anna has taken the large man by the hand; Hettie is at his side. Together they walk up the terrace steps, the two girls munching their apples, while the small man hurries behind. Looking down on the scene, Gus catches Anna's eye. She has nothing for him now. Her face is glowing. She's never looked so alight, so alive. At last, she seems to say, she's where she wants to be: in the arms of her father. Gus may be nothing, but she's something special. She's the daughter of Lionel Glanz.

Seven

CLAIRE

*T*hrough the skylight in Roger's study, the stars ascend like smoke from a chimney, a glittering, glistening stream of light. Thank God Claire's migraine is gone—more aspirin, chased with another glass of white wine finally did the trick—otherwise she wouldn't be able to bear it. She'd be in bed with the lights off, the curtains drawn, the covers pulled over her head. Even the wolf has left her in peace, remaining downstairs, sleeping under the dining table, while Claire climbed the spiral metal stairway to the loft, turning, turning, turning. Roger keeps the wolf away. Sometimes she thinks that's the only reason she married him, although that can't be true, can it?

Or even if it is true, surely it can't be everything. Surely there must be more.

Roger's at his desk, his shoulders hunched in that way he has when he's working, thinking, so lost in himself, he doesn't even know she's there. She has brought him an apple, sliced into thin wedges on a plate. She pads across the floor, puts the apple on the desk, rests a hand lightly on his shoulder. "Hard day?"

He keeps his eye on his manuscript, finishing his thought, his head with its thick shock of dark hair bowed over his desk, his hand moving across the page in his

88

characteristic tiny, precise, monkish script. A jar of pens—he will use only one kind, a rolling tip that trails ink like a fountain—sits at his elbow beside a stack of notebooks, also the only kind he will use, each one with a leather cover and elastic band securing the pages. He would have made a good priest, Roger, if he hadn't become an historian. He has the scholar's pale skin and blinking, nearsighted gaze. His movements are light and lithe—he excels at the quick, balletic turns necessary for the squash he loves to play—his fingers long and tapering, with thin, birdlike bones.

Endlessly Roger parses things, thinks and rethinks them, then thinks them again. There's always another possibility in his mind, always another level, another alternative, another side. He would happily spend his days calculating how many angels could dance on the head of the pin if there were places where one still did those things. Or rather, did them in the presence of women. Roger loves women, and they love him. Even at her worst, Claire's grateful he chose her. It was never preordained that they would marry or even, for a long time, certain. Roger is perceptive. He's known in academic circles for his insight: he sees things other people don't. The only thing he doesn't see, she thinks, is her.

He straightens, smiles, takes a bite of apple, covers her hand with his own. "Not too bad. You?"

"Okay."

He puts down his pen, pushes back from his desk, takes the glasses from his nose, rests them beside his notebook, rubs his eyes: all these gestures, so familiar to her, so sweet, and precious. She loves him, truly she does. "I've been thinking about last night," he says.

"Don't." She walks over to the railing at the edge of the

loft and stands with her back to him, peering downstairs. The wolf ambles out from under the dining table as if she knows Claire is looking for her, yawns, stretches, her eyes gleaming, her fur glinting like silver in the starlight. "We talked about it when we got married. We agreed."

"People change."

"Maybe you do. I don't." She turns around, looks at him. "I'm too old."

"Forty is hardly old these days." He rubs a hand across his forehead, another gesture, so intimate, so revealing, it pulls at her heart. He's trying to hide his hurt, doing a poor job at it. She can hear it in his voice, read it in his eyes. She feels sorry for him, feels sorry, period. It can't be easy, being married to her. He's so bright, so used to coming up with solutions to seemingly unsolvable problems. In contrast to his wife, the Cold War must seem simple. He didn't ask for this. He doesn't even deserve it. Nathan is right. Roger's a good guy. There's nothing wrong with wanting normal things—at least for most people. "You could at least think about it."

She feels her back stiffen. "I can't. You know that."

"They have ways of handling these things. I wouldn't ask you if I thought—"

She raises her hands, pleading with him to be reasonable. "Look at me and Anna. Do you really want that to happen all over again?"

"Who says it will?"

"Who says it won't?" She wants to leave but doesn't want to go downstairs where the wolf is waiting. She walks to the stool that Roger uses to reach the high shelves in his bookcases and sits down. The stool is low, and sitting on it makes her feel small and childlike. She wraps her arms around her knees, drawing herself tightly together, like she used to do late at night when she was in bed and was supposed to be sleeping but instead was awake, listening to Anna and Julius fighting. "Cassidy called me today."

"Cassidy?" Roger looks at her with surprise. "Why?"

"Anna's sick." All at once she's tired. She had no idea how tired she was. The day is too much. All of it. She wants to sink from the stool onto the floor, crawl to Roger like a penitent, bury her face in his lap. "Nathan says she's dying."

"Dying?" His eyes open wide in shock. "Oh, Claire, I'm sorry. I didn't know."

She drops her head to her knees. "Maybe it's better this way. I won't have to wake up every morning thinking: Here's another day where my mother refuses to speak to me." This is absurd and she knows it. Even she won't go so far to beg pity. She sits up, looks at him. "She's been asking about Sasha."

"Sasha?"

"Her brother."

"Anna had a brother?"

"A long time ago. He died when she was a teenager. They never talked about him. No one in the family did. It's so strange." She pauses, thinking about it: it really is. "Anna said his death was never explained."

"Why?"

"I don't know. It doesn't make any sense. There's nothing *to* explain. It was an accident. He drowned. They were living in Marby then, in that big house on the Long Island Sound, before Lionel got elected. Hettie said his death was awful for everyone. Lionel lost his only son, and Frieda almost didn't recover from grief. Then they sent Anna away."

"Away? Where?"

"To one of those places. You know. A hospital for children." She stands up, turns to the bookshelves, runs her finger across the spines of Roger's books, the textures of cloth and leather reassuring her with their physical presence. The known, where so much is unknown. "Frieda was terrible. Hettie and Anna always said so. She did so many awful things. Lionel was their white knight, rescuing them."

Roger comes over, puts his arms around her. "What are you going to do?"

"About Sasha?"

"About Anna."

She throws up her hands. "What can I do? Leave her alone, I guess. That's what she wants. Nathan said so. It's better that way."

"For Anna maybe. What about you?"

This is a question she can't even begin to answer and so doesn't even try.

"Come here." He sits down in his chair, pats his knee.

She hesitates then comes over, settles herself on his lap.

"Are you okay?"

"Yes." She leans back, buries her face in his neck. "No. I'm sorry about the baby."

His arms are around her again, warm, comforting. "We don't have to talk about that."

She nestles in to him. "I love you. I just can't."

Roger, his voice soothing, says, "Shh."

She twists around so that she can see him. "I still don't get it. If Anna has a question about Sasha, why not ask

Hettie? Why ask me? I don't know anything about him. How could I? She acts like—"

"Yes?"

"Like she thinks I should."

"Don't get started, Claire." She can hear the worry in his voice. "Leave it alone. I don't want it to be like last time."

"Nathan said the same thing. It won't be. I promise."

"You'll tell me?"

"I'll tell you."

"You won't wait."

"No." She never was good at lying. She looks away so that he won't see her eyes.

"Anna dying." Roger shakes his head in disbelief. "It won't be easy, Claire. Despite everything, she's still your mother. When Miriam died—"

"That was different. You loved your mother. You got along. Anna and I—"

"It leaves a gap in the world. It changes everything. This space opens up, and nothing can fill it. It's like everything has shifted, and suddenly you're in a new place."

A new place. He means the lair of the wolf. Claire manages a faint smile. "I miss Miriam, too." She takes his hand.

"Talk to Grimmsley about it."

"Grimmsley?" She snorts. "Ha."

Roger still looks worried, but he lets it go. He moves his hand to her breast. "Want to go to bed, counselor?"

"I think I'll sit up for a while."

He kisses her. "Okay." After he leaves, she sits alone in his chair. It still has his warmth, his smell, that wonderful scent of the outdoors from his long walks home from the bus in the evenings. It ought to be enough to keep the wolf away, Claire thinks, but as soon as he's gone, she hears her ascending the stairs, her nails clicking on the metal treads. Claire reaches for the phone. She doesn't know what she's expecting—what she's thinking—whose voice she wants to hear when she dials.

Anna answers. "Hello?" she says and then again, "Hello?" One more heartbeat Claire waits, listening to the silence, and then she hangs up.

The Journal of Baruch Zalman

PART TWO

Outside the sky is lightening. Soon the others will awake. Dora will arise, as will Keiner, and he will vanish into the woods; we decided last night, Keiner and I, that he had best spend this day hidden. I will need to help my wife bathe and dress as these tasks have become increasingly difficult for her. Then the men of the village will trudge sleepily into the sanctuary to begin their morning prayers. On any other day I would join them, and then turn to my garden, which is much in need of my attention. The cabbages swell, the beans lengthen like bony fingers on the vine, and the bee hives drip with honey. Summer is ending, and the change of season, I know, is not far away. Almost two weeks ago we began blowing the shofar during our daily prayers, awakening our spirits to the High Holydays. But today is not like any other, and so I think of you, dear Reader, and press myself to write.

Was it truly only four months ago that Raisel and I were still caught in the icy grip of winter, one of the worst we have ever known? Snow piled shoulder high in the village, and the river all but vanished beneath a thick scrim of ice. For the first time in memory, wolves came down from the mountains, and all night long we heard their voices resounding in the dells, striking fear into the villagers' hearts. One audacious beast ventured into the village itself, stealing chickens from the henhouses, dragging the bloodied carcasses of newborn sheep across the snow. Most of the women who saw it said it had the eyes of a wild animal, but others said it must be enchanted for it had the eyes of a man. Later these very same women claimed it was Dora's doing, that with her witchery she had brought the wolf with her. But this I know is untrue, for the wolves arrived long before Passover began, and Dora didn't come until well after.

I remember the day well. It was the eve of the Sabbath, the sixth day of the counting of the Omer. Ever since Passover ended, the weather had taken a turn for the better, and the snows had finally begun to melt. The scent of spring had come in the air, awakening in me the desire to go out into the mountains and spend the day in silent contemplation. My wife begged me not to go, for she was terrified of wolves, but I had no fear of beasts. As for the old wives' tales of enchantment—I put no stock in such nonsense. So I wandered the paths along the river, filling my heart with the peace of the natural world while I filled my soul with dreams of Paradise.

By the time I returned to the village, it was late, the sky growing dark. I quickened my step homeward. Lately Raisel had grown forgetful and was easily confused. She might forget to light the Sabbath candles or light them in a dangerous place where fire might take hold. As I came down the village lane, I saw two women sitting on a bench in the synagogue courtyard. I had never seen either one before. The older was middle aged, the younger a maiden of sixteen perhaps, or seventeen. Mother and daughter. This I surmised not so much from their appearance, for the girl looked little like her mother, but from the way the older woman clung protectively to the girl's arm.

"Please, sir," the mother said, rising to her feet as I approached. "Rav Zalman. They told me to wait for you here. Most honored rebbe." She bowed.

"Baruch will do," I said with a smile, seeking to ease the distress that was plain on her face. She must have come from afar. She had the weary look of the traveler, was dressed in a heavy cloak and thick shoes, and carried a small bag. "I gave up such titles long ago."

"Rav—Baruch," she said. She glanced at her daughter, who still sat quietly on the bench, her eyes downturned. "I have come to beg for your help."

"And surely you will have it," I answered, "as much as I am able to give. But the Sabbath approaches, and I must make ready."

"Yes, of course." The woman bowed again. "My apologies. I would have come sooner, but our departure was delayed. We have been on the road all day."

"Please." I opened the door to the synagogue, ushering the two women inside. I took them through the sanctuary and up the stairs to the women's gallery. "Wait for me here." Then I joined my wife and together we lit the candles.

Soon it was the time for the evening service. One by one men from the village straggled into the synagogue until finally we had the quorum of ten required to begin. A few women trudged to the balcony where they took their places with curious looks at the strangers. I rose to stand at the *bimah*, the table that stood in the center of the sanctuary before the holy ark, and began chanting the familiar Hebrew words with which we welcomed the Sabbath: *Yedid nefesh, av harachaman*: Soul mate, loving God. But I had trouble praying with intention. Time and time again my eyes strayed to the balcony where the two strangers sat. The mother, I could tell, was well versed in the service, for her lips mouthed the words. Her daughter, however, paid little heed to the prayers. Instead with eyes as bright as a bird's, she looked around the sanctuary from the burnished wooden beams on the ceiling to the pews on the floor. Most of all she seemed entranced by the oil lamp, the Eternal Light, which hung above the ark. Again and again she lifted her fingers to the flickering flame, casting shadows on the ground. The play of light and shadow seemed to amuse her, for a secret smile crossed her lips. But something about her movements unsettled me, although I knew not why.

When the service ended, the villagers left with calls for a peaceful Sabbath. I summoned the two women and escorted them to my abode at the back of the synagogue. There, in the kitchen, my wife awaited us, standing beside the table where our dinner had been laid. She must have realized we would have guests, for she had set two extra plates. As we took our places at the table, I chanted the Kiddush over the wine, and after my wife had recited the blessing for the bread, we began to eat.

The older woman said little throughout the meal, speaking only to thank us for our generous hospitality and to apologize again for intruding upon our Sabbath. I was sure she must be famished, but she would take only a little food. Her daughter, however, tucked into her meal with relish, and when she was finished, looked about her with the same bright eyes and secret smile, as if she were much satisfied with the place. I was most struck, however, by the transformation that had overtaken my wife. Her eyes never left the girl; as soon as she had finished a portion, Raisel placed another on her plate. Raisel's eyes, as if a reflection of the girl's, had become brighter than I had seen in years, and on her lips flickered the same secret smile.

When we had finished eating, we recited the grace after meals, and once again I noticed the mother easily chanting the prayers, but the girl was silent. She had yet, I realized, to speak a word. Raisel poured us cups of tea from the samovar then retired to the bedroom so that the two women might speak to me in private, leaving the door ajar as propriety demanded.

"My name is Gittel Aizic," the older one began, "but I was born Gittel Haimoviçi, in Iaşi." She looked at me curiously. "Perhaps you know my family?"

"Perhaps," I agreed, but Haimoviçi is a common name, and rather than take the time to determine exactly which branch of this family Gittel belonged to, I let her continue.

"This is my daughter, D'vorah," Gittel said, with a nod at the girl. "We call her Dora."

Ah, *D'vorah*, the fierce and mighty bee, famed judge of Biblical times. The girl bore a weighty name indeed. Perhaps too weighty. At the sound of her name, she directed her eyes modestly to her lap. *Dora*, with its echoes of Romanian longing, seemed more fitting. As I looked from mother to daughter, I was struck again by the difference between them. Gittel had fine features, pale skin, and delicate hands, but Dora's complexion was dark, her cheekbones as

99

wide as a Slav's, her eyebrows remarkably high and arching. Gittel wore her hair covered as befitted a married woman, but Dora's hair fell unbound to her shoulders. It was a thick, glossy auburn color, by far the girl's best feature, and its glow in the candlelight reminded me again of the coppery gleam of the Eternal Lamp of which she had seemed so fond.

"I was born, as I said, in Iași," Gittel continued. "I was also married there. My husband was a good man, a tradesman, well versed in metal work. We had a good life, a house of our own, with an atelier downstairs where he pursued his craft. We had no debt and had even managed to put money aside for the baby, which, as we had long hoped, was finally on the way." She cast a glance at Dora, who still sat quietly at her mother's side, her eyes downturned. "My husband was an honest laborer. We asked for nothing and caused no trouble. But in the end none of that mattered." Here Gittel raised her chin, and a defiant light came into her eyes. "One morning a knock came to our door. Constables. They declared we were vagrants and were to be expelled. Vagrants! When we had our own business and our own home? How could such a thing be? The law, they said, was on their side, but I think it was more on the side of our Gentile neighbors who, I know, had long coveted our house, and so had arranged this trickery."

The couple was forced into a wagon along with a dozen or so other Jewish victims of the same decree. For over three days they were driven southwards, Gittel clutching at her pregnant belly. At length they reached the border town of Galați where, to the jeers of the crowd, they were loaded onto a boat and sent adrift onto the Danube.

"The boat was too small," Gittel said. "If not for my husband, we would have all drowned. But he sacrificed himself for the rest of us—for our unborn child." Once again Gittel stole a glance at Dora, who seemed most discomfited to hear the story, and kept her eyes averted. "He threw himself into the water, and the river took him away. I never saw him again." A dark look of pain crossed Gittel's face, and she pressed her hand to her eyes. "A Turkish commander from the other side of the river took pity on us. He sent a soldier in a rowboat to take us back to Galați. The constables—even they had finally had enough of human suffering. They let us go."

Gittel fell silent, giving me a moment to reflect on her story. I knew about such expulsions, of course, although not specifically the one of which she spoke. Still, it was hardly unique. For centuries Romanian Jews had had no recourse before the law. We were good enough to provide the state with a source of labor, taxes, and conscripts for the army, but not good enough to merit citizenship. Confiscations of our property, public beatings and humiliations: all passed unremarked by the authorities. Was it any wonder Jews fled Romania like from a house afire? With my stubborn refusal to migrate, perhaps I was the foolish one. But how could I leave the grave of my grandfather—of my daughter? How depart the very place where I had spent each day expecting the Messiah to show his face?

"I had no wish to return to Iași. The place left a bitter taste in my mouth," Gittel said. "So I decided to remain in Galați. Dora was born there. In time I married again. My second husband has a tavern. We have two more daughters. Together we have made a life for ourselves. A good life, yes, but hard." Her voice dropped to a whisper. "We have our troubles."

Once more Gittel stole a glance at her daughter. We had come, I sensed, to the crux of her story. But she appeared reluctant to go on in the presence of the girl. I turned to Dora kindly and said, "Go in to my wife. She will have something to show you."

Obediently the girl went in to the next room where Raisel and I had our bed, wardrobe, and a small vanity table, topped by a mirror, where Raisel fixed her hair and adorned herself. Soon Dora was sitting at my wife's side, looking through a box of trinkets that Raisel kept: ribbons, rings, buttons, and other such things. With Dora so occupied, I said to Gittel, "You can continue. There's no need to be afraid."

"Thank you." She gave me a smile that trembled with both fear and bravery. "The problem," she said in a voice so low I had to lean in to hear it, "is Dora."

So I had surmised. What had the girl done? Fallen in love with a Gentile? Gotten herself with child? She would hardly be the first. But usually families resolved such problems on their own, sending the girl far away, for example, or arranging for a hasty marriage. There was hardly need to travel half way across the country seeking help.

As if she read my mind, Gittel colored. "Dora's a good girl," she said hastily. "I don't suspect her of any impropriety."

"I see." I nodded.

"A good girl," Gittel said again. Then she sighed. "At least I know she wants to be."

And so it all came out. Dora was, indeed, trouble. The difficulties began when she started school. She wouldn't pay attention to her lessons or listen to her teachers. They complained she was full of daydreams, off in her own world. Eventually they sent her home. Gittel's husband said if the girl wouldn't learn, she would have to earn. He put her to work in the tavern washing dishes, but Dora chipped the crockery and shattered the glasses. So she was apprenticed to the cook. Soon, however, the cook sent her packing. Dora over salted the stew and spoiled the cabbage. Under her watch the flour grew moldy, the corn rotted, and mice infested the storehouse. She was given a broom and told to sweep; hours later she would be found outside, playing in the sunshine with a piece of colored glass, while dirt accumulated on the floor. Mopping, sewing, shopping: there was no task, it seemed, that Dora was fit for. Finally her stepfather sent her into the tavern to serve drinks. But theirs was a rowdy crowd of sailors and dockworkers who leered at the young girl, pulling at her apron strings and pinching her behind. This Gittel could not abide, and so she pleaded with her husband to let Dora stop.

If there's nothing else to be done with her, the stepfather declared with a grim look, then we'll marry her off. Gittel was appalled. She feared Dora was too young, but she had no choice. She consulted one matchmaker after another, but none could find a match. Dora, it seemed, had acquired a reputation in the community for laziness and obstinacy. What mother would marry her son to a girl who couldn't even keep house?

Now the stepfather raged. They had two more daughters—*his* daughters, he reminded Gittel—and how would they ever find husbands for them if Dora remained unmarried? She was ruining the family; she would have to learn to bend to his will. His will, Gittel learned, could be harsh indeed. He locked Dora for days in the cellar; fed her bread and water; took her into the pantry, closed the door, and beat her. It was no use. The girl refused to change.

"She *couldn't* change," Gittel whispered. She had become convinced of it. There was something eternally childlike about her oldest daughter. It was as if Dora had reached a certain age in her mind and gone no farther. In desperation, Gittel began consulting doctors and rabbis, taking money from the till to pay the fees, since her husband declared he wouldn't spend another penny on the girl. The last rabbi she spoke to told her to take Dora to Iași, to pray at the grave of her ancestors. That night Dora was subjected to a particularly vicious beating; for hours Gittel heard her whimpering cries. When morning came, she gathered up the girl and fled to her sister in Iași. There they stayed for three weeks while Gittel prostrated herself daily in the cold and ice on her ancestors' graves. She forced Dora, too, to kneel down and pray. To no avail. Nothing changed.

The caretaker of the cemetery, an elderly man, was witness to this terrible spectacle. Finally he took pity upon Gittel and told her of Baruch, the holy man of the mountains, the only person left in these parts who still had a connection to the Master of the Name. Gittel determined to travel to Alba-Bistrița and throw herself on the great Rav's mercy, begging for his aid.

"Mercy you most certainly don't need," I said, as Gittel's story came to an end, "for I will willingly do anything I can to help you."

But I was sorely troubled. I was appalled to hear I had acquired the reputation of holy man in Iași. I was no healer!

Had not the death of my own daughter proven that? Worse than that was my conviction that Gittel was right, and there was nothing to be done for Dora. How many times, in my years at court, had I seen cases like hers before? Mothers brought me their unmarriageable daughters, seeking a miracle: girls with a cleft palate or club foot; girls who were deaf, dumb, or blind; girls with the falling sickness like me or who were troubled in the mind. Some of them raged, some were unrelentingly obstinate, and some ran after men; others gave themselves over to melancholy, refusing to eat or drink or stir from their beds. Still others remained like children in their minds even as their bodies grew to womanhood.

Was Dora such a one? Somehow I thought not. The girl struck me as being full of daydreams as Gittel had said, but not lacking in intelligence. I glanced into the bedroom where she and my wife sat entranced together, examining the treasures in Raisel's trinket box. Again I was struck by the look on Dora's face—her secret smile. But Raisel astounded me. In her eyes was a look of joy such as I hadn't seen in ages. I remembered the way Dora had looked at the Eternal Light in the synagogue and felt uneasy.

I stood up. "We will speak of this again," I told Gittel. I directed her to the home of a widow in the village who occasionally took in boarders. "Tell her I have sent you. She will keep you and your daughter tonight. Come see me tomorrow, after the Sabbath has ended." With that, the two women left.

That night I fell asleep to the sound of wolves howling in the mountains. For the first time in years, I dreamed of Bathsheva. I felt my daughter's arms around my neck and

the touch of her lips to my cheek. Once again I heard the
tinkling of the kitten's bell that heralded her approach. The
dream transported me to a world that was so vivid and real,
I was sorry to wake and find myself again in this earthly
existence. Then I realized why Dora's play with light and
shadow in the synagogue the night before had unsettled
me: once Bathsheva had held her hands up to the Eternal
Flame the very same way.

I had no more time to think of that. To my great shame,
I discovered I had overslept. I hastened into the sanctuary
where one of the men of the village had already begun
chanting the morning service. He stepped aside to accord
me my place at the *bimah*, but as before, I had trouble
concentrating on the prayers. Again and again my eyes
strayed to the women's balcony, searching for Gittel and
Dora, but neither appeared.

That afternoon I thought long and hard about Gittel. I
knew what was expected in these cases—what she would
expect. She would want an amulet for Dora, a container
holding a parchment conveying a special blessing. I spent
hours hunting through writings of the sages for the
appropriate language. But my heart wasn't in it. I knew
Gittel was right, and nothing would change Dora.

Finally I turned to an account my grandfather had
written of the life of the Baal Shem. Once again I was
taken with the great Master's humility, his profound love
for nature and his fellow man. He embodied the true role
of healer. With his help, women conceived babies, children
recovered from deadly illnesses, merchants gained fortunes,
maidens found husbands. He saw deeply into the souls of
his petitioners, recognized when foreign spirits abided

there, and knew how to redeem them. My grandfather's words brought to mind the rabbi who'd once claimed to remove a spirit from me. I was grateful that Gittel, at least, seemed to have no such expectation.

In the end I took a parchment with a prayer for healing and secreted it in a vial. When Gittel and Dora returned, I would give them this amulet and send them on their way. It was a small offering, but perhaps it would give them comfort. As I put the vial aside, I looked in on my wife. She was sitting with her trinket box again, and on her face was the same joyful smile, the same brightness in her eyes. But something about her worried me, and I feared that she was losing herself, becoming ever more like a child, easily confused.

When night came, and three stars appeared in the heavens, I recited the *Havdalah* prayers ending the Sabbath. Then I went outside to the courtyard where I found Dora sitting on the bench as before.

"Where is your mother?"

"She told me to wait for her here."

It was the first time I had heard her voice. It was lower than I might have expected, and huskier. She seemed embarrassed to speak to me, and kept her eyes downturned.

I, however, felt a growing sense of alarm. I took her into the synagogue and told her to wait for me there. Then I hastened down the lane to the home of the widow. "Where is Gittel Aizic," I said, "the woman I sent to you yesterday?"

The widow looked at me with surprise. "She left early this morning. I thought you knew. I heard some peasants say they saw her traveling on a cart."

"On the Sabbath?" I was shocked to hear it.

107

The widow shrugged. "All I know is that she is gone."

Quickly I returned to the synagogue, where I found Raisel and Dora at the kitchen table with the trinket box. Raisel hardly noticed my return. Her face was alight, as if glowing from within. Dora had the same bright eyes, the same secret smile. "Raisel!" I said. But she didn't answer. Instead she reached into the box and pulled out a bell on a ribbon—Bathsheva's bell. She held it out to Dora, and with a flick of her wrist, rang it. Then darkness flowed in, I succumbed to a fit, and fell to the ground.

Eight

.· .·.

GUS

*D*inner is served in the dining room, where the French doors have been left thrown open, an avenue to the musky, cool, darkening world, lights winking in the distance on the water. The table is set with rose china; in the center, freshly cut roses swim in pools of water captured in glass bowls, reflecting the candelabra light. Lionel sits at the head of the table; to his left is Anna, to his right Hettie. Frieda sits beside Anna, Gus beside Hettie, and beside Gus sits Max Zharkov, Lionel's associate, practically an afterthought, all but put out in the cold.

In Lionel, Gus sees the source of Anna's high arching eyebrows, the pronounced bridge of her nose. His face is round and ruddy, his lips ruddy, too, and full, radiating good cheer. His hair is thick, his mustache curved stylishly at the tips. Mr. Slocum glides in and out of the room, floating serene and restrained from diner to diner, silently carrying trays of food. The food itself is an array of delights; a cold fruit soup followed by a leg of lamb adorned with homemade quince jam, buttery carrots, and parsley new potatoes.

Wines come throughout the evening, Lionel pouring, insisting that everyone partake. Then he calls for champagne—there is so much to celebrate. Anna is home. No, more than that: Anna is home, and she is eating.

109

Throughout the meal Anna has eyes only for her father; Gus might not even exist. He's thankful for that, watches giddy with relief as Lionel cuts the choicest pieces from his own plate, feeds her like a bird, plies her with water diluted in the French style with a dollop of wine, with a sip of champagne from his own glass. Lionel reaches over, cups Anna's face in his hands, touches her shoulder, her arm. Has there ever been such love of a parent for a child, so warm, embracing, transparent? Gus is surprised to see Frieda look away, hiding her face, but when she turns back she is smiling. Meanwhile Anna is glowing, they all are, especially Gus, the hero of the day. Lionel has made him so, will not stop praising him, "Our brilliant Baltimore doctor, the one who brought Anna home."

"Yes," Gus replies, his face coloring in the heat of the alcohol, the flattery. That is to say, "No, sir, really, I was only doing my duty." But he can't help feeling *Yes*, he was the one who said Anna should come home, who believed that once here she would eat again. Not Dr. Kanner, not even the famous Dr. Meyer. Only Gus. The homecoming is due to his instincts, to his judgment. In the light of Lionel's adulation, the last remnants of Gus's doubts recede and vanish. He was right. He saw. He believed.

"Now," Lionel says to Gus, growing serious, "you must work your magic on Frieda." He turns to his wife. "You must go back to work, my darling. You see that Anna is all right—that everything will be all right." To Gus again: "Frieda is nothing without her art. It sustains her, gives expression to her being. She has sacrificed much since— since the spring. She has put her work aside. But now it's time to embrace life."

Frieda smiles. As she pulls out a cigarette, Lionel leaps to his feet to light it for her. In the spark of the flame, Gus sees a softening in her eyes, the flare of a vision, a dream. Lionel is like that, a creator. He speaks the word and it becomes so. Is there anyone who could resist him?

Gus wants it to go on and on, this evening, the fellowship and good cheer, the ever-flowing bottles of wine and champagne. But of course it can't. The meal ends with a cheese course and then an assembly of cakes and pastries: a Viennese table. At Lionel's insistence, Mrs. Sauer, the cook, appears in the swinging door to the kitchen and takes a bow, her frizzy red hair barely contained in her cap, her face equally reddened, blushing, her eyes fixed coquettishly on her mistress.

Then the final pastry tray is passed. Lionel, full of love, pulls Hettie onto his lap and Frieda, frowning, extinguishes her cigarette and says, "Lionel, she's too old for that." Anna's face darkens. Is that a flash of anger in her eyes? No, it's just a trick of the candlelight.

Lionel laughs, saying, "Mother is right. She's always right." Hettie gives her father a peck on the cheek and jumps down, and Anna is entirely unperturbed. Then both girls, smiling, are sent up to bed. Frieda stands, excuses herself, says she is sorry but she is exhausted, she will go up now and see to the girls. The three men rise to their feet.

"Wait for me in the library," Lionel says to Max. "Max and I have to talk," he adds with an audible whisper to Gus. "It's regrettable but unavoidable. But first, dear Doctor, I am all yours."

Max bears the insult without comment and exits the room. A dour man, he has uttered hardly a word throughout the meal. From their sole conversation, Gus has learned that Zharkov is some kind of party functionary from Albany, sent here to hold consultations on Lionel's senatorial campaign.

The candidate guides Gus out of the room, his arm around the young doctor's shoulders, holding him close. They come to a stop on the broad expanse of Oriental carpet in the grand entrance hall, beneath the portrait of Lionel's mother, the enigmatic Dora. The gilded mirror on the wall shines with the light of the chandelier, the polished wood staircase rising as if to heaven. "You're the one," Lionel says. "The miracle worker." He turns to Gus, his hands planted firmly on both shoulders. "We owe it all to you."

"Please," Gus protests, "no." But Lionel's eyes are on him, impossible to resist. The man's gaze is magnetic, almost sensual in its force, making Gus feel as if he's the only person in the world—the only person that matters. This, Gus thinks, must be how Anna feels when she's in her father's arms.

"I thought at first they would send a more senior man," Lionel says with a reflective air. "Maybe even the great Dr. Meyer himself." He steps back, drops his arms. To Gus the loss of intimacy feels like a chill, as if the heat and light has been sucked from the room. Then Lionel's smile returns like the sun—how badly Gus craves it already, the warmth and approbation of that smile. "But I understand now. It's youth that's required. The ability to see anew. To see afresh." He leans in close to Gus, conspiratorial. "The Thaler Psychiatric Institute. I can just see it. It's just what Johns Hopkins needs. Someone should endow it, eh, Doctor?"

"I—" Gus is taken aback and doesn't know what to say.

As he struggles for an answer Lionel winks and then laughs, a loud guffaw.

A joke. Of course. It was nothing but a joke. Gus bursts into laughter, too.

"So it's back to Baltimore tomorrow, is it?" Lionel says, serious now.

"Yes, sir."

"Excellent." He claps Gus on the back. "I'm sure your superiors will be pleased. Job well done and all that, right?"

"Yes, sir, thank you, sir, I hope so."

"Good, good." Lionel favors Gus with his beaming smile again.

Lionel is ready to go, Gus can sense the great man wanting to leave; one more word and he will be gone. The thought of his departure feels unbearable, and almost as if to keep him there, Gus says, "The apple. How did you get Anna to eat it?"

"What's that?"

"If you don't mind my asking. How did you convince her? What did you say?"

"Nothing to it, my boy." The grin on Lionel's face broadens. "I told her to be good. I said I wanted her to be a good girl. I said I expected it of her."

The penitential girl in the courtyard, being good, being oh-so-very good. Is there a connection there? For some reason, the thought unsettles Gus. It vanishes in a flash as Lionel leans in close, takes his hand, shakes it with an almost painfully powerful grip. He nods towards the library. "Max. Can't leave him waiting." With a roll of his eyes, he shows Gus how deeply he regrets it. "Good night, Doctor. Safe travels tomorrow."

"Thank you, sir, and good luck—" There's no use in going on. Lionel is gone. Gus watches his broad back vanish into the library. "On the campaign." He finishes the sentence in a whisper. He glances at his watch. Eleven o'clock. How did it get so late? He should go straight to bed. He has a long drive tomorrow. But sleep, he knows, is the last thing he will be able to do now. So he slips out the French doors onto the terrace, and goes outside for a walk.

In darkness the world is transformed, the house, the grassy slope, the sea wall, the Sound. The world inside Gus is transformed, too; he has become a person he doesn't recognize, confident, ebullient, happy. He strides down the rocky steps to the pier where just a few hours ago Anna sat with her sister. He has come to clear his head, to think. He has much to think about.

From the pier another set of rock steps leads down to the water. When the tide is low, there must be a small beach here, a thin strip of sand. Now the tide is up, swallowing the beach, licking at the rocks, which are deeply black and jagged, threaded with silver, their wet surfaces glistening in the moonlight. Caught in the crevices are gleaming tidal pools filled with tiny black snails, silvery darting fish, algae waving delicate fronds like arms. On the top of the rocks, as steep as a cliff, runs the sea wall. High on the hill—Gus cranes his head to see it—rides the house on the shoreline like an ocean liner, the windows lit, imparting a warm yellow glow to the night sky. The sight disorients him, makes him feel as if the world is turned upside down, placing him firmly underwater. It's the effect of the whiskey followed by wine and rounds of champagne. No, it's the effect of Lionel

Glanz. He would have this effect on anyone. Didn't Frieda say her world turned upside down when she met him?

Gus is still trying to assimilate it, the rush of sights, sounds, tastes, and sensations that constituted their meal. Most of all he is trying to assimilate the vision of Anna eating, the intense relief that flowed through him at the sight. He stands on the pier, leans back his head, tips his face to the night sky, and looks for the wolf constellation Meyer mentioned. He's unable, of course, to find it. He never was any good at stargazing. On a clear night he can pick out the big and little dippers, the north star, the brush of white across the sky that is the Milky Way. There's no Milky Way here. The air at the shore is too heavy and thick.

He still feels giddy. He won't deny it. He laughs out loud. It's the relief, of course, of Anna's recovery, but also the alcohol, and Lionel. Gus can see why Frieda would want only him. The voters will, too, Gus thinks, once they get to know him. He pities the man who is his opponent in this campaign.

He's almost forgotten in his intoxication that Anna has yet to speak a single word. No, not forgotten, just choosing not to think of it. She will speak soon, he's sure of it. The main thing is that Spring Meadow is off the table. The crisis has been averted.

Bed. At last he longs for it. The house is dark as he comes up the terrace steps. The Glanzes have all gone to sleep, their servants and guest, too. Gus heads to his room, remembering to take the front stairs as Miss Chase directed. Ah, Miss Chase. He will be sorry not to see her anymore. Perhaps one more time in the morning before he leaves? A pity that he has to go so soon. Something might have come from that. He shakes his head, puts the thought aside. Tomorrow he'll return to Baltimore. Everything is unfolding exactly as he wanted it to. So why does he feel a sense of uneasiness—and regret?

"You're going to send her away, aren't you?"

Gus has made his way down the long hall with its tall grandfather clock, which watched him pass as silent as a sentinel, has found the servants' quarters, has wound round and round the warren of rooms and finally come to his own, only to find Hettie sitting in it, cross-legged on his bed.

"I—what—excuse me?"

"That's why you're here. To send her away."

"Anna?"

"Who else?" She glares at him, stubborn, furious. How stupid could he be?

Neither the alcohol nor the lateness of the hour can explain this apparition on his bed, all too painfully real. She's dressed in her nightgown, her hair, a muddy brown color, falling in tangled waves around her face. Her feet, bare and grass-stained, have trailed sand from the beach onto his bed. Did she go down to the Sound before coming upstairs? He shakes his head, clearing it. "Send Anna away? Why on earth would I do that? I'm the one who brought her home."

"But she's going away, isn't she?"

He is feeling distinctly irritable. Hasn't he been through enough today? Must he submit to interrogations from an eleven-year-old girl, one who is clearly both demanding and unreasonable? He wishes she would go away. "I don't see why she would," he says, his voice clipped, turning his back to her, busying himself with washing his hands.

Out of the corner of his eye he sees her glowering, her anger intensifying, sliding into contempt. "You don't know anything. You don't even know that Mummy's sending us to boarding school."

"Boarding school?" He turns, the towel in his hands. No one has said anything about boarding school.

"In the fall." She looks satisfied; she has his attention now. She speaks slowly, with the air of explaining something to a dunce. "Mummy and Daddy are selling the house and moving to New York City. We're going to boarding school. Only Anna can't go if she won't speak. The headmistress won't take her. Daddy spoke to her about it specifically. It doesn't matter what he says. She won't change her mind. Mummy says Anna can't stay in Baltimore because she won't eat there. If she won't talk she can't go to school. That means she has to go to that other place, the one in the meadow. But I don't want to go to boarding school if Anna doesn't." She bites back tears. "I don't want to go away by myself."

"I most certainly did not—" Gus stops. Hettie has said too many things. He needs a moment to sort it all out.

She sniffs. He searches his pockets for a handkerchief, is unable to find one—When will you ever learn to dress properly? he hears his mother chiding him—hands Hettie the hand towel, which she uses to wipe her nose then gives solemnly back to him. "Mummy and Daddy fight about it all the time. He says she can't go there, to the place in the meadow, and Mummy says she has to. Everyone thinks Daddy decides things but he doesn't. Mummy does. She says we can't go to New York City with them. She says they're probably going to move to Washington anyway. Daddy's going to be a senator and I'm supposed to be happy about it but I'm not. Not if it means I have to go to boarding school." The tears are falling now, and he gives her the towel back. She presses it to her face, her voice coming out muffled. "Not if Anna can't come."

He pulls out the chair at the desk, falls into it, sits there dumbfounded. He can think of nothing to say.

"It's not fair. Anna is Daddy's favorite and Sasha was Mummy's and no one cares about me."

Ah, of course. The middle child. Difficult to get attention in a family under normal circumstances, let alone at a time like this.

She gives a last wipe to her face, wads up the towel and drops it onto the bed. "Are you going to make her talk?"

"Make her? No. But she will. She'll decide on her own." This is said firmly. He stands up. "You need to go to bed."

Nodding, she slips her feet to the floor, pads silently out of the room.

He picks up the towel, hangs it by the washbasin, brushes the sand off the bed, does all these things without thinking, that is, his body moving automatically while his thoughts are engaged elsewhere. Spring Meadow? The Glanzes can't possibly still be thinking of sending Anna there. Not when she is eating again.

Then it occurs to him: no one said they weren't.

Heat comes into his face. Impossible. He will speak to them about it tomorrow.

He feels angry, betrayed. His thoughts are still racing as he washes up, gets ready for bed. He's exhausted but sleep now is impossible. He sets the chair before the desk, sits down, opens his briefcase, pulls out his journal. It's a black leather-bound booklet, small enough to be secreted in his pocket. He began writing in it at Phipps shortly after Anna became his patient, recording his impressions, his feelings, and his doubts—the kind of thing it wouldn't do to record in her official case file. He had some vague notion of being like Freud, of one day publishing these narratives of his treatments, of his findings being universally read and admired, resulting in new psychiatric breakthroughs. The grandiose side of him again, spinning out of control. He shakes his head.

For now the journal will suffice as a means of sorting out his thoughts. He pulls the latest set of Anna's paintings out of his briefcase, lays them on the table. Lately they've become darker, the backgrounds blackened as if from fire or night, the wolf in the center depicted in browns and greys with menacing sulfurous yellow eyes.

As he writes, his mind quiets, exhaustion gradually overcoming his body. He doesn't remember falling into bed, doesn't remember falling asleep, but all at once he is awake again. He has had a nightmare, a terrible one. In it he is once again a child, a young boy, in his sister's room. She's lying ill in bed, and there's a wolf in the room with her—with both of them. The wolf is menacing Rosa and he needs to protect her. He looks desperately for a weapon but can't find one, and the wolf is too big, he is too small, he can't possibly defeat it on his own.

It's remarkable how vivid the dream is, how real. It jars Gus awake, leaving him trembling, sweating, the sheets tangled. He gets out of bed, draws a glass of water from the tap, stands by the basin calming himself, drinking it. The doctor in him immediately begins analyzing the dream. It's not a difficult task; the symbolism is obvious. He's been thinking too much about Anna, of course. And Rosa. The wolf is death, coming for his sister. The powerlessness—the inability to find a weapon—reflects the way he felt when death took her away. The wolf represents death to Anna, too. Her brother's death. She is plagued by it, by the delusion she refuses to give up, that she is somehow responsible for it.

He puts down the water glass, walks to the window for a breath of fresh air. Is he dreaming still? There, at the bottom of the hill, is a figure, walking on the sea wall. It's Rosa. It's a ghost, a wraith, a spirit. No, he realizes with a start. It's not a phantom. It's a girl, and she's very much alive.

The stairs—the stairs—for a minute Gus cannot find them, and only much later will he remember that he dashed down the set for the servants, at the back of the house. His heart pounding, he runs towards the Sound. Anna is on the sea wall, sleepwalking, poised at any moment to hurl herself down.

Judge, jury—and executioner, too. Just like Meyer said.

The tide is going out, and below her a thin strip of sand emerges from the bottom of the rocks, the waves caressing it then retreating with a hiss. The danger she is in makes him shudder, his heart catching in his throat. He doesn't know which would be worse, tumbling into the water when the tide is up or onto the sand when it is out. Either way there would be the rocks. One would hardly survive a fall from the sea wall onto them.

He knows from experience with her sleepwalking

episodes at the hospital not to hurry, not to jar her into wakefulness. That only increases her terror, precipitates the dangerous unpredictability of her movements. He takes a breath, composes himself, gathers his presence of mind. The goal is to insert himself seamlessly into the narrative of her dream, curving its trajectory, giving it a safe, satisfactory ending. He's used to this process, just as she is used to him. Carefully, gently, murmuring softly, he reaches up, takes her in his arms, pulls her down from the wall. Once safely on her feet, she allows him to guide her, following him obediently back into the house and to her bed. "Sleep," he whispers as he tucks the sheets around her, giving her the hypnotic suggestion. "Deep, dreamless sleep." At the sound of his voice she sighs and relaxes, a slight smile gracing her lips, her breathing steady.

Outside her room, in the hall, he buries his face in his hands. Around him the house is deeply silent, drowned in sleep. Thank God no one else saw what happened. What would they think of him if they did? He thinks back to dinner, to his surge of grandiosity. What a fool he has been. He has been blind to so much—he has been blindsided by both Lionel and Frieda. The truth is, they have both been seducing him, she with her tender touches and brimming sadness, he with his ebullient praise and flattery. The Thaler Psychiatric Institute? The thought makes him feel ill. The Glanzes are at war; Hettie has made that clear. Gus is their pawn, Anna the prize. At this rate, Frieda is winning. Anna will go to Spring Meadow if he can't keep her safe.

He pulls himself up, his resolve growing clear. He won't let that happen. In the morning he will get a key to her room. He will ask Miss Chase for it; he will count on her discretion. He doesn't want to give Frieda any reason to fear for Anna's safety—to send her away. He will get a nail and hammer and secure the window. There will be no return to Baltimore—not yet. He must do more than get Anna to eat. He must make her speak.

Nine

"*A*ny side effects?" Grimmsley says.

"No," Claire says. "Not really." Unless the wolf counts as a side effect. Right now the wolf is nosing around Grimmsley's office, inquiring, sensing, probing. She lifts her muzzle to eye the artwork he hangs on his walls—prints by Klee is it, or Miro?—Claire never can tell the difference between those two. The pictures, colorfully abstract, float on a soothing background of creamy white wallpaper. Everything in Grimmsley's office is meant to be soothing, from the sound machine that sits in the corner, emitting a soft hiss, to the sisal rug on the floor and the drapes on the window, sheer enough to allow light in but thick enough to reduce the view outside to a blur. The furniture is teak, the kind that used to be called Danish modern, although it's hardly modern anymore: Grimmsley's desk, the chair Claire is sitting in, the couch that she never, ever lies on. Everything is soothing, and everything is anonymous. As far as Claire can tell, Grimmsley doesn't keep a single personal item in his office, not a datebook, coffee mug, coat, photograph, not even a key. His desk is distressingly bare. The sign of a man with no personality at all. Or does he have something to hide?

Maybe he just doesn't want to give anything away.

The wolf slinks around the side of Grimmsley's desk to sniff at his leg, looking up to gauge his reaction. Grimmsley doesn't even notice. Claire could have told her not to waste her time. What can you expect from a psychiatrist named Grimmsley? He probably doesn't even see her. Grimmsley may have a lot of talents, but being perceptive isn't one of them.

"Trouble eating? Concentrating?"

She shakes her head.

"Tremors? Unsteadiness?"

"No. Nothing like that." It's not Grimmsley's fault. He has this little list. He has to check things off. It's the way medicine works nowadays. The doctors pretend to be in control, but the truth is, they're like marionettes. The insurance companies pull the strings.

"You're drinking plenty of water. Sleeping well. Watching your salt."

She nods.

He narrows his eyes. "No thoughts of harming yourself?"

"Of course not." She smiles at him in what she hopes is a reassuring way. "I'm a pro at this, remember?" She shouldn't have said that. It reeks of cockiness. Over-confidence. It raises red flags. Sure enough, he frowns.

"You're still on a low dosage. We can increase it, if you think you need it."

"No really. It's fine. *I'm* fine." Actually the opposite is true. Claire isn't fine. She's much, much better than that. Ever since the day she got caught for shoplifting—ever since the day she stopped taking her pills—she's been feeling wired, excited, fired-up, sure of herself. She can't remember when she felt this good. If she knew that quitting Xynolith would make her feel like this, she would have done it ages ago. Although a nagging voice in her head says there will be a price to pay for that, that one day she'll wake up regretting it. That one day it will go downhill and when it does, it will be bad. Very, very bad. It's the same voice that chides her each morning and night when she flushes another pink pill down the toilet instead of swallowing it, keeping careful track so that Roger won't notice. He says he doesn't count the pills in the bottle but she knows he does.

"I'm fine," she says again, keeping her smile carefully within bounds. "Really." Fine, fine, fine. It's her mantra nowadays, not just to Grimmsley and Roger but to everyone who asks, including Nathan and Alec, her boss, too. Fine. She's been fine for weeks now, ever since she heard about Anna. Ever since she stopped taking her pills.

Grimmsley gives her the little grimace that in his book passes for a smile. "Okay then." He's a horrid little man with long, greasy hair that he combs over his bald spot. About the only thing Claire looks forward to when she sees him is his comb-over. Will it be holding together today or will it have split into pieces, revealing the shiny skull underneath? It's a little betting game she plays with herself. Today she gave the comb-over a thirty percent chance of being intact. She's sorry to see that she was wrong. It's still holding up.

"Good," Grimmsley says. He takes out his prescription pad and all business now scribbles on it. "I'll give you a ninety-day supply this time. We can talk again before it runs out. You'll need to get your blood levels checked again, of course."

"Of course," Claire agrees. The good little girl doing exactly as she's been told. Or not. Three months. A vote

125

of confidence. She wants to cheer, has to exert every bit of self-control she has not to. It's the longest period she's been granted on her own since she got out of the hospital in the winter, when she had her breakdown. They don't call them breakdowns anymore, of course. They call them "episodes" or "events," as if her life were part of a newspaper story or a series on TV. A psychiatric event, Grimmsley says with a grimness befitting his name. He still doesn't know what caused it, and Claire isn't about to tell him. If she didn't tell Roger, why would she tell Grimmsley? Besides, it's not as if there's anything to tell. She'd missed her period, that's all, and when she realized she was pregnant, she'd taken care of it. A simple procedure at a clinic; she was in and out in a few hours. An aspiration, the doctor called it. Claire could relate to that. I aspire, she thought, to many things. Right now, not to be pregnant. We will evacuate, the doctor said somberly, the contents of your uterus. *Evacuate.* Claire loved that word. So clinical. So anonymous. She imagined her uterus emptied like a bus or a train after a bomb threat, the inhabitant fleeing, abandoning her body like a burning building, a ship under attack. Not once did the doctor use the dreaded a-word. *Abortion.* She almost wanted to hiss it at him, just to see him jump. There certainly was no mention of embryo, fetus, or, God forbid, baby. Only contents. She might as well be a box filled with cast-off books, broken appliances, old clothes. She'd agreed to it all, a thin smile on her face as she signed the consent form, a sharp headache pulsing suddenly behind her ears.

Afterwards she'd resumed her life, going to work, returning home at night, having dinner with Roger, reading, watching television, going to bed. Feeling great, feeling perfectly fine. Then one morning she woke up to find the wolf in bed with her. More than that, lying on her chest, holding her down, so that Claire couldn't get out of bed herself. Not just couldn't: wouldn't. Not just wouldn't: didn't see the point. Didn't see the reason for it at all.

She told Roger she was feeling under the weather, nothing serious, just a twenty-four hour bug; she would stay home and rest for the day. She called work and told Alec the same. No one was suspicious when the twenty-four hours turned into forty-eight and even seventy-two, Roger tending to her sweetly and solicitously, bringing her tea and aspirin, offering to stay home from work to take care of her—offers she determinedly fended off.

She didn't want Roger; she wanted to be alone. She wanted to be in her bed. She didn't want to talk to anyone, she didn't want to think about anything. She felt useless, incompetent, worthless. She wanted to go away. She wanted to sleep.

What she really wanted, although she didn't admit that to anyone, not even the wolf, was to go away, permanently, irrevocably, to a place where no one would find her and she would never have to come back.

On the fourth day of her self-imposed exile, Roger came home from work to find her assembling every pill they had in their medicine cabinet into a pile on the kitchen counter. It was dumb. It was beyond dumb. It wasn't even a good suicide attempt. Apparently she was even incompetent at taking her own life.

"What is it," Roger asked, weeping, as he drove her to the hospital. "What happened? What's wrong?"

"Anna," Claire said, pale and shaken, breaking into tears

127

herself. "Anna, Anna, Anna." She didn't know why she said it then, and she doesn't know now, but she kept saying it, over and over again.

Twenty-four hours in the George Washington Hospital emergency room led to two weeks on the psychiatric ward, a scan of her head, fistfuls of pills, and finally to Grimmsley. Research, he told her, suggested that people like her had "increased number of small areas of focal signal hyperintensities" in their brain tissue: areas of increased water concentration, he meant. Water on the brain, she thought, only it wasn't that, although what it was exactly, Grimmsley either wouldn't or couldn't say. In the end he simply sent her home with a prescription for Xynolith. It was the condition of her return to work: that she would visit her psychiatrist regularly and follow his orders. Take her pink pills. Alec had actually written it up as a contract and made her sign it.

The bastard.

But now she has ninety days. She's making progress. She's being stable. It's what they all want—Grimmsley, Roger, Nathan, and Alec, too. She corrects herself. And her. It's what she wants, too.

Only it isn't, not really. She wants something else. Something very different. Something that has to do with Sasha—and Anna. His death, Anna said, was never explained. Should it have been? Claire closes her eyes, wincing. She's not supposed to think about that. She promised Roger she wouldn't.

"Mrs. Sadler?" Grimmsley says. "Are you all right?"

"Yes." She smiles at him. "Of course."

Grimmsley hesitates then slides the prescription across

the desk to her. His hair almost cracks then doesn't. He reaches up oh-so-delicately and adjusts it back into place. Watching him touch his hair reminds her that she and Grimmsley have never touched. Not once. She finds it so strange to see this little man month after month, over and over again, and never touch him. They didn't even shake hands when they first met. He just smiled while she stood by helplessly, hopelessly, her hands bunched awkwardly at her sides. Does he have a germ phobia? Some kind of inner rule about boundaries, she suspects. He wouldn't want to get too close. She could lean forward, right now, reach across the desk, poke him in his soft, bulging stomach. Stir that comb-over until it falls apart. She almost does it, just to see the look of horror on his face. But she doesn't. She's a good girl. She has to be. She doesn't have a choice. She has to stay stable. Everything depends on it. Alec and Roger, too. She picks up the prescription, folds it in half, puts it in her purse.

"So, everything else is good? Work?" Business taken care of, Grimmsley can relax. Surreptitiously he glances at his watch. The insurance company allows ten minutes for medicine checks. See how far the mighty psychiatric hour has shrunk. Talk? Who has time nowadays for talk? Even in the best of times an hour was only fifty minutes. Claire sneaks a glance at her own watch. She's used up four of her ten minutes so far. That leaves six. She could walk out now if she wanted to, but she doesn't want to raise any more warning flags. She plays along.

"Good. Busy."

"You're in—misdemeanors?"

He knows she is. Or he would, if he remembered.

"Stores and whores." She smiles. "Sorry. That's what we call it. We shouldn't, of course. Prostitution, bar fights, drugs. That kind of thing. Keeping the streets clean for John Q. Public." Shoplifting, too, she could add, but she doesn't. The irony doesn't escape her that she often spends her days prosecuting people who are just like her.

"Sounds like important work."

"That's what they say." If he only knew. Working in misdemeanors is the worst of the worst, the last resort. No one wants it, and certainly no one expects to stay in it. The lawyers come in fresh out of law school, do a six- or nine-month tour in the unit, then move on to something better: felonies, clerkships, corporate jobs, promotions. Claire started with the same expectation. She would have a distinguished career, work as a prosecutor then slide into a tony position as a district attorney and end up as a judge. She would make something of herself. She was sure of it. She would do good in the world. Prosecute cases that mattered. Put away criminals. That was almost fifteen years ago. Now even Alec is younger than she is. She can hardly bear the way he looks at her, that terrible mix of pity and embarrassment. Like Thomas.

"I think they're afraid of me. At work. Ever since last winter. They act like it's contagious. They keep their distance."

"Give them time."

Time. Yes, of course. She would check her own watch but she can't do it as covertly as Grimmsley. How many minutes are left? Three, four?

"Nothing else then?"

"No." She shakes her head. "Well, yes. There is this one

130

thing. Roger wants to have a baby but I told him I can't. Because of the Xynolith."

Grimmsley's hands move to his desk. He leans forward. "Are you thinking of getting pregnant?"

"Me? No. Of course not." She breaks into laughter and is horrified to hear it go on too long, uncontrolled, a schoolgirl's giggle. Grimmsley's eyes narrow. Claire coughs, puts her hand over her mouth, bringing the laughter to an end. "I told Roger I can't because of the Xynolith. I thought it would help if you agreed."

Grimmsley frowns again, giving her the look that passes for concern. He glances at the clock. "Do you want to make another appointment—to talk?"

"No. Really. It's okay. We agreed when we got married. Roger and I. No babies. He has his career and I have mine. You know, professional couple and all that. He's writing a book on the Cold War. He needs it for tenure. And I have— misdemeanors." She glances at her watch. Eight minutes gone, two remaining. "Well, I guess that's it, isn't it?" She's leaving, even if it isn't. "Goodbye, Dr. Grimmsley." She stands up, smiles, gives him a small wave. She's halfway to the door when she turns around. "Oh. I did get some news since I saw you last time. My mother's dying. She has cancer. Apparently it can't be cured."

Even she's appalled at how nonchalant she sounds, at how airily her voice says the words. Mother. Cancer. Dying. Grimmsley bolts to his feet.

"She had a brother once. His name was Sasha. He died when she was just a girl." Claire doesn't even know why she's telling Grimmsley these things. "He drowned in an accident. But it's so strange. She said it was never explained."

131

Grimmsley is looking at her, aghast. "Claire—Mrs. Sadler—I think—"

"That we should talk about it? Why would we do that?" The only satisfaction Claire has from this whole tawdry mess is that jumping up has made Grimmsley's comb-over crack. Through the dark sections of hair a swath of pink skull glistens. What are the odds? Thirty percent. She should have put money down on that. She takes the prescription from her purse, waves it at him. "Isn't that what this is for? Ninety days, Dr. Grimmsley. See you then."

The wolf is as thrilled to be leaving as Claire is. Comrades in arms, they saunter out the door. Thelma and Louise. Who knows what they'll be up to next? Claire catches a glimpse of Grimmsley, still on his feet, a look of alarm on his face, the bare patch of skull widening. Then she turns the corner, and he's gone.

Ten

GUS

Gus spends the rest of the night sitting on the floor just outside of Anna's room, his head in his hands, his back against the wall, too afraid to leave her. Only when dawn comes does he judge it safe to return to his own room. There he falls immediately into an exhausted sleep, too deep to notice when the rest of the household begins to stir. When he finally wakes, to his great shame, he discovers it's past ten o'clock. What will the Glanzes think of him? His head is pounding, and it takes him a moment to realize the throbbing pain isn't just from lack of sleep. He's hung over.

The key to Anna's door. A hammer and a nail. He hasn't forgotten what he needs. He still can't get over his own idiocy. Secure your patient's safety. Every psychiatrist worth his salt knows that. Well, he does now, too. Every house has tools somewhere, in the basement, the garage. Once the window is secure, it will be impossible to raise the sash more than a few inches, far enough to allow in fresh air, but not far enough to allow Anna to—he breaks off his thoughts. He won't think about it. He just plain won't. He will get that key. But first he will speak to Mr. and Mrs. Glanz. There will be no Spring Meadow. Never.

He throws cold water on his face, shaves, dresses, hurries downstairs to the great hall where he runs—literally—into a young woman in a maid's uniform, hardly larger than a child. Marie. She's even more startled to see him than he is to see her, claps a hand over her mouth, takes a step back, staring. She speaks no English, he no Portuguese. She shoos him out to the terrace where he finds a table set for breakfast with only one place remaining: his. The rest of the family has already finished eating.

No food. Please God. Only coffee. Lots of it. Black. And ice water. Somehow he manages to make himself understood. He gulps down the ice water then drinks a cup of coffee while standing by the stone balustrade at the edge of the terrace, shielding his eyes from the glare of the morning sun. There's no sign of Frieda or Lionel anywhere. Even the dour Mr. Zharkov seems to have disappeared. But there below, at the bottom of the hill, are Hettie and Anna, dressed in bathing suits, sunning themselves on the sand.

It's amazing how much difference a few hours makes. The scene looks placid, idyllic, with no hint of the turmoil of the night before. The tide is out, a few clouds nesting in the hazy blue sky, waves licking as harmlessly as puppies at the girls' bare feet. Hettie's mood appears to have changed completely—not at all unusual for an eleven-year-old, Gus thinks sourly. She looks up, sees him, and waves at him gaily, as pleased as punch to be in the company of her sister. Anna looks at him, too, then, bored, looks away. She turns onto her stomach on her blanket, her head to the side, her eyes closed. What does she remember of last night, of the danger she put herself in—the danger *he* put her in? Does it seem like a dream to her, or has she simply completely forgotten it? He will have to find out. He will have to get to the bottom of whatever it was that drove her from her bed. With a shudder he recalls his own nightmare, the one that woke him just in time to save her life. Was Anna, too, dreaming of wolves? He will hypnotize her as soon as possible and hope that once in a trance, she will say. But first he will speak to the Glanzes. And he will get that key.

He leaves the terrace, goes into the house, searches for Lionel and Frieda. Neither is to be found. The house has an empty feel to it. He returns to the terrace just as Marie comes out to clear the table. "The Glanzes," he says. "Where are they?" He doesn't understand a word of the stream of Portuguese that follows. Finally he thinks to say simply, "Miss Chase?" Marie smiles, nods, and leads him to her.

Beatrice Chase is in her office, a small, tidy annex that sits just off a sunroom at the side of the house. The office has a narrow window, the view darkened by boxwoods, and a roll-top desk, crammed with drawers and cubbies, where she sits writing a letter, bent over it as assiduously as a doctor bent over a prescription. She looks up in surprise as Gus appears in the doorway, Marie disappearing as rapidly as a puff of smoke behind him. "Dr. Thaler, good morning, I thought—" Her face opens into a smile, her eyes lighting up in the way he found so entrancing—yesterday. He's in no mood for it today.

I thought you would be gone by now, is what she means. Gus has no wish to explain. "The key to Anna's room," he says simply. "I need it."

She frowns, puzzled, then nods. "Of course." She reaches into a desk drawer, pulls out a key, and hands it to him. To his great relief she doesn't ask him any questions about it. He doesn't know what he would say if she did.

He pockets the key then draws himself up. "I need to speak to Mrs. Glanz, To Mr. Glanz, too. To both of them." He makes no attempt to hide the irritation in his voice. He is Anna's doctor. His wishes will be respected. He's aware again of how he has been manipulated—and ignored. "Immediately." The sharpness of his tone startles her. She looks distinctly uncomfortable. She draws her lip between her teeth. Yesterday he found the gesture so charming. Today it only adds to his irritation. Why can't she just answer?

"I'm afraid it will have to wait," she says finally. "Mrs. Glanz has gone into the city. She drove in this morning with Mr. Glanz and Mr. Zharkov. She's gone to see John Stannis, the director of the gallery that represents her. She was supposed to have a show there in the fall, but canceled it after—well, after the spring. Now she's reconsidering." She ventures a smile. "Mr. Glanz is most pleased about it. He says he owes it all to you, to what you've done for Anna."

What he's done for Anna? Gus frowns. The last thing he needs to hear is more flattery from Lionel Glanz. It reminds him that neither of the Glanzes has exactly been forthcoming with him. Nor, for that matter, has Miss Chase.

"The girls are being sent away," he says abruptly, his voice rough. "To boarding school. Did you know that?"

"Boarding school?" Her smile fades. "I know Mrs. Glanz has been considering it. She took the girls out of school after—" She averts her eyes. "She's been most unhappy with the girls' school for some time now. She's determined not to send them back."

"And you didn't think you should tell me?" His voice

rises with anger.

Miss Chase is taken aback. The lip draws between her teeth. Then she pulls herself up, fixing him with a steady gaze. "I didn't think it was my place."

"Your place—" Gus bites off the words, fuming. All families lie. Who said that? Dr. Kanner? No, Hans van der Ploeg, the doctor Gus trained with at St. Margaret's, the one who taught him everything he knows about hypnosis. Van der Ploeg's mouth had creased into a devilish grin as he uttered the words. "Don't ever forget it, Gus. If there's nothing else you remember from your time here, remember that." Gus had, of course, immediately forgotten it— until now. But Miss Chase isn't even family; she's only an employee. His anger is entirely misplaced. None of this has anything to do with her.

"I'm sorry. I didn't mean—" He tries a different tack, softening his voice. "Perhaps we could talk?"

She has a doubtful look in her eyes but once again she nods, then stands and leads him to the sunroom.

The sunroom is a lovely place, or anyway would be, if Gus were in any mood to appreciate it. The room is light and airy, the floor made of brown quarry tile, the walls covered with thin strips of wood that have been painted white and cut into intricate, lacy patterns. On a glass table stands one of Frieda's sculptures, the figure of a woman who has twisted around to observe the lifted sole of her foot. He has no trouble now recognizing her style, the telltale knife-edges, dabs of bronze clinging to a wire frame, the signature hole in the center of the chest.

Light pours in through two sets of French doors, one

which leads to the terrace, the second to a rose garden where blooms tremble in the shore breeze, releasing a dizzying scent. The far wall is given over to a massive stone fireplace, graced by a gleaming mirror that reflects Gus's face back to him.

There's a wicker couch in the center of the sunroom, flanked by two matching armchairs. Neither of them has sat down; the tension between them has made it impossible. Finally Gus sinks into one of the armchairs, holds out his hand. "Please," he says. She hesitates, and when she sits down, he says, "Thank you." He takes a breath. He doesn't know where to begin, so just begins with what matters most. "Did you know the Glanzes are considering Spring Meadow for Anna?"

"Yes. I think so." She's dressed today in a shirtwaist dress, a pale blue color with a black belt and buttons. She drops her hands to her lap, smooths her skirt, lowers her eyes. A fly has wandered in through the open door and bats against the mirror, the buzzing outsized, echoing in Gus's head. "It's a children's hospital, isn't it? Mr. Glanz is opposed to it, but Mrs. Glanz has been insisting. A doctor recommended it to her."

"A doctor?" His voice is full of contempt. "A quack, you mean."

She looks away, twists a button on her dress. He has gone too far again; he has put her in the middle. "You have to remember that Anna has been sick for a long time," she says, speaking softly. "A very long time. Almost six months now. None of us thought it would last this long." She lifts her chin, looks at him directly. "You had her yourself for over a month." She doesn't say the obvious: that Anna wasn't cured in Baltimore. That in many ways she got worse. "I'm not trying to stand in your way, Dr. Thaler. Believe me. It's quite the opposite. I'd do anything I could to help."

He's missing something. It's there, right in front of him, but he isn't seeing it. Think, Gus, think. What happened last night? Anna went sleepwalking. Well, yes, of course, she always does; it's a part of her illness. But this time was different. This time she was sleepwalking at home. This time . . . He laughs, startling Miss Chase, who looks at him in surprise. "Sorry. It's just—" It's been there all along, staring at him in the face, looking out at him from practically every room in the house. Even the sunroom is angled to give out a view of its searing, cutting blue. The Sound. The water. Anna went in her sleep to the place where her brother drowned.

"Tell me about Sasha." In his urgency to learn about Anna, he's completely forgotten about her brother. Miss Chase would know as well as anyone. "Please." He leans towards her, his hands on his knees. "I need to know everything, especially how he died."

Once again she averts her eyes, and he sees the struggle inside her: the discretion of the employee fighting against her wish to help Anna.

"I don't want to have to tell you about Spring Meadow," he says. "You don't want to hear it. But trust me when I tell you Anna must never be allowed to go there."

For a moment longer she hesitates, then she lifts her chin, looks back at him directly. Beatrice Chase, he sees now, is guided by a strong sense of professionalism and a piercing loyalty. But she's also a woman of deep empathy, with a belief in justice. She will do what is right. He admires her for that.

"It was a Thursday. I remember because Mrs. Arturo wasn't here, and she always has Thursday off."

Mrs. Arturo. The housekeeper. Gus met her yesterday when she guided him to the terrace for cocktails. He hadn't paid her much attention—she was the kind of person who would be easy to overlook, who most likely preferred it—but he should have. She's a part of Anna's world, and anything that touches Anna has relevance. From now on, he tells himself, he will overlook nothing. Somewhere out there is the missing piece, the one that will solve the puzzle of Anna Glanz. He promises himself to find it.

"It was early March, and the girls were on spring vacation from school. The whole family was home." Miss Chase frowns. "No, not the whole family. Not Mr. Glanz. He was in Albany, for the campaign. He was due home on Friday. And this—"

"This was Thursday." Gus smiles, encouraging her. "What kind of business does Mr. Glanz do? When he's not running for senator." The fly has been taking a rest, sitting on the mantel, its wings quivering, but now it takes up its quest again to push its way into the world inside the mirror, flinging itself at the surface. How little he knows about Lionel Glanz, Gus realizes all of a sudden. How little he knows, he is beginning to realize, about everything.

"Textile mills. He supplied uniforms to the Coast Guard during the war. But there are other things, oil, coal, finance." She shrugs helplessly. "There's so much. He has an office in the city with his own staff to look after these things. I'm just here for Mrs. Glanz."

"And the politics? The ambition for national office?" He

sees her considering again before she speaks, drawing the lip in.

"He was a state senator once. That was years ago, when the girls were still small. Before—before Sasha was born. Mrs. Glanz hated politics. She hated everything about it. She told me so herself. They lived in Manhattan then, but Mr. Glanz was so much away, in Albany for weeks at a time. When Mrs. Glanz got pregnant again, he agreed to give it up." She brightens, on more secure ground now. "That's when they bought this house. When Sasha was born. She didn't want the children to be raised in the city. She wanted them to have the outdoors, the fresh air. I started working here a few years later. Sasha had just turned two."

"Two years ago."

"Yes."

He's quiet for a moment, thinking about it. "Then why would Mr. Glanz run for office now? Especially if Mrs. Glanz is opposed."

"I believe he was asked."

"By Mr. Zharkov?"

She smiles. "Yes. By Mr. Zharkov. And others. Quite insistently. They think he can win. He has—well, he has his own money for the campaign, of course. That makes a difference. But it's more than that." A hint of a pride comes into her voice. "They think he'll make a good senator. They think he can do some good in the world. They wore Mrs. Glanz down, and in the end she agreed to go along with it. The girls are older now, and she thought to send them to boarding school. Meanwhile Sasha would come with them to Washington. They would keep this house as a summer home, a retreat." Sorrow darkens her eyes. "Not anymore."

Gus understands now how Spring Meadow fits in. Ever since Sasha died and the doctors in Baltimore failed to cure Anna, Frieda must feel boxed in, as if she has no other choice. What did she say? She only wanted to live with people she loved. To keep her children safe. Well, Spring Meadow, he thought sourly, was a very safe place indeed—if you were willing to rely on shock treatments and restraints.

"So," Gus says, returning to the boy's death. The fly has given up its quest for the mirror world and wings lazily about his head; he swats it away. "It was spring vacation. Mrs. Glanz and the children were at home. And what did they do during their days? How did they"—he searches for the right way to phrase his question—"how did they occupy their time?"

"Mrs. Glanz was working on her sculpture, putting in long hours in her studio, preparing for her show. Sasha was with the nanny." The weather had been mild, with warm, sunny days, reminiscent of summer. "The girls—well, they did the usual things girls do. They took walks, read books, rode their bikes into the village. On calm days they took their rowboat to the island."

"The island," Gus says, remembering. "I've seen it. It's just off shore. There are some ruins on it, a gazebo."

"Yes. It burned down last winter. Mr. Glanz told the girls he would have it rebuilt. I'm sure he wanted to, it's just that . . . Well." She shrugs. There's no need to say anything more. "The girls love going there. They have picnics, swim." She smiles. "I think what they love most is the chance to be on their own."

"Of course." Hettie and Anna. Anna and Hettie. The two are a pair. Even Gus can see how close they are.

"They're both good swimmers and Anna is a strong rower. For over a year now she's been able to handle the boat on her own."

"So Sasha," he says, picking up the thread of her story. "On that day, Sasha was with his nanny."

"Yes." Her face saddens. "She was a French girl, an au pair. Mrs. Glanz hired her last fall. Anna and Hettie had been learning French in school, and she thought having a French girl in the house would encourage them. Anna loved French. She used to come up to me chattering little phrases, saying, '*Comment-allez vous?*'" A brief smile crosses her face at the memory. "The girls took ballet lessons, too. Anna was quite good at it. She had a growth spurt last winter and the ballet mistress said she was too tall to make a career of it, but she kept it up anyway. And she loves playing the piano. She's very musical. Mrs. Glanz hardly ever has to remind her to practice. Hettie on the other hand . . ."

Hettie, Gus can well imagine, would hardly be the kind of girl to sit still for piano lessons. Anna, however, could sit for hours, the princess in her castle, being good, being oh-so-very good. "So they were all here," he says gently. "Mrs. Sauer—"

"Yes. Mrs. Sauer. Not Mr. Slocum. He was traveling with Mr. Glanz."

"And Mrs. Arturo was out."

"That's right."

He ticks them off on his fingers. Another swat at the fly. "That leaves Marie."

She shakes her head. "No. Not Marie. The girl who was here before her. What was her name?" She frowns then smiles in relief as she comes up with the name. "Isabel."

143

"Good. Now to that day, the day he—" Gus breaks off. "Tell me everything. Take your time."

"I came in early that morning. Mrs. Glanz was already gone. She'd taken a train into the city to consult with Mr. Stannis about the show. I went straight to my office. Some of the sculptures she wanted to display were still at the foundry, and I called to check on the casting schedule. Sasha was outside, playing on the beach with the nanny. He loved it there. He was so drawn to the water." She stops, a startled look in her eyes, her hand on her mouth, as she realizes what she has said.

"And the girls?" he says, prompting her.

"Here and there, all morning long, running in and out of the house."

There was lunch, she said, describing the afternoon. Then it was quiet. The nanny took Sasha upstairs for his nap. The girls went upstairs, too. Miss Chase went back to her office to make some phone calls. It rained. Then it stopped and the sun came out. Sasha woke up and the nanny took him back outside. The girls went out again, too, rowing to the island. Later she went out to the terrace to get a breath of fresh air and saw Sasha and the nanny sitting on a blanket on the grass. He was playing with a toy fire engine; she was sunning herself. The girls were just coming back from the island. They came up the steps, and Miss Chase followed them back inside. The girls went upstairs, and she returned to her office. She had some letters to write, then one more phone call.

She frowns.

"Yes?" Gus says.

"There was someone on the line. When I picked up the

phone to make the call, someone was on it."

"On the phone?"

"Yes. The house has several extensions. There's one in my office, another in the master suite, a third in the library, a fourth by the kitchen."

"Who was it?"

"I don't know. A man. I didn't recognize the voice. It didn't make any sense. Slocum was gone, and there were no other men here."

Puzzled, she put the receiver down. A few moments later, when she picked it up again, the line was free. She was just dialing when she heard the nanny scream.

She ran outside, they all did, Mrs. Sauer, Isabel, the girls. The nanny was standing on the grass exactly where she had been before, but the boy was gone. She was screaming in French; it took them a minute to get her to switch to English. All she would say was that Sasha had been taken.

"Taken?"

"*Il a été pris.*"

Kidnapped. It was the logical conclusion.

"I thought it must have been the man I heard," Beatrice says, "the one who was on the line. Somehow he'd managed to get into the house. Mr. Glanz was a prominent politician, a public figure. He made no secret of his home on the shore. And the Lindbergh kidnapping was still so fresh in our minds."

She ran into the house to call the police. Then she called Mrs. Glanz's gallery. Mr. Stannis arranged for a car to bring Mrs. Glanz home. Miss Chase didn't know how to reach Mr. Glanz, but a man in his Manhattan office promised to get a message to him. Just as she was putting down the phone, the police arrived.

"And where was Anna in all this?" Gus says.

"She came outside when the nanny screamed."

"So before that—she was in the house?"

"Yes. Upstairs."

"You're sure about that?"

"Yes." She looks puzzled that he's pressing the point. "Anna went up with Hettie after they came back from the island. They didn't come down until the nanny screamed. I saw her coming down the stairs and then we all rushed out of the house together. I stumbled on the terrace, and Anna took my arm."

Just as Kanner said. The boy's death was an accident. Anna had nothing to do with it—nothing, that is, outside her imagination. "Please. Go on."

The next three days were terrible, the worst she'd ever lived through. Mrs. Glanz came back soon after the police arrived. "If you could have seen her face." Miss Chase closes her eyes, shuddering. Mr. Glanz returned that evening. The police scoured the neighborhood; the FBI sent two agents to the house. No one slept. They sat by the phone night and day, waiting for a ransom call. Everyone expected it. And then, on the morning of the third day, came the one thing no one had expected.

"They found him. That is, a man did. He was out walking his dog that morning on the beach and the dog—" She can't go on. "Later the police told us it was because of the currents. He'd been out there in the water all that time."

"So the man you heard on the phone wasn't the kidnapper?"

She shakes her head. "Once we knew the truth, the

146

police took the nanny in for questioning. It turned out she'd met a boy in the village. The son of a local fisherman. She'd left Sasha alone on the grass and gone into the house to call him."

"So he was the one you heard on the phone." Once Sasha was alone, it wouldn't have taken him long to—well.

"Mr. Glanz fired her, of course. I've never seen such anger in him—or anyone. It was volcanic." She shudders. "Then his lawyers had her deported."

"And through all of this," Gus says thoughtfully, as the fly buzzes determinedly back at the mirror, "Anna was still speaking?"

"I'm sorry. I don't remember. We were all so frightened. I hardly saw the girls. Mrs. Glanz kept them upstairs, trying to protect them from the worst of it."

"When did you—when did it become clear she had stopped?"

"At the funeral. One of Mr. Glanz's business colleagues came up to the family to pay his condolences. He shook Anna's hand. Mrs. Glanz told her to say thank you. She just looked at him mutely. We all thought it was the shock. We were sure it would wear off." She lifts her hands in a helpless gesture. He knows the rest.

He sits back in his chair, thinking. No wonder Anna stopped speaking. It was simply more than she could handle: the sudden disappearance of her brother, the report of his kidnapping, the presence of the police and federal agents, the terrified helplessness of the parents, the way the body was found. Her father's volcanic anger. Somewhere in the mix she'd come to see herself as responsible for the boy's death. The good girl—oh so very good. She'd become overwhelmed and had simply shut down.

"I'm sorry to put you through this," he says.

Miss Chase nods, wipes tears from her eyes.

"He must have been a lovely boy. Hettie says he was everyone's favorite." He smiles at her. "Hettie and I had a chance to chat a bit last night."

"Mrs. Glanz adored him. There's always something so special about a mother and a son. And Mr. Glanz—well, the loss devastated him. He'd always wanted a boy. He saw his future in Sasha, an heir to his business. I think a part of him died that day."

"He wouldn't consider his daughters?"

She smiles. "Oh, no, he's quite old-fashioned. He adores his girls. He only wants the best for them. In his view, they should marry well and be happy."

"The girls—were they close to their brother?"

"Yes. Well, fond of him of course. I don't know if I would say they were close. There was such a big gap between them."

Gus is quiet for a time. They both are. Is the fly gone, or has it just given up? He doesn't hear it anymore. He hears footsteps on the terrace, then in the hall. The girls have come inside, have gone upstairs. He will have to go to Anna soon, take her for her hypnosis session.

"I think you should know Anna sleepwalks." He finds it easy to confide in Miss Chase after all. He trusts her. She's an ally—perhaps the only one he has in this house. "She went sleepwalking last night. She ended up at the water. I found her there."

Her eyes widen. "Oh. Now I understand"—she colors—"the key."

"Anna holds herself responsible for Sasha's drowning."

"That's ridiculous! She had nothing to do with it. She wasn't even there."

"I know. It's a delusion." He gives her a tight smile. "Unfortunately it's proven quite durable."

She grows silent, her lip between her teeth. "Last night, when Anna went sleepwalking. You said she went to the water. Did she go to the sea wall?"

"Yes." He grimaces as he thinks of the danger. "How did you know?"

"It's a game the girls play. They walk on the wall. It terrifies Mrs. Glanz. She can't bear to see it. She expressly forbids it." She shrugs helplessly; he knows how children are. "They do it anyway."

"Is it possible the boy fell from the wall?" Gus asks. A picture is forming in his mind. "Did he climb up like his sisters?"

"I don't know. I didn't see it happen. I didn't even think about it until just now, when you said you found Anna there."

Not executioner then. He breaks out into a smile. He can't help it. The relief is impossible to put into words. Last night Anna hadn't been trying to take her life. She'd been trying to tell him something. See, Gus, he reminds himself. Look at Anna. You must look and see.

"She thinks Sasha fell from the wall." The thought is growing in him, taking on a feeling of certainty. "She might have even seen him." Quickly he takes inventory. Yes. Anna's room has a water view. "She was looking out her window and saw him climb onto the wall. She saw he was alone and realized the nanny was gone. Only it was too late—she couldn't do anything about it. Ever since then she's blamed herself." He nods. "I expect she stopped speaking at that moment. In the heat of things, no one noticed. But it's only logical."

No wonder the mutism has been so intractable. It's not entirely delusional; there's a reality behind it: the reality of what Anna *saw*. "She feels guilty because she knows her brother imitated her. Because she knew he was in danger and was powerless to help him."

Just as he had been powerless to help his own sister when she was dying.

Miss Chase leans toward him, her eyes growing bright. "Will any of this be of help?"

"I don't know. I think so." He has something to go on now. He's eager to hypnotize Anna to test out his theory. It's the most eager he's felt since he came here. He stands up. "I can't thank you enough."

She stands up, too. "Please. There's no need to thank me. If you can do anything for Anna—" She smiles. "That will be more than enough for me."

"There's one thing you can do."

"Of course, Doctor."

"You can call me Gus."

She's blushing. Her smile broadens, wide enough to bring out the amber light in her eyes. "Then you must call me Beatrice."

"With pleasure." He takes her hands, holds them briefly, liking the feel of her skin against his, warm and secure.

He's almost out of the room when something else comes to his mind. "Yesterday." He turns back to her. "You said you don't live in. Why not?" She's clearly a practical person, economical; surely it would make more sense.

The blush on her face deepens. "Mrs. Glanz is a wonderful woman. She's also a bit—" she hesitates "—temperamental. I suppose it's the artist in her. She has a tendency to imagine things."

"About—?"

"Her husband."

"I don't understand."

Her voice lowers to a whisper. "She thinks he's unfaithful."

"And is he?"

"Never. Not at all." She shakes her head firmly. "He's completely loyal to his family. If he ever did—stray—Mr. Slocum would know. He goes everywhere with Mr. Glanz. Mr. Slocum is quite upstanding. He would never work for a man who was unfaithful to his wife. Unfortunately Mrs. Glanz has a way of—well, she sees things that aren't there."

"You mean Isabel." The maid before Marie. Gus understands now. Isabel didn't just leave her job: she was fired. By Frieda.

Beatrice looks relieved that he hasn't made her spell it out.

"And you think, that if you lived in . . ."

She lifts her chin. "Mr. Glanz has never done anything to make me feel in the least bit uncomfortable. He's a wonderful father. He loves his children. And Mrs. Glanz adores him. But yes, I like my job. I *need* this job. I wouldn't do anything to risk it."

As Gus leaves the room, he notices the fly again. He was wrong about it. It isn't gone, it's still there, flinging itself hopelessly, miserably at the mirror, over and over again. He stiffens his hand and with a quick motion crushes it. The body falls lifeless to the floor. The sight brings Rosa to his mind. His sister—an insect—what kind of connection is that? Only death. Only death.

He walks back through the great hall to the stairs. As he climbs to Anna's room, under the watchful eye of Dora, the woman in the portrait, something Beatrice said lingers in his mind. Or rather, something she didn't say. She said Lionel was loyal to his family, and that he loved his children. She also said Frieda adored him. But she didn't say he adored her.

Eleven

*F*ortunately Roger sleeps like the dead. He comes home at night exhausted from a workout in the racquetball court or shuffles down from the loft bleary-eyed after a long evening battling the Cold War at his desk and tumbles into bed. Seconds later—literally seconds, Claire has counted them—he's sleeping, and he doesn't stir until morning. The sleep of the innocent. The sleep of the just.

Whereas Claire can't sleep at all. Claire can hardly close her eyes. The wakefulness of the wicked.

The insomnia kicks in hard after her last visit to Grimmsley. At first she tries to fight it. We all need our sleep, don't we? Good girl that she is, she summons every ounce of strength she has and forces herself to lie still, unmoving in bed beside Roger, her eyes pinched shut, willing herself to fall asleep, listening to his dreamy murmurings, his sweet, slightly nasal, boyish breaths. Counting sheep. Counting defendants in the misdemeanor court, each case more mind-numbing than the last. Eventually, when sleep doesn't come, she gives in and opens her eyes. The wolf is already there, standing on the floor beside her, her muzzle only inches away, lightly panting.

The wolf is a creature of the night, a creature of the darkness, of the hunt. The wolf wants to go out.

Night after night, Claire creeps upstairs to the loft. Feet tucked up under her, she sits on the floor, gazing through the skylight at the night sky, stars gleaming in the heavens, the bare branches of trees waving in the wind like sea fronds. Years ago she took a college astronomy class simply because the professor was known for giving out easy A's, and she had a science requirement she needed fulfill. She still remembers a few of his lectures, can summon up the names of a handful of stars: Castor, Pollux, Betelgeuse. Now that it's winter, Orion dominates the southeast sky. Lupus is gone, faded like the flowers with the onset of autumn. The wolf constellation. The Babylonians called it Mad Dog, the Greeks *Therion*—the Beast. "Did you know that?" she asks the wolf.

By three or four in the morning, Claire's tired enough to crawl back into bed, catching a few hours of sleep before Roger awakes. Surely, she thinks, the lack of sleep will accumulate; surely in time the insomnia will dissipate; surely she will sleep again. Instead, as the sleepless nights wear on, she finds herself feeling less tired, not more. Jazzed up, energized. Soon she can't sit still. Night after night she paces the floor.

Out, the wolf says. A walk.

It's only a matter of time before Claire slips on a pair of jeans and heels, puts on lipstick, gloves, and a coat, casts a glance at herself in the mirror, and takes to the streets.

At night Georgetown is rich in shadows, the air thick with the smell of dead leaves moldering in the gutters, the pavement damp from cold wintry rains. Here and there streetlamps cast yellowish pools of light onto the ground. Claire passes through them, heading for Wisconsin Avenue where late-night restaurants are still aglow, music spilling from bars, pedestrians crowding the sidewalks, laughter, chatter cutting through the air. Cars jam the narrow, twisting street, and as she passes by, she brushes against their cold metal sides, shivering. She wants to be inside where the people are, wants to be warm, drinking, talking, dancing, laughing, but the wolf won't let her.

No, the wolf says, not here.

Claire slinks down the hill and crosses M Street to the C&O Canal. This section of the canal—an old, abandoned waterway that cuts through the center of Georgetown—has been gentrified, cafes and galleries sprouting where once warehouses and factories stood. During the day the towpath boasts walkers and joggers, nannies pushing strollers, women promenading with shopping bags hung from the crooks of their arms. But farther to the west, the canal reverts to its original self, dark and sinister. Crime reigns. More than one of Claire's cases has taken place on its seedy banks: vandalism, drug deals, muggings, assaults. Just what the doctor ordered, the wolf says with a smirk as she turns onto the towpath, trotting purposely forward.

Only it's not what the doctor ordered at all. Grimmsley would be horrified if he knew Claire was spending her nights walking the canal. He would want to talk to her about it. He would mention taking chances, putting herself in danger, a hidden desire, as with her shoplifting, to get caught. But Claire isn't talking to Grimmsley. She isn't even seeing him. She still has over sixty days left on her ninety. Besides, what is there to fear with the wolf at her side? She follows the wolf onto the towpath, walking close behind.

She isn't talking about Anna either. Or Sasha. She isn't

even thinking of them. She told Roger she wouldn't. Don't get started, he said, and so she hasn't. He didn't want it to be like last time: the pills, the ambulance, the ER. That's one thing Claire can say for certain: it most certainly isn't. She's never felt like this before. She's never walked the canal at night.

Darkness rules. On either side of the canal run massive brick buildings with boarded-up doorways and grated windows, weedy vacant lots, sooty smokestacks reaching into the sky. The stars are muted here, their light blocked by tangled thickets of trees. The water in the canal is as thick as coagulated blood, pooling stagnantly between the locks. The air smells of mold, of the swamp the city once was, of sour, sodden garbage. The wolf is enchanted. She comes to life, her nostrils flaring, her senses prickling, acute.

One night she comes to a sudden stop, eying the darkness. She crouches, takes a few stiff-legged stalking steps, then takes off sprinting, her nose to the ground. In a moment she has returned with some kind of animal in her mouth. Gently she lays it, still twitching, at Claire's feet. What is it? A mole? A rat? Claire doesn't want to know. Shuddering, she looks away. The wolf gazes up at her, her eyes full of love. Seeing her offering refused, she shrugs and devours it.

The towpath skirts the Potomac River, passes under the viaduct where cars rattle overhead, headlights jerking from side to side. Beneath the overpass, a bundle of trash reveals itself to be a person, sitting up, dark eyes staring. Men congregate in the shadows, shoulders hunched, sharing a pipe. The crack leaves a sweet, burned smell in the air. Claire breathes in deeply, drawing near. The men gaze at her with idle curiosity. They aren't afraid; they know she belongs to the night as they do. *Just one toke*, she thinks, like at the college parties she used to go to where joints were passed from hand to hand. But some vestigial voice— is it Grimmsley's?—warns Claire away. She ducks her head, giving the smokers a wide berth.

One night she sees a man standing by a falling-down shed, the lighted tip of his cigarette tracing an arc in the darkness. She casts her eyes to the ground as she hurries past and so is surprised to find him suddenly in front of her, blocking the path. "Late night?" he says with a low growl. "Unh-huh." He stinks of old whiskey, of iron and dirt and sweat. Tenderly, with an air of wonder, he reaches up to touch her red hair. With a gasp she shrinks back, then twists sideways to shoulder past him, but he catches her by the elbow, his grip hard.

"Let me go," she says. "Let me—"

"Like you is," he says, suddenly releasing her with a grin, backing away with his hands up. "Unh-huh."

She sprints ahead until he's out of sight then stops, her heart pounding, her stomach heaving, doubled over, her hands on her hips. She thinks she will be sick. "And where were you?" she says to the wolf. "Just when I need you." *Like you is.* All at once she bursts into laughter, adrenaline surging like a drug. "What is that supposed to mean?" She shakes her head, wondering.

Twice she hears the crack of gunfire. Once too close for comfort. She spins on her heel that time, hustling back the way she came. Sirens sound while red and blue police cruiser lights sweep through the night. Surely, she thinks, someone will find me. But no one does. By the time dawn pinks up the sky, she's back home, flooded with disappointment and relief. When Roger awakens, she's already in the shower or in the kitchen, making coffee, another pink tab of Xynolith flushed away.

"You're up early," he says, nuzzling her. "Sleep well?"

"Mmm," she replies, kissing him, so that she won't have to lie.

Like you is.

They don't talk of the baby anymore. They don't talk of anything. They treat each other as if they're both exceedingly fragile, made of china or blown glass. They treat each other with the utmost politeness and careful consideration. "Would you like?" they say. "Only if you don't mind." Sometimes she catches him looking at her from across the room, watching her, studying her, the way he studies a particularly knotty problem in the Cold War. When he sees that she sees, he colors and looks away. They hardly ever make love anymore. The baby is in the way, stuck in the bed between them as surely as if it were alive. They don't speak of Anna. And they most definitely don't speak of Sasha. It was never explained, Anna said. As far as Claire is concerned, it never will be.

Every Sunday night Nathan dutifully calls, making his reports. Anna is doing fine, he says. The first few rounds of chemo have gone well. She's tolerating the medicines, has had hardly any nausea. She hasn't lost her hair yet. She's just tired. She sleeps a lot.

Sleep. The very thought of it leaves Claire trembling, weak with longing. She doesn't want sleep itself—she's not tired enough for that—but she wants what sleep brings: hours of disappearing into herself, of oblivion. She would almost take having cancer if it meant she could sleep, too.

The wolf, on the other hand, has no trouble falling asleep at all. As soon as they return from their nighttime rambles, she flops onto the living room rug. Soon she is dreaming, her paws gently quivering, her nose tucked under her tail. Whereas Claire can't sleep at all. Claire has forgotten what it feels like to sleep. Has forgotten what it feels like to dream.

Twelve

∴

GUS

The hypnosis session, Gus decides, will take place in the library. He considered treating Anna in her room, but worried it might present too many distractions. All those books, dolls, and records; household staff going back and forth down the hall. Seclusion and privacy are what he needs.

The library is a smallish room—well, large by any other standard, but small in comparison to the rest of the house—that sits off the great hall, adjacent to the sunroom. Along one side French doors give out to the rose garden, but these Gus closes easily by drawing the drapes, rendering the atmosphere cool and shadowy. In the middle of the room stands a green felt billiards table and rack of cues; in the back a bar holds crystal decanters filled with various kinds of spirits, glowing in the dim light like jewels. The air smells thickly of whiskey and tobacco, paper and chalk. Bookshelves climb to the ceiling. To Gus's surprise, there is very little art in the room—only a few miniature oil seascapes—and no sculpture at all. Not a single hint of Frieda. This room, he realizes, belongs to Lionel. He recalls the aspiring senator disappearing into it the night before with his associate, Zharkov. The thought unsettles Gus, and for a moment he regrets his choice. He remembers the uneasy laughter in the dining room when Lionel pulled Hettie onto his lap, the flash of anger in Anna's eyes. He shakes his head. It was nothing, of course, his imagination running away from him, the effect of the candlelight and the wine.

At the front of the room is a hearth made of black rock, flanked by a sofa and a pair of matching wing chairs. Gus runs his hand over the sofa, which is covered in brown leather, and finds it smooth and inviting. Perfect. Anna will lie comfortably there. He draws one of the wingchairs close and then reconsiders and pulls it back a bit. He wants to be close enough to Anna to see her clearly in her trance, but not so close that she feels scrutinized. He angles the armchair so that she will not be directly in his line of sight, then sits down and waits for Beatrice, who has offered to fetch Anna for him.

He is eager for the session to begin, full of the confidence that comes from knowing that he finally has solved the riddle that is Anna. One more hypnosis session will seal the deal. The irony is not lost on him that under ordinary circumstances he might never have hypnotized Anna at all. By the time he arrived at Phipps as a young resident, hypnosis had long been banned at the clinic—a ban Gus never thought to question. All that changed when he was sent in the midst of the war to St. Margaret's Psychiatric Hospital in Washington, D.C., for two years of public health service.

St. Margaret's, Gus discovered, treated a large number of war veterans suffering from battle fatigue. To most of the psychiatrists, the men were a stubborn puzzle, but one, Hans van der Ploeg—affectionately known to the staff as

"The Flying Dutchman" for his wild wings of white hair—achieved a fair amount of success. Van der Ploeg was old enough to have treated soldiers in World War I, casualties of what was known then as shell shock. Shell shock, battle fatigue. It made no difference to the Dutchman. He hypnotized his soldiers, taking them back in their trances to the source of their war trauma, walking them—talking them—through it. Over time they got better.

Occasionally van der Ploeg invited the hospital's young trainees to soirées at his home for port, cigars, and demonstrations of hypnosis—the kind of parlor tricks serious psychiatrists like Meyer thought gave their profession a bad name. One trainee, Gus recalls, munched with delight on a raw potato, calling it the most delicious apple he'd ever had, under van der Ploeg's nefarious influence. Another woke from a trance in great embarrassment to find himself braying like a donkey. Gus, to his shame, discovered he was particularly susceptible to van der Ploeg's manipulations. While his fellow trainees sang and clapped to drinking songs, Gus danced a most unprofessional jig. And once he completed a complete walk around the block in bare feet, wearing his shoes like a hat.

By day, quietly, studiously, Gus watched the Dutchman at work—watched many of his patients recover from their trauma. In time he began administering hypnosis himself, and was pleased to discover he, too, had success. He became adept at self-hypnosis, a technique that served him well when he suffered occasional bouts of insomnia. One morning, after observing van der Ploeg at work on a particularly difficult case, he took the Dutchman aside. "What made you decide to treat your patients with hypnosis?" he asked.

Van der Ploeg smiled and shrugged. "Whatever works, works."

Whatever works, works. The words stuck with Gus when he returned to Baltimore and resumed his training at Phipps. He was sorry to put hypnosis aside, but not too sorry. Each hospital, he understood, had its own "flavor," derived from the philosophy of its chief, in this case, Adolf Meyer, who had a decidedly scientific bent. Gus's job was to absorb as much of Meyer as he could. Perhaps one day he would resume the Dutchman's techniques, but for the time being, he was content to put them aside. He was no rebel. He still practiced self-hypnosis after hectic days when he found himself unable to sleep.

Then Anna Glanz was admitted to Gus's service and proved herself resistant to the usual clinic offerings: occupational therapy, hydrotherapy, musical concerts, courtyard walks, occasional doses of medicinal sedation. Given her mutism, talk therapy was out of the question. Art therapy gave Gus a glimpse inside her mind: the ever-menacing wolves. He began wondering if she wasn't suffering from the same kind of trauma that affected the veterans he'd treated at St. Margaret's, men who'd often witnessed the deaths of comrades in arms. Survivor guilt, van der Ploeg called it, when his patients questioned why they had lived while others had died. Could Anna's psyche have been injured in a similar way by the death of her brother?

Gus decided to put his theory to the test. One night, when the clinic was quiet, he let himself secretly into Anna's room. He was relieved to see she was willing to put herself into his hands and submit to hypnosis therapy:

the penitent girl, being good, being oh-so-very good. He was even more relieved when he discovered she was easy to hypnotize. Over the next few days he returned nightly to her room, putting her into a trance. Soon, to his delight, she began to talk. She didn't say much, and often he had trouble following her meaning, but wolves were a persistent theme. They were, he decided, a symbol of the guilt she felt for her brother's death—the same delusion that affected so many of St. Margaret's war veterans.

Anna clearly benefitted from hypnotherapy, and soon many of her symptoms began to wane—her tendency to pick at her lips until they bled, the torturous sleepwalking. Outside her trances, however, her mutism stubbornly persisted. No matter how hard Gus tried, he was unable to change her belief that she was somehow responsible for her brother's death. Over and over again he took her back in time to the day the boy died; just as they reached the crucial point of his death, however, she exhibited distress, and he had to break off the sessions. Then to his dismay she stopped eating, and he had no choice but to bring her home. But now he has something to go on. He knows what happened to Anna. He understands why she blames herself, and he is sure he can convince her she is not at fault. Literally and figuratively, Beatrice has given him the key.

Just as Gus thinks of Beatrice, she appears in the doorway with Anna beside her. "I told Anna you wanted to see her," Beatrice says brightly, speaking effortlessly with the optimism and reassurance Gus struggles so hard to perfect in his own bedside manner. "I'll be back later," she says to Anna, then steps back, leaving the two of them alone. Gus has asked Beatrice to keep Hettie occupied while he is with Anna; the last thing he needs is an interruption by a stubborn and impetuous eleven-year-old. Beatrice has promised to take Hettie into the village for an ice cream, and a moment later Gus hears the front door opening as they go out.

Anna lingers in the doorway, looking at him warily, a hint of suspicion in her eyes. She's still wearing her bathing suit from the morning, covered by a simple floral shift. Her arms and legs are bare. Sand dusts her knees and elbows; she has beach tar on her feet. Her hair is undone and falls in loose tangles around her head.

"Thank you for coming to see me," he says, rising to his feet. He smiles at her, but the smile isn't returned. She doesn't want to see me, he thinks. Now that I've brought her home, she's done with me. She wants me to be gone. "I'd like to propose something to you. I'd like to hypnotize you one more time. I'm glad to see you home again—glad to see you so much improved. But we still have much to accomplish."

Anna looks away, her fingers fiddling with the strap to her dress. It occurs to him that she might very well refuse the treatment. He has no way of forcing her. No matter what, he won't tell her about Spring Meadow. He doesn't want to frighten her. He's sure Spring Meadow will be off the table soon.

He sits back down in the wingchair, waiting patiently and silently, giving her time to make up her mind. He wants her to know the decision is hers. For a moment longer she hesitates, then she steps forward and lies down on the sofa.

Good girl, Anna, Gus thinks. The penitent girl, being oh-so-very good. "Let's begin." He leans forward, possessed by a strange excitement, a rising anticipation. She's close enough now that he can take in her scent, damp and musty like the sea. Her skin has a rosy hue from the sun. "Think about your breath, Anna. Listen to my voice. One, two . . ." Soon she is breathing softly, her body fully relaxed, her eyes taking on the glazed look they always have when she falls into her trances. "One, two, three, four . . ." He can stop counting now—he should stop counting—if he were at Phipps he would. But he wants her to go deeper than she's ever gone before. He wants to take her back to the moment of her brother's death, and for that he needs the fully calming power of the trance. "Listen to my voice, Anna. Breathe." His voice descends to a whisper. "One, two . . ."

Despite the coolness of the room, Gus is sweating, his tie gripping his throat. He swallows hard, loosens the knot. A strand of Anna's hair has fallen across her face. He reaches for it—extends his hand—then pulls it back. Then he reaches out again and with delicate, surgical precision, brushes the tangle away.

At his touch, Anna stirs and sighs.

All at once he stands up, walks to the billiards table and leans over, his palms pressed against the polished wood. The room is too close, too quiet. Was it a mistake to come here? From a great distance comes the sound of water running. Mrs. Sauer must be in the kitchen, preparing lunch. Upstairs a door opens and closes. Mrs. Arturo is there, making her rounds. He hears a faint burst of Portuguese: Marie is with her.

On the sofa, Anna stirs again, her breast rising and falling with each breath. Gus pulls himself up, wipes a hand over his face, returns to his chair. Speaking quickly now, he reminds her of the signals they established long ago for their hypnosis sessions: a lift of the right hand to indicate "yes," movement of the left hand to indicate distress. He practices the signals with her, and she responds as directed, indicating that she hears and understands.

"Good, Anna. Let's proceed."

He has decided to approach the moment of Sasha's death slowly, from an oblique angle. He will begin by taking her back first to her sleepwalking the night before. "I want you to think back to last night. You left your bed. Were you dreaming of wolves?"

Her mouth opens, and for a moment he believes she will speak, but she simply closes it again. By her side, her right hand flutters.

"You went outside. You walked to the Sound. Did the wolves chase you there?"

Her right hand rises and falls.

He checks her breathing: steady. Her body is relaxed. "Were you thinking of your brother?"

A hesitation as if she's considering, then her right hand rises.

"Good, Anna. I want you to think of him. I want you to remember the last time you saw him."

All at once she stiffens. Her back arches, and her face tightens. Her left hand twitches. If they were at Phipps, he would stop this line of questioning immediately. Instead he leans closer, his voice low. "You were in your room."

Her left hand relaxes. She takes a deep breath. Her right hand flutters and is still.

"You looked out the window."

167

The right hand rises and falls.

He sits back, wipes his face again with the back of his hand. "Your brother." His voice feels thick. "You saw him through the window. You saw him outside."

Her right hand moves: Yes.

"The nanny, Anna. Was she there? Did you see her with Sasha?"

There's no movement at all: No.

He watches her intently. "Think carefully now. Did you see your brother fall?'

At the sound of the question, her face twists into a grimace, and a tremor passes through her. He's about to break her trance when he realizes neither hand has moved: No. It's just as well. The trauma might have been even worse if she had. She must have turned away from the window to go for help, but it was already too late.

"It's not your fault, Anna." He speaks to her with all the authority he can muster. "You can't be held responsible for something that happened when you weren't even there. Do you understand me?"

For a moment there is nothing, then Anna sighs deeply, and the tension leaves her body. Her right hand rises and hovers in the air.

Gus takes her through the boy's death several more times, from different angles; he even talks about how by climbing on the wall Sasha might have been imitating her. "None of this," he tells her firmly, "is your fault. The nanny was supposed to be watching him, and the nanny failed." He doesn't hold anything back. Anna takes it all in with no further sign of distress, her right hand indicating that she understands. When he's done, when he can think of nothing more to say, he says, "It's over now, Anna. You can stop punishing yourself. You can let the wolves go."

Gus is exhausted. He rubs his hand over his eyes. Outside, in the hall, a door opens. Beatrice and Hettie have returned. He hears their voices as he brings Anna out of her trance. As she sits up, he smiles at her. "Well, Anna. How are you feeling?"

Still caught in a post-hypnotic daze, she looks at him dumbly as if she doesn't know who he is, where she is.

"Go ahead, Anna." His smile broadens. "You can speak now."

Her mouth opens, closes, and opens again. Nothing comes out. Her eyes darken with a look of panic. Then she stands up and runs from the room.

"Anna—" Gus says. He runs after her into the hall, but she has already gone upstairs. He can hear her with Hettie. Hettie is chattering, talking about her trip to the village. From Anna comes nothing but silence.

"Gus." Beatrice is in the hall waiting for him. She smiles at him happily. "How did it go? Did she—?"

Gus shakes his head.

Her face falls. "There's a way." She puts a hand on his arm. "You'll think of something. I know you will."

As far as Gus can tell, he will think of nothing. "Please, excuse me." He can't bear to talk about it now. "I need some air."

Outside the sun is shining unperturbed in a broad blue sky. A beautiful day, Gus thinks, well aware that he's in no mood to appreciate it. He needs a break from the Glanzes—from the oppression of their overbearing, luxurious mansion.

The house has begun to feel claustrophobic to him. He walks down the long drive then turns south onto the shore road and travels farther down the point. It feels good to be outside. Maybe with fresh air, his mind will clear.

What went wrong, what went wrong, what went wrong? The words echo in his mind to the rhythm of his feet. He's angry. No, not angry, disappointed. Yes, angry, terribly so, and the object of his anger is Anna. She should have spoken. He'd found the solution to her problem; had seen into her mind; had solved the riddle of her silence. What kind of perversity would keep her from acknowledging that?

Never blame your patient. Who said that—Kanner? No. Van der Ploeg. At the time Gus thought the idea was absurd. Who would be so callous as to blame a sick person for her illness? But now he knows the answer: he would. If it's blame he's looking for, he need go no farther than himself. She didn't speak because he hasn't gotten it right. He's struck by the maddening feeling that he's close—so close—and yet so blind. He's missing something right in front of him. Anna knows what it is. Only she, of course, can't tell him.

Or can she? All at once Gus is seized by the thought that Anna's silence, her intractable mutism, her sleepwalking, even her trances: it's all an act. She can speak; she's just choosing not to. She's making a fool of him, making a fool of all of them. But why? What possible purpose could it serve?

Ridiculous, ridiculous, ridiculous.

The truth is, Anna hasn't failed; he has. And failed miserably. Lionel knew what to do. He got Anna to eat. And what has Gus done?

Nothing, nothing, nothing.

As he walks farther down the road, the point grows narrower. On the Sound side, the houses become more modest, creeping closer to the road. Small clapboard cottages line the river. Behind a weathered wooden fence, a yellow dog barks. The road ends at a small beach, a scrubby piece of land, broken by dunes and outcrops of rocks. In the open air, the sun is intense. Gus sits on a rock, pulls off his jacket then his tie, yanking at it when the knot proves stubborn. How absurd to wear a suit in the summer on a beach. So much for his professionalism, his air of gravitas.

If only there were a drug that would make Anna speak! Even Rosa had medicine for her pain, a brown bottle that his parents kept on a shelf in the kitchen. They doled the drops out anxiously one by one at prescribed intervals according to the doctor's orders. It was never enough. Night after night she lay sleepless in her bed, moaning with agony from the cancer that had migrated deep into her bones.

But there's no medicine for patients like Anna. Even the great Dr. Meyer had nothing to offer.

Suddenly there's a flurry of wings—a gull landing on the beach. With beaky precision it roots in the sand and snatches up a rotting fish head. Soon another gull arrives and grabs at the head in a tug-of-war. Then with a squawk the birds drop their prize and take to the air. In their wake comes the yellow dog, bounding across the dunes. Someone has let him out. Gus looks up and sees a man in cotton trousers and a cap, wielding a fishing rod, following behind.

"Morning," the man says. He takes up a position nearby on the sand, plants the rod in the sand.

Is it morning still? Yes, Gus thinks irritably, it is. He

gives the man a brief nod then looks away.

"You're not from around here, are you?"

The dog has found the fish head abandoned by the gulls and crunches it with great pleasure. Gus manages a pinched smile. "No."

"I didn't think so." The man says the words with satisfaction. "After forty years on this point, you get to know everyone." When Gus doesn't answer, he adds helpfully, "I was born on this river. Fished here my whole life."

And maybe now you'll go back to it, Gus thinks wearily. "Is that so?"

He shouldn't have said anything. He's encouraged him. "Yes, sir. Name's Archibald, by the way." He grins. "You can call me Archie." Archie finds a rock nearby, settles himself on it in a friendly fashion. Then he narrows his eyes. "You're not one of those reporter fellows are you?"

Reporter? Gus shakes his head. "No."

"Didn't think so." There's that air of satisfaction again: a man who prides himself on his smarts. "You don't look like one."

"You've had reporters here?"

"Thick as thieves."

"How so?"

"You don't know, do you?" Archie hoots with laughter. "You don't even know who lives on this point."

Gus doesn't answer. He doesn't have to. Archie will tell him anyway.

"Lionel Glanz, that's who. You can't tell me you haven't heard of *him*."

Gus gives Archie a wan smile. "I might have."

"Should have seen this place after he jumped into that

Senate race. They came out here in droves. A pack of wolves, that's what they are. Newspapermen, all the way from the city. And the photographers." He reaches into his pocket, pulls out a handkerchief—good man, Gus thinks, to carry one—wipes his forehead, then puts the handkerchief back. "Just about drove Sally crazy."

Sally? Not a person. The dog. At the sound of her name, she licks her lips and looks lovingly at her owner.

"So you know Lionel Glanz, do you?" Gus says.

"Me? You're kidding, right?" Archie hoots again with laughter. "Sound folk don't mix with river folk around here."

That doesn't seem to require a response, so Gus doesn't give one. It's too damn hot, even for a dog. Sally trots over, drops in a spot of shade, and lazily pants, her eyes half closed.

"Where did you say you were from?" Archie says.

I didn't, Gus thinks, but there's no point in arguing. "Baltimore."

"I've got a cousin there. Works in a steel plant." He thinks about it. "Says the fishing's good in the bay."

Gus shrugs. He doesn't fish.

"Can't be as good as here," Archie says, with the air of settling an argument—one he's often had with his Baltimore cousin, Gus expects.

"No." Gus smiles. "I suppose not."

The gulls are back. Sally lifts her head then sighs and closes her eyes, content to chase them in her dreams.

"Do you think he'll win?" Gus says.

"What's that?" Archie seems to have been dreaming a bit himself.

"Glanz. Do you think he'll make the Senate?"

Archie blows out air through pursed lips. "Don't see why not. He gets whatever he wants." He lowers his voice. "He's a bully, you know."

Gus's ears prick up. "Is he?"

"Take this piece of land. The one we're sitting on. It belongs to the village. We were going to build docks on it after the war. Could have been a boon to us all. More fishing, more boats. Glanz didn't want it. Said it would 'spoil the place.'"

"And?"

"He went down to city hall. Anyway his lawyer did. Man in a suit." He looks suspiciously at Gus. "You're not one of *them*, are you?"

Gus laughs. "No." That much he can freely admit. He's no lawyer.

"I don't know who got what out of that deal. One thing I can tell you, he knows how to throw his money around, he does, Lionel Glanz." Archie waves his hand at the point. He doesn't have to say anything more. It's obvious: no docks. His eyes narrow again. "What do you expect from a Jew?"

"Come again?"

Archie detects a note of warning in Gus's voice. He backpedals. "Don't get me wrong. I don't mean anything by it. Those people had it bad in the war."

That, Gus thinks sourly, is one way of putting it.

"But not here. Not in America." He looks defensive. "Take what they want here, don't they? Take just about everything."

Gus has had enough. He stands up, brushes the sand from his pants. Sally lifts her head and looks up at him as if to say, Leaving so soon?

174

"Course I did feel sorry for him," Archie says.

"Really?" It's hard for Gus to keep the sarcasm out of his voice.

"When he lost his boy."

Gus sits back down. "What would you know about that?"

"Not much. Like I said, Sound folk and river folk don't mix." Archie's smiling now; he knows Gus is going nowhere soon. "Drowned, right there in the Sound. His body was out there for days." He gives Gus a ghastly grin. "I was the one that found him."

A man, Beatrice said, out walking his dog on the beach . . . So it was Archie. Gus shudders. How gruesome.

Archie nods, satisfied; he's gotten the effect he wanted. "Anyway, Sally did. Right there, by those rocks." He lifts his chin at the spot. "The police came out, the Feds, too, said it was a kidnapping. In the end they blamed the babysitter. Said she took up with Charley."

"Charley?"

"My boy." Archie's voice sours. "They tried to make the whole thing his fault."

Ah, Gus thinks. Charley. The voice on Beatrice's phone.

"That's the way it always is around here," Archie adds bitterly. "Something bad happens to one of them Sound people, and we're to blame for it." He points his finger at Gus. "She was the foreigner. She was the one had no reason being here." He shrugs. "They got rid of her all right. Before she had a chance to say anything."

"What's that?"

"The girl. The babysitter. Glanz sent her right back where she came from. Charley was broken up over it." He retreats. "I'm not saying there was anything going on in that house, but if there was, we'd never know now, would we?"

Gus has no answer to that question. He thinks for a minute then stands up. "Nice talking to you."

"Same," Archie says. "Baltimore." He chews that over. "Hey—you never did say. What are you doing up here?"

Gus walks off, gives Archie a wave of the hand, but doesn't look back.

He spends the rest of the day in his room. For a while he tries to write in his journal, but nothing comes of it, his thoughts just keep going in circles. He hears sounds on the stairs, the girls coming and going. Beatrice comes upstairs, and he hears her talking to Mrs. Arturo, something about putting the house on the market in the fall. Gus thinks of going to Beatrice, of telling her about his conversation on the beach, but doesn't know what he would say. That he met an old man who hated the Glanzes for their money, who was bitter and anti-Semitic, full of suspicions and conspiracies?

He puts the journal aside. He's too tired to write anymore, too tired to think. He never should have gone on that walk. The sun, the heat. He draws a glass of water from the tap, stands by the window drinking.

Hettie and Anna are outside, walking with linked arms across the grass. As he watches, they climb onto the sea wall and walk along it, balancing like tightrope acrobats. Just seeing it makes him feel sick. Is he getting nowhere with that girl? All at once Hettie stumbles. Gus raises a hand, his heart thudding, his breath caught in his throat. But Anna reaches out to steady her sister, and the girls jump back down safely to the grass, run around the side of the house, and disappear.

It's no use. He has to admit it. He's done here. He's incapable of making Anna speak. He will go back to Baltimore, a dog with his tail between his legs. First he will speak to the Glanzes about Spring Meadow. He owes Anna that much. There will be no sending her there. Beatrice has said that Frieda will be back in time for dinner; Lionel is out campaigning with Zharkov and won't be home for some days. Good, then. He will speak to Frieda tonight.

He lies down on his bed, closes his eyes, drifts into sleep. In his mind he's a boy again, attending a burial. It must be for Sasha. Gus sees the tragically small coffin, the grave gaping like a raw wound in the earth. The cemetery is ringed by an iron fence, overgrown with lilacs that bloom with a sickeningly sweet scent. Nearby stand the child's parents, clinging to each other in their grief. Only it isn't Frieda and Lionel; it's Gus's parents, his mother and his father. Inside the grave the coffin grows, extends, becomes large enough to encompass Rosa's body. Someone presses a clod of earth into Gus's hand. "The grave, boy, in the grave. Throw it in there."

His mother's legs buckle; his father's face is wet with tears. The soil in Gus's hand is thick and heavy, riddled with tiny white worms. It stains his fingers. He's just a boy, such a small boy, what can he possibly do with dirt like that?

"There," the voice says again. "Throw it." Gus steps closer to the grave, lifts his hand, is just about to drop the clod of earth when he wakes with a start to the sound of a knock.

"Gus. Open up."

He sits up. "Beatrice?"

"Please." She raps on his door again, louder this time. "I have something to show you."

177

He runs a hand through his hair, comes to the door. "Yes?"

"Look." She thrusts a piece of paper at him. "I just found it." She's breathless; she must have run up the stairs. "It's from the girls' old school. Their records. Mrs. Glanz had them mailed here. I'm supposed to forward them to the boarding school. I was packaging them up when I saw this."

Records? The girls? He's having trouble pulling it all together. He takes the paper, looks at it. It's a letter, no a note, hastily scrawled on a piece of school paper. *Anna Glanz*, the note reads. *Anna Glanz*.

"It's her French teacher. She says Anna is refusing to participate in class. She says she won't speak a word. She wrote it to the principal. She wants someone to contact Anna's parents."

For over a week now Anna Glanz is not speaking, Gus reads. *I suggest someone to call her parents.* He looks at Beatrice. "So?" Everyone knows Anna won't speak.

"The date. Look at the date."

Vendredi. "That's Friday, isn't it?" His French never was any good.

"Yes." Her face is triumphant, glowing. "Don't you see?"

See what? He looks again. The note is from Friday, from the last day of school before spring vacation. He doesn't see, and then all at once he does. His eyes widen, and his brain jolts awake.

"Anna—" Beatrice says.

"Anna—" Gus repeats. He puts his hands on her shoulders. "Anna stopped speaking—" He pulls her close and then, to the surprise of both of them, kisses her. Then he steps back, full of wonder, and finishes his sentence. "Anna stopped speaking before Sasha died."

The Journal of
Baruch Zalman

PART THREE

I have spent the better part of the day writing. Only twice have I been drawn from my task. First to prepare a simple breakfast for Raisel, Dora, and myself. Then to take a walk in the woods where I hoped the peacefulness of the mountains and the voice of the river would comfort and strengthen me. I found a rock beside the running waters where I could sit with pen in hand, my journal balanced on my knees. And so I continue.

After Gittel vanished, dear Reader, leaving Dora with me, I waited three long days for her return. Meanwhile I kept the girl with me. What was I to do with her? She had no money—the small bag Gittel had left with her, I discovered, contained nothing more than a few items of jewelry and clothing—and I couldn't afford the fees to board her at the widow's house. Gittel was right: her daughter was no housekeeper. She didn't lift a finger to help either Raisel or me. But Raisel didn't seem to mind. She spent the days at Dora's side, her hand on her arm or encircling her waist. For hours I heard the two women whispering together. Or rather, I heard Raisel whispering, while Dora seemed content to listen. More than once I heard Raisel murmur

179

our daughter's name. Then I grew afraid that my wife had truly lost her mind, and had gone to a place from which I might never retrieve her.

On the morning of the fourth day I asked my wife to stay at home with Dora, for I would be gone for many days. She paid me little heed, and didn't even ask where I was going. As long as Dora was with her, she was content. I left the village on foot, but soon had the good fortune to encounter a logger transporting wood out of the mountains. He took me as far as the town of Roman, where I purchased a train ticket for Negresti. There I spent the night on a bench in the railway station and early the next morning boarded a train for Iași. By midday I had arrived.

I was determined to find Gittel and persuade her to come back with me to Alba-Bistrița and fetch her daughter. I had no idea why she had abandoned the girl. All I knew was that Dora had to go. Each minute she spent with Raisel put my wife at risk.

It had been years since I had last been in Iași. Since that time the city, the former Moldavian capital, had grown, and to my eyes become transformed. The old cobblestone streets had been paved and lit by lamps. Horse-drawn streetcars ran on rails in all directions. Everywhere was the hustle and bustle befitting a prominent commercial town. Carts and carriages clogged the intersections while new houses— tall and big and bright—sprouted like mushrooms from the ground. It took me a while to find my way through this jumble to the rabbinic court where I had lived for so many years.

At least nothing at the court had changed—or so I thought at first. From the outside it looked quiet and peaceful. It consisted of a courtyard surrounded by a synagogue, stables, ritual bath, and kitchen. At the back stood the house, fronted like a palace with six white columns, where once I had ruled as rebbe and where my nephew Ezriel now served. As I came through the gate, however, I was shocked to find everything in turmoil. The courtyard was in disarray, heaped with baskets and crates and trunks. Hasidim in long black kaftans ran hither and thither, shouting and calling to one another, fetching and packing more things. In the center of this whirlwind stood a man issuing orders and ticking items off on a list. I approached him and asked to see the rebbe. Without even bothering to ask who I was or what my business might be, he told me Ezriel was unavailable; he was in council with his advisors. I could wait, he added, if it pleased me, although the look he gave me indicated he held out little hope.

He had no idea who I was; he hadn't even been born, I reflected, when I last ruled in this place. Should I enlighten him? "I'll wait," I said. For well over an hour I sat on a bench in the corner of the courtyard, feeling confused and dismayed, while the running and fetching and shouting went on as before. Then the man returned and told me the rebbe would see me now.

Inside I was troubled to see that the house was equally in disarray. I followed the man past rooms that once had been outfitted with rich carpets, wall hangings, and gleaming furniture but now were as empty as husks. Other parts of the house were full of frenetic activity. In one room a woman busily wrapped dishes in paper. In another a man oversaw the packing of books into trunks. In still another women sorted clothing into bags. Finally we came to the

181

grand hall where once I had received petitioners and where my nephew now sat. Here the man left me, and after a moment, I stepped inside.

The hall, I was relieved to see, still looked much as it had when I served as rebbe. As I came in, memories crowded in, and I paused to slow the beating of my heart. There, in the center of the room, was the long table where once I had expounded Torah to my followers. At the back of the room, bookshelves filled with leather volumes climbed to the ceiling, served by a rolling ladder. *My* books—the thought leaped irrationally into my mind as I recalled the years I had pored over them, feeling again my foot on the rungs of the ladder, the pages turning in my hand. The carpet had a familiar heft under my heel; the faces of my father, my grandfather, and his father before him, looked out at me with kind glances from portraits on the walls. Even my beloved brother, Ezriel's father, was depicted there, raising in my breast an especially painful sense of loss. Only the smoky smell in the room struck me as strange. It came from sealing wax my nephew was wielding at his desk as he affixed his signature to a stack of documents and sealed each one in turn. I had never had need of such an official instrument.

When he saw me, Ezriel's face lit with pleasure. "Uncle." He stood and embraced me tenderly. "This is an unexpected honor."

The last time I had seen him had been at my brother's funeral. Then he had been not much more than a boy, trembling as he faced his new responsibilities. Now I saw that he had grown into the full flower of manhood. His beard was dark and full, his face ruddy. Any fears he might have once felt seemed to have vanished, replaced by a quiet sense of confidence. Here is a man, I thought, who unlike me has no trouble wielding authority and power. But I could scarce bring myself to return his greeting and simply blurted out, "What is happening here?"

Ezriel took a seat at the head of the long table and bade me sit beside him. "I am leaving for the Holy Land." His face took on a grave cast. "Forty men are accompanying me. Once we are settled, we will send for our wives and families."

I was so shocked, I forgot my own troubles and stumbled to my feet. "What kind of madness is this?"

"Please, Uncle." He took my arm and guided me back to my chair. "I would have sent word to you, only"—a note of sadness crept into his voice—"I didn't think you would understand."

"What is there to understand?" I had to stop myself from leaping to my feet again. "That you are leaving the home of your father—of your grandfathers?" I waved a hand at the faces on the wall. "That you will abandon everything they worked for generations to create?"

Ezriel turned away, and his face colored. I sensed his discomfort; no one, I realized, had spoken to him this way for a very long time. Then he looked at me with eyes that were both determined and resigned. "There is no future for us in this place, Baruch. You know that as well as I. Even in your mountain retreat, Jews have no life."

"No life! We have the only life that matters: service to the Lord."

"The Lord?" Once again Ezriel's face colored, this time from anger. "If this is the meaning of God's service—I can no longer accept it. We choke here. My people are choking. How can we do God's work if we can't even live?"

Now I, too, grew angry. "What kind of arrogance is this to believe you can take God's prophecies into your own hands? There is no return to the Promised Land until the Messiah comes. So we have known—so we have prayed—for centuries."

"Ah, yes, the Messiah." A harsh light came into Ezriel's eyes, frightening me, and his voice was tinged with sarcasm. "Your Great Master, your Baal Shem. How many years have you waited for him, Baruch? Didn't he once promise to return, too?"

I caught my breath. Darkness encroached on my vision, and I feared I would have another fit. "You will suffer for such blasphemy," I said. "Your people will suffer. Nothing good will come of this. You will bastardize the land, turning it into nothing more than a nation among nations."

"And would that be such a bad thing?" Ezriel said, but the harshness had left his face, and a sad smile played on his lips. "I know, I know. I have my fears. Don't you think I wait daily for the Messiah's return, too?" He took my hand, pressed it, then let it go. "I am sorry, Uncle, but we have made our decision. We took a vote. We decided to leave as soon as possible after the end of Passover." A look of wonder came into his eyes. "Perhaps next year we truly will celebrate in Jerusalem."

I was confounded and fell silent. I didn't know what to think, what to say. I knew Jews were fleeing Romania, but it never occurred to me that my own family, the court, would be at risk. "Who will take over as rebbe after you?"

A look of pain came into Ezriel's eyes, and his voice

184

dropped to a whisper. "My sons fight amongst themselves." As I had feared. Already the noxious fruit of his folly poisoned his followers. But there was nothing I could do about it.

Ezriel sighed. "I am sorry that you find me like this, Uncle. I would have wished for an easier goodbye. Nevertheless I am glad to see you." Again he pressed my hand. "What brings you to Iași?"

He had asked the question as custom required, but I could sense his heart wasn't in it. Already his eyes crept towards his desk, and I knew he wished to return to his work. "I am searching for someone," I said, "a woman who was born here in Iași. Gittel Haimoviçi."

"Haimoviçi." Ezriel pulled at his beard, reflecting. "I will make inquiries for you." Then his face softened. "How is Raisel?"

"She grows old," I said. Then I, too, softened. No matter what, he was my brother's child, and it did me good to see him. I smiled at him. "As do I."

"Be well, Uncle." Once more Ezriel embraced me. He turned his back and returned to his desk. But as I left the room, I heard him whisper, "Forgive me."

I found my way to the courtyard, where again I waited amidst the hustle and bustle. Eventually a man appeared, bearing a slip of paper. He handed it to me without a word, and without a word I left.

"Liebman's Bakery" the paper said, followed by the name of a street. As I walked towards it, I consoled myself that at least Ezriel had chosen to go to Palestine. He was sorely misguided, but he still wished to do the work of God. Tales I had heard from the New World were far worse.

Jewish women uncovered their hair; men shaved their beards, lay down with Gentiles, and conducted business on the Sabbath. Worship of the Lord had been replaced by the worship of idols, especially money. I was sorry now that I had chastised Ezriel. Who was I to criticize him for abandoning the court when I had done the very same thing? Perhaps my nephew was right, and God needed a reminder that His people suffered, and they wouldn't wait forever.

In time I found the bakery. The air inside was warm and tangy with the smell of fresh bread. A young girl, twelve years old, perhaps, stood at the counter. Behind her, through an open door, I glimpsed a burly man with a red face loading loaves of bread into an oven. Working beside him was a boy a few years older than the girl. On the floor beside her, a small boy amused himself playing with a lump of dough.

"Is your mother at home?" I said to the girl.

She turned to the boy on the floor. "Go get Mama."

The smell of bread had made me hungry, and as the boy disappeared up a narrow flight of stairs, I bought a roll and munched it. Soon a woman with a baby on her hip came down, followed by the boy. As he took up his dough again, she turned to me with a curious look. "You asked for me?"

"Is there a place where we could speak in private?" I said, with an eye on the children.

"In private?" A suspicious look came over the woman's face.

"It's about Dora," I said, dropping my voice low.

She bit down hard on her lip and glanced towards the man working the oven. Then she handed the baby to the girl and said, "Follow me."

186

She took me down a dark hallway to a storeroom that was crammed with bags of flour and sugar and had a sour scent of fermenting yeast. There she lit a lamp and stood with her arms crossed over her chest, eying me warily. I introduced myself. As I had suspected, she was Gittel's sister. The resemblance between the two women was unmistakable: both had the same fair skin and delicate features. But P'ninah—for that was her name—appeared, if such a thing were possible, even harder used. Her hands were roughened from work, her ankles thick, her dress, covered by a long apron, frayed.

"I'm looking for Gittel," I said. "Is she here with you?"

P'ninah shook her head. "She left many days ago. She said something about going to the mountains. Dora went with her."

"Yes. But when she came back—"

"She didn't come back." A worried look crept into her eyes. "What has happened?"

I told her then about the arrival of the two women in the village and how Gittel had disappeared, leaving Dora behind.

"Alone?" P'ninah bit down hard on her lip. Then she raised her chin and looked at me directly. "What did Gittel tell you about Dora?"

Her eyes had grown hard in a way that made me uncomfortable. "That she's a good girl, only she daydreams too much . . ."

"Daydreams?" P'ninah laughed, scoffing. "That's the least of it. Did she tell you the girl's a thief?"

"A thief?" I was shocked to hear it.

"My gold necklace went missing when Dora was here.

187

How do you account for that?"

I thought of Dora's bag. There had indeed been a gold necklace inside.

P'ninah rolled her eyes. "She's just as crazy as her father."

"Her father?" I said. "He was a martyr—he sacrificed himself—"

"Is that what Gittel said?" Once again she broke into a scoffing laugh. "Killed himself is more like it. He would have done it sooner or later." She touched a finger to her head. "My sister, it pains me, but she makes bad choices in her husbands. First the crazy one and now the second . . ." She gave me a meaningful look.

I was still trying to fathom what she had told me and could think of nothing to say.

P'ninah averted her eyes. She twisted the strings of her apron then let them go. When she spoke again, resignation had come into her voice. "Gittel brought Dora here weeks ago. She wanted me to take her." She waved a hand towards the bakery. "Does it look like I have room for more children? I told her to take Dora home. She said she couldn't. It was impossible."

"He was beating her," I said slowly. "The stepfather. He locked her in the pantry. Gittel feared for her life."

"Her life?" P'ninah left the question hanging. "No, not exactly."

"But if—" All at once I understood her meaning. It wasn't beatings that Gittel feared behind that locked door, it was something far more insidious . . . I felt myself growing faint and sat down on a bag of flour. "So Gittel couldn't take her back."

For a long time P'ninah didn't answer. Then she sighed.

"That necklace—it wasn't worth anything. The gold isn't even real. It's just painted tin. I would have given it to Dora gladly if only she'd asked." A look of sorrow came over her face. "I would have taken her, even so, but my husband . . ." Her voice trailed off.

"Please," I said. I stood up. "Don't blame yourself."

I excused myself and left. That evening I took a train back to Negresti where once again I slept in the station. The next day was Friday. I traveled by train to Roman where I spent the Sabbath at the home of a widower near the main synagogue. Sunday morning I started on foot for Alba-Bistriţa; it was the Sabbath of the Christians, and none of the farmers who might give me a ride were about. Late in the afternoon I encountered a peasant with a cart who agreed for a fee to carry me a way up the road. After more hours of walking, as night fell, I arrived home.

I had been gone for five days. I was worried about Dora and even more worried about Raisel. How would she have fared without me? I was sorry now that I had gone to Iaşi. I didn't know what to do with what I had learned. I couldn't keep Dora. That much was clear. I would have to send her somewhere, but where? No matter how I turned the question in my mind, I could find no answer.

If I had been shocked to return to the rebbe's court, I was even more shocked when I entered my own home. Everything was in turmoil. Dirty dishes littered the kitchen. The cupboards were empty as if Raisel had been searching for something and had turned everything inside out. Pots and pans stood in heaps on the floor; crockery covered the table. Raisel appeared to be oblivious to this state of affairs. She was sitting in the bedroom with Dora, absorbed in conversation, her hand on the girl's arm, a secret smile on her face. "Husband!" Raisel said when she saw me. She rose up joyfully to greet me, but at the sight of her, my limbs grew cold. Her hair was uncovered, her face pale and drawn, her eyes burning bright as if with fever. My wife, who had ever taken pride in her appearance, was wearing a crumpled, stained skirt, and had put on her blouse backwards.

I was even more horrified to see Dora. On her finger was the ring I had given Raisel when we married. P'ninah's necklace gleamed at her neck—and something more: Bathsheva's bell was tied to her wrist with a ribbon. It tinkled as she came toward me. Color rose in my face, and I grew angry. "You—" I sputtered. I tore off the bell. "Leave this house at once!" I opened the door to push her out. She would have to go somewhere—anywhere—at that moment I didn't care. I only wanted her gone.

Just then Raisel's pale face turned to ash. She moaned, fell to the ground, and crawled to Dora on her knees. "Baruch, no!" Weeping, she kissed the hem of her dress. "Don't send her away. Don't you see? It's our daughter. Bathsheva, our beloved. She's come home to us, Baruch. She's come back."

Thirteen

CLAIRE

$\mathcal{A}$ cold January morning. Deep in the winter. Claire has forty-one days left in her ninety-day countdown with Grimmsley. At least she thinks she does. It's getting harder and harder to count these days, to order her thoughts, to get them to march in a straightforward fashion from point A to point B. One, two, three, four. Is ninety minus forty-nine really forty-one? She's fairly certain it's been over two weeks since she had a full night of sleep, although she naps at her desk. Or so it seems. She's startled from time to time to find herself staring at the clock with fifteen minutes, twenty minutes, a half hour completely unaccounted for. Disappeared. Gone.

Thank goodness she's somewhere safe today, somewhere familiar, the D.C. misdemeanors courtroom. She's come in for a series of status hearings. Status hearings are routine. She's done them thousands of times before. She could do them with her eyes closed. She could do them in her sleep.

If only.

"It's a question of responsibility," she says now, standing to address the judge. "Your Honor. I submit. A question of accountability."

It's not just time Claire's been losing lately, it's her sense of self, of where she is, what she's supposed to be doing. She takes a deep breath, clears her head.

"A question, Your Honor, I submit. Respectfully. About people getting away with things. Not just that, Your Honor, no, far more than that. About *us* letting them get away with the things they've done."

She has a colleague with her today, an attorney named James. James, is it, or John? Jason? Something with a J. Maybe Justin. He's new to misdemeanors, freshly minted, just out of law school, just passed the bar. He looks freshly minted, too, his shoes shiny, his shirt stiffly starched, his suit pressed, his face cleanly shaven. She's supposed to be mentoring him, showing him around, showing him the ropes.

"You're lucky," Alec said to Justin/James/Jason when he introduced her. "Claire's one of the most experienced prosecutors we have." He skewed his eyes sideways at her, a look she knew well: Don't screw this up.

"What they've done," she says now. "Your Honor. I submit. People. The harm they've caused. Are we just supposed to sit here? Look at the children, Your Honor. The weak, the innocent. Please. I'm asking you. Is there nothing we can do?"

She steals a glance at Justin/James. She hopes he's learning something, taking notes. Poor thing must be terrified to be in court. He gives her a wide-eyed stare, swallowing hard, his Adam's apple moving up and down.

"What they've done," she says with a grim shake of her head. She paces the courtroom before the bench. "Your Honor. Respectfully."

It's the seventh, eighth, ninth hearing of the day, she's lost count, no reason to count them, all of them are the same, all of them proceeding nicely—take that, Alec—going without a hitch. Only once did she miss her stride. Thomas came in to testify on a trespassing charge, and Claire found herself staring at him dumbstruck. Did he remember her shoplifting arrest? She had trouble looking him in the face, asking him the questions she needed to ask. But he simply said his piece and left the courtroom. He must have forgotten. Only the barest hint of a suppressed smile as he passed by her let her know he hadn't.

The rest of the cases went smoothly: drug possession, bar fight, more trespassing, shoplifting, another bar fight. Yes, Your Honor, No, Your Honor. Next? Going like clockwork—until this one.

It's an easy case, open and shut as Alec would say. A woman with a drug habit, not particularly bad as these things go. She might have even gotten away with it except for one thing. Every night when she went out to visit her "friend"—her drug dealer, she meant—she left her kids at home, alone. She has two children, a four-year-old boy and a toddler girl. Even so, she might not have gotten into trouble if she'd only bothered to feed them first. Hearing the hungry children cry night after night finally got on the neighbors' nerves. They called the police.

Everyone expects Claire to make a plea offer. The judge, the defense attorney, even Jordan/John. The defendant doesn't have previous convictions, she's expressed her contrition, her sorrow, her regret, has written a letter to the court to that effect, has entered a drug treatment program, has been taking parenting lessons. Crossing her T's, dotting her I's. Community service? Maybe. Probation? Certainly. No one expects the case to go to trial. Certainly not Claire.

Until the wolf walks into the courtroom.

Shocked, Claire looks up. The wolf has never come in here before.

She saunters down the aisle, past the onlookers who sit in rows with their heads in their hands, past the defendants who huddle in the overheated room in their winter overcoats, as if leaving them on means they'll get out sooner. She strolls to the marshal who stands, face vacant, by the empty jury box and sniffs at him in disdain: I'm not afraid of you. She casts a scornful eye on the court stenographer who is hunched over her keyboard, furiously typing. Then she stops at the front of the judge's bench.

Judge Benson. Claire knows her well. She actually likes her. Benson is an older woman, calm, fair. Once, during a recess, she passed pictures of her grandchildren around.

The wolf stares up at Benson and then, as Claire claps a hand to her mouth, springs up, landing directly on all four paws on her bench.

"The children," Claire says suddenly. "Your Honor. What I'm saying."

The wolf noses through Benson's things, sniffing her datebook, her stack of pre-trial reports, her rubber-banded clutch of pencils, the box of tissues and glass of water she keeps close at hand. Nothing there to interest a wolf. Bored, she flops down, making herself comfortable, her paws hanging over the edge, panting lightly, surveying the room.

"Accountability." Claire talks fast, a magician's patter, employing misdirection, hoping Benson won't notice. "Breaking the law. We can't let people get away with it. Are we going to let them get away with it? The things they do. Cruelty. Unfairness. I submit. Just because they have money. Just because they have privilege. Just because they have connections, and believe me, they do. They have pull. High up. I'm telling you." She gestures at the invisible jury in the empty jury box, lifting her hand high over her head. "All the way to Congress. Did I mention a senator?" She smiles in a conspiratorial way. "You know who I mean. The one from New York." She frowns. "But does that mean they should get away with it? Should they be allowed to walk away scot-free? There have to be consequences for the things people do. I submit. It's my job. What I'm here for. To hold people accountable. Respectfully."

Money? Connections? Congress? What is she talking about? The defendant has none of those things. She hardly has a decent pair of shoes to wear in the winter weather, has dressed in what must be her finest clothes, a pink dress with a shimmer, more suited to a prom date than a day in court. She looks at Claire with her mouth agape, her arms across her chest, hugging herself in fear. Something bad is happening, she doesn't know what it is, but she assumes it will come back to bite her as most bad things do.

Her attorney—court appointed—has come to his feet as if to object and stares at Claire with his mouth open, aghast. He's an older man, portly, with greying hair. Claire's seen him around before. He used to do felonies, but now he's on his way to retirement, taking it easy in misdemeanors, running out the clock, padding the bills.

Claire knows she isn't making any sense, but she can't stop herself. "Justice, I tell you. Give people the justice they deserve. Just because they're dying. So what if they're dying? Who's to say they're dying anyway? Who's to say it isn't just another ploy, another way of avoiding the consequences of the things they've done? It's the perfect alibi, don't you see? I'm dying, dying." Claire speaks to the jury that isn't there, her voice rising, mocking. She paces about the courtroom, raising her arms, gesturing to the invisible jury. "They've done terrible things, awful, cruel, terrible things. People have suffered. Lives have been wasted. There has been pain. Much pain. Years of it. Years of pain and wasted lives. Are we just supposed to walk away from that? Where is the justice in that? I submit. Where is the justice?" She stops, takes a breath, turns back to the judge. "Like you is."

"I—" Judge Benson studies Claire, her face creased in a thoughtful frown.

"Sasha." All at once it comes to Claire. Anna's brother. She'd forgotten all about him. How could she? How is that even possible? "He died," she explains to Benson.

"Mrs. Sadler." Benson gives Claire a long look. "I think . . ." She falls silent, considers. "Are you all right?"

"It was never explained. That's what she said. How he died. Why he died. She didn't ask Hettie. Not even Nathan. She asked me." A look of wonderment comes into her eyes. "She thought I might know." She shakes her head. "No. She thinks I *should*."

Benson studies her a moment longer. "Approach." She beckons to Jason/James. "You, too."

Justin/John looks like he will faint. He stands up, trembling, his face pale.

"Mrs. Sadler?"

But Claire hasn't moved. Suddenly her mind is clear. Everything is perfectly clear, the clearest it's been in a long time. She knows who she is, what she's about, what she needs to do.

Meanwhile, the wolf has mysteriously gained new powers of levitation. Silently, with great grace, she rises from the judge's bench and hovers in the air. She spins around once, twice, enjoying her newfound release from gravity, regaling in it. Then she sails through the courtroom and out the door.

Claire tips back her head, turning on her heel, watching her soar. "Like you is," she says. Then her feet leave the floor, and she flies after the wolf.

Fourteen

Gus

That evening, when Frieda comes home, Gus is still in his room, reading through his journal, looking for any sign, for any clue, for any explanation of what he now knows is true: Anna stopped speaking before Sasha died. He hears the sound of her footsteps coming upstairs and then her voice as she speaks to Beatrice outside in the hall. "He's still here?" Frieda says. There's a note of shock in her voice—and a distinctly unpleasant tone. Beatrice murmurs something in return. "Very well. Tell Mrs. Sauer there will be two for dinner."

A moment later Beatrice knocks on his door. "Mrs. Glanz has gone into her studio. She's decided to have that show in the fall after all." She draws her lower lip between her teeth. "She says that she'll see you at dinner." She ventures a smile. "Working is good for her. I'm sure she'll be more . . . amenable later. I'm sorry—"

"Don't be. You've done more than anyone could have expected." He takes her hands. "More than *I* could have expected."

"I have to go home now." She colors. "Mrs. Arturo—"

"Will come for me. I know." He smiles. "Don't worry. It will be all right."

"Yes." She lifts her chin. "I believe it will."

With a start, he realizes he's still holding her hands. He's coloring now, too. Still smiling, he releases her. More than anything, he wants to reach up, touch that lip held so charmingly between her teeth. Should he kiss her again? Does she want him to? Before he can answer the question, she's gone.

Dinner is late, and by the time Gus joins his hostess on the terrace, it's past seven o'clock. Daylight is fading, the terrace lit by torches. Moths, drawn to the light, dart in jagged circles about the flames. It's just the two of them, seated outside at a glass table, served by the mournful Mrs. Arturo in her silent crepe-soled shoes, appearing from nowhere like a specter, startling Gus with a tray of roast chicken, peas, and mashed sweet potatoes. The girls have gone for a picnic dinner on the small piney island that sits just offshore. Hettie and Anna. Anna and Hettie. They have built a small driftwood campfire near the ruins of the gazebo. Gus can just make out their shadowy shapes beside it, their rowboat tethered to a rock, the faint smell of the smoke wafting across the water.

"Anna stopped speaking before Sasha died," Gus says. "Did you know that?"

"Of course." Frieda places a cigarette between her lips and leans in close, a warm, intimate gesture, letting Gus light it. Beatrice was right. Working in her studio has improved her mood. Or maybe Frieda has decided it is simply more politic to hide the displeasure she felt when she learned he was still in her house—to keep him on her side. "You mean you didn't?"

Gus thinks back. What had Kanner said? Everything

he knew about Anna came from her father. The mother was too undone, too distraught to speak to the doctors. Did Lionel know about the early onset of Anna's mutism? Did he deliberately conceal it?

"Did your husband know?"

"Lionel? He might have." Frieda thinks back, a wreath of smoke obscuring her eyes. "No. I don't think so. Lionel was gone several weeks before Sasha—" She bites her lip, falls silent. "He was in Albany, in meetings for the campaign."

As Beatrice had said. "This wasn't the first time Anna stopped speaking." The thought is dawning on him, taking on the feeling of a certainty.

"No. But never like this."

So Frieda knew. Why hadn't she told him? Well, why should she? Perhaps she thought it was self-evident. Once again the thought occurs to him that Anna's silence is willful, a deliberate, stubborn act. But why? What could she possibly be trying to accomplish?

"Tell me about it. Tell me everything." He smiles at her, swallowing down his own displeasure, a politic act of his own. "Please."

"It started last winter," Frieda says with a resigned air—the look of a person who has been found out, who has nothing left to hide. She hasn't bothered to dress for dinner and is still wearing her work clothes: a loose white shirt, a pair of cotton pants, sandals. She has pulled her hair back from her face in a bun; there's clay buried beneath her nails. She smells of it, a rank, earthy smell, like muddied ground after a rain. "Anna has always been a passionate girl, intense, tempestuous at times. But then something happened, and she changed. She grew angry, morose. For days at a time she stopped talking. Mostly to me."

"You told me she was happy."

"Did I?" She gives him a sad smile. "Yes, I suppose I did. But Anna was happy. I don't mean she wasn't. She was just being a teen-ager. I thought it was normal. Hormones raging and all that."

"And her father? Did she stop talking to him, too?"

Frieda laughs. Is that bitterness in her eyes? She's so hard to read, in the dim light doubly so. "Anna and Lionel have always been close. Very much so. She never stopped talking to him."

"Until this time."

"Yes. Until she stopped talking to everyone." Frieda rubs her cigarette out in the ashtray. She hasn't touched her food. She lifts her fork and knife, bends over her plate, then puts down her silverware, leaves the table, and walks to the terrace edge. After a moment Gus follows, standing beside her as she rests her arms on the stone balustrade. "I blame myself, you know. I always have."

On the island one of the girls has lain back on the ground while the other sits upright, poking at the fire with a stick. Hettie? Anna? In the shadowy light it's impossible to tell. The girls are too much alike, Hettie as usual copying her sister, wearing dark slacks and a light sweater; the colors have bled away in the darkness. A spark passes between them. An ember from the fire? No, a cigarette. They're sharing it. They must have filched one of Frieda's. Both girls have loosened their ponytails, letting their hair flow down freely to their shoulders. Macbeth's witches. Double, double toil and trouble. Gus can't stop the words from playing in his mind.

"You're Jewish," Frieda says all at once, "aren't you?"

He looks at her in surprise. What does that have to do with anything? "Yes."

"I thought so. You have that look Jewish people always do, the mournfulness, the sense of being judged, of being found wanting. Of imminent despair." She laughs. "Don't take it so hard. We all have it, don't we?" She grows quiet. "After the war, after what happened to us, I suppose it only makes sense." Her eyes grow wide in wonder. "The only one I've ever met who doesn't have it is Lionel. He's so full of life, of confidence, of optimism for the future. Even when Sasha died he didn't stop believing it would all turn out right in the end, that our lives would be lived for the good. *His* life. It's what fuels him on the campaign."

She pulls another cigarette from her pocket, lighting it this time on her own. "I asked if you were Jewish because I wanted to know if you'd understand. Sasha was named for someone who died. Alexander. My younger brother."

Ah, yes, of course. Jews always named their children for dead relatives. Gus himself was named for Gustav Schein, his mother's grandfather, and Rosa for an aunt of his father's who died at a young age. If he ever has a daughter, Gus thinks suddenly, he will name her Rosa. He's surprised he hasn't thought of it before. The idea brings tears to his eyes, and he blinks them away.

In the torchlight Frieda's face glimmers with her own tears. "We lived in Providence then, on the trolley line. Mother left me in charge of him. I was six years old. He was just a toddler. He wandered onto the tracks." She closes her eyes, her face a mask of pain.

"She shouldn't have done that," Gus says automatically.

"She shouldn't have left you to watch him. You were too young."

She shakes her head, dismissing him. "I lost one Sasha and then I lost another. I still feel the pain of my brother." Her voice drops to a whisper. "I don't know if I'll be able to survive the loss of my son."

Did his mother survive the loss of Rosa? Not, Gus knows, without a price: the death brought a diminishment, the reduction of an essential part of who she was. She never forgot. Even now, Gus knew, the slightest thing brought back the memory of Rosa, the sharp stab of his mother's grief: the wind in the trees, a shadow on the sidewalk, the sound of a sonata she used to play.

Frieda wipes her eyes. "I decided I would never have children. I didn't trust myself. But then Lionel came and . . . He changed everything." She smiles. "He always does."

On the island, sparks fly from the campfire and subside. "Anna was born after Lionel and I had been married less than a year," Frieda says. Her voice grows distant, as if she were speaking to herself, as if she'd forgotten Gus was there. Three years later Hettie followed. Frieda threw herself into mothering. They lived in Riverport, Rhode Island, then; they had no money, Lionel had yet to make his great fortune. Frieda was young—too young, she understands now—to be a mother. She didn't know how to conduct herself; she didn't know what to expect. And it was so hard to live in Riverport. She didn't know anyone. The world revolved around Lionel, and so often he was gone. She felt isolated, alone. Lionel's father had died years before. His mother died shortly before she and Lionel met. Lionel had a sister, but she was cold, a suspicious, judgmental sort, and didn't take to Frieda. Meanwhile, Lionel worked night and day in the store, leaving her for long periods of time on her own.

"I didn't know what to do with myself. Even then I had a faint idea that I would be an artist. But there never seemed to be any time." The girls were so young, so demanding, so needy. She didn't know how to handle them. They ran wild, refused to listen. She began to resent them. "Lionel would come home at the end of the day. I would be exhausted, beside myself. He told me to leave them to him. He would take care of punishing them. He took Anna into the bedroom. He shut the door." She winces. "He beat her. I could hear it—I could hear her screaming. I should have stopped him. I should have opened that door. I'll never forgive myself."

"Anna got beaten," Gus says slowly. "Not Hettie?"

Frieda sighs. The truth is out now; there's no use denying. She turns to him, speaks frankly. "Anna was the older girl. Lionel said she needed to be a model to her sister. He held her responsible."

He's a bully, Archie said. What was the word Beatrice used to describe Lionel's anger? Volcanic. Well, Gus thought sourly, men like Lionel don't get where they are by being milksops. But to turn that anger onto a child— onto his own flesh and blood? The thought sickens him. He pictures Anna in the courtyard, the penitential girl, being good, being oh-so-very good. What child wouldn't be good if she thought a beating would otherwise ensue? The man is a monster.

"I love my husband," Frieda adds quickly, speaking with a defensive air, as if she intuits Gus's feelings. "Don't get me wrong. I love my daughter, too. I blame myself. I put her in that position. I never should have."

She ploys him with her sad smile again, trying to elicit his sympathy. He has little to offer. His view of Frieda is shifting, changing. Lionel may have been the bully, but she was complicit in the beatings. She should have stopped him. She should have protected her daughter. What did Frieda say when he met her? I only want to keep my children safe. How miserably she has failed.

He looks away, his eye drawn to the corner of the terrace where Frieda has set her sculpture of the striding man. In the flickering light of the torches the figure looks surprisingly vibrant and alive, as if at any moment it might jump into motion, bearing with it the gaping hole in the center of its chest. He imagines Frieda sculpting it, capturing Lionel's great strength of purpose and energy—his equally great capacity for cruelty.

"Eventually Lionel sold the store," Frieda says. "He made new investments in Riverport. His business grew. We left for Manhattan. The girls went to school. The beatings stopped. I began taking sculpture lessons." It was a happy time, reflected in the serenity in her face as she tells him about it. The family found its footing. Lionel and the girls grew close. Frieda convinced herself that the beatings hadn't mattered, that Anna had forgotten them.

They will always matter, Gus thinks. It's not the kind of thing one gets over. Even if the body heals, scars persist in the mind.

"Then Sasha was born."

She was afraid at first, she confesses, to have another child, fearful the same problems would erupt. But she was older now, more experienced, more relaxed as a mother. With wealth came servants, nannies to take care of the children, giving Frieda time at last to pursue her artistic career—a career, Gus sees now, her children have paid for dearly. Lionel was delighted finally to have a son. To her surprise, Frieda discovered that she was, too. "With Sasha I finally understood what it means to be a mother—the joy one can have in one's children. The joy I'd failed to feel with my girls."

"And then you lost him."

"Yes." She raises her hands in a helpless gesture. "Sometimes I think he was taken from me in punishment for what I did to his sisters. For the mother I'd failed to be."

On the island the girls have finished their picnic. They kick dirt on the flames, killing the fire. Then they pack up their basket, climb into the rowboat, and head for home. That's Anna at the oars; Gus sees her straining against the current, summoning the strength in her thin arms. He has thought all along that she takes after her mother, the intensity of her emotions, the fragility of her sensibility. But now he wonders. Is there a core of iron inside her, a strength of purpose, a great willfulness inherited from her father? Did he beat it into her?

Gus has made so many mistakes with Anna. He knows that now. He let the death of her brother blind him to what came before—to the violence she suffered at the hands of her father. But Frieda is right. No matter what happened in the past, Anna and Lionel are close now. She loves her father, and he loves her. Lionel saved her life. She ate for him—for no one else but him.

It's time for him to go. Once Anna bit into that apple, he

should have been gone. But that doesn't mean she should be sent to Spring Meadow.

"I know about Spring Meadow," he says. "I know you've been considering it for Anna."

Frieda rests her hand on his arm, pressing lightly. "I know it's not Phipps. It's not what you're used to. But I've looked into it carefully. They use modern methods there, scientific methods. They've made great breakthroughs with electricity, with surgery."

Gus grimaces. He can't bear to hear it. "They won't help her."

"I have to do something, don't I?" She drops her hand. Anger flares in her eyes. Then the anger is gone, and she smiles at him in apology. "I can't leave my daughter like this, Dr. Thaler. She's in pain. I'm her mother. I know she's suffering. What kind of life will there be for her if she can't speak?"

"Take her with you. When you leave this house. Take her to Manhattan."

"Impossible." She shakes her head. "Lionel is very much opposed to Spring Meadow. He can't bear to be parted from Anna. I understand that, but I can't help it. I've had to insist on it. I've told him he can't have us both—can't have both Anna and me." She pauses, letting the implication sink in. It's not just Lionel's marriage that's on the line. It's the campaign. Who will vote for a senator embroiled in a divorce? When Frieda speaks again, her voice has taken on the tone of a plea, begging him to understand. "I can't give up on my daughter. I *won't* give up on her. I'll find someone who can help her. I won't stop looking until I do."

There's nothing more to be said. Gus steps away from

207

the railing. "I'll be leaving in the morning."

"I expected that." She nods, a gracious farewell. "Please don't think I'm not thankful for everything you've done, Doctor. I am."

On the way back to his room, Gus passes by Frieda's studio. She's removed the cloth covering the sculpture on the table and for the first time, he can see it. It's the figure of a seated woman holding a child: a Pietà. The mother is bent over her son, who lies lifeless on her lap with his head thrown back in the agony of death, one arm falling to the ground. Mary and Jesus. Frieda and Sasha. In the center of the mother's chest is Frieda's telltale, jagged opening. Not a window to the soul, Gus knows now. The mother's heart has been ripped out.

She's heartless.

Fifteen

CLAIRE

"Stars, Hettie," Claire says into the phone. "I see stars." She looks up and sees the constellations floating on the ceiling high above her head: Aries, Gemini, Aquarius, Pisces. They're all there—all except Lupus. "They're here, Hettie. I can see them. But I can't find Lupus. What happened to the wolf?"

"Claire, darling," Hettie says. There's a long, considered pause on the phone. "Are you all right?"

"It's backwards, Hettie. The sky. It's upside down. Orion's there, and Pegasus. But where's Lupus?" Claire's beginning to panic, swallows hard to hold down her fear. "What happened to the wolf?"

"Darling." There's another long pause on the phone. "Listen to me. Are you home? Are you safe? Tell me where you are."

"The wolf. She should be here. I know it's not right. I know you can't see Lupus in the winter. But I have to." Claire's voice trembles. "I need to know where she is."

"Of course you do. And I'll help you find her. I promise. But first I need you to look around. Tell me where you are. What do you see?"

What does Claire see? People, people everywhere, crowds of them, rushing every which way, turning left, turning right, going up, going down. Men in crisp suits with briefcases, men in tight jeans with satchels they carry like purses, men with nothing at all in their hands. There are women with babies strapped to their chests, women pushing strollers, women tugging children by the hand. Carrying flowers, carrying boxes, carrying parcels, carrying bags. Women in suits, women in dresses, women with sneakers on their feet. A pair of students saunter by, speaking earnestly in French. *Jeudi. Vendredi.* Children in school uniforms scurry by, herded by harried teachers like a flock of lambs. Strolling incongruously slowly comes a man with a pipe. Another holds an umbrella unfurled high over his head as if it's raining.

For a while Claire was a part of the crowds, borne aloft like a leaf on a torrent. She saw lights and windows, the faces of clocks, milky glass, gleaming marble, silky bronze. She was inside—no, she was outside—no, inside again, only it felt like outside, the air pulsed like a windstorm, voices hummed with an electric buzz, the ground vibrated. The smoky smell of oil and tar was in her hair. Her legs trembled, she had a bad taste in her mouth, she thought she might faint. Up and down staircases she went, through doors, through archways, down corridors without end. Not this way, lady! Spinning around, turning, turning. What the hell! Then she saw the stars. She stopped, turned her eyes heavenward, and there they were. She stood utterly still, the center of the maelstrom, the currents parting to flow around her, everything else falling away.

Puzzled, she saw a bank of phones in the distance, silvery, shiny, fading in and out, bobbing up and down though oceans of people like a ship in a storm. She took a deep breath, plunged in, swam to them and called her aunt. "The wolf," she says now to Hettie. "I'm trying to find her, Hettie, really I am." Tears come to her eyes. "I don't know where she is."

"Claire. Darling. Listen to me. Are you seeing anyone?"

"Just stars. Taurus. Gemini. The Milky Way."

"Not stars, darling. A doctor. Do you have one?"

"No. I mean, yes. Grimmsley. He gave me ninety days."

"Grimmsley?" Hettie laughs. "Oh, you poor dear. With a name like that."

"He never sees the wolf," Claire says, "not even once, and now even I can't—" And then she can. The wolf is right there, in the midst of the crowd, stalking Claire, coming straight at her, weaving through the herds of people, her belly taut, her gaze intense, her muzzle lowered.

"Claire. Think. Where are you? I need to know."

"She's here, Hettie." Panic rises like bile in the back of her throat. "The wolf. She's—" Her words are drowned out by the sound of a voice, booming from somewhere, booming from everywhere, startling her, echoing in her skull.

Metro North. Track twenty-seven. Melrose, New Rochelle, Rye, Marby. Track twenty-seven. Metro North.

Hettie takes a breath. "Metro North? Oh, darling. You poor thing. You're in Grand Central Station. You came all the way here."

The wolf bares her teeth at Claire, snarling, the hackles rising on her back. "Hettie. Please." Claire shrinks back against the wall. "I think it's going to be bad this time."

"Stay right there. I'm coming."

"No hospitals. I can't go back."

"No hospitals."

"Promise?"

"Promise."

"Hurry, Hettie." Claire's heart is pounding, her hands shaking, she can't breathe. "She's coming. I think it's going to be very bad."

"Don't move. Don't do anything. Keep watching those stars. Wait for me, darling. I'm on my way."

In the corner is a short bald man sitting in a chair.

"Grimmsley." Claire sits up in the bed. "It's you."

Grimmsley smiles. "Hello, Mrs. Sadler."

"You cut your hair. No more—" Claire waves her hand towards the blank spot where Grimmsley's comb-over used to be.

He rubs a rueful palm over his bald pate. "It's easier this way."

"I like it." She smiles at him. "You look good." Then her face falls. "I'm sorry."

"Sorry?"

"I stopped taking my pills."

"I know."

"You're not mad?"

He shakes his head. "Not mad."

She smiles again. "I'm glad to see you, Grimmsley. I think I really am."

It's been weeks since Hettie fetched Claire from Grand Central Station, where she must have come by train after leaving Judge Benson's courtroom, although she has no memory of that. Two weeks, Claire thinks, maybe three. She's lost track. She's lost track of so many things. Shh, Hettie says, every time Claire asks. Don't worry about that.

Let it go. All she knows is that she's been safely ensconced in Hettie's house for a long time, sleeping most of the time, waking when Hettie comes to bring her something to eat, chicken noodle soup, tea and cookies, toast, coddled eggs. Claire has no appetite for any of it, would rather not eat at all, but Hettie insists, and so Claire does. Anything for Hettie. Only for her. She even takes the pills Hettie gives her twice each day, morning and night, the familiar pink Xynolith and for a while another one, small and bitter and orange, swallowing them down obediently while Hettie watches before returning to the twilight of sleep. This is all Grimmsley's doing, the prescriptions and the private nurse, too, who glides in every few days, asks Claire a litany of questions—mood? sleep? appetite?—takes a blood sample, then glides away like the moon slipping behind a cloud. Claire has heard Hettie talking to him on the phone. But no hospitals. She has followed through on her promise. Claire is grateful for that. And for Grimmsley, hovering invisibly in the background. Only no longer invisible. Here. Present. Decidedly so.

"You came to see me," she says to Grimmsley.

"Your aunt thought I should. You weren't ready to come to me, so she said I should come to you."

Claire smiles. "Hettie can be very persuasive."

"Yes, she can."

"What did she offer you? A new car? A house on the shore?"

Grimmsley laughs. "Actually she made a very generous contribution to my research foundation."

"You do research?"

"I do."

"Into what?"

"Manic-depressive illness."

"Ah." Claire sinks back against the pillow. "No wonder you like me. You do like me, don't you, Grimmsley?"

Grimmsley smiles.

She's back in her old room, the one she shared with her cousin Sabine when Sabine was still alive, before she hung herself in the shower of the last hospital Hettie entrusted her to. Oh, Sabine. Even now the thought of her brings tears to Claire's eyes. Sabine's beads and mood rings still fill jewelry boxes on the dresser, her tie-dye dresses and peasant blouses cram the closet, breathing out the faint, musky scent of the patchouli oil she wore as perfume. Shelves holds her flute, her crystal collection, her books on spirituality and the occult, her novels by Kerouac, Kesey, Pynchon, Hesse. On the walls are the strange and terribly beautiful drawings she made directly on the plaster once her mind began to go, the ones everyone thought Hettie would paint over but never did.

Has it really been twenty years? It's been almost that long since Claire last saw Franklyn, who left New York as soon as he was able, moving to San Francisco to take up the life of a West Coast financier, following in his father's footsteps. Arnold Zucker. The New York City banker. The one who brought Hettie to this brownstone on the Upper East Side with its elegant crown moldings, hardwood floors, and floor-to-ceiling windows. Uncle Arnie. Gone six years now, dead of an aneurysm.

"Did Hettie tell you I used to live here?"

"She did."

"I ran away from home when I was seventeen. Anna

214

was—" Claire breaks off. She's never told Grimmsley about Anna and Cassidy. She doesn't know if she ever will. "I couldn't live with her anymore. Hettie took me in. I never went back."

She looks to see if Grimmsley is listening. He is.

"They used to fight about it. Hettie and Anna. Anna wanted Hettie to send me home. She wouldn't. After that, Anna never spoke to me again. She's good at that—at not talking to people, I mean. She just shuts you out and then"—Claire cuts her hand through the air like a blade—"That's it. No more you. She's dying, you know. I told you that, didn't I?"

"Yes, you did."

"And her brother. Sasha. He died when she was just a girl. Anna thinks I know something about it, but I don't. How could I?" She sits up again, smooths out a wrinkle in the comforter. "It will be better, I think, when she's gone. Better for me. Does that make me a bad person, to say that?"

Grimmsley doesn't answer, his face as inscrutable as ever.

"Hettie called Roger when I got here, and Roger called me. He's mad at me. Mad that I stopped taking my pills. I don't blame him. But mostly he feels guilty. He thinks it's his fault. Because of the baby, because he brought it up, and he thinks he shouldn't have. And he's sad. So very sad. He didn't say so, but I could tell." She falls silent. "He wants me to come home. He wants to see me. I told him I couldn't. I mean, I do, I want to see him, I just can't right now." How can she explain to Grimmsley how safe she feels here? Ever since she got to Hettie's, she hasn't seen the wolf. For the first time in months, she hasn't even been afraid the wolf will come through the door.

"Rest now," Grimmsley says. "We'll talk more when you come home."

Claire smiles. "And take my pills. You forgot to say that."

"And take your pills."

"Will I see you again?"

"As soon as you come home." Grimmsley stands up. "When you're ready, Mrs. Sadler. We'll talk then."

Sixteen

That night Gus sleeps heavily in his narrow bed in the servants' quarters of the Glanzes' house. Just before dawn he awakes with a start. He showers, dresses, packs his things. The horizon above the Sound is just lightening as he leaves his room. The house is still sleeping. The night before, without telling anyone, he locked Anna's door. Now silently, without waking her, he unlocks it. On his way out he leaves the key and a note to Frieda on the table in the front hall. In it he has confessed everything about the sleepwalking. Anna's future is in her mother's hands now.

He starts the engine to his car furtively, hoping the noise won't draw attention, easing the car quietly down the long drive. Slinking out like a thief in the night, like a coward, like the failure that he is. He needs gas and will have to stop for it before heading south. He'll find a phone, call Kanner, tell him to expect him back to work tomorrow.

Or will he?

Why not just pack it in now, before they fire him? He's already broken so many rules at Phipps. What would Kanner think if he knew the truth? Not only has Gus failed to cure his patient; his negligence has endangered her life. He still shudders when he thinks of her walking on the sea wall in the midst of a dream. Surely he is the sorriest psychiatrist

217

there ever was. Maybe he could make his living like his mother, giving music lessons. He's a passable violinist. No one, he thinks sourly, ever died because of a poorly played sonata.

He feels a sense of relief as the long stone wall bordering the Glanz estate fades from view. He's not sorry to be leaving the Glanzes, putting their secrets and cruelties and lies behind him. His one regret is Beatrice. He won't have the chance to say goodbye. When he thinks of how he kissed her—of how her face looked, so joyous and full of hope—his heart sinks. He will write to her when he gets back to Baltimore, he decides, even as he knows he won't. He's too much of a coward even for that.

It's still early when he reaches the village. He passes a cluster of houses, a boatyard, a junkyard, then a gas station on the side of the road. The station is dark, still closed, but farther down the road lights burn at a diner. He parks in front, goes inside, finds an open booth, sits down. He'll wait here until the gas station opens.

A waitress appears at his table, and he orders coffee, black. He waves away her offer of a menu. He doesn't feel like eating. Is this the place where Beatrice brought Hettie yesterday for her ice cream? There are a dozen or so booths like the one he's sitting in, a long counter at the back. Except for an older woman, her hair caught up in a hairnet, who sits across from two small children, the rest of the booths are empty. But the counter is filled with men sitting hunched over plates of pancakes, sausage, eggs. A pair of cops on the beat. Factory workers. Gus remembers seeing a concrete plant on his way into Marby, a quarry beside it. Not fishermen; they would already be on their boats. From the kitchen comes the sound of bacon frying, and the smoky, fatty smell lingers in the air.

Someone has left a newspaper on the table. *The Marby Village Voice.* He pulls it over, glances at the headlines. "Glanz seeks campaign endorsement in New York City." At the bottom is another story about Lionel: "Glanz to engage in labor talks." Idly Gus begins to read it. According to the *Voice*, Lionel recently acquired title to a bankrupt textile mill in Riverport. He's decided to close the mill down for good and find a new tenant for the property. The textile workers are asking for talks, hoping to save their jobs. Over four hundred of them. Good luck with that, Gus thinks sourly. Try negotiating with a monster. He pushes the paper away.

The waitress is back with his coffee. "He lives here, you know," she says, with a nod at the paper.

"Who's that?" Gus says, although he's already thinking: Don't tell me. I don't want to know.

"Lionel Glanz." She taps the headline. "He's running for Senate."

"Is that so," Gus says, letting the weariness in his voice show. He hopes she will take the message and go away. No chance of that. She's even worse than Archie, chummy, fiftyish, he guesses, rail-thin, with sharp features and dyed blond hair. She could use with a better brand of dye. She puts the coffee pot down on the table, rests her hands on her hips, makes herself comfortable.

"Not everyone likes him, you know."

You don't say.

"But I do."

Okay, he thinks, I'm game. "Why is that?"

"Because of all the good he's done here. People forget about that. Half the boys in this village use the boys' club he built. He supports the police fund—and the police fund supports widows and children. Last year he bought the fire department a brand new fire truck. They didn't even have to ask for it." She leans in closer, lowers her voice. "I've seen him weep with my own eyes."

"Weep?" This is the last thing Gus expected to hear. The monster, crying?

"You betcha. Just last year. A friend of mind, used to work here, got cancer and died. It happened that fast." She snaps her fingers. "Left two young children. Them, there, with their granny." She nods at the children in the booth. "Glanz came to the funeral. He didn't even know her, but he came anyway. And he wept. I saw it myself. Afterwards he sent the family a thousand dollars. I saw the card. 'For the poor orphans.'" She shakes her head. "I'm not kidding."

Gus doesn't know what to say to that so he says nothing.

"Some people don't like him because they wanted to build docks on the point and got voted down," she adds in a conspiratorial tone. "They blame him for it, but most of us were against those docks. That's where we go on picnics, on our day off. There are plenty of docks on this river already."

So one man's bully is another man's savior. Gus is still trying to make sense of her story, this vision of Lionel Glanz weeping. For the poor orphans? What is that supposed to mean? Maybe Glanz is one of those sociopaths, Gus thinks sourly, the kind that can't muster feelings for real people and so drum up phony ones for figures in their imagination. "Think he'll win?"

"Senator?" The waitress shrugs. "The whole state has to

get behind him for that. But he'll get a good showing in this village." She lifts her chin again, defiantly this time. "I'll vote for him."

Would you, Gus thinks, if you knew he beat his daughter?

"Course he hasn't had it easy."

"How so?" He doesn't really care. He opens the paper, starts to read, hopes she'll notice and go away.

"His son drowned last spring. Terrible thing. I heard all about it from Joey." She's got that air of conspiracy again, tinged with self-satisfaction. She's in on something most people aren't. "That's Joe Cataldo. We went to school together. He's on the police force. Detective. The one that investigated the drowning. Everyone said the babysitter did it, but Joey had a different idea."

Gus blinks. Then he puts the paper aside. "What do you mean?"

"Joey said someone else was behind it, someone in the house."

"Could we get some coffee here?" One of the men at the counter is frowning, shaking his empty mug.

"Oops. Sorry." She gives Gus an apologetic smile. "Gotta go."

"Wait." He grabs her arm. "Someone in the house? Who?"

"Don't know." She frees herself, looks back over her shoulder as she walks away. "Joey said it didn't matter. He couldn't prove it anyway."

Gus drops a few coins on the table for the coffee, leaves the diner, and gets back into his car. The gas station is finally open. Automatically he drives in, waits while the attendant fills his tank. There's a phone booth at the corner, and after he's paid for the gas, he walks over to it. He'll make that call to Kanner now. He drops a few coins into the phone and picks up the receiver. Then he swears under his breath and puts it down.

The village is larger than he thought. As he drives farther down Main, streets branch out on either side, shady avenues lined with rows of cottages. He passes a laundry, a market, a craft and hobby shop, a garage. A bread factory spills a yeasty smell into the air. The village center has a library, a bank, a park with a playground. On the opposite side is the police station, a low brick building, set back from the road. He parks in front.

The station might have been a retail store once, selling hardware, home goods, plumbing supplies. It has that look. Inside is a display room that's been converted into a waiting room, pegboard walls, tiled floor, a few chairs scattered about. One is occupied by a man wearing a watch cap, his shoulders hunched, his face hidden in his hands. At the back stands a uniformed cop behind a counter. Gus walks to him, wrinkling his nose at the seated man, who exudes the rank, ripe smell of beer and piss.

"Excuse me," he says to the cop. "I'd like to speak to Joey." Damn. What was his name? "Catalpo. He's a detective here. I'd like to speak to him."

"Cataldo." The cop smiles. He's a big man, gap-toothed, his fleshy face glistening already in the early-morning heat. "Don't feel bad. Everybody gets it wrong. Half the time he does, too." He jerks a thumb across his shoulder. "In the back."

Gus follows a narrow hallway past an empty office, a grimy restroom, a shelf holding a hotplate and a pot of burned coffee. Past that is a second office with a man in it, sitting behind a desk. "Mr. Cataldo."

"Who's asking?"

"Gus Thaler." Gus takes out his wallet, hands the detective his card.

Cataldo studies it. "Baltimore. Johns Hopkins Hospital." He puts the card down on the desk. "You're a long way from home, Dr. Thaler."

He pronounces the name wrong, the *th* soft like Theo, with a smirk on his face as if he knows the difference, and he's done it on purpose, just to rankle him. Gus doesn't know what to make of that. A long way from home, yes. Cataldo hasn't exactly asked why, so Gus doesn't bother answering. "I'd like to ask you some questions."

The detective is pudgy and balding, in his mid-forties, Gus guesses, wearing an open-collared, short-sleeved shirt, a gold school ring on his right pinkie finger. He has the slightly unkempt, disordered look of a man missing a wife. His office is unkempt, too, cluttered and run-down, with boxes piled along one wall and a set of filing cabinets crammed in the back. The clutter has migrated onto his desk, which is stacked with papers, coffee cups, bowls of rubber bands and paper clips. He must like to fish. The one bright note in the mess is a photograph of Cataldo fishing with a couple of friends. One must be his brother. Looks just like him. The other is tall and gangly with a pronounced Adam's apple. Cataldo holds a fish by its tail. The fish is big. Other than that, Gus has no idea. He doesn't know anything about fish beyond what appears on his plate.

"Questions?" Cataldo takes out a handkerchief, wipes the perspiration from his forehead. "Usually I'm the one asking those." He grins. "Don't worry, Doctor." He waves Gus into a chair. "I'm all ears."

"I've been called in to consult on a case," Gus says as he sits down. He's not sure what to say—how to say it. "It concerns the Glanzes."

The detective steeples his fingers.

"I need to know about their son. The one that died."

"And what exactly is it that you want to know?"

"Everything."

"That's a tall order." Cataldo leans back, studies him. "And I should tell you because?"

"Because it's important." Gus presses forward, his hands on his knees. "Because someone's life might hang in the balance."

"This isn't a dime novel." Cataldo snorts. "No one's life ever hangs in the balance."

Gus sits back, thinks, tries another tack. "It's all public, isn't it? Your investigation. It's paid for by taxpayer money isn't it?"

Cataldo gives him an easy smile. "You a lawyer, too?"

"Please. Someone told me you had an idea about it. That it wasn't an accident."

"Someone. Would that be Mr. or Mrs. Anonymous?"

"They said you couldn't prove it."

Cataldo studies him with narrowed eyes. "You're not going to give up, are you?"

I should, Gus thinks. "No."

"Consultant, huh?" Cataldo pulls a rubber band from the bowl, stretches it back and forth between his fingers. "Consulting on what, exactly?"

Gus doesn't answer.

224

"Doctor-patient confidentiality, I take it?"

Gus nods.

Cataldo rolls his eyes. "Okay. I'll grant you that. Tell me what you know about the Glanz family."

Gus shakes his head. He doesn't know where to begin.

"You know the man's running for Senate, right? That he's just about the richest man on the point—and that's saying something."

"Yes." Please, Gus thinks. Just tell me.

"Not too many people have the nerve to come in here asking about Lionel Glanz." Cataldo leans back with an appraising air. "I give you that."

Gus holds up his hands. He doesn't have much choice.

"I like my job. You know what people like Glanz do to people like me?"

Gus winces. He's beginning to think he does.

Cataldo juts out his chin. "Don't get me wrong. I'll stand up to anyone, long as I have the facts to back me up."

Gus nods. He believes he would.

"Oh, hell." Cataldo shifts in his seat, his chair groaning. "Want to give me that doctor-patient privilege too?"

Gus leans forward. "No one will ever know what you tell me. They won't even know I was here. I promise."

"Anything you learn here comes from Mr. Anonymous." Cataldo grins. "Make that Mrs. Anonymous."

"Agreed."

Cataldo stands up, opens a filing cabinet, takes out a file, puts it on his desk. On the top, in bold capital letters, is written: GLANZ. He sits down, opens the file, flips through it. Gus watches as pages of typescript, handwritten notes, newspaper clippings fly by. It's all he can do to stop himself from ripping the file out of Cataldo's hands, reading it for himself. Cataldo leans back in his chair, closes his eyes with a thoughtful air. Gus is perspiring now, too. Unlike Cataldo, he has forgotten his handkerchief.

All at once Cataldo opens his eyes and snaps the file shut.

Alarmed, Gus sits up. "Wait."

"Don't worry, Doctor." Cataldo grins again. "What you want to know isn't in there anyway." He taps his head. "It's in here." He leans closer, drops his voice. "You know the Glanzes have children, right?"

Gus nods.

"There was the boy. Now there's just the two girls. One's a teenager, the other's a few years younger. They used to go to the village school. My neighbor's wife teaches over there." He shakes head. "The Glanzes took them both out in the spring. If they hadn't, the school would have made them. Those girls are nothing but trouble." He ticks the points off on his fingers. "Vandalism, disrespect, acts of cruelty, smoking in the bathrooms, playing with fire. The older one's the worst. She tormented a girl in her sister's class so badly, the family had to take the girl out and send her to another school."

"Why wouldn't they—"

"Try what? Calling her parents? Calling Lionel Glanz? And say what exactly? Those girls run like hellions through this village. They come in, shoplift, take what they want from the stores. It's gotten so bad, the shopkeepers send Glanz a monthly bill to settle up."

"And does he—does he pay?"

Cataldo gives a lazy shrug. "Why wouldn't he? Money

226

doesn't mean anything to people like him."

Gus wipes his forehead with the back of his hand. The smell of beer and piss from the waiting room is leaching into the office. He's beginning to feel ill. He could be on the road to Baltimore now. He *should* be on that road. "You said they played with fire."

Cataldo smirks. "So you know about that, do you?"

Gus thinks back to the night before, the girls on the island, sitting by their campfire. The burned ruins just beyond it. "There's a gazebo—on an island—by the Glanz estate. It burned down."

"Lionel Glanz owns that island. No one goes out there but him and his family. Who else would start a fire out there?" Cataldo shakes his head. "The village sent the fireboat out. Otherwise the entire place would have gone up in flames. Normally the department would hold an investigation into arson like that."

"But," Gus says slowly, "the department got a new fire truck instead."

"Good for you, Doctor." Cataldo nods approvingly. "You're beginning to see how things work around here."

"The boy." Gus swallows hard. "You said you would tell me about his death."

Cataldo settles in his chair. "It was a big hullabaloo, worst we've seen in a long while. First we get news of a kidnapping. Babysitter says someone took the boy. We wait three days for a ransom call. The feds come in." He rolls his eyes. "I'd like to see them do that for a child in this village. In the end it was all a lie. The girl made it up. We brought her in, questioned her. A French girl. Never could get anything out of her. Not like we had a lot of time to do it. Glanz had his lawyers in right away. Had her deported."

"But you thought someone else was responsible. Not the nanny. Someone else in the family."

"Like your Mrs. Anonymous told you: I never could prove anything."

"But who—"

Cataldo leans forward. "There's something going on in that house. Something isn't right. I can't tell you what it is, but after fifteen years on the force—you develop a sense for it." He taps the side of his nose. "I was in that house for three straight days. Night and day. Waiting for that ransom call. Once I managed to pull the older girl aside. I questioned her. She didn't say a word." He shakes his head. "I've never seen anything like it. I don't know if it was out of loyalty or fear, but she was silent as a stone. So, yes, I thought there was more behind the death of that boy. Who was she covering up for?" He sits back. "That's what I want to know."

Gus's head is spinning. Anna covering up for someone? Who? How? Why? He stands up. "Thank you for your time, detective."

Cataldo stands, too. "I'll tell you one thing, Doctor. The coroner ruled Sasha Glanz's death an accident. That means it's closed—at least as far as this department is concerned." Not as far as Joey Cataldo's concerned. Cataldo gives Gus a look to make sure he's caught his meaning. Then he picks up Gus's card. "Phipps Psychiatric Clinic. You one of those head shrinkers?"

Gus grimaces. "I'm afraid so."

Cataldo grins. "Well, then, if you don't mind, I'll hold onto this." He slips the card into the file. "Way things are around here, I just might need to consult you myself."

Gus is halfway down the hall when he hears Cataldo calling to him.

"Dr. Thaler."

He's pronounced the name right this time. "Yes?"

Cataldo's standing in the hall, friendly now, looking after him, his thumbs hooked into his pockets. "Where are you off to? Baltimore?"

Yes, Gus thinks, wishfully. Then: No. Despite everything, despite his failings, his evident incompetence, he's a doctor. He has a duty to fulfill. He will do what he needs to for his patient. He will do whatever he can for Anna. "Actually I'm headed farther north."

"Where to?"

Find the source and you will find the cure. "To Riverport."

Seventeen

CLAIRE

Hettie fills Claire's arms with silk blouses, lambswool sweaters, gabardine skirts.

"Hettie, stop!" Claire says, laughing. "I can't possibly afford all this."

"I know." Hettie gives her a look that brooks no argument. "That's why I'm buying."

They're in Hettie's favorite store, Henri Bendel. Over the past two weeks, they've been to movies, they've been to galleries, they've been to shows. Day after day, Hettie marches Claire through Central Park, insisting she get fresh air, sunshine, exercise. Down Lexington and up Madison they go, window shopping, wading through crowds on the sidewalk, walking arm in arm. No one can argue with Hettie, certainly not Grimmsley, who cautioned against plunging Claire too quickly back into life, and not even the wolf, which has disappeared—forever? Claire can only hope. The weather cooperates marvelously for a Manhattan winter, delivering unseasonably warm temperatures, glorious sunshine. The Hettie prescription, Claire calls it, as powerful as the pills. And she means it. With each day she feels her mood lifting, her strength returning. Even the nightmares have finally receded, the ones that plagued her as powerfully as hallucinations when she first got to New

York, leaving her sweating and trembling in her bed. In the worst one she stood before a tribunal of grim-faced people who judged her with stony stares.

You're a bad person. Your mother's dying and you've abandoned her.

In vain, Claire protested: Anna doesn't want to see me! She asked specifically that I stay away.

Doesn't matter. Doesn't matter.

Even now the words echo like a chant in her mind.

You're a bad person. Bad, bad, bad.

She owes her recovery to the Xynolith, she knows that, just as she knows she needs it and mostly likely always will. Still she can't help hating the way it makes her feel, slightly numb as if she's swaddled in cotton. Muted like a trombone. Wah-wah. Part of her will always want to stop taking it. She'll always hear that voice whispering in her ear: You could be so much sharper, so much more alive. But she won't listen. She'll count on Grimmsley to help her with that. For now she has Hettie, who stands there resolutely every morning and every night, watching her swallow down the little pink pills, even though Claire says she doesn't need babysitting anymore, she can be trusted.

Trust. Hettie won't waver. She's had a lifetime of seeing how far that goes.

The packages are wrapped up, paid for, arrangements made for delivery to Hettie's brownstone. Then they are off again to another thing Claire can't afford but Hettie insists on: lunch at the Russian Tea Room.

Outside the front door of the restaurant a boy with a Mohawk is gathering signatures for a petition, something about refugees. The doorman, dressed in a fur hat, tall black boots, a long red coat with gold braid, sweeps them past, ushering them in with the sweep of a hand. The dining room is hushed and opulent, the décor rich with jeweled tones of crimson, gold and sage. At tables decked in white linen and gleaming silver sit patrons similarly gleaming in silks and pearls. The maître d' takes them to a booth with leather banquettes—booth, not table, Hettie says firmly—chandeliers glowing overhead, a thick russet carpet softening their footsteps. The air is redolent with the scent of cardamom and baked apple. Waiters in tuxes glide across the floor.

Hettie wastes no time ordering for the two of them. She knows exactly what she wants and sees no reason to wait. Borscht, gravlax, blini, omelettes with sour cream and caviar. Cheesecake for dessert. Steaming cups of café au lait.

"Drink," Hettie says when the coffee arrives. She narrows her eyes, a schoolmarm, instructing. "It's good for you."

It is. Claire drinks it in, the milky coffee, the warmth, feeling herself relax, feeling coddled, letting Hettie spoil her, knowing it will have to come to an end, and soon, but enjoying it as long as it lasts.

"I called Alec this morning," Claire says. "My boss. I told him I wasn't coming back. He would have fired me anyway." She gives Hettie a rueful smile. "I don't blame him. I didn't exactly live up to my contract."

She called Jordan, too—that, it turns out, is his name—and apologized. He is, she discovered, surprisingly sweet. He sounded genuinely glad to hear from her, and sad about the turn of events as he so delicately put it. He thanked her for being his mentor. Imagine that. She almost laughed out loud. But she didn't. She thanked him for being such a good colleague, wishing him the best.

Be kind. If there's nothing else she can learn from this latest episode, she thinks, it's that.

"So, no more misdemeanors?"

"No more misdemeanors."

"What will you do?"

"I don't know." Something better, she thinks. Anyway, she hopes so. She won't worry about that now. "I've been thinking about Grand Central Station—about how I ended up there." They haven't discussed it yet. Hettie hasn't brought it up, has been waiting, Claire knows, until she was ready to talk about it. "I think I was on my way to Marby. I must have taken the shuttle crosstown from Penn Station."

"Marby?" Hettie falls silent, thinking about it.

"I think we should talk about it."

"Yes."

"About Anna, I mean."

Hettie nods. "I know."

One of the things Claire loves most about Hettie— although she's never told her so—is how much she reminds her of Anna. In a good way, that is. In Claire's mind, Hettie is Anna transformed, her malevolence bleached out, resulting in a kinder, more compassionate version of herself. If Anna is despair, Hettie is hope. Like Japanese puffer fish. Properly prepared, it's a delicacy; improperly, it's poisonous.

There's no denying the two women are sisters. Both are terribly vain, imperious, impatient; those traits come from Frieda, of course. From Lionel come their olive skin, broad cheekbones, full lips, and high, arching eyebrows. The eyebrows are a Glanz tradition. Claire has them, as did her cousin Sabine. So did Claire's great-grandmother Dora.

233

Claire remembers seeing them in the oil portrait of his mother Lionel kept in his house until the day he died. No doubt they go back even farther in the Glanz family line. Claire imagines a medieval Glanz rabbi bent over his text, his eyebrows giving his face a look of constant surprise.

Both Hettie and Anna are beautiful women, striking in an exotic way. Even at sixty, Hettie turns heads. She has an edge of glamor Anna lacks, perhaps from her years of living in Manhattan. She loves designer clothing, dresses with flair. Also without pretension. Today she's carrying a Bottega Veneta handbag and is wearing leather boots, diamond earrings, a hunter green knit dress with a cowl collar that shows off her figure. Her sable coat is piled on the banquette beside her. Just like Hettie to wear sable, and just like Hettie to crumple it up carelessly beside her.

If only, Claire thinks, not for the first time, I'd been born to Hettie instead of Anna. But that didn't help Sabine, did it?

Some things are larger than us all.

"Have you heard from Anna?" Claire says.

"Yes," Hettie answers carefully. "Some."

"Nathan used to keep me up on her treatments, but I haven't heard anything for a while." Call Nathan, Claire thinks suddenly. It's been ages since she talked to her brother. He must be worried about her.

"The chemotherapy stopped working." Hettie opens her handbag, realizes there is nothing in it she wants, closes it again. When she looks back at Claire, her eyes are bright with pain. "They're trying her on a new drug, something experimental. Nathan got her on the trial. She's on oxygen now. It's slowed her down. She doesn't get out much anymore."

Claire fights a surge of panic that even the Xynolith can't dull. "She still has time, doesn't she?"

"I hope so." Hettie gives her a sad smile. "No one knows."

Claire leans in. "Did she tell you she asked me about Sasha?" She gives her a grim smile. "Not personally, of course. She sent Cassidy to do her bidding."

Hettie ignores the last remark. "Sasha?" She looks surprised. "Why would she do that?"

"I don't know. She said his death was never explained."

"Never explained." Hettie mulls over the words. Then she nods. "I can see why she would say that."

"Why? He died in an accident."

"Yes, that's right," Hettie say slowly, "but there was always something else about his death, something more . . ." She shakes her head. "Anna knew more about it than I did."

"What do you mean?"

"They blamed it on his babysitter. She was a silly girl, an au pair from France. It was the spring. He was outside, playing on the grass. She was supposed to be watching him. She wasn't. She told the police he'd been kidnapped. But it wasn't that. He'd fallen into the water and drowned."

"Then what else could there be?"

"I don't know, but Anna took his death hard. Too hard, if such a thing is possible." Hettie grows quiet. "I asked her once about it, but she wouldn't say, as if she thought it was better if I didn't know. Anna always looked out for me. She mothered me in a way Frieda never could." Hettie presses a hand to her forehead, her eyes pinched shut. "It's one of the hardest things for me to accept, now that she's dying. That she won't be there to look out for me anymore." She wipes away a tear. "I think it's hard for her, too."

235

Maybe, Claire thinks, if Anna hadn't been so busy mothering other people, she might have had a little left for her own daughter. But she doesn't say that to Hettie. She already knows. There's no point.

"The worst of it was when she stopped talking," Hettie says. "You know Anna. She gets mad and then she stops."

Yes, Claire thinks. She knows that very, very well.

"But this was different. She shut down completely. She wouldn't even talk to me." Hettie fiddles with her coffee cup, running the tip of her finger around the rim and then letting it go. "They sent her away, to a hospital. There was nothing else to be done. She was gone for weeks. Then a doctor brought her back."

"A doctor? To the house?"

"A psychiatrist."

Claire smiles. "No wonder you called Grimmsley."

"He had red hair, like you. And a funny name. Shorter, taller, something like that." Hettie laughs. "Dr. Taller. Maybe that's just what I called him. He was tall. That much I remember. Anna said he was in love with her."

Claire rolls her eyes. "Leave it to Anna to think that. Who in the world couldn't possibly be in love with her?"

The waiter returns with fresh coffee, and the two women fall silent while he refills their cups.

"It must have been awful, when Sasha died," Claire says. "To lose a child like that. I can't imagine. Frieda must have been a wreck. And Lionel? Sasha was his heir. His only son. And then for Anna to go away." Claire twirls her spoon thoughtfully in her cup. "Anna always was Lionel's favorite. Not that he didn't—" she adds with a hasty look to her aunt.

Hettie takes her hand. "It's all right. I know my father

236

loved me. But I wasn't Anna. Sasha's death cast a shadow over all of us. It changed us, dividing our lives in two, a before and an after. After he died, nothing was ever the same again."

Claire imagines a scale, held by a Goddess of Justice, off-balance, swinging from side to side then suddenly tipping over. The puffer fish releasing its poisonous toxin. But what caused the poison to be released, the scale to tip? Surely there was more than Sasha's death. Plenty of families endured losses equally devastating without falling apart.

"When Anna was in her hippie days," Claire says, "after she divorced Harold, and that fire destroyed our house. Remember how she bought that van and took Nathan and me on the road?" She shakes her head as if she still can't believe it. All she remembers is how oppressed Anna felt by Harold, her second husband, the one who came after Julius, Nathan and Claire's father. "She was single again. She decided she wanted to have fun in life. She wanted to be spontaneous and free. She thought it would be good for us. For her, maybe, but for Nathan and me? He was fifteen. I was twelve. There we were, with our mother, driving across the country in a Volkswagen bus with psychedelic paint on the side, from the East Coast to the West and back again. Did it ever occur to her that we were missing school? We lived in that van for over six months. We would have stayed in it longer if she hadn't run out of money. We were in Las Vegas then. She called Lionel's office, got his secretary to wire us plane tickets."

It wasn't the first time Lionel had bailed Anna out. She had established the pattern early on, acting recklessly, then counting on her father to rescue her when things fell apart.

The first time was when she left Julius. They were living in Seattle at the time, and Julius was away on business, when Anna suddenly scooped up Nathan and Claire, boarded a plane for Washington, and turned up on Lionel and Frieda's doorstep. Claire was only three, too young to remember, but Nathan did. He said Frieda wanted them to go back. She told Anna she had no right to abandon her husband like that and should try harder to make the marriage work. Marriage, Frieda said, wasn't what anyone thought it should be, and it was time Anna got used to that. But Lionel never could say no to Anna. In the end he went behind Frieda's back, hiring a high-priced lawyer to handle the divorce. Julius didn't stand a chance.

Claire never saw her father again. Last she heard, Julius was still in Seattle, had a thriving business and a second family, too. Nathan actually went to see him once. When he came back he was tight lipped and refused to talk about it. Claire always said she would go, too, but she knew she wouldn't. She wasn't half as brave as Nathan when it came to things like that.

Then there was Anna's second husband, Harold. Sweet, sweet Harold Klein. Such an innocent. He'd actually taken parenting seriously, had tried to be a good father to both Nathan and Claire. It didn't matter. It certainly didn't endear him to Anna. For all Claire knows, it might have made things worse. Maybe Anna was jealous; maybe she wanted Harold to herself. More likely, she just got bored. Harold was an ordinary, reliable, nine-to-five guy. He insisted on homework, on dinner on the table at six, on synagogue attendance, on the importance of family. It didn't take Anna long to decide she'd had enough.

The second divorce was especially nasty. Harold actually fought back. But in the end Anna—with Lionel's help again—prevailed. Just after the divorce was finalized, their house burned down. Anna called the fire an act of providence—a signal from above that they should put the past behind them and launch into a new life. She threw Claire and Nathan into a van with the few possessions they had left and took to the road. But Claire knew Anna didn't believe in God. The fire was her excuse to embark on exactly the kind of life she knew Harold would find the most appalling—and terrifying.

"Sometimes I wish Lionel hadn't done it," Claire says, "bailed her out, I mean. Things might have been better for us if she'd been forced to settle down. But she always knew she could count on him. Anna and Frieda—those two never got along. But, oh, how Anna lit up when Lionel was around."

The flight from Las Vegas was the last one. Soon after, Lionel died, felled by a stroke while he was still in office. He was only sixty-seven. He left generous bequests to his daughters, but the bulk of his estate passed to Frieda. Anna would have enough to live on but not enough to squander. She knew that with Frieda in charge there would be no more coming.

Lionel's death unmoored Anna. In the midst of her grief she sold the van and bought a house in Midfield, Kansas. Midfield? What could Midfield possibly offer Anna Glanz—offer any of them? In those days it was little more than a cow town. Railroads and cattle trucks rumbled through the city; night and day the air smelled of blood and manure from the stockyards and slaughterhouses downtown. But Anna always had been driven by impulse, and with Lionel gone, one place must have looked as good as another. Perhaps she just wanted to keep her distance from Frieda. Midfield was certainly the last place Frieda was likely to show up. With her husband gone, Frieda sold the Washington house and moved back to Manhattan. Soon she was ensconced again in the art scene.

Anna hated Midfield. Her misery was palpable. She had trouble sleeping, trouble eating, wandered the halls at night. She lost weight, grew skeletal. She kept to her bed with the door closed and the shades drawn, picking at her lips until they bled. For days on end she refused to speak. Nathan was worried, but the truth was, Claire didn't care. She was tired of being held hostage to Anna's impulses, to Anna's moods. All she wanted was to stay in one place, and if Anna had to hover on the edge of death for that happen, then so be it.

That fall, Claire and Nathan finally went back to school, forging Anna's signature on their enrollment forms. Gradually over the winter Anna emerged from her funk, although she never completely regained her old vitality. She haunted the house as much as lived in it. There was no talk of leaving Midfield, no talk of going back on the road, of new horizons. What was most surprising to Claire was that there was no talk of a new husband, either. Anna had never lived alone for such a long period of time. Two years later Nathan graduated high school and went off to college, leaving Claire for what she expected would be three more reasonably bearable years with Anna.

But then, she hadn't expected Cassidy.

The waiter comes, deposits the check discreetly on the

240

table. Claire knows better than to try to pick it up. Hettie pays, then arm in arm they walk outside and wait while the ever-attentive doorman hails them a cab.

"Home?" Hettie says.

Soon Claire will have to leave Manhattan. She hasn't told Hettie yet, but Hettie knows. Hettie will be worried when she goes, and so will Claire. But that doesn't mean it doesn't have to happen.

Call Nathan, she thinks again. And then, call Roger. Her heart sinks when she thinks how she has abandoned her husband, sinks even farther when she thinks of the baby. None of this is Roger's fault. Nathan's right. All Roger wants is normal things. She doesn't know if she can make her marriage work, but she owes it to Roger—to both of them—to try.

"Actually, if you don't mind"—she takes Hettie's arm—"I thought we might make one more stop."

The Journal of
Baruch Zalman

PART FOUR

*E*vening approaches. I have returned to my home, where once again I write at the kitchen table. In the next room Raisel sits beside Dora, brushing and plaiting her hair, and otherwise petting and caressing her, for she knows their time together grows short. Keiner has not yet returned. He will not do so, I know, until darkness is firmly upon us. I have just come from davening *mincha*, and the recitation of the afternoon prayers has refreshed and strengthened me. With thoughts of you, dear Reader, who one day, God willing, will read this account, I continue to write.

Was it truly possible, as Raisel believed that day, that the soul of Bathsheva, our beloved daughter, had returned to us in the body of Dora? Do you believe it, dear Reader? Did I? Let me begin by speaking not of what I believed but of what I knew to be true—that is to say, with the teachings of the Master, the great Baal Shem.

All men, the Master taught, are the abode of wandering souls. At the time of Creation, sparks of souls came into being. These sparks abide in the breasts of people but also in trees, fish, plants, animals, even water and stones. They strive through redemption to be reunited with their Creator,

242

creating at times harmony but more often discord. My grandfather never drank from a well without first uttering a prayer so that the spirit in the water would not flow inside him.

It is well known that Rabbi Luria, may his name be for a blessing, saw the dead in his midst. If he were walking in a field, he might say, Here is a man named so-and-so who was righteous and a scholar but because of his sins has been transmigrated into this stone. He could gaze at a distance of 500 handbreadths at a single grave among thousands and see the soul of the interred standing on the earth. The dead, he said, are not departed from us, but live in close proximity.

So my grandfather taught me. All souls enter Gehinnom upon death, where they abide for a year, purifying and redeeming themselves before admittance to the Paradise of Gan Eden. Only in some cases may entrance to Gehinnom be denied. The first case concerns the souls of people who have committed sins too great to be purified in the usual manner. These souls wander the earth until such time that they receive redemption. The second case concerns righteous people who died before fulfilling their destiny. These souls, too, wander the earth seeking to perform the final deeds that will perfect them.

Such a one, my wife believed, was our daughter, Bathsheva. Surely she had been destined for greatness if only her life had not been cut so grievously short. Why wouldn't she wish to come home after so many years of exile, to bring us joy at the end of our lives and sweeten our mouths with a taste of Paradise? In Raisel's mind Dora wasn't just Dora, a simple girl from Galați. She was also Bathsheva, our beloved daughter, who had died at the age of eight a half century ago.

As for me—what did I believe?

I believe the Lord is capable of miracles such as mortal man can hardly imagine. So it is written in our Holy Books: Who is like thee, O Lord, among the mighty? Who is like thee, glorious in holiness, awe-inspiring in renown, doing wonders? So sang Moses and the children of Israel as God split the Red Sea, and they marched through on dry land, but Pharaoh and his chariots were swallowed by the returning waters so that not a single one survived.

In ancient times the gate between death and life was easily opened. This I believe. On the eve of a great battle with the Philistines, Saul, desiring to know the future, consulted the witch of Endor. So it is written: Conjure for me the soul of Samuel, he demanded, speaking of the prophet who had recently passed on. As a ghost rose from the ground, the witch cried out, and Saul asked, What do you see? The witch answered, An old man wrapped in a cloak. Then Saul knew it was Samuel and bowed his face to the ground in homage.

In my grandfather's time spirits of the dead announced their presence to the living in many ways. It is well known that the Master himself bore the soul of David in his breast. From time to time the soul of the great king would be called forth into battle. Then the Master would fall silent, his eyes would become unseeing as if he'd traveled to a distant place far away, and his disciples would have to wait patiently until his senses returned. This my grandfather saw himself many times.

But Rabbi Luria lived hundreds of years ago in Safed, distant from us by thousands of miles, and the Master has been gone for over a century. Did I believe in these modern times that the soul of a person who has died can enter the body of another and take over its limbs and senses? Was it truly possible that my daughter had returned?

Over the next few weeks, I kept Dora with us. I grew accustomed to seeing her face at our dinner table and to watching her sleep on her straw pallet by the stove. Raisel clung to her and would scarcely allow her to leave her sight, while still regarding me with suspicion, ever afraid I would send her away. To satisfy the curiosity of the villagers, I let it be known that a distant cousin of my wife had sent her daughter to help us in our dotage. Truthfully we were in need of such help, since Raisel had lost the ability to care for the household or herself. But Dora had little to offer. She spent her days, as Gittel had said, off in her own world. I wondered if this imaginary world wasn't a place she had conjured for herself when her life in the tavern grew too painful to bear.

Meanwhile my life was stretched to the breaking point as I struggled to keep up the synagogue while caring for Raisel and our home. In the garden the beans and corn and cabbages grew wild and the beehives were untended. Feeding another mouth diminished our small supply of coins. I wished to find work for Dora, and eventually convinced Raisel to let the girl go for a few hours each day. First I placed her in a dairy, but the owner's wife soon sent her back, saying the cows refused to give milk whenever Dora was there. Next I sent her to a goatherd, but his wife complained that at the sight of Dora the goats behaved in a strange and disturbing fashion, standing up and walking about on hind legs like a man. The shepherd's wife also refused to keep her, saying that when Dora herded the sheep, they baaed in human voices.

Soon rumors circulated in the village that there was something wrong with the girl—that she had the power of enchantment, or was even a witch. But I wondered if the farmers' wives didn't have other reasons for sending Dora away. As summer came, and she shed her heavy garments, the full ripeness of her maidenhood was revealed. She wasn't a particularly beautiful girl; there was something coarse about her dark skin and broad features, and her eyebrows, high and arching, struck an odd note on her face. But her hair was lush and thick and fell in shining auburn waves down her back. In the sun her bare throat and arms gleamed. More than once I saw a farmer turn his head when Dora passed by and this, I expect, the farmers' wives saw as well.

So Dora remained with Raisel and me. If Dora was indeed an enchantress, my wife was under her spell. Raisel liked nothing more than sitting at the girl's side, whispering to her, touching her hand. She combed out her hair, fed her tidbits from her plate, and presented her with gifts. Soon, in addition to my wife's ring, Dora sported Raisel's finest scarves and costliest perfumes. It was no use asking Dora to give these things back; if I did, Raisel grew angry and accused me of betraying her. In time Dora accumulated a sizeable collection of treasures, which she kept in a niche behind the stove: beads, feathers, shiny stones, jewelry, bits of broken glass. Like a magpie, she coveted anything that glistened or gleamed.

Gittel was right: there was something eternally childlike about Dora. Was it the influence of Bathsheva's spirit, which, according to Raisel, had taken up residence in the girl's breast? Even I had to admit there was much about Dora that bore an uncanny resemblance to my long-departed daughter. There was the way she played with the light and shadow of the Eternal Lamp. Dora never acquired a kitten, but she befriended every dog in the village. As the days warmed, she spent hours dancing in the synagogue courtyard, twirling her scarves, jingling the bell on her wrist, secretly smiling and humming to herself.

Eventually, just as Bathsheva once had done, Dora began accompanying me on my mountain walks. Gradually I became accustomed to having her at my side. Soon I found myself telling Dora the stories of the Master that I'd long desired to share—the ones I would have told to Bathsheva if she had lived. I don't know how much Dora understood, but she listened with a willing ear. If nothing else she seemed to enjoy the sound of my voice. When I turned to look at her, she smiled.

One afternoon we passed by the cemetery. I hadn't visited my grandfather's grave in many months and was overcome with the desire to do so. Dora followed me through the gate and waited as I stood at my grandfather's grave with my head bowed, engaged in silent meditation. When I looked up, she was gone. For a moment I grew afraid, but then I saw her on the ground beside me. She was kneeling on Bathsheva's grave, pressing her forehead to the earth.

"I am sorry," she said, looking up at me, "for the pain you have suffered."

How could Dora know this was the place where Bathsheva lay buried? She had never been to the graveyard before, had never learned to read. Tears coursed down my cheeks, and I was overcome by a mixture of joy and sorrow such as I had never known. I reached down and drew her to her feet. It was the first time I had touched her, and as I felt the warmth of her skin against mine, I remembered Bathsheva's arms around my neck.

"Come daughter," I said. The words fell naturally from my lips. "Let's go home."

When summer came, the wolves retreated to the higher mountains, and our sleep was no longer disturbed by their howls. But the beast that had plagued us over the winter remained. He had developed a taste for farm animals, and from time to time would steal a chicken, calf, or lamb.

Then the unthinkable happened.

A few days after our visit to the cemetery, as Dora and I returned from one of our mountain walks, we found the village in an uproar. A shepherd had just found the body of a boy—killed by the wolf—in a field. He brought the child to the synagogue, and as we entered the courtyard, the men of the *hevra kadisha* were gathering him up to prepare him for burial. I caught a glimpse of the mangled corpse—one of the worst sights my eyes had ever beheld. The boy's mother rolled on the ground, tearing at her hair and clothes. Her husband's face was as white as a stone.

The next morning I presided at the boy's funeral. That evening we held services at the home of the slain boy so that his parents might have a minyan to recite kaddish. When I returned to the synagogue, several men from the village accompanied me. Their faces were grim. Such a calamity, they said, must never occur again. Someone must go into the mountains and hunt down the wolf. We looked at each other with frightened eyes. In truth, none of us were hunters. We were forbidden to eat the meat of wild animals and so had never learned how to kill them. We didn't even have proper weapons. Then one man stood and said, "I know of someone who might help."

So Keiner Glanz came into our lives.

I never did find out exactly where he came from. Even his name was a mystery, since I knew no other Jews named Glanz and *Keiner* in our language means *No One.* "*Keiner,*" I said to him once. "What kind of name is that?"

He just smiled and said, "The only one I've ever had."

Rumors swirled about him. Some people claimed he came from a family of fourteen children, but others insisted he was an orphan whose parents had been killed in a pogrom. I heard he grew up in the northern mountains, that he came from the southern plains, even that he hailed from exotic lands far to the east. No one knew how he made his living. Some said he was a robber, others a smuggler, still others a hunter or trapper. I was told he was a Hindoo, or a follower of Mohammed, a secret converso, a part of a Romani tribe. The only rumor I can dispel with confidence is the last. Keiner was a Jew, no more and no less. This I ascertained myself, for while he had little patience for synagogue services, he refused to touch forbidden food, treated every person he met with kindness and respect, and observed the Sabbath as a day of rest. He was in many ways the most moral man I'd ever known.

Still he was unlike any Jew I had ever met. There was something wild about him. He dressed like a peasant in felt boots, a cloth coat, and fur hat. He was a small man in his late twenties, surprisingly wiry and strong. Once I saw him—on his own—lift the wheel of a cart that had become mired in mud. His hair was red, his face round, he had prominent ears. These, I believe, embarrassed him, for he kept his hair long to cover them. He had no fear of animals. When he walked through a barnyard, the geese settled and the horses nickered. The only time I saw him uneasy was around people. When he arrived in the village, many offered him lodging, but he chose to stay in an abandoned barn. Because I like it, was all he would say when I asked why. I never saw him without a rifle under his arm.

Were we friends? I hesitate to say. Men like Keiner, I believe, are incapable of friendship. But we were comfortable together. We understood each other. This I believe is true. At least I believe he understood me.

We had plenty of time that summer to develop our friendship, if that is what it was. The wolf proved to be a wily beast, and it took Keiner many weeks of patient hunting before he returned triumphant to the village with its pelt slung over his shoulder. Until then, he left early each morning for the mountains and returned late in the day, just as the sun was setting. He would take a seat in the synagogue courtyard, drink from the well, clean his rifle with a rag, and eat the simple meals he preferred: bread and cheese, wild berries, mamaliga with a slice of onion or lard. Together we whiled away the evening hours, engrossed in conversation. Or rather, I spoke, for Keiner was a man of few words. Still I told myself he took pleasure in my company, for why else would he spend so much time at the synagogue? Then I realized—foolish old man—that Keiner had his eye on someone else.

Dora.

Was it *beshert*—predestined—that these two would find each other? According to our sages, forty days before a boy is born, God ordains his bride. I can well imagine the Lord, with a smile, choosing these two for each other. Both were misfits, unsuited for anyone other than each other. I believe they fell in love the first time Raisel sent Dora to the courtyard with a jar of honey so that Keiner could dip his bread. Raisel encouraged their budding romance and often found reasons to send Dora outside when Keiner was there: to draw water from the well, gather flowers for a vase, cast bread crumbs for the birds. Why wouldn't Raisel want our beloved daughter to find love in her life? Soon I, too, began to steal away so the lovers could be alone.

It is one of my fondest memories still, seeing Keiner and Dora sitting side by side, while the last of the sun warms Dora's skin, her hair gleams in the fading light, and her face glows with its secret smile. In her presence, Keiner is overtaken by a boyish shyness, making him appear much younger than his years, while she—this girl who had said hardly more than a dozen words in my presence—chatters away in earnest conversation.

If I had any doubts about Keiner's intentions, they were laid to rest after he killed the wolf. I expected him to leave us then. Once he had confided to me that he planned to leave for the New World as soon as he had the funds. I assumed the fee for the wolf was all he needed. Instead he lingered in the village, keeping up his routine of walking through the woods during the day while spending the evenings with Dora. Soon he was the one she accompanied each day into the mountains instead of me. Eventually when Keiner returned at night to the barn where he slept, she

251

accompanied him there, too. Should I have stopped them? Should I have married them then and there? I suppose so, yes. But something stayed my hand. Perhaps it was the knowledge that once she was married, Dora would leave us, and I was reluctant to see her go. More than that: I feared parting from Dora would be a sorrow too great for Raisel to bear.

Then one day Raisel pressed her palm to Dora's belly while her eyes filled with tears, and I knew Dora was with child. How could I take Dora away from Raisel now?

I had never told anyone what I'd learned in Iași about Dora's stepfather, and Dora had never spoken of it to me. Did she confide in Keiner? One morning he came to me, his face dark. "What," he asked me, "do you know about Dora's family?" I was frightened and reluctant to say. I told him her father had died, and she'd been raised by a stepfather. "His name," Keiner demanded. "What is it?" I didn't want to say, but he wouldn't leave me in peace until I did. For hours afterwards he paced the courtyard in silent fury. "Look after Dora," he said. "I'll be back in a few days."

Days turned into weeks. We were still waiting for Keiner's return when word came from P'ninah that Gittel's husband had been murdered, and the authorities were on the lookout for a red-haired man. Keiner? Two days later, as the village bells tolled midnight, he appeared at the synagogue door. He looked exhausted, his clothing muddied and torn. I thought surely he must be hungry and offered him bread and olives, but he refused to eat. I trembled to ask him where he had been and what he had done, and he said not a word. Finally he downed a glass of rose-hip wine and stood up. Dora wanted to go with him, but with a grim look he bade her to stay. "Keep Dora with you," he said to me as he left. "I will come for her tomorrow. It isn't safe with me."

Not safe? When I heard the words, my limbs grew cold. Could Keiner truly have killed Dora's stepfather? I knew he had to go. If the authorities found him here, we would all suffer. Entire Jewish villages had been punished before for deeds far less than murder. Fines, imprisonments, torture, hangings—anything was possible. Yes, Keiner would have to go, and Dora, whose belly swelled daily, would have to go with him. But how could I convince Raisel? She understood nothing of the danger we faced. As Dora went back to her pallet by the stove, I took Raisel back to bed. "It is time," I told her, "for Dora and Keiner to be married and start a life of their own."

Raisel was delighted and nodded happily. But when I said they would have to leave us, she grew angry and confused. "Why can't Bathsheva stay here?" Over and over she asked the question. "And what of our grandchild, Baruch? What will happen to Bathsheva's child?" When I insisted it had to be so, she wept bitterly and turned her face to the wall.

Eventually Raisel fell into an uneasy slumber, but I couldn't sleep. I crept into the sanctuary where I stood before the holy ark, rocking back and forth on my heels. I couldn't keep Dora. That much was clear. But I couldn't let her go, either, not as long as Raisel believed the spirit of our daughter inhabited Dora's breast. Nothing I could do would change Raisel's mind. So I believed—until I remembered there was one thing that might.

Eighteen

. . .

GUS

*E*veryone has a story. Everyone *is* a story. So van der Ploeg used to say as he merrily hypnotized his veterans, ferreting out their stories one by one, bringing them to light, transforming them from narratives of illness into narratives of recovery. Or anyway from narratives that couldn't be borne at all to ones that could be borne, even if only barely. As far as Gus can tell, it's the only thing those two great psychiatric thinkers, Adolf Meyer and Sigmund Freud, agreed on: the importance of a patient's story.

To Freud, what mattered most were the stories we told ourselves: what we left hidden and what we revealed; what part of our world was real and what part imagined or dreamed. Meyer located his narrative in the body, in the delicate structures of the brain, in blood, and flesh, and bone. He sought the patterns laid down by nervous pathways over decades—sometimes over generations—determining moods, thought patterns, personality traits, behavioral types. You meet a patient in the middle of the story, Kanner liked to say. Reconstruct the beginning and maybe, just maybe, you can influence the end.

What, Gus wonders, is Anna's story? What is his? He has plenty of time to think about these things as he drives north from New York into Connecticut on his way to Riverport, heading towards what he hopes will be the source of Anna's illness, and the one person who can tell him more about it: Lionel's sister. He passes by long stretches of farmland and coastal villages, moving from the deep shadow of forests into wide tidal estuaries where the Atlantic Ocean appears with arresting vividness, a bright and glittering topaz blue.

He's not surprised after all to learn from Cataldo about Anna's great capacity for cruelty. He suspected it all along, glimpsed it in her remoteness, her distant coldness. Anna would have learned the behavior from her father—would have had it beaten into her. Gus pictures the penitent girl in the courtyard of Phipps, the reservoirs of pain and suffering in her eyes, the desperate need for atonement. He thought she was the victim of a delusion. Now he wonders if she isn't riddled with guilt for very real actions she's committed in the past. Fires. Theft. Torment. The wolf she dreams of might very well be herself.

Then there's Sasha. Cataldo believed Anna wouldn't speak because she was covering up for someone. But for whom? Hettie? There's no doubt the two girls are close. But what could Hettie possibly have to do with Sasha's death? Cataldo said there was something going on in that house. Something with Sasha, he meant. What were the chances that Lionel, having beaten one child, wouldn't beat another? Cataldo must have suspected Lionel of abusing his son. Did Anna know? Witnessing her brother's torment would no doubt revive memories of her own trauma. Worse than that, it would put her in an impossible position. Tell the truth, and she risked betraying her beloved father, tearing her family apart. Keep the truth hidden, and the beatings would continue. The conflict could very well be enough to render anyone dumb, the vocal cords paralyzed, incapable of speaking a word.

And what about Sasha? What would the beatings have done to him? Meyer said children were capable of being judge, jury—and executioner, too. He meant suicide. The youngest case Gus had ever encountered was an eight-year-old girl who drank lye when her parents died, and she was forced into a foster home. Sasha was only four. Could he have purposely leapt to his death?

It doesn't matter, Gus thinks all at once, what Sasha did. It only matters what Anna *thinks* he did. Then there's the lingering suspicion Gus can't fully shake that Anna's silence isn't the result of a pathology at all. It's a deliberate, malicious act. But why? What could she possibly be trying to accomplish? There are too many possibilities, and he has no basis to decide.

And what of himself? What is the story, Gus reflects with self-irony, he is telling about himself? What drives him to seek a cure for Anna Glanz? Why, despite everything—his doubts, his mistakes, his shameful failures—does he still feel responsible for this girl? Is he trying to be the man who plucks victory from the jaws of defeat; the one who, despite abundant proof to the contrary, still hopes to convince the world that he's a competent physician? How long will he hold himself to the vow made by a nine-year-old boy—the promise to alleviate the manifold suffering of the world? There's a thin line between courage and foolishness.

Gus finds himself thinking back to the bottle on the kitchen shelf that held Rosa's pain medicine in the weeks before she died. He remembers how he became fixated on it—and on the clock beside it—counting the hours, the minutes, at times even the seconds until his parents would dole out the next dose. It never came soon enough. For a time Rosa would be still, and then the whimpering would begin again.

If there's one thing he's learned through his years in psychiatry, it's this: We think of ourselves as radiant suns, as singular sources of streaming light. We are in fact constellations of stars, some of which war with one another.

Which souls are at war in his breast? In Anna's?

He crosses the Rhode Island state line, reaches Providence, and turns east, passing over the mouth of the Somers River at Temperance Bay. On the far side emerges Riverport, a bustling, industrial town, growing from the harbor at its heart, a jumble of ferry terminals, warehouses, docks, and massive brick mill buildings—some of which belong to Lionel Glanz.

By the time Gus arrives, it's evening. He's exhausted, has been on the road all day. He finds a roadside motel, checks in, has a forgettable dinner at a café next door. Outside the motel is a phone booth. Frieda said Lionel had a sister—but she never mentioned the woman's name. He pages through the phone book, looking for her. Not a single Glanz. Of course. She would be married by now, would have changed her name—if she were still in Riverport at all. He goes to his motel room, lies in bed, his mind circling, circling, coming up with no solution, with nothing new. Finally, lulled by the throaty engine growls of trucks rumbling by on the road outside, and a strong dose of self-hypnosis, he falls into a fitful sleep.

In the morning he has a quick cup of coffee at the café then gets back into his car. Up and down the narrow streets of Riverport's city center he drives, past apartment buildings, tenant houses, shops. He passes a laundry, an automat, a stationary store; shops selling fishing tackle, hardware, roofing supplies. None of them has anything to do with the Glanzes. The river, reduced to a sluggish trickle in the heat, gives off an industrial stench. The city has a downtrodden, desperate feel. Hardly a block goes by without at least one collection of boarded-up windows, blackened with paint, like rotted teeth in a jaw. A desultory breeze stirs trash in the gutters. Not every town in America regained its prosperity in the war. Riverport would make ripe pickings, Gus thinks, for a man seeking to turn a profit on other people's backs. For a man like Lionel Glanz.

How Frieda must have hated it here. As Gus travels down the shaded, dusty streets, he thinks of her need for color and light, beauty and art. He imagines her thin, angular frame walking on the dull city sidewalks, a shopping bag in her hand. Impossible. If Lionel hadn't left this place, Frieda would have withered as surely as a flower deprived of water.

All at once he sees a tin sign hanging over a storefront. *Glanz Emporia.* The sign is dented and faded as if it hasn't been repainted in years. Beneath it, in the shop window, is another sign, this one hand-lettered. *Mercado Abela.*

He parks the car, goes into the *mercado*, pushing his way through the cramped aisles. Barrels of salted cod, bins of potatoes, tins of sardines. An elderly woman, swaddled despite the heat in a thick cloth coat, hunches over a wire basket, picking with knobby fingers through garlic bulbs. The floorboards are uneven, blackened with grime. The air has an oily, fishy smell.

At the back of the store, behind a display case, a

butcher, an aproned woman with fleshy hands, is running meat through a grinder. She looks at Gus with a hint of curiosity—and hostility—as he draws near. A man in a suit. She doesn't know what he's there for, but she doubts it's to buy.

"Excuse me," Gus says. "I'm looking for someone. Her name is—it might be—Glanz."

"No Glanz." The butcher shoves a bowl full of ground meat aside, puts an empty bowl in its place.

"The sign." Gus realizes he sounds ridiculous. He's begging, but he can't help it. Surely this isn't the end. He can't have come so far only to have nowhere else to go. "The one above your store. It says Glanz."

"No. Not Glanz." The butcher frowns, shakes her head, points to the hand-lettered sign in the window. "Abela."

"Lionel Glanz. You must know him. He's in New York now. He's running for Senate. He grew up here. He has a sister."

The butcher shrugs, her face opaque. "No speak English." She slices another slab of meat, feeds it into the grinder.

"A sister." Gus raises his voice over the sound of the machine. "*Schwester.*" No, German won't do. "*Soeur.*" Wasn't that French? What was *mercado* anyway? Italian? Portuguese? "*Sorella.*"

"Irina. Her name is Irina." It's the elderly woman with the knobby hands. She has come up behind him, is peering up at him through rheumy eyes. "Irina Glanz. She used to work here. That was years ago. I knew her mother."

"Irina." Gus turns to her. He takes her hands. "Irina Glanz."

"She's married now." The elderly woman smiles up at

259

him, beaming, looking almost girlish at his touch. "Her name is Irina Kanovich, and she lives in the Highlands."

Gus finds the Highlands, a neighborhood of modest houses and tree-lined streets north of the city, a high peninsula of land flowing east from the bay. Mr. and Mrs. Dov Kanovich. He locates their address in the phone directory, drives directly to the house, a clapboard cottage with green shutters and a peaked roof. The house looks unpretentious—a place for people with few means—but also tidy and well cared for. When he rings the bell, the door opens just a crack. "Who is it?" a woman with a sour face says, peering at him through the gap. "What do you want?"

Gus slips her his card. Well, he thinks, Frieda did say Lionel's sister was a cold, suspicious sort.

"Phipps Psychiatric Clinic." The woman's voice is just as sour as her face. The door swings open, and she looks out at him with a smug, self-satisfied air. "I always figured I'd hear from you people. What's he done now?"

"Who?" Gus struggles to take it in, this vision of Lionel Glanz in a woman's body, his thick, muscular frame translated into heavy-set legs in thick stockings, a wide waist swaddled by a housedress, a short neck, greying hair wound in tight curls like the advertisements he sees on billboards for cheap permanent waves.

"Lionel." Irina gives him an impatient wave of her hand. "What's he done? Landed himself in the loony bin?"

"Mrs. Kanovich. I'm sorry for the confusion. I'm not here for your brother. I'm here for his daughter. For Anna."

"Anna?" She blinks. "I—I didn't know." Her face crumples. "Are you sure?"

"I'm afraid so."

She pats at the pockets of her dress as if she's lost something important but doesn't remember what it is.

"Then you'd better come in."

Gus follows Irina through a small foyer into a room with a stale, disused air, the kind of place that is only occupied on special—and rare—occasions. A dusky blue sofa covered in a plastic slipcover sits by a coffee table bearing cheap cut-glass bowls, the kind banks give out free for new accounts. Opposite it stands a wing chair, also covered in plastic. There's a fireplace holding fake flowers, a pair of framed photographs on the mantelpiece. The wallpaper must have been cheerful once, a pink pattern of fleurs-de-lis, but now it's faded to a brownish stain. The feeling Gus gets is of a woman who is trying to keep up appearances, aiming for gentility even when money is tight.

The only spot of vitality comes from the garden, visible through the open window. A riot of roses and zinnias gives out a deliciously perfumed scent. Irina must love flowers. And birds. A half dozen birdhouses, hanging from an oak tree, are populated with chattering finches and doves. On the ground a pair of sparrows splash in a birdbath.

She has disappeared into the back of the house. Gus waits on the sofa for her to reappear. When she does, she hands him a glass of iced tea, then sits in the chair opposite. She's brought nothing for herself. She's the kind of person, he thinks, who's used to doing for others—and expecting little in return.

"Dov. My husband. He's out." Her fingers work at her dress, picking at the fabric with an air of apology.

Not at work, Gus notes. Just out. "That's quite all right,"

he says with a smile, doing his best to set her at ease. "You're the one I'd like to talk to, in any case."

She nods, still not meeting his eye. "What's happened to Anna?"

He doesn't know where to begin. He doesn't know how much she knows. He puts his glass on the table, folds his hands in his lap. "You know that her brother died."

"Sasha." She looks up at him so that he can see the sadness in her face. "Yes. It was awful. Unbearable. They had the funeral here, in Riverport. He's buried in the family plot."

"Anna took it hard. His death, I mean. She stopped speaking. Her parents sent her to us—to the hospital. I became her doctor. We had her for some time, but we couldn't do much for her. I decided to bring her home. I'm still trying . . ." He ventures a small smile that isn't returned. "I thought you might be able to help."

She looks down again to her lap. He's struck again by the great weight she seems to bear, the fatigue in her body, her bones. "I don't see how I can."

"I think the root of her illness is here." He searches for the words, not sure of how to say what he needs to say. "In the things that happened to her before the family left Riverport."

"I wouldn't know about that. I saw little of Anna when she lived here. Little of Lionel." Her voice takes on a bitter edge. "Frieda made sure of that."

Frieda made the breach sound like Irina's fault, calling her sister-in-law harsh and judgmental. Now that Gus has met her, however, he wonders about that. Irina strikes him as not so much judgmental as hard worn. She seems to have gotten little pleasure out of life—and has given up thinking she ever will. "Surely you saw them sometimes."

"Yes, sometimes." Irina stands, adjusts the photographs on the mantelpiece, waits for a moment, then sits back down. She wants to make sure he sees them. The first picture shows a pair of boys, standing in a stiff pose in their best clothes. Irina's sons. The resemblance is unmistakable. Even from a distance Gus can make out the distinctive Glanz look, the high arching eyebrows and broad cheekbones. In the second picture one of the boys has become a father. He stands trim and proper beside an equally proper wife, holding a baby in her arms. Irina's grandchild. She's a grandmother. She wants Gus to know that. She wants Gus to know that while Lionel may have great wealth, she has something he doesn't: a loving family.

"We lived downtown then. We all did. Lionel and Frieda, too. They were poor once, too." She has left her bitterness behind and speaks to him directly, simply stating the facts, allowing him to draw his own conclusions. "Anna used to walk past my house on her way to school. Hettie was too young to go, and Anna would be alone. Once in a while I would see her." Her eyes darken with sorrow and regret, the face of a woman who wanted desperately to intervene but was unable to. "Anna walked so slowly in the afternoons, dragging her feet. This sad little girl, so thin, her dark hair tangled, falling over her face. She kept her eyes down, on the sidewalk in front of her. She looked so unhappy—like she dreaded going home."

The penitent, Gus thinks. The habit started even then. Of course Anna didn't want to go home. She knew the beatings that were waiting for her. This is a delicate subject.

He wonders how to bring it up without offending Irina, so that she won't simply deny the truth out of hand, closing ranks with her brother. "I think Anna was treated poorly at home. She may have been beaten."

"Beaten?" Irina gives him a puzzled look. "No, she never did anything like that."

"She?" He's confused. "Who—"

"Frieda. She did all kinds of things to those girls. Locked them in closets, made them sit for hours in a chair facing the wall. Put their arms in braces when they were toddlers so they couldn't suck their thumbs. But beatings? No. She never did that."

He's still trying to make sense of what she is saying. In his confusion, he simply blurts out, "Not Frieda. Lionel."

"Lionel? Beat Anna? Who told you that—Frieda?" Irina's eyes flash with anger. "She couldn't control those girls—she couldn't *mother* them. She left that up to Lionel. He was the one who took care of them, who fed and bathed them in the evenings, who put them to bed. He knew what Frieda did to those girls when he was at work—how she abused them. Finally he told her to leave them alone. She wasn't to touch them. He said he would punish them for her. He said he would beat them—he would beat Anna. She was older, the role model. She would be held responsible. He took her in his bedroom, closed the door, hit her with his tie, and told her to scream. But he never hurt her."

Gus sits in stunned silence, his hands on his knees. "How do you know this?"

"Because I told him to do it. I told him it would be the only way to get Frieda to stop. And it worked. He said so himself. Lionel would never hurt anyone, certainly not a child." She lifts her chin, indignant. "His own child? Never. He loves those girls. They're his life. They're all he has left, now that Sasha's gone."

All he has left. Not his wife? Gus remembers Beatrice telling him how much Frieda loved Lionel. The question left open is how much of her love is returned. A vision comes to him of Anna and Hettie on the first night he was in Marby, Anna running across the grass to greet Lionel when he came home. The apple, Anna biting into it, the look in her eyes—the relief. At last her father is there. She is safe. She is loved.

Did Anna's streak of cruelty come from her mother then? What of Sasha? Did Frieda abuse him, too? Could the boy have jumped to his death to escape his mother? Gus is having trouble making sense of it, trouble relinquishing the picture he has fixed in his mind of Lionel as the abusive one. "I've heard people talk about your brother. They say he's cutthroat, ruthless. I've read about him in the papers myself. The labor disputes, the bankruptcies."

"It isn't easy being a Glanz in this town, I can tell you that." Irina gives him a thin smile. "But business is business and family is family. Lionel knows the difference." She shrugs. "Riverport's a tough place. Not everyone agrees with Lionel. But the mill era is over. He knows that. He's trying to push this town forward. He never said it would be easy."

"Then why—" Gus shakes his head. Then why, he wants to ask, won't Anna speak? But he knows there's no point in asking. Irina doesn't have any answers for him. He has come so far, and yet he has come nowhere. He feels like the blind man in the story who touches an elephant, running his hands over the animal's leg, trunk, tail, never succeeding in piecing the parts together into a complete whole. Only Gus is even more at sea. Every time he touches the animal, it changes, shifting and metamorphosing into something else entirely.

"I'm sorry to have intruded like this." He stands up. "I appreciate your taking the time to talk to me."

Irina stands, too. "I'm sorry about Anna. I'm sorry about both those girls. Hettie, too. God knows I'm sorry about Sasha." She raises her hands helplessly. She's been sorry, Gus suspects, for a very long time. She shows him to the door. "What's going to happen to Anna?"

"Frieda's going to send her to Spring Meadow. It's a hospital for children." She will, Gus realizes now. Without a doubt, Frieda will send Anna away, and there's nothing he can do to stop her. Anna's in the way. She always has been. As long as Anna's there, she will capture Lionel's affection, and Frieda will be left out in the cold.

"Spring Meadow." Irina says the name in a pleading way. She looks so lost, so distressed. Her hands are fluttering again, patting the pockets of her dress. "It's a nice place, right?"

"No." He sees no reason not to tell her the truth. "It's not. It's a terrible place. I don't know if she'll survive it."

He's halfway down the walkway to his car when he hears her calling to him. "Wait." She's standing on her doorstep, wringing her hands. "You said you're Anna's doctor. You said you wanted to help her."

"Yes." He gives her a gaunt smile. Even though he knows the answer is absurd. Help Anna? How can he possibly do that?

"Then there's something you need to see."

266

Nineteen

$\mathcal{T}$he taxi deposits Claire and Hettie directly in front of the Whitney Museum of American Art. Claire has never much cared for it. She finds the architecture austere and forbidding, shadowy slabs of granite overhanging the entrance like inverted steps, casting an air of oppression. The few windows are absurdly tiny and oddly placed, like portals in a ship—or a prison. Is it any wonder that this is where Frieda's sculpture has ended up on display?

She takes Hettie's arm, and the two women sail inside.

Frieda. Even now the name evokes a sense of apprehension in Claire, a frisson of fear. She has few memories of her grandmother, virtually none that are pleasant. When she was a child, she hardly ever saw her. Anna kept her distance. Whenever she did go back to Washington, it was Lionel that she wanted to see. She saw no reason to hold back on her feelings and regaled Nathan and Claire with tales of Frieda's harshness, her driving ambitions, her manipulative, punishing behaviors. Claire learned early on to fear her grandmother. Whenever she came into the room, Claire found a reason to slip out. Visiting Frieda was like having an audience with the Red Queen. You never knew when she would chop off your head.

Little changed when Claire moved in with Hettie. By

267

then Lionel was gone, and Frieda had taken an apartment in Manhattan. She retained her prickliness, her need for control, her insistence that no matter what, she knew best. Hettie wasn't particularly close to Frieda, but she wasn't afraid of her the way Anna was. From time to time she took Claire to see her. Claire remembers her grandmother as a bony woman with sharp edges. She wore her hair in a tight bun, streaked with grey. Her face was taut from facelifts; she had prominent veins in her hands and hooded, arrogant eyes.

Frieda was still sculpting then, working in the studio she'd built in her apartment. When she didn't have her hands plunged in clay, she was on the phone, talking, arguing, badgering John Stannis, the gallery owner who represented her. She wheedled prospective clients, flew to Europe for the Biennale, held endless meetings with trustees from the Whitney, the MOMA, the Guggenheim, the nascent Hirshhorn, all of whom were vying for her art collection. Not just her own work but also the work she had amassed over the years with a judicious use of Lionel's wealth and influence: the Picassos, Rothkos, Stellas, and other contemporary artists of distinction. Frieda had nothing if not a brilliant eye. She didn't want money—she never wanted money; she didn't need it—but she desperately wanted prestige. Already she was working on her legacy. It was the placement of the art that mattered to her, the cataloguing, the exhibitions, the display.

In the end she decided she couldn't trust anyone but herself. She surprised the Manhattan art world and settled on a deal with a local university where she retained total control. With the remains of Lionel's fortune, she built the

Glanz Center for the Arts, overseeing every stage of the construction from the purchase of the land in midtown to the architectural drawings. She made no apologies for it. In her mind everything her husband had done—the businesses, the legislative accomplishments—was transient. She would create something permanent, a temple to the arts. To her art. When it was done, the Glanz Center contained exhibition space for her entire collection; studios for aspiring artists; scholarships for students; a library; and endowed chairs for a trio of permanent faculty members, one in sculpture, one in painting, and one in film. It opened in 1981, and the following year, with everything finally in place just as she had envisioned it, Frieda died.

Fifteen years later people still flock to the Center for its rotating exhibitions, for the view of the permanent collection, and Frieda's sculptures. But there is nothing at the Glanz that Claire wants to see. She has her eye out for the sole sculpture by Frieda Glanz that the Whitney retains, the piece it bought early on before her career rocketed to its later heights.

It's on the third floor. Claire and Hettie take the stairs.

To Claire, the interior of the Whitney is as unappealing as the exterior: cavernous, cold, echoing. The rooms have black, industrial ceilings; sterile white walls float on dark floors. There's virtually no natural light. When she emerges with her aunt onto the third floor, she discovers an exhibition consisting of hundreds of bowls, some filled with colored paint, others with a viscous brown liquid. She has no idea what they're supposed to represent. The bowls line the floor, in some places standing in stacks like pyramids. The brown ones give off a malodorous scent. She wrinkles her nose as she hurries past. The smell is either accidental, the result of spoilage, or deliberate, a part of the artistic effect. It's impossible to know.

The sculpture she's looking for is in an alcove, at the far end of a room devoted to post-Modern painting. *Pietà*, the plaque on the wall reads. *Frieda Glanz. American sculptor. Born Rhode Island 1907, died New York 1982.* Claire comes to a standstill in front of the sculpture and, with Hettie beside her, looks at it in silence. As always, Hettie waits for her to speak, to say the things that need to be said. "It's him, isn't it?" Claire says finally. "Sasha."

Hettie nods. "I've always thought so."

Claire has always found Frieda's sculpture to be as cold and sharp-edged as her grandmother. This piece is no exception. The lines are angular and harsh without a single note of softness. Perhaps that's what makes the work so compelling: its unapologetic authenticity.

"It made her reputation," Hettie says. "Frieda had a modest following before, some success, but nothing like what came afterwards. This was the first piece acquired by a museum. The Whitney bought it in the fall from the show she had after Sasha died."

"A Pietà," Claire says. "I always wondered about that. Frieda never made any bones about being Jewish. Why would she choose such a traditional Christian image? What was she trying to say?"

The sculpture is in bronze, the patina darkened with age from gold to black. It's almost life-sized, the figure of a seated woman holding a child. The boy lies on his back across his mother's knees, the arms and legs splayed out, the head thrown back, revealing the throat, the agony of the death. But it's the mother that draws the eye of the viewer, the expressive tilt of her head as she gazes down at her son, the signature hole in the center of her chest, the almost unbearable depiction of pain and sorrow.

"Leave it to Frieda to make it all about herself," Claire says. "Me, me, me. Anna gets that from her, you know."

"I've often thought that she shouldn't have had children. Don't get me wrong. I'm glad that she did." Hettie smiles. "But she wasn't suited to it. We all knew that. In another time, another era, she might have remained childless. But in those days, what choice did she have? She did the best she could."

"You're awfully forgiving," Claire says with a roll of her eyes.

Hettie shrugs. "She was my mother after all."

"That hasn't kept Anna from blaming her."

"Anna had it harder than me."

Claire reaches out to touch the sculpture, hoping it isn't alarmed. She draws a finger down the line made by the mother's arm to the waist of the boy. The metal is cold with a tense, textured feel. "Tell me about him."

"Sasha?" Hettie smiles in a sad way. "Honestly I can't remember much about him. I was so young when he died, and it was such a long time ago." She steps back, reflects. "He was just a boy. A little boy. He liked to do the things boys do. I remember that. He played with balls. He had a little red fire engine. When he pushed it on the floor, he made engine noises with his mouth. What else is there to say?"

Hettie shakes her head. "I always thought—when he died. There was a wall behind the house. By the water. The house was on a big hill, and the wall was at the bottom. Anna and I used to walk on it. There were rocks below. It drove Frieda crazy. She was so afraid we would fall. But we didn't care—that is, Anna didn't care—already she was so defiant, and I followed along. But later I wondered if that was why Sasha drowned. Because he wanted to be like us. He walked on the wall when he shouldn't have, with no one there to stop him, and then he fell. Then I thought maybe that was why Anna took his death so hard. Because she felt responsible."

She still does, Claire thinks. Why else would she ask about him? She steps back to join her aunt, viewing the sculpture from a distance. "It's such a powerful piece. It tells a story. I can see why the Whitney would want it."

Hettie nods. "She did good, your grandmother. She wasn't easy to live with, but she made something of herself, and she left something of herself behind. Both of them did, your grandfather, too. There are people in New York who still benefit from the work he did in Congress."

They did good, Claire thinks, yes. Lionel and Frieda, too. But they exhausted their goodness on their public lives. Their private lives were much different. Hettie has made her peace with the past, but has Anna?

Overhead a chime sounds, a trilling line of notes. A voice comes over the loudspeaker, announcing the closing of the museum. Hettie and Claire make their way down the stairs. At the bottom is a poster announcing an upcoming photography exhibit, and Hettie stops to look at it. "Cassidy had a show recently," she says carefully, "at a small gallery in Midfield. Anna told me about it last fall. She came to see me when she learned she was sick—they both did. She was very proud of him."

272

"A show?" Claire snorts. "What was it this time? Pictures of rainbows? Puppies and girls with bows in their hair?"

"It hasn't been all bad," Hettie says softly. "He's been good for Anna."

"For Anna? Maybe. And why not? After everything he's sacrificed. But what about Cassidy? He was going to be someone. He was going to make a difference, take pictures that mattered." Claire feels her anger rising. Fuck you, Xynolith. "Anna had no business marrying him, Hettie. You know that as well as I do. He was Nathan's college roommate. For God's sake, he was Nathan's friend. He was practically a child. She took advantage of him. She destroyed him. And not just Cassidy, but Julius and Harold and—"

In her mind Claire sees a photograph in black and white, a girl with a full mouth, luminous hair, promise in her eyes.

"Not everything's the way you think it is, darling." Hettie takes Claire's arm, guides her to the exit of the museum. "You have to leave room for that. Not just Anna. Me, too. Anna and I, when we were growing up—"

Hettie pushes the door open, and they emerge into rush hour traffic, the sidewalk full of people hurrying by, taxis and buses rumbling in the street. She tucks her hand in the crook of Claire's elbow, and they begin to walk. "We did awful things. Terrible things. *I* did. I hate to think of it, even now." She breaks off, her voice full of sorrow. "I have my regrets. Sabine. Sasha. And your mother. When I think of how she suffered—it's unbearable. There are things I've never told anyone—"

Claire turns to her aunt, takes her face in her hands. "Don't do this to yourself. You don't deserve it."

273

Hettie smiles, her eyes full of tears. "I hope you're right."

They come to the corner, wait for the light to change, then cross the street. "Shall I hail a taxi?" Hettie asks.

"I'd like to walk a little more," Claire says. "If you don't mind."

At the corner is a busker in a worn top hat and tails playing Paganini on a violin. Automatically Hettie reaches into her coat pocket and throws coins into the violin case at his feet; she never passes anyone in need without giving. Is that, Claire wonders, what Hettie saw in her when she showed up on her doorstep so many years ago? Another lost, forlorn person in need of the generosity of her home, her pocketbook, her heart? The last thing Claire wants to do is add to Hettie's pain, but how can she avoid it?

Claire takes her aunt's arm, draws her close. "I have to go."

"Yes," Hettie says. "I know." There's a hint of sadness in her voice, of resignation, too. Once again a chick is leaving her nest, flying outside her embracing, rescuing reach. "Home?" she adds hopefully.

Home, Claire thinks wistfully, yes. Roger is waiting for her, and she knows he won't wait forever. But how can she go home when she has nothing to offer him—when nothing has changed? If she climbs into bed with Roger now, all she'll find is the same heap of unanswered questions and unnamed fears blocking the space between them.

If only Anna had never asked her about Sasha! Claire suspects her mother's dying request is nothing more than a last act of selfishness on her part. But something happened the day that boy died, something terrible that no one in the family has ever talked about. Claire can no longer deny it. Hettie knows it, and so did Frieda. If nothing else, her Pietà is the physical expression of that fact.

Don't think about it, Roger would say if he were here. Let it be. He would be worried about her. But Claire has listened to Roger's warnings before, and where has that gotten her? It's no use. Anna has opened a door, and now all Claire can do is go through.

"No," she says to Hettie. "Not home. Not yet. I'm going to Marby."

Twenty

GUS

Gus and Irina are on the way to the apartment she and Lionel grew up in. There's something there, she tells him, that he needs to see. What it is, exactly, she leaves unsaid, and the set of her jaw lets him know it will remain that way. He will find out when he finds out. There's no reason to argue; he must simply put himself in her hands.

They are nice hands to be in. Irina, he discovers, as he drives back to the city center with her beside him, is a wonderful storyteller. The Riverport of her childhood, she explains, differed markedly from the Riverport of today. As they drive down the congested avenues, she points out landmarks, bringing each one to life with a narrative braiding the present with the past. He finds himself listening with pleasure, enjoying the ride. The streets rumble with busses, pedestrians darting across the crossings. On one corner a man with a trumpet belts out a lone fanfare. Irina has changed from her housedress into a navy blue dress with big white buttons along with blue pumps, a white handbag and gloves, a pillbox hat topped with a tiny veil like a crown. She looks, Gus thinks with a smile, positively regal.

The route takes them past one empty mill after another, hulking brick buildings with broken windows and boarded-up doors emerging from scruffy lots. Smokestacks with the

276

names of long-gone factories painted in black point like dead fingers at the sky. Old tenement houses still crowd the neighborhood, as dilapidated and gloomy as abandoned barns. In one of these, Irina was born.

"We had a single room," she says. "No running water, no electricity, a pump in the courtyard, an outhouse in the back." The tenements were overcrowded, poorly heated, with little ventilation. Not a green blade of grass in sight. Her earliest memories are of fetching water from the yard in a tin bucket that once held horse feed, slipping on ice in the winter, scuffing up dust in the summers. When she went to the outhouse, she pressed a sliver of perfumed soap to her nose to ward off the smell.

She has no complaints. She had no complaints then. No one did. Certainly not Jews. No matter how bad the conditions, no matter how miserable their daily lives, no matter how polluted the rivers or congested the housing or filthy the streets, Riverport was better than the place those Jews had come from. Riverport was the New World, the *goldene medinah*, the Promised Land. Riverport was America. And in America a Jew could find work. In America a Jew could live; in America a Jew could *breathe*. After ten hours of slaving in a factory, attaching felt to the brims of hats or sorting sheep shit from boxcars of wool or sewing ticking onto piles of mattresses, a Riverport Jew could come home with a dollar in his pocket and not have to worry that he'd be thrown from his home or robbed of his possessions or tossed in the river for it.

"They arrived here in the fall of 1894," Irina says, "Keiner and Dora Glanz. My parents. Ma was already pregnant with me."

"*Keiner?*" Gus says in surprise. "What kind of name is that?"

"Do you know Yiddish?" Irina says.

"No, but I grew up speaking German. Usually I can puzzle it out." What he doesn't tell her is how his parents, with their elegant *Hoch Deutsch* and high Viennese manners, looked down on their Yiddish-speaking kin, disparaging their language—a medieval German dialect mixed with Hebrew—along with their primitive religious rites and old-fashioned, peasant ways.

"It means *No One*. It was just Pop's name. He never told me how he got it. He never told me anything about himself—at least not anything that mattered. I always thought he must have been an orphan: no one's child. Ma was practically an orphan, too. She said her father died before she was even born. Pop acted like someone who grew up without a family. He wasn't good with people. He didn't know how to talk to them. He had trouble," she pauses, searching for the right words, "getting along."

He didn't know how to talk to people. Is this, Gus wonders, the origins of Anna's mutism? He files the thought away to return to later, when he has time to think about it. Irina's story is marching on, and he doesn't want to miss a word.

"Even when I was little, I knew better than to ask Pop about the old days—before he and Ma came to America. Neither of them would talk about it. All I knew was that they came from somewhere in Romania. I remember one day a man came to our door, asking for Pop. I was only five or six at the time. He was a *landsman*." She looks at Gus to make sure he is following.

Countryman, she means: a fellow Jew from the Old World.

"I thought Ma would faint dead away. Pop took him outside. I followed. I didn't know what that man wanted, but I was terrified." It was a winter day, a snowstorm brewing, daylight fading. She sensed something menacing in the stranger, feared he'd come to do Keiner harm. She crouched in the doorway of their building, shivering in the wind as the two men argued. "I think he wanted money. He acted like—" She struggles to put into words something that baffled her as a child. "—like he had something over on Pop. It sounded terrible, like Pop had killed someone. Pop just laughed. He said no one cared about that kind of thing here, this was the New World and the whole place was full of criminals. Pop was a small man—even Ma towered over him—but he was strong. No one ever got the better of him." This last is said with evident pride. "He balled up his fists and that man took off." The tension eases, and she laughs. "I've never seen anyone run so fast in my life."

Was this the origin of Lionel's ruthlessness? Another reason for Anna's cruelty? Certainly, if her grandfather was a murderer . . . Gus leaves this thought, too, for another time. Irina has returned to her story, and he leans in, listening closely.

"Ma and Pop landed in New York, but Pop hated city life. He wanted to have a farm." She gives Gus a small smile, filled with the pain of unfulfilled dreams. This is the way the world is, her eyes say: it gives you so little of what you want. "Pop heard there were jobs in Riverport, so they came here. I was born a few months later. A few weeks after that, Ma turned eighteen. Pop learned English eventually, but Ma never did. She couldn't read or write. She relied on me. '*Vos heyst err derzogn?*'" Irina laughs again. "I swear sometimes I can still hear Ma saying that."

Vos heyst err derzogn: What did he say? Once again German gives Gus the clues to puzzle it out. He imagines little Irina accompanying her mother through her day, making requests at the markets, negotiating purchases at the shops. "Pop found work in a textile factory, operating a cotton loom. Ma stayed home and took care of me." Again the small smile, this time tinged with resignation. "Ma wasn't much of a housewife. It's just the way she was. I don't blame her. When I think about it now, she was practically a child herself. But there was something more . . ." Again she falters as she searches for the words. "Most of the time I had the feeling she lived in a world of her own."

A world of her own? Gus pricks up his ears. Like Anna? He'd like to ask Irina more about that but doesn't want to press.

"Don't get me wrong. My parents loved each other." Irina gives Gus a sideways glance. "I know they did. But Ma . . ." Her voice trails off. She has come, Gus thinks, to the heart of the matter. He listens carefully, trying to understand not just what she says but even more importantly, what she leaves unsaid. "It couldn't have been easy for her, living with Pop. He had his eye on that farm, and we just couldn't afford it."

Keiner became a penny-pincher, saving every penny he could for his dream. Dora hardly had enough money to buy the necessities for family life. "More than once I went to bed hungry. I can promise you that." Keiner saw no need to spend money on extras—frivolities, he called them, savoring the English word. "Pop always said, 'Why buy new when second-hand was perfectly fine?' He didn't see the point of anything. Hair ribbons. Lace. Anything pretty. To him it was all a waste."

Dora, on the other hand, liked pretty things. She craved them. "Ma had an eye for color, for anything bright and shiny. I remember one time she came home with armfuls of tinsel. Pop was furious. What a waste of money. Didn't she know the *goyim* used that stuff for their Christmas trees?" Irina laughs. "Ma didn't care. She just thought it was pretty."

Eventually Keiner's penny-pinching took a toll, and Dora began shoplifting. "Nothing expensive," Irina says with a defensive air. "Nothing that mattered."

Ah, Gus thinks. So theft is a tradition in the Glanz family. What were all of Lionel's acquisitions, anyway, if not a kind of thievery? He might operate within the law, but he stole nevertheless, taking every bit he could from working men, from their hard labor, the sweat of their brow.

"She had a box full of treasures. *Shane*, she called them. Pretty. She'd take them out when Pop was at work." Beads. Baubles. Feathers. A gold chain. "She had a silver bell that she wore on a ribbon around her wrist. It drove Pop crazy. Ma didn't care. She wore it anyway."

A silver bell . . . Gus thinks back to the portrait in the Glanzes' front hall, the woman with the bell on her wrist, the secret smile on her face. Was that the secret she was hiding—all the things she had stolen?

"One day Ma was in a five-and-dime when she put a broach into her bag. It was only costume jewelry, but the shopkeeper didn't care. He had Ma arrested." Keiner had to pay the shopkeeper for the broach—along with a hefty bribe to get him to drop the charges. Soon after that the family fled Riverport. "Pop was afraid to stay any longer. He took the money he'd saved up and bought some land."

The land was in New Hampshire, a remote, mountainous place, enough acreage, Keiner thought, to enable the family to survive. He was wrong. "The soil was thin and rocky. Nothing Pop planted took. Even the cow he bought sickened and died." Six months later they were back in Riverport— back to the factories and the tenements. "We didn't have a choice. Ma was pregnant again. I think it surprised them both."

Again Irina gives Gus a sideways glance. "It had been so long since they'd had me. Lionel was born in the fall of that year. It was 1901. Something about Ma changed. She wouldn't admit it, but I think she'd always wanted a boy. He became the center of her life." She shrugs letting the rest go unspoken: that she never was. "Pop never spoke of leaving Riverport again, but I knew he wanted to. Sometimes he'd take me downtown, and we'd sit on a bench watching the trains come and go. 'Look, Irina,' he'd say. 'You can go all the way to California. They have oranges and almond trees there.' I half expected to wake up one morning and find him gone. But he wouldn't leave Lionel and me. He knew Ma would never be able to take care of us on her own." She has tears in her eyes as she speaks, and she wipes them away in a self-conscious way as if she's ashamed.

Wouldn't leave Lionel and me, Irina says. Not: Wouldn't leave Dora. Gus finds himself thinking of Beatrice. What had she said about Frieda? She loves him. Not: They love each other. Was this some kind of pattern in the Glanz family? Had it been set early on?

"Pop went back to saving, this time to buy a store. He was determined to have something of his own." Living in a one-room tenement with two children was impossible, and finally Keiner relented and moved the family to a larger place, an apartment with three rooms. "I thought it was a palace," Irina says, her eyes shining. "I had my own bedroom. Can you imagine?" But Keiner still kept a tight fist on Dora's pocket book, and soon she was stealing again. "Ma spent entire days in the city, walking the streets with Lionel in a buggy, going in and out of the shops." Irina shakes her head. "She was quite a sight. She'd wait until Pop was at work, then she'd dress up in her feathers and beads. Ma had her own style. Everyone in town knew her. She had a funny way of walking. She'd hurt her toe when she was just a girl and never walked straight afterwards."

Meanwhile Irina went to school in the mornings and in the afternoons kept up the house. "I did all the cooking and the washing, too," she says with another shrug. "It wasn't hard."

Wasn't hard? Irina is acting deliberately nonchalant, but once again Gus wonders about the parts of the story she is leaving out. If nothing else, the housework robbed her of a childhood. What else had Dora taken from her?

She was eleven years old when Keiner put a down payment on his first store. "Glanz Grocers. We sold dry goods. We sold *everything*. Canned food. Candles. Kerosene." Keiner bought firewood and coal by the truckload. All for resale at a tidy profit. "Ma was supposed to run the store while I was at school. Pop still had to work in the factory to make the payments on the loan." But Dora had no interest in the shop. She left that to Irina. "I'd come home after school, take inventory, stock the shelves, wash the floors."

Even so, the store was failing. Left on her own, Dora was as likely to give things away as sell them. She'd disappear for hours on end with Lionel in tow, leaving the store unlocked. Entire shelves of goods would disappear. "I remember Pop got in a shipment of apricot preserves. He stood to make a good dollar on that. Then they were gone. He couldn't get over it. Not a single jar—and not a penny to be seen." They managed to hold on until Irina finished eighth grade. "I dropped out of school and began working in the store full-time. Pop didn't want me to. He said it wasn't worth my education. But the store was all he had. I couldn't let that be taken away from him. He'd already given up so much."

With Irina at the helm, the family began to make money. Soon Keiner paid off the loan, quit his factory job, and came to work beside her. "The first night, when we closed up, it was just the two of us. Ma was home with Lionel. Pop opened a bottle of champagne so we could celebrate. I'd never had champagne before." Her eyes widen in amazement. "I was only fifteen."

A picture is forming in Gus's mind of the Glanz family, Irina and Keiner on one side, Dora and Lionel on the other. Once again he finds himself wondering about Dora and Keiner. Irina said her parents loved each other. But then why the sideways glances? Why insist on something if it was evidently true?

In time they sold the first store and bought a bigger one. Glanz Grocers was big enough now to merit hiring a shop clerk. "Dov. I was seventeen when he came to work for Pop. Two years later we married. Pop reached into his pocket and gave us money to rent our own place. We had two rooms."

Soon Irina was staying home with a baby of her own while Lionel went to school, and Dov and Keiner ran the store. Then Keiner bought the adjacent property, tore down the wall, and expanded. Glanz Grocers now occupied three connected storefronts, and in honor of that fact, Keiner decided to change the store's name. "Glanz Emporia," Irina says. "Pop was so proud when he put up that sign."

One day Dov came home, tearing his clothes. It was 1915. "He couldn't speak. War was raging in Europe, and everyone was terrified that America would join in. I thought he'd been drafted." Instead he took her back to the store, where she found Keiner slumped on the floor behind the counter. "Gone, just like that." The tears fall freely, and this time she's unashamed to let Gus see them flow. "Pop wasn't even fifty."

Lionel dropped out of school. "He said he was going to work in the store. He never would have done that if Pop was alive. Pop wouldn't have let him. I told him not to. I told him how I'd missed out on my education, but he wouldn't listen to me. All he cared about was Ma, and Ma thought it was a fine idea. She thought Lionel was smarter than all his teachers. She said he didn't need school anymore. She said he was destined for greatness. She said it so many times, he began to believe it."

Destined for greatness. That would certainly explain Lionel's outsized self-confidence, his radiant sense of purpose. Not a bad set of personality traits for a man running for Senate. Add to the mix his father's relentless business drive, and you had a fairly complete picture of Lionel Glanz. Gus cuts his musings short to turn his attention back to Irina.

285

"Dov never did get drafted. He was too old, and Lionel was too young. So we were lucky in that. Dov was a hard worker and a good salesman. After the war he and Lionel expanded again. Now we had a whole city block. By the time Lionel turned twenty-one, we had a dozen employees."

Lionel still lived with Dora in the same three-room apartment he'd grown up in. "I told him to get a place of his own. I said no girl would ever marry him if he lived with his mother, but he said he didn't care about that. I tried talking to Ma. I said, 'You've got to let Lionel go. He needs a life of his own.' She just laughed." Again Irina gives Gus a sideways glance. "She said she wasn't the one keeping Lionel home."

With Keiner gone, Dora began to steal things openly. Expensive things, too. Silver. Watches. "I told Lionel to talk to her, to make her stop, but he said Ma had had a hard life and deserved what she wanted. He just told the shopkeepers to send him the bills."

Ah, Gus thinks, just as he had done with Anna and Hettie. It must have seemed normal to him.

"Dov and I were still in an apartment, too. We had two boys now, and I wanted a house, but Dov kept pouring everything back into the store. Even then I had a bad feeling about it, but he wouldn't listen. I said we needed something of our own, that we shouldn't be tied so tightly to Lionel. 'He's your brother,' Dov would say. 'What are you worried about?' Then the depression hit, and the city went bankrupt. I didn't think such a thing was possible. Everywhere you looked, men were out of work, people begging on the streets. The store took a hard hit. We cut back, fired our employees. I went back to work. There was no chance of a house now. Every penny we had went into keeping the store afloat.

"Then Ma died. For a long time she'd been complaining of stomach pains. She wouldn't go to a doctor—she was afraid of them. I think she'd been afraid of them ever since she was a child. She ended up in the operating room anyway, but when the doctors opened her up, they found cancer everywhere. There was nothing they could do."

Irina tells the story in a matter of fact way, but Gus sees the pain in her eyes. How little, he thinks again, the world has given to her; how disappointed she has been in her dreams.

"Lionel turned thirty the day we buried Ma. I went back to work after the funeral. I knew it wasn't the right thing to do, but I had no choice. Dov and I had to keep going. Too many children were living in the streets. We couldn't let that happen to our boys."

For several days after the funeral, Lionel didn't show up for work. At first Irina thought he was home observing *shiva*. "Lionel had never been religious, but this was Ma, and I knew how close they'd been." Then one week stretched into two, and two stretched into three. "After a month, I thought, Enough already. I went to the apartment. I knocked on the door." There was no answer. For the first time, Irina was afraid of what she might find inside. She still had her key. She opened the door.

"You can't imagine it," she says, her voice hushed. "The apartment was a mess. Trash everywhere, dirty clothes heaped in the corners. Everything stank. I think Lionel was eating food out of tins. Empty ones were strewn all over the floor. I found him in bed. He looked terrible. He smelled, too. I don't think he'd bathed in weeks. I tried talking to him, but he wouldn't say a word."

Ah, Gus thinks. A fit of melancholic despair. Add that to the man's elation and you had a perfect case of *la folie circulaire*: the severe mood swings that so often accompanied manic-depressive disorders. The illness must run in the family—along with mutism. More clues to Anna. Slowly he feels a picture of the girl forming in his mind. The thefts. The dependence on her father. The fearfulness and desperate need to feel safe. The remote retreat into an inner world. He files it all away to return to later. Irina is still speaking, and he needs to concentrate on every word.

"I called Dov. We took Lionel home with us. Dov practically had to carry him. He could hardly walk. Over the next few weeks I stayed with him night and day. I wouldn't leave his side. I was afraid of what might happen if I did." Afraid her brother might kill himself, she means. "A month later Lionel returned to work, and soon after he moved back to the apartment. He took care of himself after that, but he'd changed. It was as if—well, when Ma died, I think something in Lionel died, too." She falls silent, and Gus has a feeling she will say something more. Instead she shakes her head. "Then Lionel started dating. I took that as a good sign."

The first few women he went out with didn't have much to recommend them. "Hardly the kind of girl you'd bring home," Irina says with a sniff, leaving Gus to wonder if Lionel hadn't taken to loose women—maybe even prostitutes. Then he started bringing Frieda around. "I don't know how he met her. She was a Boston girl. College-educated. Refined. She always looked down on me."

Irina shrugs. "I figured he'd latched onto Frieda because of Ma. She always used to say he would go places one day—that he was worth something. He must have decided he needed a wife to go with him, maybe even show him the way. Lionel never did have much—" she purses her lips "—*polish*. So he married her." Irina laughs. "I couldn't get him out of that apartment but Frieda sure did. She took one look at that place and turned up her nose. She made Lionel move to a nicer part of town. He left everything exactly as it was. He just locked the door and walked away. But he kept paying the rent. Frieda wanted him to stop, but he wouldn't. I saw them argue about it once. I've never seen Lionel get so angry in my life. She never brought it up again."

Lionel and Frieda. Gus finds himself wishing Irina would hurry up. She is coming to the part of the story he knows for himself. But he reminds himself to be patient. It's not just *what* she says that matters, but *how* she says it. Even more importantly: what she doesn't say. He listens closely.

"Frieda hated Riverport, and I think she got Lionel to hate it, too. One day Dov came to work, and Lionel told him to go home. He said he'd sold the store. Just like that. He hadn't even asked us. Dov got into him. He said he had no right." Irina gives Gus a wan smile. "Turns out he had every right in the world." Keiner hadn't had a will, but Dora had, and in it she left everything to Lionel. "Ma cut me out completely. I guess she thought Lionel would take care of me." Irina's voice trails off. For the first time since Gus has met her, she has nothing to say.

There's no need to wonder now what Irina is feeling. Gus can well imagine it, the shock and pain of Lionel's betrayal. It wasn't the kind of thing a person was likely to get over—

ever. The family had a fault line running through it from the beginning, Gus thinks, pitting Lionel and Irina against each other. Keiner and Irina; Dora and Lionel. So went the pairings.

"Even in the depression, a block downtown was worth something. Lionel pocketed the proceeds from the sale. Soon it was clear he had other plans. So many of the mills were shuttered, turned over to the city for back taxes. The city was dying to get rid of them. He bought one. An old textile factory. I thought he was crazy. What was he possibly going to do with that place? Two hundred fifty men used to work there. Word flew around town that Lionel was a savior, that he was going to get the mill running again and put the men back to work. Instead he dismantled it. He sold the machinery down south and made a bundle. Then he found a tenant for the empty space—a tire manufacturer. Dov knew the owner. We'd sold their tires in the store. Lionel took the profit from that deal and bought himself another mill. This one became a bottling company."

By now people in Riverport were beginning to resent Lionel Glanz—to fear him. The new factories employed a fraction of the workers compared to the old. Word traveled around town that Lionel Glanz was a liquidator, that he was making a fortune on the backs of hardworking Riverport men.

"Lionel didn't care. Frieda didn't either." As Irina speaks of her sister-in-law, Gus hears the bitterness she spares her brother creep into her voice. "No one could stop him. He did it a third time. By then he had a million dollars. He told me so himself. 'What do you think, Irina,' he said. 'Your brother's a millionaire.' *Millionaire.* He had no shame saying that word to me, even though he knew Dov and I were still living in a tiny apartment with our two boys, trying to survive."

"After Lionel sold the store," Gus says. It's been so long since he's spoken, his voice cracks, and he coughs to clear his throat. "Did your husband find work somewhere else?"

"Dov's a good salesman," Irina says, "but you can't sell things if no one's buying. No one in Riverport had money in those days. No one was hiring."

"How did you live?"

"I cleaned houses for a while." She manages to keep her pride intact as she tells him this. He imagines that she managed to keep her pride intact even as she was doing it. "Dov fished. He likes to fish—he's out fishing today. Most of the time, we got by."

Dov never got over it. "He wanted me to hire a lawyer and go after Lionel. He said half of that million dollars rightly belonged to me. But how could I? He was my brother. And he had the law on his side."

She went to Lionel only once, after he and Frieda moved to New York. "We'd run out of money. We were about to be evicted. Lionel was in the state legislature then. I told him Pop would have never stood for it—to let me be put out on the street. Lionel wrote me a check. We used it to buy this house." She gives Gus a sad smile, her voice betraying her embarrassment at making this confession. "He still sends us monthly checks. Anyway, the bookkeeper in his office does. It isn't a lot, but it's enough to get by. So in the end, I guess you could say he took care of me after all."

They have come to the place Irina wants him to see. They have been there for some time, parked on a narrow street, the houses crowded so close together, a person leaning out of one window could touch hands with someone next door. It's the apartment Irina and Lionel grew up in. The one he lived in with his mother; the one he refused to sell.

The apartment is on the second floor of a clapboard cottage, which is set in a littered lot, weeds emerging from sunbaked dirt. Concrete steps lead to a porch covered by a skewed metal awning. Beneath it a cat yawns in the shade, eying them with narrowed, yellow eyes. A lone boy, playing a game of stickball on the sidewalk, glances at them then turns away, batting the ball against the steps and catching it on the bounce.

Irina steps out of the car, and Gus follows her. A light wind stirs, bringing the rank smell of rubbish and cat urine into the air. She stands on the sidewalk in front of the cottage, clutching her bag, her shoulders square, her chin lifted. She looks like a boxer about to enter the ring when she knows she's been outmatched. Her face is full of bravado, but Gus can see the fear in her eyes. She's steeling herself for what's to come.

"Ready?" she says.

It's a good question. Gus has come so far in his search to find the answer to Anna, but now that he's here, he's not at all sure he wants to go on. Despite the heat, the muggy, miserable afternoon, he feels a chill. She still hasn't told him why she brought him here, but her fear is contagious. So are Anna's wolves. He feels them circling, coming ever closer and closer, the beasts she paints so obsessively, that haunt her nightmares.

Irina waits patiently as he makes up his mind. He knows she won't judge him if he turns away. She might even be relieved. "Are you Anna's doctor?" she asked when they first met.

"Yes," he'd said, even though he didn't really know what that meant. He has a feeling he's about to find out.

He gives her a smile—a bit of bravado of his own. Then he nods. "Let's go in."

Twenty-One

CLAIRE

The sky is overcast, spitting rain, as Claire crosses the Harlem River, heading east towards the coast. She has left Manhattan after the morning rush hour and expects the drive to Marby to take a half-hour at the most. But she has forgotten about New York City traffic, likely to slow to a crawl at any time of the day or night. Forty-five minutes later she's still creeping through the city on the Cross Bronx Expressway. Even with the windows rolled up there's a damp, gritty odor in the air, the sour smell of diesel.

She wonders who had this rental car before her. She could have taken the train to Rye and avoided the traffic, but then she would have had to rely on a taxi to get her to Marby, and what then? It's not as if she can just be dropped off at the house to pay a visit. She has no idea who lives there now, how they might react to a stranger on their doorstep. It's been fifty years since the Glanz family occupied the house on the point. For all she knows, the house isn't even there anymore.

On either side of the highway neighborhoods stretch to the horizon, a grid of congested streets, blinking traffic lights, grimy buildings and factories. She wonders what the drive to Marby was like in Lionel's time. Was Co-op City already there? Probably not. The towers of the apartment complex disappear in the foggy sky, a city unto itself as the name says, spilling traffic onto the road. Her grandfather was nothing if not practical. He would have chosen Marby for the ease of the commute. Easy, perhaps, in his day.

It's a relief to reach the bay, to turn finally to the north. The air lightens as she nears the water, even as the sky remains resolutely grey. She passes through coastal towns, the traffic finally easing. Hettie has given her the address to the house in Marby but little else. It was on the shore road, she said, furrowing her brow as she thought back. A big white house, covered in stucco. It sat on a hill, far back from the road. There was a stone wall along the front. She gave up with a helpless shrug. She couldn't remember anything else. "Maybe that's a good thing," she concluded with a laugh. "Maybe it's better not to know."

In the trunk of the car is the suitcase Hettie gave her, packed with her new clothes and a small travel case holding toothpaste, toothbrush, shampoo. She's dressed in the clothes she wore when she arrived in New York, a black skirt and sweater, raincoat, black pumps. Tucked into her purse is the scarf she stole from Hettie's dresser drawer just before she left.

The theft brings a humiliating stab of guilt. She feels greedy, not to say ungrateful, as if Hettie's outpouring of love and generosity over the past few weeks hasn't been enough. As if she still needs something more. She sighs. She's not even sure how the scarf ended up in her purse. Her brain is still foggy from the Xynolith. Maybe that's the beauty of the medicine. It doesn't change the awful things you do; it just helps you forget them.

She weaves past a truck, spray flying from the wheels onto

the windshield. Last night she called Roger, feeling relieved to hear his voice, hoping he was relieved to hear hers, too. When she told him about her plans to go to Marby, he fell silent. Don't go, he said. Come home so we can talk about it. He's worried about her. He's afraid she hasn't been on the Xynolith long enough to stabilize. More than that: he's worried about *them*. He's still hurting from the wound she gave him when she told him not to come to New York. What kind of marriage do they have if she doesn't feel safe turning to him in times of need? Roger's been more than deceived; he's been betrayed. She's not the only one who has doubts about their marriage, about whether or not it will survive.

And all that was without factoring the baby into the mix, a topic neither of them dared to bring up.

Then she called Nathan. She told him she was at Hettie's, that she'd spoken to Grimmsley, and was back on her meds. She didn't tell him she was going to Marby. If she finds something there, she will tell him. If not, well, there's nothing to say.

When she asked about Anna, he grew quiet. "She's accumulating fluid in her lungs," he said. "She's been to the hospital twice to have it drained. She's had some pain, some difficulty breathing. She's scheduled to have a permanent drain installed sometime in the next few days."

"To solve the problem?" Claire asked.

There had been a long beat of silence before Nathan answered. "Nothing will solve the problem, Claire. All we can do now is try to keep her comfortable."

Comfortable. The word sent a surge of panic through Claire like an electric wire. She knows what it means: it's doctor code, signifying the end is near. What if she finds something in Marby, but it's too late? She reaches into her pocketbook and puts her hand on Hettie's scarf, taking comfort in its presence. Roger is right. Going to Marby is risky. But not going is worse.

She reaches Marby and turns onto the shore road, heading south onto the point. On her left is the Long Island Sound, on her right the Marby River, fog rising from the water like steaming breath. She passes the remains of an old fishing village, a scattering of clapboard cottages set amidst gentrified houses, sailboats and yachts docked in back. No more working boats here. But the point is still beautiful. The road is lined with winter-bare trees, which must make a lovely, leafy bower in the summer. Claire can understand why Frieda and Lionel would want to live here. The air feels fresh and peaceful, hushed with the kind of privacy only the very rich can afford.

She brings the car to a stop at the address Hettie gave her. There's the stone wall she spoke of, the house in the distance, sitting high on the hill, shielded by boxwoods. A long gravel drive winds towards it, a tennis court on one side, a stand of quince trees on the other, towering copper beeches behind. The house is still stucco, although the white has given way to pale rose pink. The wall along the road has been changed, too, topped by a cast iron fence with pointed tips. A gate blocks the drive.

Claire steps out and walks to the gate, lifting the collar of her raincoat against the rain. On the post is an intercom with a buzzer. Does she dare? What will she say if someone answers? Her heart racing, she presses the button. Nothing. From a distance the house looks closed up as if no one has been there for ages. She tries the button again, pushing hard, holding it down. The gate is locked. She gives it a shake, the metal cold in her fist, rattles it, then lets it go.

So that's it. The end of the road, as they say. For some reason she laughs, long enough for tears to come to her eyes. The fat lady has finally sung.

Absurdly the thought comes to her to scale the fence. Seriously? Houses like this have security. There would be alarms, sensors, cameras planted all over the property. And if she gets caught? She might have quit her job, but she's still a lawyer. She could be disbarred.

The laughter dies away, and she wipes her eyes.

A black sedan glides past, the driver eying her through tinted windows. Time to go. She gets back into her car, drives farther down the point in search of a place to turn around. At the end is a spit of land, a stretch of beach between the river and the Sound. She needs a breath of air. She pulls the car over and walks onto the sand. At least the rain has finally let up. She shakes the damp out of her hair, pulls her coat closer against the chill.

The beach is studded with shrubby grasses, a lone sneaker, tangles of fishing line. A line of browning seaweed marks high tide. Waves hiss across the sand and retreat. The air smells of rotting shellfish. Here and there rocks jut up in haphazard heaps. She chooses a flat one and sits down. She tries not to think. What is there to think about, other than of how she has failed?

All at once the ground trembles and a streak of yellow barrels past. Claire jumps to her feet. The wolf? No, a dog. A big yellow dog and a man, in his late sixties, she guesses, in a knitted cap and dark green windbreaker, following

298

close behind.

"Sorry. I'm afraid we've startled you."

"No. It's all right. I just thought—" Claire shakes her head. "Never mind." She smiles. "Looks like a nice dog."

"She is. Exceptionally so, if I say so myself. Her name's Sally. Sally the Fourth, that would be, or maybe Sally the Fifth." He laughs, his face creasing in a smile. "Tell you the truth, I can't remember anymore. I've lost count. We had the first Sally when I was just a boy. It's silly, I know, to keep calling your dog the same thing over and over. Sally doesn't seem to mind."

Hearing her name, the dog comes over to nudge Claire's hand, grinning, her tail wagging as if she agrees.

The man holds out his hand. "Charley."

Claire takes it, liking the warmth of his fingers, the rough calluses of a man who works with his hands. "Claire."

That seems to be enough for a while. The two of them watch in silence as Sally noses in the sand, finds a dead fish, rolls in it with glee. Charley throws up his hands. "Bath time when we get home."

Claire laughs. "That would probably be wise."

Charley laughs, too, the laughter seeming to come easily. "You're not from around here." It's a statement, not a question. Charley, Claire guesses, is the kind of man who, given the chance, likes to chat. Well, why not. It's not as if she's in a hurry to head back home. "I grew up on this point. My dad used to fish here, but the fishing's been gone for a long time now. I'm a gardener by trade. A 'landscaper' people around here call it. Gardener's good enough for me. It gets me around." There's that easy laugh again. "You get to know everyone after a while."

"You're right. I'm not from here. I mean, yes, I am. Well, no, not really."

Charley smiles. "There's a story behind that."

"My family lived here a long time ago."

"And?"

"You wouldn't have known them." Then, realizing how silly she must sound, she adds, "Maybe you did. My grandfather was a senator."

"Ah," Charley says slowly. "Lionel Glanz."

Her heart quickens. "You knew him?"

"I wouldn't say that. Sound folk and river folk don't mix, as my dad used to say. He wasn't right about a lot of things, but he was right about that." He gives Sally an affectionate rub. "You must be Hettie's girl."

If only, Claire thinks. "Actually I'm Anna's."

"Anna?" He looks surprised. "Sorry. It's just that I have a hard time seeing her getting married, having children, and all that."

Claire smiles. "You're not too far off."

"Anna and Hettie." Charley shakes his head. "They had a reputation on this point, you know. Bit of a hellion, both of them, if you don't mind my saying so."

"I don't."

"Your grandfather was something else. Lionel Glanz. Senator Glanz. He was quite a presence here. Made us famous for a while—our little village in the news and all that. Most people looked up to him." He laughs. "Can't say my father did. He went head to head with Lionel Glanz. Dad had a plan to develop this beach into a fishing port. He thought it would save the Marby fishing industry. Your grandfather opposed it." He waves a hand at the open stretch of land. "You can see who won."

"I'm sorry."

"Don't be." He shrugs. "Nothing was going to bring the fishing back. And I have to admit I'm glad the beach is here. I know Sally is. Here, girl." Sally has wandered off, but at the sound of his voice she reappears, bounding across the sand. Charley smiles at her. Then his face grows serious. "Course we all felt sorry for him when he lost his boy." He raises an eyebrow. "That would be your uncle now, wouldn't it?"

"Uncle?" For a moment Claire is confused. She has no uncles. Then she remembers: Oh, yes, she does. Or rather: she did. "Sasha?"

Charley nods. "Sad story, that. It had us all turned around for a time."

Claire feels a sudden constriction in her throat, making it hard to speak. "You knew him—I mean, what happened to him?"

"Me? Not all of it, no. But I knew someone who did."

Someone who did. Claire mulls that over as she leaves the beach and follows Charley onto the shore road, walking back to her grandparents' house. She has left her car behind. "Don't worry," she tells Charley when he objects. "I'll come back for it." What she means is, Hurry up, tell me everything you know.

Charley, however, is in no hurry, and makes that plain as he ambles along the point. "No one can afford to live here anymore," he says. "None of *us*, anyway." The sun has finally come out, casting shadows on the ground from the leafless trees. The air smells ashen. Sally bounds ahead, her nose to the ground, ever hopeful for squirrels. "When my dad died, we had to sell the house to pay the taxes. Perfectly good house. Didn't matter. The buyers tore it down and built a new place."

He snorts. "Not bad, if you happen to need a dozen bedrooms and a six-car garage. I live in Port Chester, come over here to work. My wife says it's nonsense, I could get plenty of work closer to home. I suppose she's right." Sally chases a squirrel up a tree then stands at the bottom transfixed, looking up. "Leave it, girl. Let's go! It's sentimental claptrap, I know, but I like coming here. Still feels like home."

They round a curve and then there it is again, the pink stucco mansion on the hill. Charley peers through the gate. "Family's in Florida for the winter. Cold's too much for them."

"I thought they might be," Claire says. "I tried the buzzer."

Charley grins. "Doesn't mean they don't want their property looked after while they're gone." He takes a ring of keys out of his pocket and puts one in the lock.

Claire looks at him, dumbfounded.

"And that, as they say, is that." He swings the gate open and steps aside, ushering her in like a magician with a broad sweep of his hand.

Sally leads the way up the drive, her paws scuffing the gravel. "The tennis court wasn't here in your grandparents' time," Charley says as they walk past it, a smooth clay surface, glistening wet, fenced in chain link. "The quince trees were your grandmother's. She made the most amazing jam." Charley speaks confidently in the manner of a tour guide. He knows what he's about. "The roses were hers, too. She took care of them herself. Wouldn't let anyone else touch them. Always had to have fresh flowers in the house, Ronnie used to say."

Roses? Jam? Claire's having trouble taking it all in. The roses look healthy, spiky brown knobs cradled in mulch. The pruning would be Charley's work. She smiles at him. "Ronnie?"

"Véronique. She was French. Ronnie's what I called her. I had a thing for her, you might say."

He smiles in a shy, modest way, a blush coming to his cheeks, and Claire sees the young man he was once—the one who was in love. "Ronnie was Sasha's nanny?"

"*O-pear*, they called her. Never did understand what that meant. But yes, she took care of Sasha." They've come to the end of the drive, where the house reaches out as if to embrace them, long wings projecting on either side. From closer up it looks grander, also older, exuding an air of bygone elegance. The stucco is flaking, the rose color fading in patches to a sickly green. Dark stains leach from the downspouts. Boxwoods crowd the French doors, making it impossible to see inside.

"Hard to keep these old girls up. Sea air and all," Charley says with an apologetic look. "Sorry, but I can't take you in. I don't have keys. Housekeeper stops by once a week or so to look in."

"No, please, don't worry." It's just as well. The idea of going in overwhelms her as if the house were inhabited by ghosts. She tries to imagine her grandmother tending roses, making jam. Had Frieda really been so domestic once? When did she turn so cold and hard? Was it because of

Sasha's death—or something else?

Pity me, the mother in the Pietà says. Pity what I have become.

What about Anna—and Hettie? What was it like for the two girls to grow up here? Like living in a castle, Claire thinks.

Or a prison.

"Well, then." Charley seems relieved that she isn't disappointed. Together they walk to the back of the house, where the hill drops down to the Sound. "The copper beeches have been here forever." His voice drops, and he hesitates, as if he's lost his confidence. The mood is changing. Maybe it's just the beeches, which have a wild air, their limbs sketching dark lines across the sky. Perhaps it's the foundation of the house, which looms beside them, brooding black slabs of stone. Above it the pale pink house floats like a ship lost at sea. Light and dark, black and white. Claire is losing her bearings. Which vision is real?

"Swimming pool's new," Charley says, picking up the pace again, leading her down the hill, "but the pier hasn't changed. The wall and the steps are the same, too. Solid rock. I'd like to see someone change that." He laughs as if he's glad to have something to laugh about. Sally has raced to the head of the steps and turns back to peer at them anxiously, her muscles quivering. "No girl. No chasing gulls today." Charley clucks at her, disapproving, as a flock of birds roosting on the pier bursts into flight, a flurry of white, like snow driven upwards.

Sally follows the gulls with her eyes then slumps dejected to the ground, her nose between her paws. Claire is drawn to the sea wall. She puts her hands on the stone, leaning her weight onto it, her palms flat. The wall is cold and slippery, wet from the rain, and she shivers. So this is it. Where it happened. The place, Hettie said, that changed their family forever, cleaving it into two, a *before* and *after*.

The Sound looks dark and dangerous, wintry and frothing. Just off shore brambles choke a small, piney island, the blackened remains of some kind of structure visible in the thicket. Beneath her rocks thrust upwards, wickedly black, studded with tidal pools filled with shadowy fish, thinly waving algae arms, glimmering snails. The sight is beautiful and terrifying at once. In her mind Claire sees a small body tumbling to the water, and she shudders.

"Hettie says my mother used to walk on this wall. They both did." What could have possibly possessed them? Claire pictures a pair of girls on the wall, their bodies whipped by wind, thin and angular, like semaphores. Her knees weaken in fear. Then she sees herself walking the canal night after night. What had possessed *her*? Was she any different? "Hettie says that's why Sasha fell. He wanted to be like them. He climbed onto the wall and then—" She raises her hands in a helpless gesture.

"No. Impossible." To her surprise, Charley is frowning, speaking with vehemence. "The wall's much too high. He couldn't get on it. He was too little. Ronnie told me so herself. She said he used to try, but he never made it. They tried to make it her fault when he fell, 'cause she came inside to call me on the phone. But she never would have done that if she didn't think it was safe."

Claire steps back. Charley's right. The wall reaches to her waist, easy enough for a teen-aged girl to climb on, but a little boy? "Then how—?"

He gives her a grim smile. "That's the question, isn't it?"

"What did Ronnie think?"

"She didn't know."

"Then why did she tell the police he'd been kidnapped?"

"She didn't. She said he'd been *taken*. What she meant was *taken and lifted up onto the wall*. She tried to explain, but her English wasn't good enough." His face colors in anger. "Not like they gave her much of a chance. The police took her in for questioning, and then your grandfather's lawyers swooped in and had her deported."

There's something else in Charley's face—something left unsaid. "Are you saying Lionel deported her on purpose? That he was afraid of what she might say?"

Charley shrugs.

"But what could Ronnie possibly—"

The anger flashes again. "Like I said, I don't know what happened. Only Ronnie did. I would have asked her but they took her away. I never saw her again."

"The police officer," Claire says slowly, "The one who took Ronnie in." Her mind is racing, her instincts as a prosecutor taking hold. "Do you know who he was? His name?" If the police questioned her, they must have suspected a crime. And if they suspected a crime, they would have launched an investigation. And if there was an investigation, there would be a report. Maybe still. Maybe somehow.

Charley breaks into laughter, so loudly, Sally jumps up and joins in with a bark. "No chance of forgetting that. He nicked me a number of times in my wayward youth." He flashes Claire his crooked, charming smile. "His name was Joey Cataldo. Detective Joseph P. Cataldo of the Marby Police Force."

Twenty-Two

GUS

The boy playing stickball moves away as Gus and Irina approach the cottage, following them with his eyes. As they climb the steps to the porch, the cat startles, jumping up with a yowl, skittering away. Irina pays it no mind. She rummages in her pocket book for a clutch of keys, puts one in the lock, and opens the door.

Gus follows her into a dimly lit vestibule, the air stuffy and rank. There are two mailboxes in the wall, but apparently they are little used. Circulars, newspapers, unopened letters litter the floor, gathering dust. In the corner stands a broken umbrella, a lone rubber boot. Irina turns to him, apologetic. "It used to be nicer than this. It used to be—" She gives up. There's no point in trying to explain. He will see for himself.

The door to the ground-floor apartment is on their right. Straight ahead, a steep set of stairs rises to a landing. Gus follows Irina up to another door. She bends over, the key rattling in the lock, then swings the door open and steps aside, allowing him to enter before her.

So this is it, he thinks, the apartment the family moved into when they came back from the failed farm—when Lionel was born. A palace, Irina called it. Only someone who had been living in a one-room tenement would call

307

it that. The apartment is small, and they have come into the center of it, a kitchen which doubles as a sitting room. Against one wall, Pullman style, are an oven, refrigerator, sink, cabinets. A window gives out a view of the back yard, a square of bare dirt crossed by a clothesline, the clothes hanging limply in the hot sun. In the shade of the house sleeps a dog on a chain. The air on the second floor is even hotter than below, stale with disuse. Irina throws the window open, but there is no breeze, and the air hardly stirs.

Gus is surprised to see dirty dishes in the sink. "Someone lives here?"

Irina gives him a small smile. "Not exactly."

He doesn't understand her then all at once he does. "Lionel."

She nods.

"How often does he come here?"

"A few times a month. He's been coming here for years. Half the time Frieda thinks he's on the campaign trail, he's here."

The walls are painted a bright yellow: someone's idea of cheerfulness. The red linoleum on the floor must be there for the same reason. There's a wooden kitchen table with four chairs, a sofa upholstered in a worn floral fabric, a rolled-up cot tucked away in the corner. "Pop's bed." Irina says, with a glance at the cot. Her voice is tired, her face flat and expressionless. She might as well be speaking to him from under water. Her parents loved each other, she insisted. Now he understands why. Loved each other—yes. But something was missing from their marriage. Was the same thing missing from Lionel and Frieda's?

Gus still doesn't know what Irina has brought him here to see. She shows no sign of telling him. She puts her pocket book down on the table and goes to the sink to wash up the dishes.

"May I?" He wants to look around, but it feels like trespassing.

She waves a hand. He's here, isn't he?

He begins with the refrigerator. Inside is a carton of milk, a few bottles of beer, a dried salami, a half-loaf of bread. "I shop for him." Irina says in the same distant voice.

The checks Lionel's bookkeeper sends each month, Gus sees now, come at a price. Just bringing him here has been risky for her. "I won't say anything—"

"I don't care about that. I'm doing this for Anna."

She dries the dishes and puts them back in the cupboard. Then she turns to him with her hands on her hips. There will be no sitting down. She will give him time to do what he needs to do and then they will leave.

Three doors lead off from the kitchen. The first one opens to a narrow bathroom with a black and white tiled floor, sink, toilet, tub. Two plain white towels hang on a bar, as neatly and anonymously as a motel. Whatever Gus is meant to see isn't here. He closes the door and tries the one beside it. This must be Irina's room. I had my own bedroom, she said, glowing. Can you imagine?

The room is much like she is: plain, functional, unadorned. Nothing girlish or frivolous about it. Irina did say Keiner forbid such things; still Gus can't help feeling the sadness here of a lost childhood. The mattress on the bed is stripped, the dresser bare. He opens the closet. Empty. So are the dresser drawers. The window looks out onto the siding of the house next door. He closes the door behind him, feeling ashamed, like a voyeur. Feeling pity for her. She knows it, but won't acknowledge it. She's still in the kitchen, her chin lifted, waiting for him to finish.

He opens the last door, is about to go in, then steps back as if he'd encountered a wall. The sight is breathtaking, overwhelming. The doctor in him thinks: pathological. He's afraid to go in as if the room were contagious.

Shane, Irina said. Ma liked pretty things.

He takes a breath, steps inside.

He's heard about hoarders, about the disease that compels people to acquire things, to beg, borrow, and steal. Kleptomania, van der Ploeg called it. This is the first time Gus has seen it for himself. Every single surface in the room—windowsills, tables, dresser, shelves—is covered with things. Items. Possessions. Stuff. Most of it shiny or glistening. Glassware, mirrors, perfume bottles. Brass lamps without shades, a box stuffed with tinfoil from cigarette packs, another filled with silver-plated cups and cutlery. Gus opens a dresser drawer crammed with jewelry. Necklaces, bracelets, earrings, rings. The next drawer holds pages ripped out of newspapers and magazines. Advertisements for movies, hair products, clothing, cosmetics. In each one, a beautiful woman looks out at him with a warm and engaging smile. You can be me, her voice whispers. You, too, can be beautiful.

You, too, can be loved.

The disorder, he understands, is a disease of the imagination. Attached to each one of these objects is a fantasy. Together they constitute the glittery, fascinating world Dora created for herself in her mind. When the real world disappointed—as it inevitably did—she set out again on her hunt to acquire something new, something marvelous and fascinating, to keep her sadness at bay. He opens the closet. It bursts with dresses, shoes, hats, each one more shiny and flamboyant than the last. One he recognizes as the velvet dress Dora wore when she sat for her portrait. Ma had her own style, Irina said. Gus can only imagine.

Irina has clearly been at work here. Despite the clutter, the room is clean and dusted. The curtains at the window are pressed; the double bed is made. It's a shrine, Gus thinks all at once. The room is a shrine to Dora, and Lionel is preserving it. It feels sordid. It's making him sick. He needs to get out.

As he turns to leave, a silver bell on a shelf catches his eye. Ah. The bell Dora wore on a ribbon in her portrait. He picks it up, listens to it jingle, puts it back down. Beside it is a book, small enough to carry in a pocket. Strange. The book is plain, the kind of ledger a shopkeeper or merchant might use to keep track of receipts or sales. It has a brown cardboard cover, not a single sparkle in sight. Why would Dora keep something like that? Irina said her mother couldn't read. It looks like it might have been dropped in water. He opens it up. The pages are wrinkled and stained, yellowed with age. They're also in Hebrew. He recognizes the script. He learned how to read it years ago, when he was studying for his Bar Mitzvah. Could this be a prayer book? If so, it's unlike any one he's seen before. There's nothing printed in it, simply handwriting flowing uninterrupted from one page to the next.

A ledger book in Hebrew? Why on earth would Dora have one of those? It makes no sense. Gus shakes his head. He'll never know. He may have learned how to read Hebrew—that is, how to sound out the words phonetically—but he never learned what they meant. Becoming a Bar Mitzvah at his parents' Reform Temple didn't require that.

He's about to put the book back when all at once a word jumps out at him. *"Yeder."* Like *jeder* in German? In English it meant *every*. The next word is *"Vort."* In German, *Wort*. It meant *word*. *"Yeder vort . . ."* *Every word . . .* The script might be Hebrew, but the language is Yiddish. Of course. Gus smiles. He'd forgotten Yiddish was written with Hebrew letters.

"Yeder vort ihk shraybn do . . ."

"Every word I write here . . ."

All at once he hears a stirring in the kitchen. Irina is coming. Startled, he turns around, slipping the book into his pocket.

"Done?" she says.

He glances one more time around the room. Was this what Irina brought him here to see? He still doesn't know. Does she want him to draw a line from Dora's kleptomania to Lionel's obsessive acquisitions to Anna's shoplifting? The connection is surely there. He can't help feeling that he's missing something. But what? Whatever it might be, Irina isn't going to tell him. She brought him here; she opened up her secrets; she opened up the past. The rest is up to him. She stands in the doorway waiting for him to answer, her face placid and blank. He can think of no reason to stay. "Yes," he says. "Done."

He follows her out of the house. The boy is gone, but the cat is back on the porch. It yawns as they go down the steps to the sidewalk. As a car winds its way down the street, the

312

dog in the back yard barks then is still.

All at once it comes to him. What he has been missing. Two bedrooms. Three beds. Four people but only three beds. Irina's bed. Dora's bed. The cot in the kitchen where Irina said Keiner slept. So where did . . .

"Where," he says to Irina, "did Lionel sleep?"

She looks at him with level eyes. "I told you. He and Ma were close."

"You mean when he was a baby."

"I mean forever."

Forever. How old had Lionel been when Dora died? Thirty, Irina said. This is the reason Lionel keeps coming back. Not for the apartment, not for the campaign, not even to get away from Frieda. He comes back for Dora, to sleep in the bed he shared with his mother until the day she died.

"I'm—" Gus doesn't know what to say, but he must say something. "I'm sorry."

"I don't care about that. I stopped caring about Lupu years ago." Irina waves away his apologies. "Do what you said you would. Help Anna." She turns her back on him, as rigid as a statue, and walks away.

"Wait," Gus says. "I'll drive you home."

"I'll take the bus."

"Please."

"I'm used to it."

She's struggling to maintain her dignity. She has lost everything; she has been stripped bare, with nothing left but shame. Spending more time with him will only make it worse.

He nods. He has to stop himself from apologizing again. "Okay."

She's halfway down the block when all at once he calls to her. "Please. Wait."

She stops and turns to him.

"Lupu. You said you stopped caring about Lupu years ago. Did you mean Lionel?"

"Either way." Irina laughs, a mordent sound riddled equally with mirth and pain. "Lupu's the name he was born with. Lionel's just for appearances. How many people do you think would elect a senator named Lupu?" The laughter dies away. There's more sadness in her than anyone should have to bear. She manages one last, gaunt smile. "It's Romanian. Ma named him Lupu after her father. It means wolf."

The Journal of
Baruch Zalman

∵

Darkness is upon us. Keiner has returned, and in the kitchen he and Dora prepare for their journey. The evening prayers have ended, and I have come alone into the sanctuary to finish this account. It is fitting that I write here now, before the holy ark, in the presence of the Torah, for I have come, dear Reader, to the most difficult part of my account, difficult not only for me to write but to imagine that you will believe. Nevertheless I must beg you—beseech you—not to give up hope, but to be steadfast in your heart and mind and soul. Let my words speak to you, and through them let yourself witness the glory of the Almighty God.

That night, before dawn, I left the synagogue and made my way to the river. I knew what I needed to do. The sky was clear, and far above in the heavens the wolf constellation shone with exceptional brilliance. A good omen, I thought, as I recalled how my grandfather once told me we were descended from the tribe of Benjamin, "the ravening wolf," known for its ferocity in battle. I had never been to war, but at that moment imagined I knew what warriors felt on the eve of battle. If ever I needed a wolf's courage—and cunning—it was now. I disrobed, recited the prayers for purification, and immersed myself naked in the river's dark, rushing waters. When I returned to the bank, dripping and shivering, my skin felt exquisitely tender as if the water had stripped me bare, leaving me newly vulnerable and open to the world.

I returned home and posted a note on the door informing the villagers that I had taken ill, and out of fear of contagion, the synagogue would be closed. Raisel and Dora were still asleep, although my wife's slumber was disturbed by sighs, and I knew her dreams were uneasy. Quietly, so as not to disturb her, I dressed in the white robe I reserved for the highest of our holy days. As on a fast day, I refused to allow food or drink to touch my lips. Then I took my place in the sanctuary and as the sun rose prayed the morning service. *Baruch sheh-amar v'haya ha'olam.* Blessed be He who spoke, and the world came into being. The mystery of the words filled my soul, elevating me until I felt as if I soared among the heavens. In mercy You give light to the earth and those who dwell on it. In goodness You renew the work of creation every day.

If ever I prayed with intention, it was that morning. Praise the Lord! Praise the Lord, O my soul! I sang. I will praise the Lord as long as I live; I will sing to my God as long as I exist. One after another I murmured the psalms, meditating with heart and soul on ancient words once uttered by King David: May the Lord answer you in time of trouble; may the name of the God of Jacob protect you. Truly I found comfort there: My refuge, my fortress, my God in whom I trust.

Raisel and Dora were just stirring as I finished my prayers. Raisel called out to me in an anxious voice, and

I went in to her. "Calm yourself, wife," I said, placing my hand on hers. "I promise not to abandon our Bathsheva." So reassured, she joined Dora in the kitchen, and I returned to the sanctuary.

After checking again to make sure the door was locked and no one was about, I climbed the stairs to the women's gallery. At one time Raisel had taken pride in maintaining the small balcony, keeping it neat and clean and even adorned in the summer with fresh flowers. But for many months now she had been incapable of performing such duties, and I had failed to attend to them. So I found the gallery covered in dust, the air rank and stifling, dead flowers moldering on the windowsill. The benches were askew; prayer books stood in disorderly heaps on a shelf. In one corner a spider merrily spun a web.

I paused for a moment, thinking about the Sabbath eve so many months ago when Gittel and Dora had arrived in our village. That night they ascended to this very place for the evening service. As I watched, Gittel's lips moved in silent prayer while Dora held her hands up to the dancing flames of the Eternal Light, just as Bathsheva once had done. How long ago that day seemed! My life, I knew, had altered in that moment and would never be the same.

At the back of the gallery stood a cabinet, a repository for head coverings, candles, and *tzedakah* boxes where the women deposited coins for charity. Bending down, with great effort I pushed the cabinet aside, revealing a small locked door the size of an oven in the wall behind it.

My grandfather had taught me many things—but not everything. I remembered the day he showed me the door. I was only twelve years old, not even a Bar Mitzvah, and I could tell by the tremulous look in his eyes that he feared entrusting such a large burden to such a small boy. But he must have known his death was near, and he had no choice.

There are two kinds of knowledge, boy, he said to me that day. There is knowledge of God's law, which you must never cease striving to acquire. He placed his hand on my shoulder, and his voice grew exceedingly grave. Then there is knowledge of God Himself. Only the bravest—or most foolish—of men believe they can master such mystery. Many who have tried have come to unfortunate ends. Promise me that you understand—and will honor—the difference.

I nodded, and with that he handed me the key. Then he replaced the cabinet, hiding the door. Before the month was out, he had joined his ancestors in the world beyond the grave, and I had returned to Iaşi.

I had not looked at the door since.

Now I pulled the key from my pocket. The lock was stiff with disuse but after a few moments of prodding gave way. Behind the door was a nook, large enough to hold a sack of flour, maybe two, crammed with papers, parchments, scrolls, and moth-eaten books with tattered spines. I drew back, fearing to touch them. I recalled my grandfather's warning and wondered if I was the brave man he had spoken of or simply the fool. I should leave the papers be. But didn't the wellbeing of my wife—of all of us—merit the risk? I reached into the nook with trembling fingers and pulled the documents out. Then I carried them downstairs and laid them out on the table where each week we read the Torah.

It took me a while to sort through them. At one time the nook must have functioned as the synagogue's *genizah*—the place where old documents containing the name of God are stored, since it is forbidden to throw them out. Many were of simple nature: letters, contracts and the like. Some of these, I was charmed to see, contained my grandfather's signature, others the signature of the rabbi who had preceded him. Still others must have dated back to earlier times, for I didn't recognize the names. I leafed quickly through a few prayer books that had been consigned to the *genizah* at the end of their useful life, then turned my attention to a clutch of parchments, tied with string, that stood at the bottom of the pile. As I opened the first parchment, I realized this was the mystery my grandfather had warned me against when he gave me the key to the nook in the wall—the one I was looking for.

Accounts of spirit possession.

There were over a dozen in all, each one penned in a different hand from a different time and place. Some appeared to be fairly recent, dating perhaps to the time of the Master, for the ink on them was still dark, the parchment supple with a creamy color and oily texture, exuding the faint smell of sheep. Others must have been many hundreds of years old, for they had become dried and brittle, browning on the edges. I handled them with care, for at the slightest disturbance they crumbled to dust. In places the ink was so faded as to be illegible. But as best as I could, beginning with the oldest of the parchments, I began to read.

Today I will speak of enigmas, as I tell that which happened to me in Egypt, may God preserve me, began one. Something wondrous happened in Damascus, and I will retell only that which I witnessed, said another. Now, after all of this has been made known to you from God by the work of my hands, may my words present before you the case of foreign spirits that enter the bodies of humans.

Each parchment held the testimonial of a rabbi who had been summoned to the home of a person possessed by a spirit. The accounts related how the rabbis conducted themselves, what they encountered and observed—and even more importantly for my sake—the rituals they performed to make the plaguing spirits depart. As I read the parchments, my mouth grew dry, and I sympathized with my grandfather, who had hoped I would never have need of such things. The events the rabbis related were both marvelous and terrifying, poised on the boundary between the holy and the profane, the place where the earthly realm gives way to the divine—and to the demonic. How easy it would be to slide unsuspecting from one into the other. Surely there was great power in them, but it was power any mortal man—especially one as insignificant as myself—should tremble to assume.

Time passed as I studied the testimonials, although I didn't know it. When I was finished, I stood for many moments in silent contemplation. Then I bundled the parchments together and returned them to the nook in the wall along with the other papers I had found there. I locked the door and pushed the cabinet back to its usual place. As I came down the stairs, I realized the day was ending, and the sun hung on the horizon. Swiftly I prayed the afternoon and evening services, then feeling faint from my long fast, went outside to draw a cup of water from the well. As I drank, I looked up and saw Keiner coming down the village lane. He was carrying a pack on his back and held his rifle under his arm.

"I've come for Dora," he said.

"And you shall have her." I was enormously relieved to see him, and took his hand. "But first I need your help."

Surely a man who can kill a wolf—dare I say a human being?—is capable of many things. As quickly as I could, I explained to Keiner the situation we faced and my plan to rectify it. He listened in silence, and when I was done, nodded his assent. Together we went inside, where the women awaited us. At the sight of her beloved, Dora leapt up joyfully, and Keiner folded her in his arms. Raisel looked on smiling. Meanwhile I prepared a simple meal of bread and cheese and honey. We sat down to eat, and at last I broke my long fast. Keiner and I fortified ourselves with rose hip wine, Raisel drank cool, fresh water from the well, but for Dora I brewed a particularly potent pot of valerian tea.

"Drink," I said, handing her cup after cup. Soon she was nodding sleepily. "Put her to bed in our room," I said to Raisel. Then I set about readying the other instruments I would need.

From a drawer in the kitchen I took out a packet of sulfur powder, which I kept handy to treat ailments of the skin. I poured a thin layer of powder into a flask and set it aside. On the vanity table in our bedroom, in front of the mirror that in happier days Raisel had used when she brushed out her hair, I placed a white waxen candle. By positioning a second mirror across from the first, I created a series of reflections extending into the infinite. Meanwhile I asked Keiner to fetch a pail of water from the well, which I placed on the floor beside the bed where Dora slumbered.

With pen and ink I wrote out four prayers and positioned them around Dora's body. At her head: The Lord our God is a compassionate and gracious God, slow to anger, abounding in kindness and faithfulness, extending mercy to the thousandth generation, forgiving iniquity, transgression, and sin. At her right hand: May the Lord answer you in time of trouble, may the name of God protect you. At her left hand: True it is that the eternal God is our King. And at her feet: The Lord will reign forever and ever.

Raisel watched me with fearful eyes. "What are you doing, husband?" she asked, for she had never seen me make such preparations before.

"Don't worry," I soothed her. "I promise you no harm will come to our Bathsheva."

I put a stool in the corner of the room and bade Raisel sit on it. It was most important that she be able to see and hear everything that transpired. She looked doubtful but took her place as I requested. With Keiner's help, I moved the bed so that it occupied the center of the room, leaving me space to stand at the head. Keiner stood at the foot. The pail of water was at my right side; the flask of sulfur sat next to the candle; nearby I placed a shofar—the ram's horn we sound on the highest of our holy days—and a glass of rose hip wine lest I needed strength to get through the proceedings.

"Are you ready?" I asked Keiner. His face was grave, and I believe he braced himself. But as I said, a man who can kill a wolf must be capable of many things. He nodded his assent.

Outside it was dark, the sky overcast, nary a star visible in the sky. I lit the candle between the two mirrors and endless bright reflections of the flames imparted a magical glow to the room. The windows were open, bringing in the murmuring voices of the river and the wind. The air was thick and warm, redolent with the ripe smells of summer: dust from the village lanes, honey dripping in the hives, flowers drooping on thin stalks. In the distance an owl called out a question then was still.

Dora was on her back, sleeping comfortably, her face lightly flushed, her breathing regular. I took her wrists in my hands. Deep within her I could feel the life force of her blood surging, the pulses steady beneath my fingers. Were there truly two souls within her breast? The rabbis whose testimonials I had read told of sensing the presence of the soul within the pulse, but I had no such skill.

Softly I held her as I chanted the *Aleinu*, the prayer with which we conclude our daily service, beginning, "It is our duty to praise the Master of all," through the many passages that end, "As it is said: The Lord shall be King over all the earth; on that day the Lord shall be One, and his name One." Seven times I recited this prayer, and each time my voice rose in intensity, and I lifted my eyes, summoning every ounce of intention I could muster. Then with supreme concentration, for such a thing is no easy feat, I recited the prayer backwards, also seven times. Through all of this Dora remained unchanged, and Keiner, steely-eyed, showed no emotion, but Raisel looked as startled as a caught mouse, her eyes wide, her hand clapped to her mouth.

Finally I released Dora's wrists, stepped back, and in a thunderous voice proclaimed: "In the names of the angels, the seraphim and holy messengers, I adjure you, spirit, speak!" With a flick of my hand I flung sulfur powder into the flame of the candle, releasing an acrid, burning smoke into the room. Dora's nostrils widened, and her face paled, but her eyes remained closed, and she was silent. I checked her pulses, which were racing now with an irregular beat. I was perspiring from the heat, my eyes stinging from the sulfur. Once again I flung powder into the flame, and as vapors swirled through the room, cried out, "In the name of the Lord, honored and awesome, majestic and sanctified: speak!"

All at once Dora's body stiffened and grew as rigid as a rock. Her eyes flew open and stared blankly upwards. A great tremor coursed through her, causing her back to arch, her limbs to spasm, and the bell on her wrist to jingle. Raisel moaned in fear, and even Keiner looked shaken, but remained steadfast. "In the name of the Almighty, I adjure you—" I said, but went no further, for now I, too, was terrified and felt as if my heart would stop. Dora trembled, and her body jerked as if it would levitate and leave the bed, flying upwards. The bell rang with what sounded like a deafening roar. Then she fell back, her eyes closed, and with a deep sigh her body softened and grew still.

Silence reigned in the room. I looked at Keiner, and he looked at me. Neither of us could summon a word. One, two, three . . . to twenty I counted my breaths. Nothing happened. Dora slumbered on silently as before.

I had failed. Either I had incorrectly performed the ritual, or I was too insignificant a rabbi to bring about such a tremendous transformation. Perhaps I had simply given Dora too much of the valerian tea. Feelings of self-disgust washed over me, coupled with a mixture of relief and regret. I remembered my grandfather's warning that those who attempt such mysteries often come to unfortunate ends.

But it was Raisel—not I—who bore the brunt of my arrogance. She had never look so frightened in her life. "No, Baruch, please, don't," she said as tears coursed freely down her cheeks. I went to her and took her in my arms. I was sorry and I was just about to tell her so when all at once a voice behind me said, "Hello, Papa."

Were I to live a hundred years, dear Reader, I would never be able to say where that voice came from. Was it Bathsheva speaking? Was it Dora? Throughout my interview with the spirit, Dora never moved. Her eyes remained closed, and her lips emitted nothing but the softest sighs of dreams. And yet—there is no other way to describe it—the voice came from inside her. Sometimes it emanated from her belly, other times from her throat. *Bathsheva.* Dare I say it? The spirit of our daughter was with us. Even Raisel knew it, for at the sound of the spirit's voice, her fear vanished, and her face grew misty-eyed and full of love.

"Daughter," Raisel said.

"Mother," the spirit answered, affection, sorrow, and longing coloring her voice. "How I have missed you."

Outside a great wind had risen, sweeping away the clouds. The stars shone down now with a singular force, the constellation of the wolf framed in the window as if to watch our proceedings with its gleaming eye. On Raisel's vanity, the mirrored flame of the candle answered the stars' brilliance, casting flickering light throughout the room. Gradually the sulfur smoke dissipated, and the air became pure again. I glanced at Keiner, whose face had turned ashen, but like a good soldier, he had yet to move from his post. Raisel sat down on the bed and took Dora's hand, bathing it with her kisses and tears. Meanwhile I resumed my place at her head and took a long draught of rose hip wine.

"Bathsheva," I said, and my voice, too, reflected my sorrow and longing. "Beloved. What can I do to help you?"

A long period of silence followed, accompanied by many sighs. "I am tired, Papa. I have lived too long this earthly life. I wish to move on to the Gan Eden that I know awaits me."

"And I wish to help you," I said, "but first you must tell me how you came to inhabit the body of this woman."

Once again the spirit fell silent as if she were struggling with herself. "Please do not make me speak of such things, for they are very painful, and I fear my mother's heart will break."

Raisel clutched Dora's hand: my brave wife, who had sacrificed so much for our daughter while she lived and continued to sacrifice for her after her death. She caught my eye and nodded, giving me the strength to go on. "Nevertheless," I said, my voice firm, "you must tell us."

For a long time the spirit did not answer, and I sensed the violence of the struggle in her breast. Then with a deep sigh, she said, "Very well." And so she told us her story.

Here, Reader, before going on, I must pause, to strengthen both myself and you. The night is deepening, and in the next room, Keiner and Dora are ready to leave. They are impatient to be on their way, and soon I must release them. But I have told them they must wait until I finish, and so they do. I dare not falter now.

Dear Reader, dare I say *beloved* Reader, for surely, if you have come so far on this journey with me, we are tied by bonds not just of friendship but of love? How can I convince you that every word you are about to read is true, that it came directly from the mouth of the spirit itself? Such a thing, I know, is beyond belief. And yet it is so. All I can tell you is that each word, as it was spoken, was burned into my heart. I will never forget it as long as I live. One day, if I meet my Creator as the Master has promised that I will, I will carry these words in my heart to His side. Thus I give you this story in the spirit's words—not my own.

I will never forget, Papa, the moment of my death. I was overcome with sadness as my earthly life came to an end, but also with relief, for as you know, I had long been sickly and suffered a great deal. My sorrow was for you and Mother, for I knew you would grieve for me, whereas I looked forward to the delights of Gan Eden. Know then my surprise when I realized as the last shuddering breath left my body that I had not transmigrated, but instead was still on this earth. I was meant to give rise to a line of righteous men, scholars of the Torah, leaders in their generation; and pious women like our foremothers, Sarah, Leah, Rachel, and Rebecca. I had not yet fulfilled my destiny, and so was forced to remain.

Easily I saw and heard everything that transpired after my death, although I was unable to communicate my presence to you. I watched as my body was lowered into the grave and heard the thud of dirt on wood as you threw the first shovelful of earth onto my casket—the sound that, more than anything, made me realize I had parted from you forever. Mother had lost her strength and could barely walk, and as you took her home on your arm, I followed.

Then I waited outside while you went in.

I was never far from you, Papa, in those early years, although you knew it not. Water, I discovered, was a great comfort to me, and so I spent much of my time in the courtyard well. When the weather was fine, I wandered in the woods. Many a time I saw you there and tried to speak to you, but you did not hear me. My voice was lost in the wind in the trees, in the splashing waters of the river. I joined with birdsong in the summer and with rain in the winter. I was in the shadows and in the ice glistening in the sunlight. For a time I inhabited a deer, and she was a delightful creature, swift and innocent and light of foot; but she walked on four legs, and it was too difficult and burdensome for me, and so I left her. For years I lived in a stone, but it was cold and unbearably lonely. More than anything I wanted to touch you, to comfort you, and let you know I was with you, but I could not.

The pain of my exile from Mother was all but unbearable. Once I flew into the house in the body of a bird and perched on the oven and looked at her through my bright eye. But she was weeping and distraught, and watching her suffer was more than I could bear, so I flew away. As the years went by, her grief did not lessen, but instead grew stronger. Finally I determined to leave this place and lose myself in forgetfulness. I fled from the well to the river, where I entered the body of a fish. The fish carried me from the mountains to the plains and from there to the Danube, where I hoped to flow into the vast, encompassing nothingness that is the sea.

On this journey I saw the most extraordinary things. Men in boats casting fishing nets, great steamers chugging eastwards against the current, churning whirlpools and rocky outcrops, sprawling towns that sprang up along the river's banks. Just as I thought I had seen all the marvels this world could offer, I saw one more: a man who stepped out of a boat onto the river and stood on the water for one heartbeat then two. As he sank beneath the surface, a wolf swam to him and seized his throat in its jaws. He clutched the wolf and so entwined, the two disappeared into the depths, never to be seen again. The shock caused the womb of a woman in the boat to open, and as her waters poured out, I flowed inside her, taking up residence in the unborn child. There I have stayed to this day.

When the child was born I rejoiced, for they named her D'vorah—the judge, the righteous one—and I thought through her at last to fulfill my destiny. At first we got along well, for she was an innocent child just as I was, but then she began to change and take on the attributes of a woman. Inside her body, all was in turmoil. She was driven by monthly cycles and unfamiliar feelings. Men around her sensed the change and attempted to use it to their advantage. One, her stepfather, forced himself . . . but here I must stop, Papa, and nothing you say will persuade me otherwise, for the things I witnessed are terrible beyond words.

At last I determined to leave this body, even if meant returning to the cold and lonely life of a stone. I was searching for an opportunity to escape when I heard we would be traveling here, to Alba-Bistrița. I desired to see you and Mother one more time, and so I determined to wait. But now, dear Papa, I must go, for this body has become unsuitable. Inside it another child grows, and there is no longer room for me. So I beg you: release me and let me go.

Silence fell on the room as the spirit ended her tale. I was full of remorse, weeping, blinded by my tears. Let her go? Was I somehow responsible for Bathsheba's suffering—had my love for her kept her trapped on this earth? Raisel, too, sobbed painfully, and clung to Dora's hand. Even Keiner wiped a tear from his eye, and I knew he had been moved by the spirit's trials.

"Help me to enter Gan Eden, dear Papa," the spirit said, "and I will wait for you there, for I know both you and Mother are old, and will join me soon."

"If I help you," I said to the spirit as I wiped my eyes and steadied my voice, "will you promise to leave the body of this woman and never return?"

"Gladly."

"Where will you go?"

"Into the pail of water."

"How will I know you are there?"

"I will turn the water red."

"Beware that you do not damage the woman when you leave her body. You must exit between the nail and flesh of the little toe of her left foot."

"Agreed."

Gently I pulled Raisel away from Dora and guided her back to her stool. I told Keiner to stand back. I felt weak and lightheaded as if a fit might be coming on, and took another draught of rose hip wine to fortify myself. Summoning all my strength, my voice rising, I chanted the greatest mystery of all: the seventy-two names of God. Then I lifted the ram's horn, took a breath, and blew a long, echoing blast such as signals the end of our Day of Atonement.

At the sound of the shofar Dora's eyes opened and her body shook. Then her foot jerked into the air, and blood spurted from her toe. Terrified, I jumped back, knocking over the wine, which fell into the pail, turning the water red, and then darkness fell over me, and I knew no more.

Time passed; I never knew how much or little when I was in the throes of a fit. When I came back to myself, I was stretched out on the floor, the midnight hour drawing near.

Raisel was in our bed, sleeping peacefully, a light smile playing across her lips, dreaming, I hoped, of the World to Come where she would soon be reunited with our daughter. Dora, too, was asleep on her pallet, a bandage on her damaged toe. Keiner must have seen to that. When he saw life return to my eyes, he helped me to my feet and poured me a glass of water that I might recover myself. Then he looked at Dora. "It is just as you said."

"Is it?" I said.

Keiner smiled. "We will leave tomorrow night."

I clasped his hand. "I will be here to see you off."

Together we carried the pail to the river, and beneath the exuberance of stars that filled the heavens, emptied it out. I watched the red-stained water mingle with the other river waters, and imagined it flowing out of the mountains across the plain to the vast expanse of forgetfulness that was the sea.

"Be well, daughter," I whispered as the red stain vanished, "be free."

When we returned to the synagogue, Keiner lay down on a bench in the sanctuary to catch the last few hours of sleep before dawn. More than anything I, too, wished to sleep, but I knew I had much work ahead of me. I sat at the kitchen table, fetched this journal, and began to write.

What I did not confess to Keiner that night was the

vision I had during the fit that overtook me as the spirit fled Dora's body. If the vision of the Master I had as a child was a taste of Paradise, this was a glimpse of Hell. I saw a great conflagration, the world aflame, the bodies of men, women, and children alike turned to ash, rising through towering chimneys to blacken the sky. Then I knew, as my nephew did, that there was no future for Jews in this place. The Messiah will not come to us no matter how eagerly we await him. The future, if there is such a thing, lies elsewhere: in the golden land of America where Keiner is determined to make his home, or in the stony hills of the Promised Land where my nephew will make his.

This account is now finished. Praise be to God to whom all praise is due. I will go into the next room where Keiner and Dora await for me. In the presence of Raisel, I will unite them in marriage and give them my blessing. As they leave, I will slip this journal into Dora's bag, so that she may take it into the future with her. One day soon I will be gone, and the world I know will end, too. But you, beloved Reader who reads this testimony, and all others who take this journey with me, will know that once a man named Baruch Zalman—the son of Rav Menachem Zalman, who was himself the son of the great Rav Isak Zalman, a disciple of Rabbi Israel ben Eliezar, the Baal Shem—walked this earth. His faith never wavered, everything he saw testified to the everlasting mercy of a loving Lord, and he served his God unceasing until the day he died.

End of Journal of Baruch Zalman

Twenty-Three

GUS

*G*us steps into a phone booth in the back of a Riverport drugstore, places a frantic call to Marby, holds his breath then lets it out in a rush of relief when Beatrice's voice comes on the line: "Glanz Residence. Miss Chase speaking."

"Beatrice." Just saying her name is a balm in itself, the first step in putting the shock behind him. "It's me. Gus. Something has happened. I need to see you. I need to talk to you—" He checks himself, starts over. "I need," he says simply, "to come back."

"Hello, Gus," she says softly.

He imagines her sitting at her desk in her office in the great house on the Sound, the narrow window giving out a view of the rose garden, the late afternoon sun dying on the tiles of the sunroom. "I'm sorry. I shouldn't have left you like that. I didn't even say goodbye." He winces as he thinks of their kiss—of what a cad he has been.

There's a moment of silence on the line, then her voice comes through, quietly cautious. "I know this has been hard on you." On *you*, she says. Leave it to Beatrice to take his side: to think of him. She could have just as easily said on *Anna*. Or on *me*. She could have said: You abandoned us both. Instead he hears the hurt in her voice, and something else: a willingness to listen, to give him a second chance. He knows he doesn't deserve it.

"I was going to go back to Baltimore. I didn't think there

333

was anything else I could do for Anna. I came to Riverport instead. I met Irina."

"Irina?"

"Lionel's sister."

"Oh," Beatrice says. She's silent for a moment, taking it in. "I knew he had a sister. I didn't know her name."

"Irina's amazing. She's wonderful. She's—" He breaks off again. It's more than he can possibly explain in a phone call. "She's incredibly brave." He leaves it at that. "I'll tell you all about it when I see you." The druggist walks past, carrying a package from the stockroom, and Gus lowers his voice. "I need to hypnotize Anna one more time."

"You can't." Beatrice falls silent, holding her breath, as Gus hears voices in the background, coming close then fading away. It's Frieda, calling to Lionel. There's the sound of their footsteps, then they're gone, and Beatrice speaks to him again, her voice hushed. "They won't let you. I mean, *she* won't. Mrs. Glanz got your note—the one about Anna sleepwalking. She's terribly upset. I heard her arguing with Mr. Glanz about it. She says you've endangered Anna. She says you're never to be allowed to set foot in the house again." Again she falls silent as voices sound in the background. "Where are you?"

"In Riverport." The druggist is back, and Gus turns his head, shielding his voice. "I have to see Anna again. There must be a way."

"Wait." He imagines Beatrice's lip drawing between her teeth. The thought of the gesture makes him smile, makes him want to hold that lip between his own two lips, and soon. "Come by the house tomorrow. Mr. and Mrs. Glanz will be out. They're going into the city to look at

334

apartments." Her voice grows firmer as she makes up her mind. His smile broadens. He's so grateful to have Beatrice on his side. It's where, he thinks, he would like to have her forever.

"Gus." Her voice drops to a whisper. "You need to know. After you left—after Mrs. Glanz found your note—she had me place a call to Spring Meadow. She said she can't wait any longer. She said it's too dangerous for Anna. She's made arrangements for her commitment. They're coming to pick her up on Friday."

Friday. Three days away. "Does Anna know?"

"Not yet."

"Does Mr. Glanz?"

"I don't know. I don't think so."

"I'll drive down right away." He will fix this. He's determined to, one way or another. "I'll find a place to stay—a motel—nothing fancy. I'll come by in the morning as soon as they're gone."

"Nothing fancy?" Beatrice laughs. He hears the warmth in her voice, imagines the afternoon sun coloring her face, feels his own face coloring in response. The desire to touch her is all but unbearable. "In that case, you can stay with Mother and me."

Lionel. Lupu. Wolf.

The words echo in Gus's mind as he drives down the coast road to Marby, playing in time to the humming of the tires on the road.

Lupu. Lionel. Wolf.

So Lionel was the wolf after all.

In the end Gus isn't surprised to realize it. He should

335

have guessed it long ago. Instead he let himself be blinded by Sasha, let the boy's death keep him from seeing what he needed to see. The drowning, he knows now, was exactly what everyone said it was from the beginning: an accident. Tragic, yes, but nothing more than that. Cataldo might have had his suspicions, but the coroner knew what he was about. Sasha's death had nothing to do with Anna's silence. It was Lionel. He had been abusing her all along—only not in the way Gus thought.

Lionel. Lupu. Wolf.

No wonder she paints wolves so obsessively. She has been trying to tell Gus through her art what she can't bring herself to say.

The drive to Marby comes as a welcome relief, not only because each mile brings him closer to Beatrice, but because it gives him time to think, to assimilate what he has learned. He'll never forget Irina, will never be able to thank her enough for her courage, her devotion, the pain of her sacrifice. When she opened the door to the apartment, she opened the door to the truth. In the end, however, it was Baruch Zalman's journal that brought Anna's story into the light—that made it whole. The plain brown book, watermarked and stained, sits on the seat beside him, and he reaches out to touch it as if even now he can't believe it's real: a missive hurtled from deep in the past into the future, directly into his hands.

The journal was still in his pocket when he left the apartment. Later he told himself he'd simply forgotten it, but of course that wasn't true. Even then, as Irina walked away from him, her head erect, clinging to the last vestiges of her dignity, he sensed the weight of it in his jacket, the snug fit against his hip. He should have given it back to her, but he didn't. No use trying to analyze that, Dr. Freud. That's just the way it was.

Instead he got into his car, drove a few blocks, then pulled over by a small corner drugstore. Inside he took a seat in a booth and as the afternoon waned, over cup after cup of coffee, read through Zalman's journal. He didn't follow everything the rabbi said, and he didn't understand every word, but he understood enough. The last missing piece of Anna's story fell into place, revealing to him what he should have known all along.

Another mother, in another place, in another time, standing outside of a locked door, afraid to go in.

No wonder Frieda hadn't opened the door when Lionel took Anna inside. She must have suspected what she would find on the other side.

Think, Gus tells himself as the car wings southward through the night. Think of Anna. What do you see?

A vision of the penitential girl in the courtyard of Phipps comes to him, making her rounds around the pond, being good, being oh-so-very good. It all made perfect sense. The last thing Anna would want was to give anyone a reason to punish her. She knew what such punishments would bring.

He sees the Glanzes at the dinner table the day he arrived in Marby, Lionel pulling Hettie onto his lap, the look of alarm on Frieda's face, her nervous laughter: "Hettie's too old for that." Anger flashing in Anna's eyes. Lionel, laughing, saying "Mother is right. Mother is always right."

Frieda didn't suspect Lionel was abusing Anna—she knew. And she was afraid Hettie was next in line. The realization fills Gus with disgust. He understands now

337

why Frieda refuses to take the girls with her to New York City. What did she say? Impossible. They must be sent away to boarding school. If Anna can't go there, she will go to Spring Meadow. All Frieda ever wanted was to keep her children safe. Keep them safe from Lionel, she meant.

Gus thinks back to Anna's tug on the dress when they arrived in Marby; how she fiddled with the strap to her shirt; how he reached out and touched her hair while she lay helpless beside him in her trance. She has been trying to tell him all along about the abuse. If only he had listened. How close he came to abandoning her. He can't bear to think of it anymore.

But in the end he didn't, just as he never abandoned Rosa either.

He turns his thoughts back to Zalman. Reading the journal gave him a deep admiration for the rabbi, mixed with a deep, aching sadness. Somehow the rabbi intuited what the future held for European Jewry—the destruction of the world he held so dear. He was an astute chronicler and keen observer; born a generation later, he would have made an excellent psychiatrist. His journal read like a case history, infused with the warmth of his personality and overarching humanity. Not all of it was true, of course. Gus doesn't believe in spirit possession—does he? No, of course not. Stories like that were nothing more than a relic of the pre-scientific age, the attempt to explain behaviors people had no other means of understanding. Zalman didn't even have the vocabulary to describe what he saw: mania, melancholy, *la folie circulaire*. Could Dora's trance have been an episode of catatonia? Fascinating. Gus wishes he had been there to see it.

And yet: there was that troublesome exit of the spirit from Dora's foot, the bandaged toe. Didn't Irina say her mother limped? Gus shakes his head with a smile. He won't go down that path. Any number of things might have caused Dora's limp.

Meyer was right. Find the source and you will find the cure. What mattered in the end was Anna's story. Gus knows what it is now, knows that its origins lie deep in the past, in a great river traveling across a wide plain, a man wrestling with a wolf, the blowing of a ram's horn. What Gus doesn't know yet is how her story will end. It's no longer a question of *his* story or *her* story: it's *their* story. A shared journey. The ending will be shared, too. He will return to Anna. He will show her that he understands what happened to her, that he accepts her as she is, and that he values both her and her suffering. She will see that she doesn't need to punish herself anymore. She will see that she can speak.

He will go back to Marby. He will hypnotize Anna one more time, and then both of them will be free.

Twenty-Four

CLAIRE

"I'd like to speak to Detective Cataldo," Claire says.

The woman behind the front desk of the police station has a scar on her wrist. Injured through the line of duty, Claire wonders? Sergeant Reid, the nametag on her uniform reads. "Cataldo." She eyes Claire over glasses perched low on her nose. She's fiftyish, dark hair sprinkled with grey, cropped short to her head. "You do know Joey Cataldo passed over twenty years ago?"

Claire doesn't, but she should. Should have guessed it anyway. Sasha died over fifty years ago, more than enough time for anyone who investigated his death to have died, too. She suppresses a stab of disappointment. She's not here to see Cataldo, she reminds herself, just his records. "Then I need to see one of his case files." She digs into her purse and pulls out a business card from the D.C. misdemeanor court. It's stained and battered, but it's the best she can do. She's lucky to have it. She has a dim memory of burning the others in Hettie's apartment before the Xynolith kicked in. She puts the card on the desk, slides it across to the sergeant. "I'm working on a cold case."

"One of Detective Cataldo's?"

"Yes."

Claire looks away as Reid studies her card. Other than a

340

janitor pushing a mop in the corner, the station is empty. The mopping fills the air with the cloying smell of disinfectant, reviving a long-forgotten memory of her elementary school lunchroom, a faint nausea. Under the glare of the fluorescent lights, she feels a headache coming on.

"D.C. prosecutor." Reid puts the card down. "You've come a long way for a misdemeanor."

"Yes, I mean, no, it's not a misdemeanor." Claire's a terrible liar. She always has been. The sergeant purses her lips with a knowing air as if she can see right through her. "It's a felony. Could be murder." She bites her lip, a nervous tic. Next thing she knows, she'll be picking at it like Anna. "I'm in charge of the investigation." That much at least is true.

"Is that so." Reid looks as if she believes this as much as she believes everything else Claire has said. Then she shrugs. A prosecutor is a prosecutor after all. She turns to the computer on her desk. "You got a case number?"

Claire shakes her head.

"A name?"

Claire looks at her blankly.

"Victim?"

She has to stop herself from biting her lip again. "Glanz."

"Glanz." Reid is typing. She shows no reaction to the name. "Location?"

"Marby Point. The shore road."

The keys click. "Date?"

"Mid-forties."

She stops typing. "You do know that's fifty years."

"Yes."

Reid returns to the keyboard with another shrug: It's

your funeral, lady. "Cataldo. Cataldo." She raises her hands. "Nope."

"Excuse me?"

"We don't have it."

"You don't have—"

"A case file with those identifiers." She speaks the words slowly, with emphasis, as if that's the only way Claire will understand. "Cataldo. Glanz. The shore road. The forties." Claire can practically read her thoughts. Lawyers sure are dumb coming out of D.C. these days.

"Maybe you could look—"

"No maybe. That's it."

"But—"

"Look, Mrs.—" Reid glances at the card again "—Mrs. Sadler. Let me explain to you how it works. We used to keep our own files. On paper. We stored them in the old police station. Then that got torn down and everything got sent to the graveyard."

"Graveyard?"

"Central Archives. Upstate." She cackles. "Graveyard is what we call it, 'cause anything that goes in there doesn't come out."

"But theoretically a person could—"

"Get a file out of the graveyard? Theoretically, yes. But only if it's there."

"How can you be sure—"

"I have a list. A graveyard inventory." Reid gives Claire a sour look as if she's accused her of not knowing her job. "I used to keep it in a ledger." She taps the computer. "Now it's here."

"But maybe the list isn't perfect. Maybe something got overlooked—"

"And maybe Santa Claus visits every house on Christmas Eve just like they say." Reid runs a hand through her hair then sighs, relenting. "Mrs. Sadler. I remember Detective Cataldo, okay? I'd just started on patrol when he retired. That was—" she thinks back "—thirty years ago. I was here on his last day. He cleared everything out of his office. Handed it all over. He cared about his cases—maybe too much. He wouldn't have let anything go missing. It's all here. Believe me." She taps the computer again. "If it isn't, it doesn't exist. Never did. Plenty of Cataldo." She gives Claire a pointed look. "No Glanz."

So Reid knows the name after all. Claire's face colors. "Is there anyone else I could talk to?"

Reid pulls herself up, offended. "You mean a supervisor?"

"Someone who might have known him."

"I did tell you he's been gone twenty years, right?"

"He must have had a family."

"A son. Joey Junior. Passed."

"His partner then."

"Like I said."

Like you is. Claire has the feeling she's circling round and round, returning over and over again to the same place. "So there's no way—"

Reid purses her lips, looks at her.

"But there must—" Claire breaks off. This has to stop. She has to stop. Reid is right. Fifty years is fifty years. Finished. Done. She needs to get used to the idea. If she doesn't, she's liable to end up—well, God only knows where. Most likely with the wolf.

"Thanks," she says to Reid. She turns to leave.

Now that Claire's going, Reid relaxes, gets chattier.

343

"You're lucky you found me here. I'm probably the only person left who even knows who Joey Cataldo was." She grows thoughtful. "Except maybe Tom Marzetti. The Marzettis and the Cataldos always were close."

Claire stops. "Marzetti?"

"He's a patrolman. Grew up with Joey Junior. Like I told you, Joey Junior—"

"Passed. I know. But this Marzetti—Officer Marzetti—I could talk to him?"

"That's up to him, isn't it? He'll be in tomorrow morning. He comes in at eight. You can ask him then."

Tom Marzetti is a tall man, gangly, with a pronounced Adam's apple. His fingers are surprisingly thin and tapering. Artistic, Claire thinks. She wonders what he might have been if he hadn't become a cop. She finds herself thinking of Roger's hands, his delicate fingers leafing through a stack of documents, tracing a pen across a page in his tiny, monkish script. She banishes the thought. She isn't ready to go there yet.

"Nice place," she says to Marzetti.

Tom Marzetti smiles. "Kind of cheesy if you ask me. We used to have an old diner in the village that most of the patrolmen went to. It burned down last year."

Cheesy, yes. The Cup and Spoon. The coffee shop they are sitting in is fitted out in a faux Colonial style, oilcloth on the table, pewter mugs. Olde this and olde that. Claire has ordered olde wheat toast. It sits on her plate untouched, growing literally old. She can't manage a bite. She has gotten down a mug of coffee, black, has started on a second. The coffee is medicinal. Her head feels thick, a combination of the Xynolith and the night she spent in a nearby Marby motel. She hardly slept, disturbed by dreams she couldn't recall when daylight came. By seven-thirty a.m. she was in the police station, pacing the floor, waiting for Officer Marzetti to arrive.

She told him everything when they met. A stranger. She abandoned all pretense, abandoned all lies, and settled on the truth: Sasha's drowning, the real reason she came to Marby. She even confessed Anna's imminent death. Keeping it in had simply become too hard. Marzetti listened without saying a word, and when Claire finished he took her arm and led her across the street to The Cup and Spoon.

At least the place is cozy, quiet. Most of the tables up front are taken. They have taken one in the back, speaking in hushed voices, seeking out privacy in a very public place.

Marzetti doesn't remember Sasha's death—that was before his time—but he remembers Lionel Glanz. And he remembers Joey Cataldo. "One thing I can tell you is Joey didn't care for your grandfather." He has stuck to coffee, too, flavoring his liberally with sugar and cream.

"From everything I know," Marzetti says, "Lionel Glanz was a good guy. Did his best for the state of New York. That didn't matter to Joey. He said Lionel never would have been elected if people knew what he'd done." He winces. "Sorry."

Claire waves the apology away. "Do you know what he meant by that?"

"He kept it close to his chest, like maybe one day it would all come out, and then people would see that he was right."

"I think it might have had something to do with Sasha's death."

Marzetti looks thoughtful. "I wouldn't know."

"He never talked about it?"

"Not to me."

"Sargent Reid said he had a son."

"Joey Junior. We grew up together." He smiles. "Joey Senior used to take us fishing."

"She said his son died young."

"You remember that warehouse fire in the Bronx in the early sixties?"

Claire shakes her head.

"Three firemen lost their lives. One of them was Joey Junior." Marzetti raises his mug in a silent tribute. "My dad worked a fireboat in the Sound, and his dad was a cop. Look how we ended up. Joey Junior and I used to laugh about it."

"What was he like—Joey Senior?"

"A good cop. He cared about his job. Maybe too much. Worked his cases like a dog with a bone. Wouldn't let anything go. He was hot-headed, too. Opinionated. Said he knew what was what and that was it. But he was a good man. We could use more like him."

It's time to go. She's taken up enough of his time. She stands up, puts a few dollars on the table, waves off Marzetti's attempt to pay for his own coffee.

"I'm sorry about your mother," he says, "sorry I couldn't be of more help."

"No. Please. I've been—unreasonable in my expectations. I'm going to try to change that." She smiles. "I appreciate your listening. Appreciate your time."

They walk out together. "It's hard to lose a parent," Marzetti says. "I had a tough time when my father passed. I know it was hard for Joey when his son died. It took a lot out of him. You could see it in his face when he retired. It was like he knew there would be no one left to remember him after he was gone. I was there the day he emptied out his office. He packed up his files, handed them over to the desk sergeant. I helped him carry the boxes out. In the end there was just one left. 'Unfinished business,' he called it. He told me take it out back. I thought he was going to take it home with him—something to keep him busy in his retirement. But instead he gave the box to me. Said I could look through it if I wanted." He looks away. "Sad. He worked so hard his whole life, and in the end it was like there was nothing left. Just one box."

"And did you? Did you go through it?"

"The box? No. I always said I would but I never did. Then Joey died, and I thought I should get rid of it, but I felt bad about it, as if I'd let him down."

"So this box—you still have it."

Marzetti nods.

"Joey's 'unfinished business.'"

"Yes."

"And there was nothing more unfinished to Joey Cataldo than Lionel Glanz."

"No, there wasn't." Marzetti grins. "Want to take a look?"

Claire is back in the Marby motel, has taken a room for another night. She sits cross-legged on the bed with the blankets ruched around her shoulders, Joey Cataldo's file laid out before her. The stone before the cave.

The temperatures were dropping as she checked in, rain sliding into sleet. Now wind rattles the door, and a cold draft slips underneath. The motel doesn't have much to recommend it. Heat comes from a window unit that doubles in the summer as an air conditioner, hissing out a stream of lukewarm air. She finds herself thinking of home. Her own bed. Roger. Her throat thickens with longing. She pulls the blankets closer.

She left the Cup and Spoon promising to meet Marzetti at his house at six, after his shift ended. The rest of the day she spent in Marby walking, walking. Not thinking, that is, thinking as little as possible. For a time she sat on a bench in a municipal park alongside the Sound. The park had a marina, but it was empty now, the boats gone, in storage for the season. The playground was empty, too, the kids in school. She matched it all with an empty mind.

Eventually she realized she was feeling light-headed from hunger and headed to a fish shack at the end of one of the docks. She sat at a planked table and managed to eat most of a bowl of chowder. The chowder was good, brimming with fresh fish, and under other circumstances, she might have enjoyed it. Today it was almost tasteless.

That evening she met Marzetti at his house as they had planned. Rain beginning to fall. She stood in his garage while he searched for Cataldo's files, digging past bicycles, a lawnmower, fishing rods. Finally he pulled out a plain brown cardboard box, the kind that could hold anything: hardware, paint, junk. In this case maybe, just maybe, her future. The box held a dozen or so files, each one neatly labeled. The thickest one had GLANZ written across the top in black letters. Claire lifted it out of the box, feeling its weight, cradling it the way some women might cradle a newborn.

Marzetti swept a hand towards the door. "Would you like to come in?"

"No. Thanks." She hugged the file to her chest. She didn't know how she would react when she saw what was inside. It might be better to be alone for that.

Now she pulls the blankets tighter around her shoulders, runs her fingertips over the file, the paper slightly warped, faded to a pale jaundiced color. She promised to let Marzetti know if she finds anything he might be duty bound to pursue. Neither of them expected it. Cataldo was too good a cop. If there'd been any actionable evidence on the Glanzes, he would have found it. Anyway fifty years is fifty years. The time to prosecute most crimes is past.

Only not murder. Her fingers retract from the paper as if it's afire. There's no statute of limitations on that.

She opens the file. The contents are neat and orderly, divided into sections, secured with paper clips. She lifts up the first section, works the clip loose, releasing a clutch of old newspaper clippings with a dry, ashen scent. *The Marby Village Voice.* The first article dates to the spring of 1947. "Glanz seeks campaign endorsement in New York City." Claire's surprised to find nothing older. Then she remembers: Lionel wouldn't have come to Cataldo's attention until Sasha died. It's her first indication of the date of the boy's death. Anna would have been fifteen at the time, Hettie eleven. Anna fifteen? What had that been like? Claire can't imagine. She can hardly remember herself at that age; it felt like a muddle. And Anna was always so guarded. She never volunteered anything about her past, especially not about the time when the family lived in Marby.

"Glanz to engage in labor talks," reads the next headline. "Lionel Glanz to Meet with Governor." "Local Businessman Promises to Address New York Economic Needs." The articles pile up on the bed beside her. Cataldo must have had his eye on Lionel all that spring. The detective did more than just clip articles about her grandfather; he annotated them in ink by hand. "Lies." "Not True." The comments run down the margins. "Where's the rest of the story?" Cataldo was hot-headed, just like Marzetti said. And he hated her grandfather with a passion. "Bastard," he writes again and again. "A-hole." His favorite: "SOB."

The articles march through the summer to the fall, ending with "Glanz Family to Move from Point," and then, the final headline: "Glanz Wins Senate Seat with Strong Wall Street Backing." With the election, Cataldo must have felt Lionel slip from his grasp. It would be nearly impossible for a small-town cop to pursue charges against a Washington politician. Is that the reason Cataldo resented Lionel? For his wealth and power—his evident success? Or was there more?

She opens the next section in the file. This one also contains clippings from *The Marby Village Voice*, but all of them are about Sasha. "Glanz Heir Missing," reads the first one. "Kidnapping Suspected," says the second. Then: "Foreign Girl Brought in for Questioning." Poor Charley! Claire's heart goes out to him. She knows how he suffered. By the third day the *Voice* was reporting: "FBI to Join Forces with Local Police in Search of Missing Child." Then came: "Tragic Drowning: Body of Glanz Boy Found." The final article appeared roughly a week later. Cataldo cut all of the other pieces neatly from the newspaper with scissors, but this one has been roughly torn out as if in fury: "Death of Glanz Heir Ruled Accident."

Claire reads through each of these articles with care,

350

searching for anything she might have overlooked, might not have known. She's not surprised to learn the FBI was called in on the case. Lionel was a national figure. The disappearance of his son would very well merit federal attention. Otherwise the *Voice* tells her nothing new. The story is just as Charley said it was. Disappeared. Falsely presumed kidnapped. Found drowned. Judged an accident.

The third section in the Glanz file consists of a single sheet of Marby Police Force stationary. It's Cataldo's report of his interview with Véronique. He must have suspected her from the start. He brought her in for questioning the very next day after the boy disappeared. The report is neatly typed. It's also cut short. Just past the French girl's name and country of origin comes: "Suspect silenced on advice of counsel." Lionel's counsel, Cataldo means. Then: "Released without charge." Scrawled at the bottom of the page is a single word: "Deported." Claire can almost feel Cataldo's anger in the dark, clipped strokes of his handwriting as his primary suspect escaped his grasp.

The last section in the file contains pages from a notebook, small enough to be easily secreted in a pocket. The pages are covered in Cataldo's familiar script, sprawling haphazardly, as if jotted furtively by a man who didn't want to be seen. Cataldo must have taken the notes when he was at the Glanz household, assigned to the detail waiting for the ransom call that never came. He wasn't happy when the agents from the FBI arrived. Apparently they wanted the local police removed from the case, but Cataldo managed to keep to his post. He interviewed everyone he could in the Glanz household, ascertaining who was home on the day of the boy's disappearance, where they were, and what they might have seen.

"Isabel Branca," reads the first note. "Maid. Ironing. Upstairs. No view of water."

"Beatrice Chase," reads the second note. "Secretary. In office. On phone. Heard babysitter talking to boyfriend. No view of Sound."

Claire startles at the next note. "Elena Sauer. Cook." Mrs. Sauer? Claire remembers her well, a pudgy, awkward woman with wiry red hair faded to grey. Sauer was devoted to Frieda, excessively so, according to Hettie, who said the cook had feelings for Frieda—romantic feelings, she meant. The cook remained loyal to her mistress for years and years, following Frieda from New York to Bethesda then back to New York again. She also despised Lionel with a passion. Everyone knew that, even, Claire suspects, Frieda. Still she kept her on until the day Sauer died. Frieda, who hardly ever showed emotion, wept openly at the funeral of her cook. Cataldo makes no note of Sauer's affections. But he does make it clear that she saw nothing the day Sasha disappeared. "Cook in the kitchen, preparing dinner. Kitchen has window overlooking the water. Boxwoods too thick to see through."

Claire can well imagine it. She has seen those boxwoods herself.

That left the girls. Anna and Hettie. No one else, according to Cataldo's notes, was home that day. He got to Anna first. "Older daughter refuses to answer," reads the note in the file. What did Cataldo mean by that? He doesn't say, but Claire is beginning to know how he thinks. She imagines the detective's thoughts turning. What was Anna hiding? Even more important: *Whom* was she hiding?

All at once her aunt's words come back to her. I did terrible things, Hettie said. I have my regrets. Even Sasha.

Did Cataldo suspect Hettie in Sasha's death? Did Lionel? Did he fear what Véronique knew—what she might say? Is that the reason he had her silenced—and deported? What of Anna? Did she, too, believe Hettie was guilty of Sasha's death? Did Anna see Hettie lift the boy onto the sea wall? Someone, Charley insisted, had to have done it. Anna loved her sister. She would never do anything to harm Hettie. No wonder Anna stopped speaking. The conflict over confessing Hettie's guilt would have been more than she could bear.

Cataldo never got to question Hettie. Frieda must have seen him talking to Anna and swept the girls away. "Girls taken upstairs," reads the note in his file. "Mother refuses to cooperate." He must have suspected Frieda of covering up Sasha's death, too. If so, he never got the chance to ask her. He never even came close to Lionel. "Lawyer shuts down Glanz interviews."

Claire sits back, presses her fingers to her temples. Outside sleet scratches at the door. She draws the blankets closer. She can't deny what she's read. Joey Cataldo was convinced Sasha's death wasn't an accident. He thought the family closed ranks to protect one of their own. Everything pointed to Hettie, but he couldn't prove it. That doesn't mean it isn't true.

Maybe it's better not to know, Hettie said.

She shuts the file. What is she supposed to do now? Confront Hettie? Speak to Anna? Anna at least is dying. The truth may not matter very long to her, but Claire will have to live with it for a long, long time.

She stands up, throws the blankets to the floor, shakes a tablet of Xynolith out of her purse and carries it to the bathroom. There is the wolf, waiting for her, lightly panting. Why take only one, the wolf says with a friendly smirk, when the whole bottle would be so much better? Claire squeezes her eyes shut. Grimmsley, she thinks. When she opens her eyes, the wolf is gone.

She swallows the pill with water from the tap. She should have listened to Roger. He told her not to do this. He told her to stay home. But home, she remembers, is the one place she couldn't bear to be.

As she returns to the bedroom, she notices a piece of paper on the floor. It must have fallen out of the file. A business card. One of Cataldo's, no doubt, or Lionel's. Maybe Lionel's lawyer. She bends over, picks it up.

Gustav Thaler, M.D.

The Phipps Psychiatric Clinic

The Johns Hopkins Hospital

Baltimore, Maryland

Thaler, Thaler, Thaler. She speaks the name out loud, wrapping her tongue around the syllables, the soft, aspirant "th."

No. Not like that. Gustav is German. The "h" would be silent. Like "Taller."

Dr. Taller, Hettie said. Maybe that's just what I called him. He was tall.

Claire runs her fingers across the card.

Not everything's the way you think it is, Hettie said.

She opens her purse, takes out Hettie's scarf, runs it thoughtfully through her fingers. Claire has been seeing the past through Joey Cataldo's eyes. But Cataldo hated her

grandfather. From the detective's point of view, anything—
everything—Lionel did would be reason for suspicion. But
Hettie's right. There's another way.

What was it Hettie said about Anna? She shut down
completely. She wouldn't even talk to me.

Anna didn't refuse to speak to Cataldo because she was
hiding something. She simply couldn't. She was incapable
of speech. The realization makes Claire laugh out loud.
And Frieda? She wasn't hiding anything either. She took
the girls away from Cataldo to protect them. What mother
wouldn't want to spare her children the trauma of a police
interrogation? As for Lionel: of course he had Véronique
deported. It was a fit of well-deserved fury.

Claire sits on the bed. She's no closer to the truth than
she was before. Something about Sasha's death traumatized
Anna, something that haunts her even now as she lies
dying. But if Anna doesn't know what it is, how is Claire
supposed to find out?

She looks back at Thaler's card. How did it end up in
Cataldo's file? Did Thaler speak to Cataldo when he brought
Anna home from the hospital? Claire sucks in her breath.
He must have. He was doing the same thing she's doing
now: trying to find out what happened when Sasha died.
Once again she laughs. It's absurd, and yet it's true. She isn't
forging a new path; she's walking on one that has been very
well carved out.

Outside the wind gusts, and sleet slices to the ground.
Thaler. Baltimore. Claire tucks the card into her purse. If
anyone knew what was in Anna's mind, surely it would
be her psychiatrist. Fifty years was fifty years, but was it
possible? Could there be any trace of Dr. Thaler left?

355

Twenty-Five

GUS

*T*he rain begins just as Gus reaches Marby, a light spatter on the road that quickly turns into a deluge. Water sluices down the windshield of the car, turning the landscape into a watery scrim of darkness, layers of black on black. He drives south through the village as Beatrice has instructed him, past the police station, where light wavers in the window, a shadowy figure visible behind the duty desk, snoozing with feet up. Was it really only two days ago that Gus spoke to Joey Cataldo, that he almost—just almost— set his sights on Baltimore? How much has happened since then. He might as well be a visitor from an alien world.

Lionel. The wolf. Gus drives past the diner, bearing his dreadful burden. What will Beatrice think when she hears what he has to say—if he can bring himself to say it? Her livelihood is at stake, after all. Will she still be willing to work for the Glanzes once she knows what he knows? No matter. He will have to tell her. Abuse is most monstrous when it's hidden, and it's his job, whether he will or not, to slay monsters. That means bringing them into the light.

He skirts the shore road, crosses the river, and turns away from the Sound. Western Marby has an industrial air: mills, car repair shops, a bread factory, a bottling plant. A brown fog of light leaks from the windows of a bar. Just past a laundry he turns onto a narrow road that curves back to the east. He keeps an eye out for a cottage with an iron gate and dark green shutters, stops the car, gathers his bag, and steps outside.

He's near the river. He can't see it but he can feel it, a deepening pressure in the night. He hears the murmur of the current, the splash of rain on the surface, the peeping of frogs. The air has a liquid, mossy scent. The gate to the cottage garden opens with a groan. He dashes past a dripping birdbath to a covered porch where a Japanese lantern is alight. It's almost midnight. He hesitates to knock. He knows Beatrice is expecting him; still, he hates to disturb the household so late. As he wavers, the door springs open. "Gus." Beatrice is smiling. Then she is in his arms.

Never before, Gus thinks, has he been so happy.

He's sitting beside Beatrice on a sofa, waiting for her mother—"Evelyn," she said as he came in, "I insist"—who has gone into the kitchen to make tea. He's brimming with happiness, positively dumb with it. He can think of nothing to say. His face is flushed—*Carrot Top*—and for once he doesn't even mind. He's holding tight to Beatrice's hand. She has let him. She looks down shyly, her face warm, too. She's dressed in a simple pair of slacks and a blouse; her feet are bare. Her scent is in the air, bright and summery, as rich as the rain pattering on the roof.

Evelyn returns with tea and a plate of sandwiches. She's half a head smaller than Beatrice, trim with silvery hair pulled into a bun at the top of her head. She's wearing a navy shirtwaist dress, a sweater thrown over her shoulders. Her eyes, as she hands Gus his cup, are mischievous and warm. Take a good look at a woman's mother before you marry her, his father once advised him. That way you'll know what you're getting yourself into. If Beatrice ends up like her mother, Gus thinks, he will be just fine with that.

The front room of the house is cozy and warm. Off to the side is the bedroom where Beatrice has put Gus's bag. Ordinarily, he gathers, it belongs to her brother, but he's in the Navy, sailing the China Sea; a pin stuck in a map on the wall marks the spot. In the corner, light spills from another Japanese lantern. Both lanterns, Evelyn explains, will remain lit as long as her son is at sea. Bookshelves hold souvenirs from around the world: ivory elephant tusks, twined baskets, carved wooden masks. Dolls with exotic faces gaze out at Gus with placid eyes.

"They belong to Beatrice," Evelyn says. "Her father brought them home for her, one for each port. He began collecting them before she was even born." She smiles at Beatrice. "He always knew we'd have a daughter."

Mr. Chase was in the Merchant Marine. He died in the summer of 1940 on a cargo ship in the North Atlantic, victim of a U-boat attack. "The war before the war," Evelyn says. Her son joined the Navy soon after. He was only seventeen. "I didn't want him to go, but he said his dad would have been proud."

Beatrice was meant to go to college. "Smart as a whip," Evelyn says with pride as Beatrice colors. "I told her to do it. I said I would make it work." But Beatrice had other ideas. With her father and brother gone, she insisted on helping to support her mother. She graduated high school, took a year of secretarial school, then found work as a bookkeeper in a local pipe-fitting factory. All day long she sat in an airless

358

office, the room vibrating with machine noise. When she came home at night, her head felt as if it was vibrating, too. Then one day she saw an ad in *The Marby Village Voice* from an artist on the point seeking secretarial help. Two days later she sat for an interview with Frieda Glanz.

"She impressed me," Beatrice says to Gus with a sideways glance. "I thought she was demanding as an employer, but fair. She opened up an entire new world to me. New York City, galleries, museums. I admired her." This last is said with an air of defensiveness. "She made me feel as if I was making a difference."

"Beatrice works too hard," Evelyn says, frowning at her daughter. "She always has. She doesn't get out enough. She doesn't have fun." She gives Gus a meaningful look.

"Mother," Beatrice says, her color deepening. "Please." She draws her lower lip between her teeth in a charming pout, and it's all Gus can do to keep from kissing her.

He smiles. "Maybe we can change that."

Evelyn has finally been persuaded to go to bed. Gus and Beatrice leave the house to take a walk, following a path down to the river. The rain has finally stopped, and wind whips the sky clear. The moon is luminous, an orange half-disk. The river is wide, still retaining some of its wildness. As they walk along it, Gus talks freely to Beatrice, pouring out his heart, telling her about his decision to become a doctor, about Rosa, her long illness and painful suffering. He's never confessed so much to anyone, but he's glad to do it. It feels right. He slips his arm around her shoulders, drawing her close. Then he turns to her and gives into the urge to kiss her.

She leans into the kiss then stands back. "Gus."

"Yes, I know." He takes her hand. "We need to talk."

He leads her to a grassy knoll beneath an overhanging rock. They sit down, and Beatrice tucks her feet beneath her, her hands in her lap, waiting for him to speak. How to begin—how to tell a story that, as far as he can tell, has no beginning, whose origins lie deep in the mists of the past? He decides simply to jump in, to start with Detective Cataldo, and let the story unspool from there.

"The girls shoplifted," he says. "Anna and Hettie. Did you know that?"

"Shoplifted?" Beatrice looks surprised. "I know they brought things home in their school bags—candy, ribbons, little things like that—but I always thought their father gave them money for that."

"They were going to be expelled. That's the real reason Frieda took them out of school. They were causing trouble. Anna tormented a girl in Hettie's class."

"I know about that," Beatrice says with a frown. Her voice grows indignant. "That girl was hurting Hettie. She came home with bruises. Anna stood up for her sister. I'm not saying it's right, but the school did nothing to prevent it. Anna will always protect Hettie. The girls are very close."

"They burned down the gazebo. They did it on purpose."

Her frown deepens. "No one ever proved that."

"Then why did Lionel give the village a new fire engine?"

"They needed that! The old one was in shambles. They were grateful for it. Mr. Glanz is generous. He cares about this place. That's why he's running for Senate. He wants to be of service."

The conversation isn't going at all the way Gus expected.

He thought Beatrice was his ally. Was he wrong about that? Does she need her job so badly? Has her attachment to the Glanzes blinded her to the truth? If she doesn't believe what he says about the shoplifting and the fire, what will she think when he tells her the rest of the story?

"I know the Glanzes aren't perfect parents," Beatrice says, relenting, but she is avoiding his eye and has pulled away, setting a distance between them. "Mrs. Glanz doesn't always pay attention when she should, and Mr. Glanz is away so much. It's not his fault. It doesn't mean he doesn't love his daughters. He does."

"Yes," Gus says. "And his daughters love him, too. The question is what love means to them—what it has become."

He will simply have to tell her, flat out and direct. It's cruel, and it might mean the end of everything between them, but he has no choice. All at once she turns to him. The look on her face is enough to break his heart.

"You knew." The realization comes to him as a shock, but it's there, written plainly in her eyes, in her anguish, her guilt. "Isabel—the maid—she knew, too. That's why Frieda fired her. Not because she was jealous. Because Isabel found out." It's clear to him now. Why didn't he see it before? "You knew about Lionel and Anna. Did Isabel tell you?" He shakes his head. "It doesn't matter. You didn't *want* to know, but you did. That's why you wouldn't live in the house."

"Oh, Gus." She has tears in her eyes. "What have I done?"

He reaches out to her, and as she weeps, takes her in his arms. "Don't blame yourself. It's not your fault." He holds her close. "You wouldn't have been able to stop it."

361

She still won't look him in the eye. "Will you be able to help her?"

Will he? The net is widening, and more is on the line than just Anna. Gus lifts his chin. "I'm going to try."

Twenty-Six

CLAIRE

*C*laire wakes in the morning to sunlight glittering in the window. Overnight the sleet has turned to snow, leaving a sheet of white luminescence on the ground. The view is blindingly clear. She has no sunglasses. Who packs sunglasses in the winter? If they pack at all—which she didn't exactly do when she fled on the Amtrak from Judge Benson's courtroom. She squints as she pays the motel bill, holds a hand over her eyes as she dashes to her car. Cataldo's file is in the back seat. She may never look at it again, but she won't let it go. It is, she understands now, a part of who she is. A part of Hettie and Anna, too. Tucked in her purse, along with Hettie's scarf, is Gustav Thaler's card. She pulls down the sun visor and heads south on the highway.

The air has a sharp, knifelike feel, sun slicing through the freezing cold. Snow still lingers on the road, but she reaches Manhattan without incident, glides across the Bruckner Expressway (hello, Hettie, goodbye!) and slips across the George Washington Bridge. The view from the upper deck is stunning, fog rising from the Hudson, crystals of ice glistening in the light. She ought to slow down to take it all in but she won't. She isn't living in the past anymore or even in the present. Her mind is focused on the future, on *What if.* On *If only.* On Gustav Thaler. Fifty years is fifty years, but is it possible? Might he still be there?

Northern New Jersey has an acrid, chemical smell, factories and refineries chugging out clouds of steam. She floors the rental car on the turnpike, taking it to the limit, hoping she won't get a speeding ticket. Half an hour later the industrial parks ease up and so does she. She needs coffee, and pulls over at the Molly Pitcher rest stop. Who was Molly Pitcher? Her mind mulls over the question as she stands in line at the take-out counter. Someone she might have learned about in school if she'd only paid attention. Twenty minutes later she's back on the highway, the car motoring at seventy, the first cup of coffee gone, a second cup clutched in her fist.

She should call Roger. She should call Nathan, too. Nathan said they were keeping Anna comfortable. Claire knows the dying can only be kept comfortable for so long. What if she's too late? The thought jolts her. Then she calms herself down. There's no reason to call anyone yet. She has nothing to say. Maybe soon.

If only.

Temperatures rise as she crosses the Delaware Memorial Bridge, the freeze moderating. Snow melts to puddles on the side of the road, gives in to the sun, gives up the ghost. Mist rises like spirit breath on the fields. The woods are dripping and have a dense spring-like smell. By mid-morning she's reached the outskirts of Baltimore. She has no idea where the Johns Hopkins Hospital is, takes an exit at random and finds herself on a commercial road studded with strip malls, tire shops, junk yards. In time the neighborhood turns residential, block after block of row houses, each one fronted by gleaming white marble steps.

As repetitive as a needle stuck on a record. A city with an architectural fixation, an obsession, completely lacking in imagination. She needs gas. She pulls into a station, gets out, and as the tank fills asks the attendant for directions. It isn't until she sees the look on his face that she realizes where she is. The area is derelict and downtrodden, tiny plastic bags—detritus of the drug trade—drifting like milkweed in the gutters.

"John Hopkins?" The attendant pronounces the name without the initial "s." He gives her a look, shakes his head, crazy white lady, and points her farther south. She climbs chastened into her car, locks her doors and heads down the road.

Then she's there, or rather the hospital is, sitting on a hill, a red brick building from the Victorian era topped by a copper green dome, a pennant flying gaily like a flag. Johns Hopkins is not so much a single building as an accretion of edifices, the old mixed with the new, brick and glass towers rising over several city blocks like structures in a coral reef, linked by bridges like octopus arms. She drives around the complex once, then twice, then gets lucky and pulls into a parking spot just as someone else pulls out. A brick pathway leads her up the hill to the building with the dome. Over it sails the sky as blue as a sunlit sea. The sight disorients her, as if the world has been turned upside down and she is walking on the bottom of the ocean instead of on dry land. She climbs a flight of stairs to a doorway where people stream in and out and dodges to a desk where a guard greets her with a bored, placid face. "Where you going?"

"Phipps."

"Unh-huh." He straps a paper band to her wrist and

points straight ahead. "You just keep on."

You just keep on. It seems like good advice. Past the guard is a rotunda where a towering statue of Jesus holds court, his face turned down in decorous compassion, his marble foot offered for devotion, the big toe of his sandaled foot polished by generations of caresses, kisses, wishes, hopes, tears. The dome flies directly overhead, light drenched, a series of circular floors rising to it as if to heaven.

Past the rotunda the hospital constricts like an occluded artery into a dark, narrow hallway and then Claire is thrust again into the light, a warren of corridors populated by people who all know where they are going and are going there in a hurry: a blur of blue scrubs; long white coats; wheelchairs; strollers; men in suits. Hopkins is not so much a hospital as a city; no, not a city, a collection of villages, with residents traveling at top speed from one place to the next. She floats through the crowd and is thrown as if by a wave at the desk of another guard—Phipps? Unh-huh, hon, you just keep on—then glides past the cafeteria, the sour smell of boiled vegetables, to a desk where another guard sits—That's right, you keep on—and finally is thrust out of the hospital on the other side.

Is this a joke? She stands in the sunlight, buffeted by eddies of people going into the hospital, going out. In front of her runs a long circular drive, taxis and cars swimming up to discharge passengers, swimming away. An ambulance siren wails, growing louder by the moment. She's lost, confused, at sea. Did she remember to take her Xynolith this morning? Tears spring to her eyes. It's all too much, not just the drive this morning but everything leading up to it: her flight from Washington, Hettie's gentle ministrations,

Cataldo's suspicions, Sasha's drowning, Anna's impending death. She can't stop the tears, she's crying outside the Johns Hopkins Hospital like the fool she is. Gus Thaler? Phipps? What has she been thinking? Fifty years is fifty years.

"Lady?"

A very small child, thin and almost transparently pale, wearing a flowered headband on her bald head, looks up at her with anxious eyes.

"Are you all right?"

"Yes. Thank you." Claire wipes her eyes.

The child clings tightly to the hand of a man in a denim jacket. "Sorry." He gives Claire an apologetic smile. "She worries too much. Ever since she got sick, she worries about everyone. She thinks it's her job to comfort us."

The girl and her father sweep past her into the hospital, and when Claire raises her eyes, the Phipps Psychiatric Clinic floats into view.

$\mathcal{T}$wenty-$\mathcal{S}$even

. : .
. . *.
. *.

GUS

"*Gustav, bitte.*"

Gus is in Rosa's room. He's a little boy again—the nine-year-old boy who is watching his sister die—standing at the foot of her bed, terrified and helpless in the face of her suffering. In his hand is the brown bottle of pain medicine.

Gustav, please.

It's time for one of her doses. His parents must have sent him to the kitchen to fetch the bottle. But they aren't there. Where have they gone? Why have they left him and Rosa alone?

"*Gustavchen.*" It's her pet name for him: Little Gus. "*Bitte.*" Please.

The leukemia has made her so thin as to almost be skeletal. Beneath her skin blue bruises bloom. Her body contorts with pain, a sheen of sweat on her face. She bites her lip to keep from crying out. Then she smiles at him—smiles at the bottle. "*Gustav.*" He pulls the dropper from the bottle, and she opens her mouth like a little bird to receive it. "*Danke.*"

Thank you.

A rapping at the door wakes him from the dream. "Gus," Evelyn says on the other side. "Beatrice called. It's time."

They made the plan the night before. Beatrice would

368

drive to the Glanzes' house early in the morning, keeping to her usual routine. Once Lionel and Frieda left for the city, she would call Gus, and he would come over to hypnotize Anna.

"Coming." He stands up, feeling groggy, exhausted. He's overslept. He had trouble sleeping last night, riddled with anxiety over what this day might bring. Even his usual self-hypnosis was no help. He doesn't remember falling asleep at all—only the dream, which lingers with him as he hastily dresses. He decides to take it as a good sign. Today he will deliver relief to Anna for her suffering, just as he delivered relief to Rosa in the dream. The brown bottle is the symbol.

He turns down Evelyn's offer for breakfast—there's no time, even if he had the stomach for it—gulps down a cup of coffee, and says his farewells.

"Don't be a stranger," Evelyn says as she sees him to the door. "Come back soon."

"I will." He smiles. Of all the promises he's made since he left Baltimore, this is one he's most sure he will keep.

Twenty minutes later Beatrice greets him at the Glanzes' door. "Anna still doesn't know about Spring Meadow," she says. The anxiety is plain on her face. "I heard Mrs. Glanz talking to her this morning. She and Mr. Glanz have taken Hettie into the city with them. Hettie is to be fitted for her school uniform. Mrs. Glanz told Anna she would have her uniform fitted another time."

Just like Frieda to be deceptive to the end, Gus thinks, fuming. Still, he isn't sorry to hear Hettie's gone. He knows how much trouble she can be. As for Lionel—Gus imagines himself grabbing the man by the collar, throttling his throat, his fist connecting with his chin. It's a silly schoolboy fantasy, and he would never carry it out—would he? It's just as well he won't have the chance to find out.

"Where's Anna?"

"In her room. Shall I fetch her for you?"

Gus nods, and as Beatrice disappears upstairs, goes into the library to wait. The room is unchanged since his last hypnosis session with Anna. The armchair still sits by the couch, angled to the side, just as he left it; the drapes are still drawn. Was it really only two days ago that he believed Sasha was the source of Anna's trauma? So much has changed since then. He has been so wrong about Anna— he has been wrong about everything. Now he finally has the chance to make things right. If she will let him. He is painfully aware that he has no control over her. If she refuses to cooperate, there is nothing he can do. He can't force her. He's too tense to sit. He walks from one end of the room to the other, ending up at the French doors. The last time he was here, he felt a need for darkness and seclusion. Now he craves the light. He pulls open the drapes, and then for good measure throws open the doors.

When he turns around, she is there.

"Anna."

She stands in the doorway, dressed in her sailor shirt and navy slacks. Her hair is in a ponytail; she has flats on her feet. At the sound of his voice she frowns, her eyes skewing to the side.

"We need to talk." He takes a step towards her then stops when he sees her body tense. "Please. I understand if you're angry at me. I shouldn't have left you. I'm sorry I did. More sorry than I can tell you. But I learned . . . some things while I was away. I think I can help you now. I'd like you to let me try."

She still hasn't met his eye. Her frown deepens, and she fiddles with the collar of her shirt with a sullen air.

"I know I haven't been much use to you." Of all the things he's said to her, this must be the truest. "I was hoping you would give me one more chance."

He holds his breath. She twists around, looking behind her. She's going to leave, he thinks. She's going to walk away, and there's nothing I can do about it. "Anna—" he says again. He doesn't want to beg, but he can't stop himself. "Please."

For a moment longer she stands with her back to him, then slowly she turns around. Eyes downcast, she steps into the room and comes towards him: the penitent girl, being good, being oh-so-very good. Being obedient. Lionel has drilled it into her. I told her to be good, he said, when Anna bit into the apple. I told her I expected it from her. The pathology has been her downfall; but maybe now it will be her salvation, too.

"Thank you, Anna." Gus breathes out with a smile. He waits until she arranges herself on the couch, then he walks to the armchair and sits down.

A flock of yellow birds has taken up residence in the copper beech trees. Out of the corner of his eye Gus can see them, a blot of color against the bronze leaves. Through the open doors comes the scent of the roses, dizzyingly thick. Anna must have been outside earlier this morning. He can smell the sun on her skin, a touch of salt and sweat. He remembers how she acted when they came to Marby—how she smiled at him, tugging at her skirt, how she revealed the strap of her bra. He remembers how he responded, too, reaching out

371

and touching her hair as she lay in a trance on the couch beside him. These gestures, he understands now, were not meaningless. They were a language between them: Anna's attempt to communicate to him what she could not say.

He sits up, clears his throat, modulates his voice so that it is soft and calm, trying to still the excitement rising in him. "Very good, Anna. Let's begin."

Quite easily she falls into the trance; he turns in the chair to be sure. She looks relaxed and peaceful, her hands resting easily at her sides. How will he handle her during this session—how will he handle himself? The question has been gnawing at him since he left Riverport. He needs to get Anna back into Lionel's bedroom. He doesn't want to; like Frieda, he doesn't want to see what's on the other side of that door. But he must. He must look hard and unflinching, with courage, a steely spine. He must absorb what he sees and bear it. This, he understands, is what it means to be a doctor: to look when other people turn away, to take on another person's suffering and make it your own.

Of all the sessions he has held with Anna, this one will be the most difficult, the most risky. His goal is to take her back to the source of her trauma. He remembers how van der Ploeg hypnotized his veterans, returning them in their imaginations to the battlefield, a gentle exercise in guided imagery. He will lead her carefully by suggestion. He will go slowly. As much as possible, he will follow her lead.

He begins by re-establishing their signals, raising the right hand to indicate "yes," the left hand to convey distress. She demonstrates both for him so that he's sure she understands. "Good." He takes a breath. "Now I want you to go somewhere. I will go with you. I'll be at your side.

No matter what, I'll keep you safe."

Her right hand flutters and is still.

"You're at home with your father. You're standing outside his room. He opens the door and you go inside with him. Imagine yourself there. Imagine us going in together."

Bit by bit he walks her through it. She doesn't speak but with the use of their codes confirms what he suspected. The abuse began, he understands now, out of love, just as Irina said: Lionel's clumsy attempt to spare Anna from Frieda's punishments. When did comforting Anna cross the line into something else, something hurtful and damaging? For a man like Lionel, raised with no boundaries of his own, that line must have been impossible to discern.

Gus feels ill as the story unfolds, his stomach turning, but he holds himself to it, without faltering, sitting supremely still, barely breathing. Anna handles the session well. She doesn't speak, but she shows no sign of distress. Not once does the left hand flutter.

"It's not your fault, Anna," he says. "You aren't responsible for things adults do—for things parents do. It won't happen again." It won't, he thinks. He will make sure of it. He will speak to Lionel himself—and Frieda. They will know their secret is out. One misstep and . . . well, Gus doesn't know what he'll do. But he'll do something. He can start with the police and go from there to the papers. Let the senator-to-be think about that. "You can stop punishing yourself. You don't need to be afraid anymore."

In the distance he hears the phone ringing, then Beatrice's voice, low and urgent, answering. She must be in her office. The session has exhausted him. He leans back and closes his eyes. Then he sits up and brings Anna out of her trance.

"Well, Anna?" He smiles at her. "How do you feel?"

She sits up blinking, her eyes blank as they always are when she comes out of a trance. She looks about her with an air of incomprehension, then gradually, as she comes back to herself, her face changes. Her eyes narrow, and her mouth turns down in a frown, angry and pinched. Briefly she glares at him, then she stands up and stalks from the room.

"Anna." He sits in his chair, stunned. "Wait." What is she—what has just happened? He dashes after her, catching her in the hall, taking her by the arm. "What's wrong? Tell me." Tell me anything, he wants to say. *"Anna, speak."*

He's never seen such hostility in her before. Her body has grown rigid with it, her face full of hate. He's discovered her secret—yes—but she isn't happy about that. She's furious. She wrenches herself free and runs upstairs.

"Gus." At the sound of his voice, Beatrice emerges from her office and comes towards him with an air of alarm. "Mrs. Glanz just called. They aren't coming home tonight after all. They're staying in the city. The plans for Spring Meadow have been moved up. The attendants are coming for Anna in the morning." She tilts her head towards the stairs. "Is she—?"

He shakes his head. Frieda's a coward, he thinks, seething. She doesn't want to be here when Anna is taken away. Then, more charitably: she wants to spare Hettie.

"I'm to pack a travel bag for Anna. A trunk with the rest of her clothes will be sent later." Beatrice raises her hands helplessly, not knowing what to do.

"Go on," Gus says, rather short and unfeeling. "Do what you have to."

She gives him a last, questioning look then vanishes up the stairs. A moment later he hears her calling to Mrs. Arturo. From Anna comes nothing at all. Gus stands at the bottom of the stairs, his hands clenched at his sides. Why won't she speak? It doesn't make sense. None of it does. Her secret is out. He knows what she knows. She doesn't need to remain silent anymore, because she has nothing left to hide. He's brought the monster into the light. He's slain the dragon. There's no reason left for her silence, no reason for any of this. No reason—

Unless—

It's the only possibility left. Anna's silence isn't a symptom; it's a game. What else can it be? A perverse game, and she's been playing it from the start. Playing *him*. She isn't really mute; she's simply throwing a tantrum of the worst kind, a vile act of manipulation. Gus chews on the idea, the anger in him rising. He's been made a fool of. Well, he knows how to fix that.

He takes the steps two at a time and marches down the hallway. "Anna." She's in her room, standing by the window. Startled, she turns to him, growing pale when she sees the look on his face. "Your mother is sending you away. You're going to Spring Meadow. It's a hospital for children. It's not like Phipps, I can promise you that. You won't like it, and you won't have doctors like me. They won't care if you don't speak, and they won't care if you don't eat, either. They have ways of making you. Your father can't stop it. He can't rescue you this time. Your mother's made up her mind. She's made him choose between herself and you."

Lionel will be senator, Gus thinks, fulfilling Dora's exhortation to greatness. But he can't be senator if his wife divorces him, the scandal making headlines in the daily papers. Anna knows it. She blanches. For the first time since he brought her home, Gus sees fear in her eyes.

"If this has all been a hoax, if you really can talk, now is the time to do it."

Panic rises on her face. She looks as if she will be sick. Her hands fly to her mouth, clawing at her lips. Her mouth opens in a sustained, silent scream. The sight is chilling, horrifying. Involuntarily Gus takes a step back. Then she runs to the door and slams it shut.

"Anna." He knocks on the door. "Open the door." He rattles the knob. It's locked. She must have gotten hold of the key. "Anna, listen to me—"

"Gus? Is everything all right?" Beatrice appears at the far end of the hall, followed by Mrs. Arturo, carrying a suitcase. "Is Anna—?"

"She's in her room. She locked herself in."

"Anna?" Beatrice knocks on the door. "Are you all right?"

Mrs. Arturo drops the suitcase, gives Gus a look. What is he doing here?

Beatrice knocks on the door again, her voice rising in alarm. "Open the door, Anna, please—"

"Anna!" Mrs. Arturo shouts. She turns to Gus, hisses, "Go." She pushes him aside, joins Beatrice at the door, knocking. "Anna. You must open. Listen to me. The door—"

Gus steps back. He's no help here. He never has been. He backs down the hall, goes downstairs, flees outside to the terrace. Stupid, stupid, stupid. He hits his head with the flat of his palms. Not willful. Not a game. Then what?

Yesterday's storm has returned, and clouds darken the horizon, spilling shadows onto the Sound. Wind whips through the copper beeches, bringing the moldering scent of dying leaves into the air. Think, Gus, think. He walks the terrace from one end to the other, pacing, pacing. What did Frieda say? Anna stopped speaking in the winter. Frieda thought it was normal, hormones and all that. She meant Anna got her period. Anna got her period, and so Lionel stopped taking her with him behind closed doors. He wouldn't want her, now that she wasn't a child anymore. Instead he turned his attention to Hettie. Gus sees Anna at the bottom of the terrace steps, biting into the apple, delighted to be back in her father's arms. Then he sees Lionel pull Hettie onto his lap at dinner and hears Frieda laugh nervously, saying, She's too old for that, while Anna throws her sister a murderous look.

Anna isn't angry because the abuse happened. She's angry because it stopped. She stopped talking in the winter on purpose, as an expression of her fury; silence had been her weapon of choice before. But then something happened and the silence mutated, becoming malignant, beyond her control. Something happened—yes—but what?

Sasha's death.

Gus has come back to that again. But how? Why? He's been over every inch of it before, more times than he can count. Anna wasn't responsible for Sasha's death. She wasn't even there when he tumbled from the wall. She was in her room. Beatrice has confirmed it. Anna didn't even see him fall. Losing a brother is terrible, yes, and certainly tragic. But where is the trauma great enough to render her mute? Gus is missing something, but what?

As he paces, the storm breaks, and rain falls, darkening the terrace steps, peppering the sea wall. He goes inside and stands in the sunroom, watching the rain. Through the scrim of water his dream comes back to him again, and he sees himself at the foot of Rosa's bed, the bottle of pain medicine in his hand. Morphine. He didn't know it then, but that's what the medicine was. He knows about morphine now. He's seen it used in the hospital many times, the drops put under the patient's tongue to assuage the pain, to ease the passage from life into death.

Evelyn's knock wrenched him from the dream before it had a chance to end. Something was about to happen. What? *Gustav, bitte.* He thinks of Anna's suffering, thinks of Rosa's suffering. Meyer said it was a mistake to conflate the two, but what if he was wrong? What if the answer lies not in keeping Rosa and Anna apart but in putting them together?

Gus closes his eyes, standing utterly still, lost in thought. Then he strides into the hall and goes upstairs, moving at a rapid and deliberate pace. Beatrice and Mrs. Arturo are still outside Anna's room, pleading with her to open the door.

Mrs. Arturo shoots him a furious look, but he ignores that. "Beatrice."

Beatrice glares at him, angry now, too. What has he done? It can't be helped. He doesn't have time to explain. "I need you."

Beatrice and Gus are in the library. He has explained to her what he intends to do. It isn't difficult. He doesn't need much from her. He's adept at self-hypnosis, at putting himself into a trance. He needs her as a witness, to register what he says, to prompt him if he stumbles, to pull him back at the end if he has trouble returning. "I want to go back to a dream I had last night. I need to see where it takes me."

He arranges himself on the couch just as Anna did a few minutes earlier. Beatrice sits in the armchair beside him, her face pale, a worried look in her eyes. He takes her hand, smiling. "Don't worry. Nothing bad will happen. I promise you." Then he settles himself, closes his eyes, breathes deeply, and begins to count.

"*Gustav, bitte.*"

He's home again, standing at the foot of Rosa's bed. It's the dead of night. He's been pulled from his bed, drawn downstairs by the sound of Rosa's cries. Across the hall his mother and father slumber in their room, exhausted with worry, leaving him and Rosa alone.

"*Gustav, bitte.*"

Gustav, please.

Light from the streetlamp leaks through the window, casting a greenish glow on her face. Her eyes skew from one side to the other, a blue vein pulsing in her forehead. Her hands, her beautiful, musical hands claw at the bedclothes. Her breath is shallow and ragged. Outside, in an act of cruel mockery, spring has arrived. Crocuses emerge from the wintry soil in his mother's garden; the forsythia burst with a yellow hue. But here in Rosa's room, the air is close and stifling. From her body rises the dark odor of decay.

"*Gustavchen.*" She manages to smile as she says the word, light coming briefly into her eyes. Once again they are mischievous compatriots, sneaking down the back stairs without their parents' knowledge, running out of the house to snitch free rides on the streetcar, to steal apples from the grocer's cart, to buy tickets for the moving pictures with pennies they are supposed to be saving for music books.

"*Bitte.*"

Then her face grimaces, and the light dies.

He knows what she wants. He leaves the room, takes the stairs down to the kitchen. The drops are kept on a shelf too high to reach. He pulls over a stool, climbs up, gets the bottle, brings it upstairs. When he returns, Rosa is rigid with pain, her muscles in spasms. Still she manages a thin smile when she sees him—when she sees the bottle. "*Gustavchen.*" As he pulls the dropper from the bottle, she opens her mouth like a little bird, her hair tangled and matted on the pillow like a dark nest. He puts the drops under her tongue just as he's seen his parents do so many times.

"*Danke.*" Rosa shudders and sighs, smiling at him as the medicine takes hold. Such a sweet, loving smile. He gives her another dose, and she takes it, murmuring something he doesn't understand, then he gives her another, three, four, as many as she wants, she is so grateful as she takes each one, she looks at him with such happiness. He is making Rosa happy! He feels happy, too.

"*Danke, Gustav, Du bist ein guter Junge.*"

Thank you, Gus, you are a good boy.

"*Tut es Dir noch Weh?*"

Does it still hurt?

They are whispering so as not to wake anyone.

"*Nein.*" She smiles at him in gratitude. "*Nicht mehr.*"

No. Not anymore.

When he leaves the room, she's sleeping so peacefully, he can hardly see her breathe. Her face is relaxed, still smiling. There's a lightness to her now, an air of release, as if she has become weightless and is floating high above the bed in the air. He puts the bottle back on the shelf and returns the stool to its place. In his attic bed, as the deep, flowing silence of the house rises around him, he falls into a dreamless sleep. He is still sleeping peacefully when dawn comes, and he wakens to the anguished sound of his mother's wails.

Gus is weeping, tears running freely down his face. "I killed her."

"Gus, no, you mustn't say that. Don't think that way." Beatrice sits on the couch beside him and takes him in her arms.

"It's true. I killed her. She died because of me."

"You helped her. You did what she wanted. You stopped her suffering. You eased her pain."

"She overdosed on the morphine I gave her. Afterwards Mother and Father—their grief—they were inconsolable. They didn't get a chance to say goodbye to her properly. I took that away from them. And I couldn't tell anyone." Even now the guilt burns in him, the piercing weight of the truth he has kept hidden for so many years.

"Shh. Don't."

He cries in Beatrice's arms until he's cried himself out. He hasn't been able to mourn Rosa fully before. He understands that now, just as he understands he will be mourning her for a long time to come. But all that will have wait. Upstairs is a girl who still needs him, a girl who's been made prisoner by her own silence. Meyer was right: children are capable of acting as judge, jury—and executioner, too. Gus is living proof of that. He finally knows what happened to Anna. The answer was in him all along.

Beatrice hands him her handkerchief, and he uses it to

wipe his eyes. A handkerchief! It feels like a miracle. He smiles. If nothing else, he will marry this woman for that. He tucks the handkerchief in his pocket and takes her face in his hands. "Thank you." He kisses her gently. "I'm going to Anna now."

Twenty-Eight

CLAIRE

*P*hipps must be one of the oldest structures in the Hopkins reef. Like the building with the dome, it's made of red brick in a Victorian style. Five stories rise in a solemn fashion to a steeply pitched roof topped by corner cupolas. Altogether, the clinic breathes an air of somber, quiet discretion. Bureaucratic functionalism. Anonymity. Not quite a prison and not quite a castle either—although the earth is dug out deeply around the foundation like a moat. To keep visitors out or inmates in? A cross between a church and a town hall: a place to worship or get your parking ticket validated. To legions of people, it must have presented a reassuring sight. You could disappear inside. You would be treated in the utmost privacy. No one would ever know.

Today no one is going in or out of the Phipps Clinic. Beneath an awning of iron and glass the entranceway stands empty. Nearby the hospital laundry bellows forth clouds of starch-scented steam. As Claire approaches the door, a frisson runs through her. Once her mother crossed this very same threshold. As she grasps the handle, slick with cold, she shrinks back: Anna's touch.

Just past the doorway is a foyer with yet another desk for a hospital guard, this time unmanned. The entire clinic looks abandoned. On either side empty corridors disappear into darkness. Where is everyone? The quiet unsettles her. Shouldn't there be someone, anyone, at least one person, crazy or sane? The air smells incongruously like a bookbindery, of wax and paper.

Straight ahead lies a lobby filled with light. She wanders into it. Marble floors, Greek columns, golden chandeliers, fireplaces topped by gilded mirrors. The feeling is of an elegant pre-war European hotel ministering to the very, very rich. She half expects a tuxedoed attendant to appear with a silver tray and a linen napkin folded over his arm. But there is no one.

Past the lobby a double set of doors leads to a courtyard. She steps outside into chilled, shadowy air. Flagstones lead around a pond, where flickers of red and gold reveal koi floating in the depths. She travels the path past sleeping rhododendron and azalea bushes, a weeping willow, a Japanese maple. The snow has been slower to melt here, has left an icy crust on the dark, fragrant earth. Dusky green vinca leaves poke through, bravely offering tiny purple blossoms. A columned portico surrounds her like a cloister.

Still no one. Her senses are bristling. Anna was here. Claire can feel it.

She walks back through the lobby to the desk where a guard, a woman with a round face and spiky blonde hair, now sits, regarding her with mild curiosity.

"Oh, thank goodness." How silly to feel so relieved to see a face. Claire smiles at her as if she were the last person on earth.

"Yes?"

"I need to find a doctor." She laughs, the sound trilling

384

on just a bit too long. "Not for me, of course, I mean, yes, for me, only not like that." Is it true you can be committed without your permission? Didn't a journalist once go undercover in a mental hospital and never come out? "I mean I'm looking for a psychiatrist." This isn't helping. She rummages through her purse, pulls out Thaler's card, places it on the desk, bites her lip, falls silent. The guard pulls it over, studies it.

"Not here."

"Not—what?" Claire feels a stab of anxiety. "How do you know? I mean, shouldn't you ask? Isn't there someone—?"

The guard swivels the card, pushes it back to her. "Like I said, not here. This place has been closed for years and years. No patients here, no doctors either. It's all offices now."

As if on cue, a man emerges from a door with a folder under his arm, glides across the corridor, disappears through another doorway.

"Then where—?" Where do you keep the lunatics, Claire wants to say, although of course she can't.

"They're all in Meyer now."

"Meyer?"

"Unh-huh. The Meyer Building. Like I said. You just go on."

The Meyer building at least is easy to find. Claire floats back into the main hospital, stops to ask yet another guard directions, then wades down a long corridor to the lobby of a modern red brick tower. A sign on the wall in large black letters reads MEYER. Nearby hangs the portrait of a man with a pointed beard, standing beside a tall filing cabinet, his hand resting on a model of the brain. Dr. Adolf Meyer says the title on the frame. Meyer's face is grim, and he looks out at Claire with a fearsome gaze as if to say: How much I know that you do not.

The lobby is understated, a place trying not to call attention to itself. Grey granite flooring, anonymous white walls, a bank of institutional elevators. Even the air smells unassuming, vaguely plastic, perhaps from chairs that line the walls like in an airport lounge. Doors lead in different directions. All of them closed. What next? Take an elevator to a random floor? Claire hits the call button but nothing happens. The elevators are operated by the swipe of a badge—which she doesn't have.

All at once she hears the murmur of voices. A woman wearing a dark skirt, with long grey hair pulled back in a ponytail, walks into the lobby, accompanied by a young man in a tie carrying a clipboard. Doctors? They don't have white coats, although both have hospital ID badges clipped to their pockets. The man swipes his, and the elevator hums to life.

"Excuse me."

The two turn to her.

"I'm looking for someone." Claire knows better this time than to try to explain. She simply holds out Thaler's card.

The man shakes his head. "Don't know him."

"Before your time," the woman says to him. She turns to Claire. "Dr. Thaler's gone now, I'm afraid. He retired about six years ago, passed away—" she pauses, thinking about it "—about three."

Claire quells the panic rising in her throat. "His records, then. Would you still have them?"

The man studies her with narrowed eyes. "We're not allowed to release private medical information."

"Of course not." Claire summons the remnants of her professional self and gives him her best, lawyerly smile. "I'm interested in a particular patient." She swallows hard. "My mother."

"One of Dr. Thaler's patients?" the woman says.

Claire nods.

"I see." She falls silent. "You'd need her permission."

"That's just it. I can't possibly get it. She's far away. And she's ill. Very ill."

The elevator comes—and goes. The man watches it depart with an annoyed air. "Can't do it." His fingers drum an impatient staccato on his clipboard.

"But I'm her daughter! She asked me specifically—"

He pulls himself up. "The law is very clear."

"And if she dies?"

He's about to answer when the woman puts a hand on his arm, quieting him. Then she turns to Claire, speaking softly. "You'd need permission from her closest relative."

"Exactly. So as her daughter—"

"Is she married?"

Yes, Claire wants to say, but only if you consider a third marriage valid, especially one that makes no sense and never should have taken place in the first place. "I just want—" What exactly is it that she wants? Suddenly she has no idea. She began this search for Anna. Since then it's become something else—something far more than that. More, she expects than she would ever be able to find in Dr. Thaler's records—if she could even find them. But what?

The woman gives Claire a moment to finish her answer, and when she doesn't, smiles at her in a regretful way. "I'm sorry we can't help you. He was a nice man, Dr. Thaler.

A very good doctor. Everyone loved him. I'm sure he took good care of your mother."

So this is the end. Dr. Meyer peers down at her as if to say, What did you think? Did you actually . . .? No, Claire thinks wearily, I didn't. Not really. She is so tired, fatigued to the bone. She slumps down in one of the airport-lounge chairs. Couldn't she just stay here, rest for a while? There's no place left for her to go. No place, that is, except home, and what then? What does she have to bring to Roger? To Nathan—to Anna—to any of them? Nothing has changed. Anna will be dead soon, and what will Claire do then?

The man swipes his badge again, and once more the elevator hums. A thoughtful look crosses his face. "Thaler." It's coming to him now. "I know that name. Doesn't his wife—"

"Yes." The woman nods. "On Mondays."

"Right. Thaler. Beatrice Thaler. She's one of the volunteers. She does crafts with the children."

"Beatrice?" Claire stands up. "Beatrice Thaler?"

"Do you know her?" the woman says.

In her mind she sees Cataldo's cramped handwriting: *Beatrice Chase. Secretary. In office. On phone.*

"Yes," Claire says. "I mean, no. Not yet." Was she wrong about Dr. Meyer? Is that the hint of a smile on his lips, a particle of hope in his eye? "But I will."

Twenty-Nine

GUS

"The door," Gus says to Anna. "Open it. Now."

He has sent Mrs. Arturo away, has sent Beatrice away, too. He has no need for women and their anxious begging and pleading. He stands outside Anna's door, his voice firm and in command. "Now, Anna. The door." There will be no more soothing gestures, no more reassuring words, no more gentle coaxing. He has been locked in a battle of wills with Anna from the day he met her, waging war. So far she's been winning. He needs to change the calculus. "I'm not asking you. I'm telling you. Open the door."

There's a moment of silence, then the last remnant of the penitent girl comes forward, and the key turns in the lock. He pushes the door open and steps into the room. Anna is backed against the wall, glaring at him. She's been busy since he last saw her. Her room has been emptied out. Cabinets, drawers, shelves—all are bare, the contents tossed into the middle of her room like a giant trash heap: ballet shoes, dolls, animal figures, trinkets. Trash heap or bonfire? On the top are pages torn from books. She is clutching a box of matches in her fist.

"The matches." He thrusts out his hand. "Give them to me." Rain beats on the windowpanes, wind thumping on the sash. Her eyes flick around him. She wants to bolt but

389

he's in the way, blocking the door. He pulls himself up to his full height and braces himself. He hopes she won't get physical but he's ready if she does. "The matches," he says again, walking towards her, his hand outstretched. "Now." When he's close enough to touch her, she drops them in his hand. "Good." He gives her the one word of praise, acknowledging her cooperation. "And the key." His hand is still out. She hesitates then reaches into her pocket and produces it. He secures the matches in his pocket then walks back across the room and locks the door—leaving them locked in together. She wasn't expecting that. Her face pales. What will he do next? The key joins the matches in his pocket. "We need to talk."

She scowls at him, her arms crossed over her chest. He's never seen such anger in her before; it makes her quite ugly. She knows she's trapped. He sees her calculate. She's survived his hypnotic sessions before; she judges she can do so again. She walks to her bed, arranges herself for a session.

"No. Not like that. No more trances." Gus drags the chair from her desk, turns it around so that it faces the center of the room. "Sit." Fear flickers in her eyes. She doesn't know what he has in mind—what this means. Gus points at the chair. "Now, Anna. Sit. There." He doesn't care that he's frightening her. So much the better. He won't back down. She has no choice; she has no place to go, and she knows it. With a shrug she sits down, adopting the last, sullen, refuge of the adolescent: Fine. I don't care. He catches his breath and turns away from her so that she won't see the relief in his eyes. He doesn't want her to know he's had any doubt. He's won the first skirmish. He feels the ground shift between them.

When he turns back, she's hunched in the chair, her knees on her elbows, picking at her lip. She won't meet his eye. She's having trouble maintaining her nonchalance, and he sees the tension in her mounting. She hasn't moved. She's pinned to the chair by the force of his resolve. Out of habit he almost sits down himself. The technique has been drilled into him in his years of training: put yourself at your patients' level. Make them feel comfortable. Ease their fears. Not this time. Fear is in his favor and he wants to maximize it. He draws closer, towering over her, maintaining his superiority. She shrinks away from him, looking all at once childish and helpless. He feels a pulse of sympathy for her but ignores it, keeping his feelings in check. "The day your brother died. We're going to talk about that."

A stifled moan escapes her lips. It's the first conscious sound she's made since he met her. He will take that for progress. Her hands claw at her lips, drawing blood. The sight disturbs him, and he turns away so that he won't have to see it. "You were here, in your room. You knew the babysitter had come inside. You heard her talking on the phone. You went to the window and looked outside. You saw that your brother was alone."

He walks to the window and looks out as she must have done. Rain courses down the steps to the beach, flooding the pier. Mist rises from the rocks, flowing over the sea wall. In the fog he sees an imaginary figure walking on the wall. It's a boy, a very small boy, and he is walking all alone.

"You saw your brother outside. You saw him on the wall." His voice grows in confidence as he speaks, finally knowing what he is about. "You left your room and went down to him. You took the back stairs." The servants' stairs, he means. It's the last missing piece of the puzzle, the one that confounded him for so long: how Anna got out of the house. Beatrice insisted Anna was in her room when Sasha fell; if she had gone out, Beatrice would have seen her come down the stairs. But not if Anna used the *back* stairs; the girls would do that whenever they wanted to come or go without being seen, just as he and Rosa had once done in their own home. Just as, he suddenly recalls, he did the first night he was here, when he dashed down the servants' stairs to pull Anna down from the sea wall. "He was there. Your brother. You saw him. On the wall."

Anna moans again, louder this time, more intensely. He wants to look at her but won't let himself. He mustn't be deterred. "You climbed up beside him. He wanted to play that game with you, the one you played with Hettie. Follow the leader. You let him."

A strangled sound escapes Anna. A word? He ignores it, keeping his eye on the sea wall, watching the shadowy figure in the rain, who has now been joined by a second. A boy and a girl. "You walked back and forth on the wall. Both of you. Together." In the mist the two figures walk to one end of the wall then turn and come the other way. "But Sasha was too little. He couldn't do it like you and Hettie. He couldn't balance. He stumbled." Gus closes his eyes, remembers seeing Hettie and Anna on the wall, remembers how Hettie stumbled, how Anna reached out for her. "He stumbled and you reached out to him."

A guttural sound issues from her, almost animal. It chills him, and he wants to stop but he doesn't. So far he's said nothing he doesn't already know. Everything is just as he's pieced it together from her story—his story. Their story. He turns and looks at her. Her face is ashen, her body contorted, her lips bleeding, but she's still where he put her, fixed to the chair. "You reached out for him." He stops. What then? She said she didn't see him fall. Did she lie? He's come as far as he can without her. "What then, Anna? What happened next?"

She twists away, making a rasping sound, louder this time, half animal, half human.

"You reached out to him, Anna. You reached out to your brother. What happened then?"

All at once she flies at him, flailing, kicking his legs, pummeling his chest. He wraps his arms around her, pulls her tight, holds her close, containing the grief and anger that's tearing her apart. She's crying, saying something he can't understand, still trying to hit him, shaking in his embrace. Then she moans and her legs give way and she slides to the floor, pulling him with her. He sits beside her holding her tight, keeping her safe.

"I don't know."

The sound of her voice startles him. It's deeper and huskier than the voice in her trances, more wrenching and vulnerable. At the sound of it, tears come to his eyes. He's crying—for what? For Anna? For Rosa? For himself? She goes limp in his arms.

"What happened, Anna," he says. "What happened to Sasha?"

"I don't—" Sobs break through her words. "I don't know. I blinked, and he was gone."

Gus closes his eyes, sees Anna on the wall with the boy, sees him stumble, sees her reach out to him. As he watches, the boy disappears, and she flies up the hill to the house, then takes the servants' stairs to her room. Minutes later, when the nanny screams, she runs down the front stairs to the sunroom, meets Beatrice, and dashes outside, already locked in silence over what she can't say.

He reaches into his pocket, finds Beatrice's handkerchief, hands it to her. He holds her, gently rocking, while she wipes her eyes. Then he laughs. He can't help it. Laughter bubbles in his throat, forcing its way out. She turns to him in surprise. "Anna." He's smiling, crying, laughing all at once, wiping his eyes with the back of his hand. "I'm sorry." He knows he should stop laughing but he can't. "It's just that for once I finally have a handkerchief when I need one."

Gravely she finishes wiping her face and gives him the handkerchief. Slowly, helping each other, they come to their feet. She stands in front of him with her head bowed and her eyes downcast like a child who expects a punishment—who expects to be judged. It's his last view of the penitent girl. But he has no judgment to give. "Anna, listen to me." He says the words firmly and evenly, coming back to himself. "It wasn't your fault. It was the nanny's job to watch him, and the nanny failed."

She's quiet for a moment, taking it in. "Are they going to send me to Spring Meadow?"

"No, they won't."

"Then I'd like to go now."

She lifts her chin, looks at him directly. As her fear fades, he sees a hard edge come into her eyes, a hint of her father's arrogance, her mother's cruelty. He sees the girl she has been give way to the woman she will become. She didn't create the bonfire of toys to purge her room; she created it to purge herself. She's moving on, leaving her childhood behind.

What does love mean to Anna Glanz—what will it mean to her as she goes through life, becoming friend, girlfriend, wife, mother? Gus will never know. He can't undo the damage she's endured. She will always bear the scars. But it's over. Whatever it was that rendered her mute—and he's still not sure he knows exactly what it was—it's finished, as surely as the blast of a ram's horn.

"Yes, Anna." If this is a victory, he doesn't feel it. He feels done in, wrung out, spent. "You can go now." He unlocks the door, hands her the key, and steps aside.

Thirty

CLAIRE

Beatrice Thaler lives in Mt. Washington, a Baltimore neighborhood a half dozen miles north of the Johns Hopkins Hospital. Claire finds her address in a phone book. She finds her phone number, too, and considers calling ahead but decides not to. What would she say? She still doesn't know, but whatever it is, she feels certain it must be said in person. She doesn't even know if this Beatrice is the Beatrice she's looking for. Gus might have married any number of Beatrices fifty years ago. Part of her feels it's not worth the bother—What are the chances? You'll only just humiliate yourself—but the other part whispers: What if?

She asks yet another hospital guard for directions to the Thalers' street, and then she's off, on the road again, taking the expressway through the city, exiting at Northern Parkway. She follows Falls Road to the Kelly Avenue Bridge, drives past centuries-old brick mill buildings that have been converted to restaurants, markets, boutiques, and lofts. Past the mills, a narrow street rises steeply up a hill and then, at the crest, there it is, a white clapboard house with a mossy green slate roof, a wide covered porch, and a brightly painted red door.

Claire pulls the car to a stop, sets the parking brake, steps outside. The drive to Mt. Washington has vaulted her forward in time, taking her from winter into spring. In Beatrice Thaler's garden the last of the snow has vanished, and purple pansies with yellow centers bloom. Crocuses announce themselves along the walkway to the house; a hedge of forsythia glistens with a yellow glow. The earth gleams fragrant and dark and inviting. Beneath a retreating blue sky, the house is bathed in vivid, intense colors as if by a column of light: luminescent green shutters, shining mica windows, crimson sparks from a pair of cardinals feasting at a feeder on the porch. As Claire climbs the steps to the porch, her thoughts feel like sparks, too, surging, flying. Is this the future she has been seeking?

When she reaches the door, the cardinals burst into panicked flight and disappear over the rooftop, leaving her alone in air that is cool and shadowy with a faint peppery smell. At her feet thyme and basil grow in pots. She reaches for the bell.

What will she say when Beatrice—if it is, indeed, the Beatrice she is seeking—answers the door? How will Claire know? She doesn't get the chance to find out. A few breaths after the bell sounds, the door flies open, revealing a woman with a shock of white hair and bright hazel eyes. "Yes?" she says. "Can I help you?" Then, as Claire stands silently, struggling to speak, the expression on the woman's face changes. "Oh, my," she says. And again, "My. You are"—a hand flies to her mouth—"yes, you must be. Look at you. You are the picture of—Oh, my. You couldn't be, could you?" Then, as realization dawns in her eyes: "Of course you are." She reaches out and takes Claire's face in her hands. "You're Anna's. There's no mistaking that." Just like that, Claire is whisked inside.

"A daughter. Anna has a daughter!" Beatrice studies Claire with her hands on her hips, beaming. She's wearing a black wool skirt and a ruby red sweater, the sleeves of the sweater pushed up to her elbows in a workmanlike fashion, as if she's the kind of person who must keep busy, who can't keep still, and just now Claire has just pulled her from an important task. Her face is round, her figure comfortably plump, her hair clipped straight to her chin; a strand falls into her eyes, and automatically she sweeps it away. "I'm so glad. Are there others? Are there boys? No, don't tell me. Wait until I put on some tea. You are staying for tea, aren't you? Of course you are." She laughs. "I'm forgetting myself. Please. I don't even know your name."

"Claire," Claire says, relieved to get the word out. Her throat feels so thick, she fears she might have no voice at all.

"Claire. Wonderful." Beatrice takes her hands, leads her to a living room populated with paintings and books, a coffee table strewn with journals, pens, ledgers, binders. She pushes them aside. "Don't mind that. It's a project I'm working on, research, I promised Gus before—" She smiles in a rueful, affectionate way. "Never mind. Sit down. Please. How did you find me? No, wait. Don't tell me that either. Don't tell me anything. Just sit. I'm sorry. I'm chattering. I'll give you time to talk when I come back. I promise." With the wave of a hand, she is gone, disappearing into the kitchen to put the kettle on.

Claire sinks into the chair Beatrice has shown her to, thickly padded with a striped cotton cover, glad for the softness of it, for the way it engulfs her, so that she feels hidden and safe. She doesn't mind Beatrice's chatter, she's grateful for the time it gives her to collect her thoughts, to come back to herself. She still isn't sure what she will say to her, how she will begin. How do you tell a story when you're still muddling through the middle of it, when you have no idea, really, how it began, even less how it will end?

Her mind is whirling, and she's having trouble concentrating. All she can think is, It's her, it's really her, Beatrice Chase. Beatrice Chase Thaler. She was there. She knew my mother. She knew Hettie, she knew all of them, Lionel and Frieda and Sasha, too. Sasha! And Gus. Of course, she knew Gus most of all. Could she possibly—? Claire shakes her head, hardly daring to hope.

The living room is cozy, full of light, with a bright, airy scent. Sturdy wood beams stud the ceiling; rugs soften the polished pine floors. A stack of bookshelves holds a slew of medical and psychiatric tomes, most devoted to children, a few with Gus Thaler's name on the spines. In a glass-fronted cabinet are more books—biographies, novels, natural histories, sea tales, and folklore—as if the occupants of the house were voraciously curious about anything and everything in the world. There's a painting of the Hopkins dome in bright neon colors, a poster of a woman in a gold mosaic gown, done in a Viennese art deco style. On the mantelpiece sit exotic, antique dolls, each one wearing a different costume. Above them, as if to chart their hometowns, is a tattered map of the world, pinned to the wall.

"It's silly, I know. That map is so old, half the countries don't even exist anymore." Beatrice comes in bearing tea and lemon bars on a tray. Suddenly Claire realizes how late it is in the day, how little she has eaten or drunk—nothing but coffee on the turnpike that morning—how hungry she is, how much she loves lemon bars, and how long it's been since she had one.

As if she can read her thoughts, Beatrice puts one on a plate then adds a second "for good measure" and thrusts them into Claire's hands. "The map's a tradition in my family." She takes a seat on the sofa opposite. "We're a seafaring group. My mother used to say the Chases have more saltwater than blood in their veins. Thank goodness Gus brought me to a port town. I don't know if I could have managed otherwise." She breaks into laughter again, a comfortable, contagious sound. Claire finds herself smiling in return. "That's our son, Joseph. He's in the Navy. He's sailing there now." Beatrice points to a tack on the map stuck in the middle of the Arabian Sea. "At least so he was last I heard. Rosa's in San Francisco. She's our daughter." The laughter comes again. "Listen to me, going on and on. And I haven't even offered you your tea."

Beatrice pours out the tea—Sugar? Milk? Both? Good for you—passes one more lemon bar to Claire—You must, absolutely, I insist—and finally sits back as promised to give Claire a chance to talk. But Claire is still struggling for words, for her voice, for a way to begin. Her eye falls on a violin case propped in the corner of the room. "Do you play?"

"Me? Oh, no. That was Gus. He was quite good, although he wouldn't admit it." Beatrice rolls her eyes. "Just like Gus to think he could always do better. He played in a local quartet. They held concerts for the children around holiday time. In the summers they played in the courtyard behind the clinic. I don't suppose you've—?"

"Yes. I was there today. I saw it."

"Then you know how lovely it is." Beatrice's face takes on a rueful look of affection again. "I should put the violin away, I know, but I can't seem to bring myself to do it." She falls silent, drawing her lower lip between her teeth. It's a charming gesture, utterly transforming, and all at once Claire sees the young woman Beatrice was when she met Gus Thaler, when she fell in love with him, and when he fell in love with her. "But enough of me." She refills Claire's cup—Milk and sugar like before, yes?—and sits back, settling herself, growing still. "Now, Claire. You."

Two hours later the lemon bars are gone. So is the first pot of tea, the second one cooling. Claire never did figure out how to begin her story. She simply jettisoned the idea of beginnings and told it the only way she could: by starting in the middle and working her way backwards and forwards, letting the story unspool as it would. Listening to her would be enough, Claire thinks, to drive anyone crazy, but Beatrice stayed the course, taking it all in patiently, never interrupting, except to murmur from time to time a response of her own: How is Hettie? Children, too? I'm so glad. And then: I was sorry to hear your grandmother died.

Somewhere along the way Claire found her voice, her words becoming stronger, clearer. In the end she managed to tell Beatrice most of her story, not everything, but enough, she hopes, to make her understand. At the center, like the hard pinpoint of shell at the heart of a nautilus's spiral, was Anna, her illness—Beatrice, crestfallen: I'm so sorry to hear it—and her question about Sasha, the one that brought Claire to this moment, to this hilltop house in Mt. Washington, to this person: Beatrice Chase Thaler.

When Claire finally falls silent, Beatrice begins talking, telling a story of her own, of a fifteen-year-old girl who once lived with her family in a house by the water, who stopped speaking when her brother died, until a tall young man with red hair—red just like yours—figured out her secret and gave her back her voice. Beatrice speaks softly, with long pauses, parceling the story out, gauging Claire's reaction to it, making sure she's ready to hear more, that she wants to.

"So Lionel . . ." Claire says when Beatrice finishes. "Lionel and Anna . . ." Her voice trails off. The shock of learning the truth is profound, and she feels it reverberating deep in her bones. It's achingly tragic, terrible beyond imagining. It's also fitting. Of all the things Claire has learned about Anna since she left home, Beatrice's story makes the most sense of all. It explains so many things about Anna that have defied explanation: her arrogance, her coldness, her streak of cruelty. Lionel and Anna. Anna and Lionel. For years, Claire's image of her mother has been solid, fixed, immutable. Now she feels it changing, transforming—into what? She still isn't sure.

"Gus blamed your grandfather," Beatrice says, "but in the end he found it in his heart to forgive him. He said Lionel was a victim, too, that the abuse didn't begin with him; he was just the last in a long line." She smiles at Claire in a sad but hopeful way. "We're all part of a chain, aren't we? Bound by cords to the people who came before us, to what we know, and sometimes even more so to what we don't."

"Like the seawater in your veins?"

"Yes." Beatrice laughs. "Like that." Then she grows thoughtful. "Gus was always grateful to your mother."

"To Anna?" Is there no end to Beatrice's surprises? "Why?"

"He said she taught him how to be a doctor. She showed him that he could trust himself." She smiles. "Does she still paint?"

"Anna?"

"Yes. For a long time it was the only way she could communicate. I thought she might end up an artist, like your grandmother."

Anna, an artist? Claire shakes her head. She can't imagine Anna doing anything remotely like Frieda. Anna, Claire thinks, has spent her life fleeing from Frieda, trying as hard as she can to become everything Frieda is not. Despite everything Claire has learned from Beatrice, she still doesn't have an answer to the question that drove her here, to what happened when Sasha died, the moment, Hettie said, that forever sundered their family in two, cleaving their lives into an *after* and a *before*. In her mind Claire sees the damp, mossy sea wall by the Sound, sees the body of a boy tumbling to the rocks, swept away with the tide. And something she hasn't seen before: the figure of a girl beside him as he falls. "You said Anna was there. When Sasha drowned. That's what Gus discovered. She left the house and went down to the water. But why? What was on her mind? What did she want to do?"

Beatrice grows thoughtful. "Gus never did find out. He said only Anna could know, and she didn't say."

"She said it was never explained."

Beatrice nods. "I expect that's true. We all do things sometimes, don't we, for reasons we don't understand?"

Yes, Claire thinks as a vision of herself walking the

canal trail comes to mind. Then she shakes her head. Anna must have lifted Sasha up onto the wall. Charley said he didn't know who did it—but he didn't know Anna was there. No one did. It makes Sasha's death more than just a tragic accident—it makes it a deliberate act. "She wanted to destroy him." Gus might be reluctant to assign blame, but Claire most certainly isn't. As a prosecutor, she's staked her life on her conviction that people must be held responsible for their actions, that they should suffer the consequences. Without blame—without judgment—the social compact frays to tatters, leaving nothing but anarchy and chaos. "She wanted to take revenge. She had plenty of reasons. She'd been mistreated by Lionel, by Frieda, too."

Beatrice draws in her lower lip. "Gus thought she might have done it for Hettie."

"Hettie?" Claire's shocked to hear it. "What could Hettie possibly have to do with all this?"

"Something had to change in the family. After Sasha's death, it did."

"Are you saying Anna sacrificed Sasha for Hettie?"

Beatrice raises her hands, her palms helplessly open, as if to say she's reached the point where knowing fades into unknowing. "In the end she sacrificed herself, too, didn't she?"

Anna, Claire thinks, sacrificing herself? Impossible. Beatrice might think so, but she doesn't know Anna the way she does. "Anna and Hettie never lived under the same roof again. Frieda sent them to boarding school together, but it didn't take for Anna. After a few months she transferred to another school. She ended up at three different places before she finally graduated high school. Then she went away to college, to a girls' school in Vermont. That's where she met my father. He was in medical school."

Claire's voice rises in anger. "Sasha wasn't the only one she destroyed. There were others. My father, her second husband, her third. Cassidy Bleeker. He was my brother's best friend. They were roommates in college. He came home with Nathan after their junior year." Riding across the country on Cassidy's motorcycle, so that when Claire met him, he smelled of wind, his hair and beard streaked by sun, a camera slung across his shoulder. "Nathan had a job that summer working on an ambulance crew, and Cassidy went with him. He wanted to be a photojournalist. He was going to make a difference, document things that mattered. He sent some of his shots to the *Midfield Times*, and they hired him as a stringer."

Claire sees herself in a darkroom, sees a photograph emerge dripping from a tray, an image of herself coming to life in the shadowy light. Beside her stands a lanky young man in a stained T-shirt, his jeans falling to his hips. She feels the warmth of his body, breathes in the fog of his unfiltered cigarettes, sees the lamp cast a reddish glow on his face.

"At the end of the summer Nathan went back to school, but Cassidy moved in with Anna. He didn't have a chance." Bitterness blooms at the back of her throat. "She flattered him. She made him promises. She was the daughter of a senator. She said she'd give him an entrée into the political world. And her mother was Frieda Glanz. Frieda Glanz! No one could top that. Anna got him a show at the Stannis Gallery in Manhattan, 'Kansas Dispatches.' But after that, there was nothing. She didn't like to travel, and she couldn't bear for him to leave her. She wasn't about to go into war zones, to Third World countries, to the places he needed to go to if he was going to make something of himself. He had dreams. We used to talk about them. He was just a—"

"A child?" Beatrice says softly. She settles back in her seat, letting silence reign for a moment between them. Then she smiles again in her sad but hopeful way. "If it makes any difference, I always thought your mother wanted to save Sasha."

"She's not like that. I told you. She doesn't save anyone." Except, Claire thinks, herself. She bites her lip, looks away. "I still don't understand. Why would she say Sasha's death wasn't explained? She was there. She must have seen what happened to him. Of all people, she would know best."

Beatrice breathes in deeply. "Gus used to say we all see as much as we can. Beyond that—" Once again she raises her hands helplessly.

Claire has reached an impasse. She has learned so much about Anna, but not what she needs to know. She shakes her head. None of this is Beatrice's fault. She's clearly a kind person, one inclined to see the best in people. Claire has imposed on her long enough. She stands up. "Thank you. I appreciate you letting me in like this, hearing me out. I know it hasn't been easy."

Beatrice gives her a short wave of the hand as if to say none of that matters. Then she stands up, too. "Please. Wait. Before you go. I have something to give you." She leaves the room and returns a few moments later with a book in her hand.

The book is small enough to fit in Claire's cupped palm. The cover is warped and water stained, the pages yellowed, exuding the faint scent of candle wax. It's a ledger of some kind, one that a merchant might use to record sales. She opens to the first page. The writing inside is in Hebrew script. She knows enough to recognize it, not enough to read it. "I don't understand."

"It belonged to your great-grandmother Dora."

"Dora? How did—?"

"I don't know. Gus never told me. But I'm sure he would want you to have it."

Claire closes the book and tucks it into her purse. Her journey to resolve a mystery has ended in uncovering more. Is life always like that? She follows Beatrice to the door. The cardinals are back at the feeder, and as Claire steps onto the porch, they depart in a flurry of wings. She's sorry about all this, sorry she has drawn Beatrice into her troubles, mostly sorry that she hasn't been able to summon the forgiveness for Anna that Beatrice seems to be hoping for. "Anna and I—" she begins. How can she possibly explain in a way that Beatrice will understand? It won't work out, she wants to say. It never will. There's a reason, she wants to say, I don't have children. In the end she says simply, "It's difficult. Anna hasn't spoken to me for years and years."

"I'm sorry," Beatrice says. Her face falls. "Is there any chance you can change that?"

No, Claire wants to say. There isn't. But she doesn't want to burden Beatrice any more. She leaves the question unanswered. "Thank you," she says again. Then, like the cardinals, she's gone.

Outside the market at the bottom of the hill is a pay phone. One of these days, Claire thinks, she will get one of those mobile phones that are becoming more and more ubiquitous by the day. Who knows how that will change her life? She fishes coins from her purse, dials Roger's office. No answer. She hangs up, tries the home phone. Nothing. She glances at her watch. Six o'clock. Wednesday? She's lost track of the days. Yes. Wednesday. He's playing squash. He has a standing reservation for a court. She'll leave for Georgetown, be home before he is.

They will have to have it out. She and Roger. There's no other choice. Hettie will be heartbroken when she hears the marriage is over, but there's no helping that. In that respect, apparently, Claire and Anna are very much alike. Both of them in the business of breaking hearts.

First she'll call Nathan. She owes him that much. He's been worried about her. What will she tell him? She's too tired to think about that now. One day soon she'll go down to Houston. They can talk then. For now she'll just tell him that she's all right and that she's going home.

She deposits more coins in the phone, dials the hospital. No Nathan. Not on the wards, not in the operating room, not in his office either. Strange. He never leaves work this early. She calls his house, hears Ruth come quickly on the line. "Oh, Claire, thank goodness it's you. Nathan's been trying to reach you. He left for Midfield last night. He said if you called to tell you it's time."

Thirty-One

CLAIRE

*P*eople do things for reasons they don't understand. So said Beatrice Thaler, and so must it be. Why else would Claire find herself a few hours later on a plane to Midfield? The only possible explanation she can give is Nathan. Anna is Nathan's mother, too. Claire can't possibly leave him to face their mother's death alone.

The journey to Mt. Washington might have taken her into the future, but the flight to Midfield vaults her firmly into the past. She arrives in the depths of winter, in the thick of a blizzard, lost in a cloud. Snow streams in torrents past the windows of the plane, the lights from the wings blurring into streaks as they land—or rather don't. Just as the ground looms up, the engines roar, and the plane veers upward in a sickening spiral, thrusting her back in her seat. She's overcome with terror and then with the sting of irony: to come this far only to have it all end in a fiery crash. She almost laughs, then she does laugh in relief as the plane levels off, and the pilot's voice comes over the intercom, speaking in measured tones that only barely hide his own giddy sense of relief. "Small problem on the runway, folks. Sorry about that. We'll be on the ground in a few minutes." Which they are. Claire lines up with the rest of the passengers to deplane, her body trembling. The near miss, she decides, is a fitting homecoming. She has no idea what she's headed for, either deliverance or damnation. Either way, it's out of her control.

Home. It feels odd to call Midfield that. She lived here for only a few years as a child and hasn't been back for decades. She doesn't even know which hospital Anna is in. She calls two before learning from the third that her mother has been discharged. "Dr. Levy took her home this morning, according to her wishes." Oh, Nathan. She fetches the small suitcase she's been lugging with her ever since she left Hettie's apartment—was it really just days ago, or was it years ago, even ages?—then hurries outside to look for a taxi, only to rush back inside. She's forgotten she doesn't know where Anna lives. She moved after Frieda died and the strings on Lionel's fortune finally loosened, making her a wealthy woman.

It's almost impossible to find her in the phone book. She's not one person but many: Anna Glanz-Levy-Klein. Finally Claire finds her under "B": Bleeker A. and C. Isn't that just like Anna, radical enough to marry a man twenty years her junior, conventional enough to take his name. She returns outside, signals to the lone taxi waiting at the airport at this hour, gives the address to the driver, and climbs in.

It's after midnight, the roads all but abandoned, the windows fogged. She rubs a fist on the glass. The Midfield she sees bears virtually no resemblance to the Midfield she remembers. The city has grown, metastasized, spreading eastwards across the prairie in a scrim of light. They drive down one expressway that didn't exist then another. Claire leans back, lets the window fog over again. It's just as well. She'd rather not see the passing landscape, rather not

410

experience the memories it evokes: This is where she went to high school and this is where Nathan learned to drive and this is where Cassidy . . .

All at once she's on the back of Cassidy's motorcycle again, her arms wrapped around his waist, her head on his shoulder, feeling the warmth of his body in the summer sun, the softness of his T-shirt, his smell of tobacco and sweat. They're on a dirt road, riding to the end, where a barbed-wire fence marks off the last of the rangeland, and the prairie begins. They stop in a cloud of dust and dismount so that Claire can sit on the ground, her legs crossed, her head in her hands, while Cassidy aims his camera at her, clicking the shutter again and again.

"Lady." She can tell by the note of annoyance in the cab driver's voice that he's said it more than once. "We're here."

The taxi has come to a stop. Claire tenders the fare, takes her suitcase, steps out, and just as she turns around to say, "No, wait, I've made a mistake," the driver pulls away.

He has left her in a neighborhood of homes the size of small mansions, gathered in cul-de-sacs on surprisingly small plots of land. They are far outside the city, in what must be a fairly new development, plunked down in the middle of the prairie, emerging from the raw earth like dragon's teeth. Trees as thin as toothpicks lean into the wind, secured by cords to the ground. The houses are eclectic, each one constructed according to a different design—Tudor, Colonial, Georgian, Victorian—in an attempt, Claire supposes, to make them seem unique. The result is only to make them appear more alike, uniform in their ostentation. Anna's house is one of the largest on the street, a stone behemoth that Claire can only describe as mini-French-chateau.

So this is Anna's final incarnation: eighteenth-century countess.

The departure of the taxi has left Claire in darkness. The storm, at least, has finally abated. High overhead the wind blows, sweeping across the plains, clearing the sky. The air tastes of sage and dust and cold. It comes to her as a shock, not in its strangeness but in its familiarity. Winter on the plains. She's surprised at how quickly she remembers.

Who will come to the door? The impossibility of knowing the answer to that question all but paralyzes her. If she had one of those radically new mobile phones, she'd use it now, recall the cab. Instead she has no choice but to knock. Which she does. And then the door opens and Nathan is there and she is in his arms.

"Oh, Nathan." The relief at seeing him is almost too much to bear. "I have so much to tell you." Claire buries her face in his shoulder, the familiar feel of him telling her she has done the right thing by coming here, that maybe, just maybe, it will be all right. "The plane almost didn't land and then it did. I could have—I didn't even know where you were and then—" She steps back, smiling, wipes her eyes. "It's good to see you."

He smiles. "It's good to see you, too."

"How is Anna? Is she—?"

"Sleeping. Cassidy's sitting up with her now. Do you want to go to her?"

Claire shakes her head. She isn't sure which one she is dreading seeing most—Cassidy or Anna—but she knows she isn't ready to see either one yet. "Let's talk."

"Sure." He gives her an appraising look. "You look great.

Did Hettie take you shopping?"

"Of course." She smiles at him. "You look like hell."

"I suppose I do." Nathan laughs, rubs his hand across his head in that typical Nathan way she loves so much. "Come on. I was just about to have some coffee."

Hell. Nathan looks like he's been through it. He's wearing a rumpled button-down shirt, sneakers, slacks. He's tall, balding, with a slight hunch in his back from standing on his feet in the operating room too long. He reminds Claire of Julius. For as long as she can remember, Nathan is the closest to Julius she has been able to come.

He chatters while he fills their coffee cups, filling her in on Anna's condition, using medical terminology she doesn't understand. She doesn't mind. She sits at the kitchen table, letting the words wash over her, happy just to be with him, to hear his voice. "She didn't want to die in the hospital," he says finally. "It was her last wish. She wanted to come home. Cassidy called and told me so I flew in last night, and we brought her back this morning. She's been having trouble breathing. The cancer—it causes fluid in the lungs. Like drowning." He shakes his head. "The hospital gave me a supply of morphine, and I've been giving it to her, keeping her as comfortable as possible." He puts the coffee on the table, sits down beside her.

"Will she—will it be—?"

"Long?" Nathan shakes his head. "I don't think so. I've seen people . . ." He smiles at her, bucking her up. "Hours. Maybe a few days."

There's nothing more to be said. He falls silent, looks at her, waits. Now it's her turn to talk. Anna drowning.

413

It must be a terrible way to die. It brings Claire back to Sasha. She needs to tell Nathan about him. One day she'll tell him the whole story, from Judge Benson to Hettie and Grimmsley, Charley and Joey Cataldo, Gus and Beatrice. Especially Gus and Beatrice. For now all what matters most is the end of the story. She begins there.

Nathan shakes his head when she's done. "Lionel and Anna."

Something about the way he says it gives her pause. "You knew."

"Knew?" He frowns. "I wouldn't say that."

"But you suspected."

"I wondered. Whenever I saw them together . . . It wasn't something I wanted to think about."

"You never told me." She feels the pricklings of anger. How could he have kept something like this from her?

"What was there to say?" He lifts his hands helplessly just like Beatrice did, palms open, signifying the place where the known bleeds into the unknown.

"There's more," Claire says. "Anna was with Sasha when he died. She was there, Nathan, on the sea wall. She lifted him up. She had to. He couldn't climb up on his own."

Nathan takes a sip of his coffee, looks away.

His silence astonishes her. After everything she's just told him, does he really have nothing to say? "Are you listening to me? She might have killed him. Deliberately. She probably did. We have every reason to think—"

"Do we?" He rubs a hand over his eyes. "Honestly, Claire, I don't even know if it matters anymore. Anna's dying. Whatever happened—whatever she did—she'll take it with her. We have to think ahead now, to what comes after, when she's gone."

"Doesn't matter?" Her astonishment slides easily into anger. "How can you say that? It's not just Anna, it's us. If she's a murderer, what does that make us?"

Nathan pushes back his chair, carries his cup to the sink, turns back to her with tired eyes. "It was a long time ago, Claire."

No, she wants to say, It wasn't. It was yesterday. It was today. It's now. "I didn't start this," she says, a righteous note in her voice. "Anna did. She said it was never explained. She wants to know what happened to Sasha. That's what Cassidy said. She specifically asked me—"

"Claire—" There's a note of warning in his voice. He's about to say something wounding, something they'll both regret. He shakes his head. "I have to go. I told Cassidy I'd spell him in a while. I need to get some sleep while I can."

"Wait." Claire stands up. All at once she feels a surge of panic. He's leaving her? "What should I do?"

"Do what you want. Go in and see her. Or don't. Wait for me. I'll take you with me later."

Halfway to the door, he stops and turns around. "I'm sorry." He's apologizing for the thought he had, for the words he didn't say. It always comes to this. Claire pushes him and pushes him, and then he's the one who apologizes when it should be her. "I know this is important to you. Talk to Anna when she wakes up. Maybe it will mean something to her that you cared enough to try to find out."

If she'll talk to me at all, Claire thinks as Nathan leaves. Maybe none of this matters to Nathan; maybe he can put it all behind him. But he and Anna have always been close. She never stopped speaking to him.

Anna's kitchen is large enough to feed a small army, all gleaming granite and stainless steel. Cold. Don't they have heat in this house? Claire pours herself another cup of coffee, the last of the pot, more for warmth than anything else, and wraps her hands around the mug. At the back of the room is an entire wall given over to windows, bringing in the vast darkness of the plains, the heady sprinkling of stars. The other walls hold photographs, landscape shots of prairie, sagebrush, sky. The photographer must have used a special kind of lens. The pictures are arresting, sharply realistic yet also disorienting, with an eerie, otherworldly quality, like a moonscape. Even without the characteristic signature at the bottom of each frame, Claire would know Cassidy's work. She shakes her head. It doesn't matter if the photos are good. This isn't the life he was meant to lead.

The coffee in her cup has gone cold, and she pours it out in the sink. Should she make more? Nathan might want some when he gets up. As she rummages in the cupboards for coffee filters, she hears footsteps. Nathan. Thank goodness. He's come back. He must have decided he couldn't sleep. She'll apologize this time. She will. And then—

"Hey, Nate, is there any coffee left?" Claire turns around just as Cassidy enters the kitchen and pulls up with a start. "Oh. Claire. Sorry. I didn't know you were here."

"I just got in." She takes a breath, spies the filters on a shelf, pulls them out. "I took a cab from the airport."

He smiles. "It's good to see you."

She closes the cupboard in a stiff, deliberate fashion, maintaining her politeness, maintaining her distance. She won't reveal her feelings. He doesn't deserve them. "I'm sorry about Anna." It's the right thing to say, so she says it.

"Yeah, me, too." His smile fades. He sits down at the table, puts his head in his hands.

"I was just about to make coffee."

"Thanks. I could use some." He looks up at her, an edge of hopefulness in his eyes. "Thanks for—" Thanks for coming, she thinks, that's what he wants to say, but he doesn't. "I'm glad you're here." He settles on that. "Anna will be, too."

Will she? In the end it's not up to Cassidy to say. Claire runs water in the pot, measures out the grounds, leveling each spoonful, standing by the counter while the coffee drips. Cassidy looks away, an awkward silence settling between them. So few words, and they've already run out of things to say.

They were always so different, Cassidy and Nathan; from the beginning it was hard for Claire to see how they became friends. Nathan so tall and thin, with a bony frame, Cassidy a head shorter with rounded contours. The years haven't treated him kindly. She takes some satisfaction in that. The pudginess of his body has become pronounced, settling in a thickness in his neck, a laxity in his face, a protruding belly. He has aged. He would be a fitting companion to Anna now, Claire thinks. People would hardly notice the age difference between them. His hair has gone grey, thinning at the crown of his head, but he still has his signature flair, the ponytail that drapes down his back. At one time it drew Claire like a beacon, seeming to promise all kinds of forbidden pleasures. Now it looks faintly ridiculous. If Anna has reinvented herself as a countess, Cassidy has become a cliché, an aging hippie. He's even dressed for the role, barefoot, in khaki pants with frayed hems and an untucked flannel shirt.

417

"I was looking at your photographs," she says, just to break the silence. "Hettie said you had a show."

"They were nice to take me." He smiles at her in a shy, self-deprecating way.

"No, they're good. Really they are. You've captured something."

"Thanks." He pulls a pack of cigarettes out of his pocket, shakes one loose. "Do you mind?"

She shrugs. It's his house.

"I should quit." He lights the cigarette, inhales with a grimace. "Nathan's been after me to do it. I know, it's crazy, especially now, with Anna—" He turns away, wipes his eyes with a thumb. "I will." He flashes her a small smile. "Hell, there's always tomorrow, right?"

Tomorrow. It was always Cassidy's mantra, even back then, the word uttered with the same self-deprecating smile whenever something went wrong, when things didn't go as planned, when Nathan aced his courses and Cassidy barely passed his, when the deadline for applications to graduate school came and passed, and he hadn't filled out the forms. They used to argue about it until the small hours of the morning, Nathan and Cassidy, going back and forth about the future and what mattered most in life, Nathan already so clear and directed in his path, while Cassidy was wild with possibility, refusing to be pinned down, driven by dreams of social justice and transformational change. Meanwhile Claire would sit and listen, her eyes traveling back and forth between them, these two young men who seemed to her at the time to fill the whole world.

"Have you heard from Hettie?"

The question jolts her back to the present. "Yes."

418

"She's been calling every day, asking about Anna. I took Anna to see her last fall, you know."

Claire startles. She didn't.

"We'd just found out about the—about Anna's diagnosis. She wanted to see Hettie, so I took her to New York. Mostly I left them alone, walking the streets while they talked. I still couldn't believe it—that Anna had cancer, I mean. That it couldn't be cured. Mostly she was fine. She just had this little cough. And she got tired easily. But other than that . . ." The coffee has finished dripping. He stands up. "Milk, right?" He busies himself pulling a jug from the refrigerator.

It hurts that he remembers. She moves aside while he puts two cups on the counter, pours milk into one. He still takes his black. Some things, apparently, never change.

"Hettie and Anna." He shakes his head as he sits down with his cup. "They were something, those two. Always hatching some kind of plot, acting like they were up to no good." He gives her a wan smile. "I think they both knew this would be the last time they would be together. We were supposed to go straight home afterwards, but instead Anna said something about going to Marby. So I rented a car."

Claire is still standing, her coffee untouched. She was going to sit down but now she has become wary, alert. It seems safer to stay on her feet.

"I'd never seen their house on the point before. Had you?"

"No." It's not untrue. At the time she hadn't.

"Impressive." His cigarette is almost out. He takes a last pull, crushes the butt in a nearby ashtray. "Lionel must have been something else."

419

Something else. Yes. Cassidy never met Lionel. He died before Nathan went to college, before Cassidy came into their lives. Would Anna—could Anna—have said anything to him about Lionel, about what went on between them? Claire thinks not. Should Claire? It would be both surprising and hurtful, and part of her wants to have just that effect. Do you know he abused her? she could say casually, lightly, just like that, reminding Cassidy that despite all the years he has been married to Anna, he doesn't know everything, that she has kept secrets from him and kept them well.

"We walked around. I took a few pictures. Anna wanted to go down to the water, so we walked down the hill."

"To the sea wall?"

"Yes."

"So you saw it."

"Only for a minute. The people who live there had been out, but then they came back. Anna didn't want to bother them, so we left. I knew she'd had a brother once and that he'd died while they were living in that house. I didn't know anything more about it. She never told me. I thought it might be the reason she wanted to go back—because of him. I asked her how he died, and she said, 'It was never explained.' So I called you."

"You called—"

"I asked Hettie first, but she said Anna knew more about it than she did. Then I asked Nathan, but he didn't know, so I tried you. I figured over the years someone, anyone, Lionel, Frieda, might have said something and maybe you—"

"You called—" Claire says again. Her mouth has gone dry. "You were the one who wanted to know what happened to Sasha. Not Anna."

"Anna?" He shakes his head. "No, not really. I mean, I don't know. Maybe she did, too, but she never said so."

This can't be happening. Cassidy. Really? Cassidy wanted to know? Not Anna? It can't be true. Seriously. Fucking seriously. It just can't be. "You know I lost my job over this."

"Your—what?"

"Never mind." Claire laughs. There's nothing else to do. It's not worth it. There's no point. She laughs again. Then she's laughing so hard, she begins to cry.

"Are you all right?" Cassidy stands up, a look of concern on his face.

"Fine, I'm fine." She wipes her eyes. "You know what? I was wrong about your pictures. They're crap. I mean, they're beautiful but they're still crap. You know why? Because they don't matter. They're decoration. Pretty decoration on someone's wall. Did you sell any of them? Because if you did, I bet the people who bought them were grateful. I bet they said you'd brightened their lives. You'd made them feel good. They could look at your pictures of prairie and sagebrush and sunrises and sunsets and not have to think about all the crap that's going on in the world—wars and illness and people suffering and people—"

Stalked by wolves. She almost says it, catches herself just in time.

"Claire." He stands up. "Listen. I'm sorry. I know things didn't turn out the way you wanted—"

"The way I wanted? What about what you wanted?"

"I didn't—I wasn't like that. I never was."

"That's not true. You were. You let it all go. You sacrificed everything. In the end, that was the part I couldn't believe, that you gave it all up for one fucking New York show. You let yourself be bought, just like that—"

Cassidy turns away, fumbling in his pocket for another cigarette, trying to light it, his hands shaking, finally throwing the cigarettes and the matches onto the table. "That show wasn't any good. Didn't you see the reviews?"

Reviews? Claire's surprised to hear him say it. It never occurred to her to think about his reviews before. She didn't even know he'd had any. By the time the show opened, she was living in Manhattan with Hettie. She vaguely recalls Hettie talking on the phone to Anna, saying something about Cassidy's show, but Claire was too angry to listen.

"I was never going to be any good." There's an edge of bitterness in his voice, a pleading note. Can't she, just for once, understand? "That stuff I used to say about photojournalism, about changing the world? It was kid stuff. Half the time I said it just to piss Nathan off. He knew it. We both did." He picks up the cigarettes, his hands still shaking, finally manages to get one lit. "Nathan was the serious one. He was the one who was going to be somebody—he did become somebody. I was the goof-off."

Claire won't believe it. She refuses to. "You could have been something. You had dreams. We had dreams."

"Oh, Claire." He takes a breath. Then he puts the cigarette down, comes over, cups her face in his hands. "You were so pretty. I'll never forget the day I took those pictures of you. You're still a beautiful woman, you know that?" He smiles at her. "And smart. You were always so smart. Even Nathan said so. He always said you had the brains in the family. You were going on to great things. I never would have been able to keep up with you."

"That's not true." She's crying again. "You sold out."

"Sold out?" He releases her, steps back. "No."

He's going to say he loves Anna, that he fell in love with her then and that he still loves her now, but Claire can't bear to hear it. "You were supposed to choose me."

He takes a breath, falls silent. Then he retrieves his cigarette and walks to the window, his back to her, looking out into the darkness, his fingers trailing smoke. "I know. I'm sorry."

Pity. She hears it in his voice. It's the one thing she can't stand, especially not from him. "Twenty years. You didn't speak to me for twenty fucking years. Not a single word from you or Anna—"

"You told us not to." He turns around, looks at her in genuine surprise. "You said specifically not even to try. And then you took off, and Anna was crazy with worry, and we didn't know where you were, even Nathan didn't know. We didn't find out until weeks later when that doctor in New York called and said you'd been living on the streets."

The streets. She has no memory of that part. What she remembers is leaving Midfield in the middle of the night, hitchhiking across the country, a vague idea about seeing Hettie in the back of her mind. Hettie the rescuer, even then. Only she never made it to Hettie, she ended up in Bellevue instead, her first psychotic episode, using the ward phone to call Hettie day after day, begging her not to let them send her home.

"Anna wanted to go and get you right away, but then Hettie called and told her not to. She said you wanted to go home with her. Anna didn't like it, but in the end she agreed. Even the doctors said it would be best, and we both—"

Best. Yes. Claire remembers how relieved she was to get out of the hospital, how grateful to be at Hettie's apartment, where she finally began to come back to herself. And something else. Anna calling, day after day, begging Claire to speak to her, Claire refusing, Hettie saying into the telephone: Not yet, give her time.

"We both thought you'd come home eventually. We thought you had to, that you'd—" Come to your senses, he means. Get over it. Isn't that what everyone thinks when she's in the midst of one of her "crises," even Roger? She hears his voice, his exasperation, his fatigue: Claire, please, stop. Just think for a minute. Be reasonable. As if thinking isn't precisely the problem; as if any of this is under her control. "But days went into weeks and then months . . ." Cassidy shakes his head. "After a while we gave up. Anna said we had to. She was afraid—afraid of upsetting you. She said that if this is what you needed to be happy, then so be it. She would leave you alone. She didn't want you to end up—she didn't want anything like that hospital to happen to you again. So she kept away. We both did."

Claire's still crying. "You didn't even try."

"I did try. Remember? I called you last fall. Anna was sick and I thought that maybe—well, maybe you would finally talk to her. Honestly, Claire, that whole thing about Sasha was just an excuse. Mostly I just wanted to see if maybe you would finally give in and speak to Anna." He shakes his head. "You hung up on me."

Claire wipes her eyes, pulls herself together. It's not true. This is not her fault. She's not the one who sinks into painful silences, who keeps secrets. Suddenly she's filled with anger. What is she doing here? What was she thinking? She has nothing to say to Anna. Anna didn't even want to know about Sasha. Nobody did. Cassidy just made the whole thing up. "Tell Nathan—" Never mind. She'll call him later, tell him herself.

She rushes outside. She has her purse with her, has left her suitcase behind, so much the better, she doesn't want any reminders of this ridiculous, misbegotten journey. She turns down the street, walking in the snow, her feet wet and freezing. Overhead stars gleam in an icy sky. Suddenly she feels a burst of moist warmth against the back of her legs. The wolf is right behind her, panting, dogging her heels.

She picks up the pace, begins to run. The wolf settles into an easy lope. Claire will never outrun her. Isn't that what wolves do best, run for miles and miles and miles, chasing down their prey? She reaches the end of Anna's street. Which way now? In the distance is a chain of lights, cars moving on a highway. Otherwise there is nothing but blackness. She jogs towards the light. Xynolith, Xynolith. Even Xynolith isn't up to this. From deep in the prairie comes a howl. The wolf pricks up her ears. Then she lifts her head, extends her throat, and howls in return.

Jogging, jogging. No matter how far Claire runs, the lights seem to come no closer. In all directions extends the relentlessly flat, forbiddingly cold plain, reaching to the ends of the earth. The wolf is at home here. She sidles past Claire in a friendly fashion and takes the lead. There's still a warm current of air on the backs of her legs. She turns around, sees a second wolf behind her. Howls come from all directions now, dark grey shapes loping towards her through the darkness. The wolves gather around her, brushing their coarse fur against her body, filling the air with their animal stink. She's one of them now. There's no going back. She's joined the pack.

Finally she stops. She can't run anymore. She's exhausted, out of breath, her heart pounding. She bends over, rests her hands on her knees. Then she starts moving again, walking as quickly as she can, slipping and sliding, slogging through the snow on the side of the road. At last the lights on the highway coalesce, revealing a service station at the end of an exit ramp. Claire drags herself past the gasoline pumps and shoves open the door. Inside is a boy, a high-school student from the look of him, sitting behind a counter, studying a textbook. He lifts his head and blinks at her with surprise. He's trying to figure her out. Where's her car? How did she get here?

"Do you have a phone?" she says.

"A phone?" He's still puzzled, not sure what to make of her. He hesitates. Claire's seen that hesitation in people before. It's the way they look at her when they're trying to decide whether she is, as the psychiatrists always so delicately put it, a danger to herself or others. When they're trying to decide whether they should call an ambulance or the police.

She smooths down her hair, pulls herself together, manages a crooked smile. "A phone. Yes." She clears her throat, forces herself to speak slowly. "I need to call a cab. After that I'll leave. I promise."

He's still hesitating.

"Please. Really. I just need to call."

He frowns, uncertain, then says, "In the back."

The service station doubles as a small country store. Aisles containing cans of automobile oil, fan belts, groceries, stove parts, run through the middle. Claire walks down one crammed with dusty displays of tourist fare: shot glasses decorated with longhorns, T-shirts bearing the logo "There's No Place Like Kansas," cheap earrings in the shape of sunflowers. She picks up a pair of earrings and almost pockets them, but the boy is watching, so she puts them back. The aisle is too narrow for the wolves, and they fan out around her, flowing through the store, six, seven, eight, a dozen, sniffing at cereal boxes and bars of soap, turning their noses up at toothpaste and mouse traps. The phone is on the wall next to the restrooms. Claire fumbles in her purse for her wallet and fishes out some coins. She forgot to ask the boy for the number to the taxi company, but there it is, scrawled helpfully on the wall, alongside other useful numbers: Feed, Baling, Church of our Lord—All Souls Welcome!, Home and Gutter Repair.

She doesn't know where she is. When the dispatcher answers in a sleepy, bored voice, she tells him to hold on. "Where am I?" she calls to the boy.

He looks at her.

"This place. Where is it?"

"Tell them highway six-twenty-five. Exit seven."

Twenty minutes, the dispatcher says. Claire hangs up the phone. Will she be able to hold it together that long? She has no idea where she'll go once the cab gets here. She'll deal with that later. She can't think that far ahead. She walks back to the front of the store, taking a different route through the aisles this time, keeping a distance from the jewelry.

"Coffee?" the boy says gently.

He's decided she isn't a threat after all and just feels sorry for her. It's when people feel sorry for her that Claire feels worst of all. "Yes," she says. "Thank you."

He fills a paper cup from a pot behind the counter and tries to give it to her, but her hands are shaking, and she can't take it, so he puts it down. She tries to get money out of her wallet to pay him, but she can't manage that either. The wolves crowd around her, pushing and jostling. They don't want to be here; they don't like being inside. They want to be on the road again, or even better, on the prairie, sloping into the wilds of the night, to dark and distant places, where it's cold and icy and silent, and no one will ever find them.

All at once Claire drops her purse, and the contents spill out: wallet, tissues, the stub of her boarding pass, lipstick, calendar, pen, that broken watchband she still hasn't gotten repaired. The brown bottle of Xynolith springs open, pink pills skittering across the floor. Dora's book lands open, spread-eagled. Claire has forgotten all about it. In the rush to Midfield, she hasn't even looked inside. Not that there is any point. She knows she can't read it.

The wolves gather around the book, curious, sniffing, and as Claire shoves them aside to scoop it up, a piece of paper falls out. Drawing paper. The kind children use for crayons and watercolors. It must have been tucked between the pages. Claire opens it and the face of a wolf, menacing, threatening, stares out at her against a blood-red background. She turns the picture over and sees a name written on the back: Anna Glanz.

I'm not like her. Claire has spent her life believing that. *I'm not like Anna.* She's staked everything on it. What if she's been wrong?

She stands for a moment stock still, then she folds the

picture, puts it back into the book, and shoves it along with everything else into her purse. "Never mind the coffee. I have to go now." I have to go back, she means. To Anna. She understands that. For the first time in her life she sees that the threads connecting her to Anna, despite her attempts to break them, are intact and always will be. She's bound to Anna—she's bound to all of them: Lionel, Frieda, Hettie. God knows she's bound to Dora. In death as in life. Now, she thinks, with a rising sense of urgency. I have to go. There's so little time left. Where is that taxi? She extracts a dollar, hands it to the boy, manages a smile. "Thanks."

As she walks to the door, headlights appear outside. Thank goodness. Finally. But it's not a taxi. It's a pickup truck. A woman dressed in a parka, boots, and powder blue scrubs gets out, reaches into the cab of the truck, pulls out a baby, then balancing it on her hip, rushes inside. Claire steps aside to let them in. The baby, wearing a yellow snowsuit with bunny ears, gives out a milky scent of talcum powder and drool.

"Hey, Henry," the woman says.

The boy behind the counter smiles. "Hey, Mrs. Collins. Late shift in the ER again?"

"Yeah." She nods in a friendly way at Claire. "They just called me in. The charge nurse couldn't make it so that means I'm on." She turns to the baby. "Mallory was fast asleep and now she's awake and now she's going to Nana's, isn't she?" She jounces the baby in her arms in time to her words. "Mallory, Mallory." At the sound of her name, the baby coos and smiles. "Daddy's away on a long haul and won't be back until Saturday. So Nana it is."

"Coffee?"

"Nectar of the gods. You bet."

Henry pours out a fresh cup while the woman jiggles the baby. "You're going to Nana's, aren't you? Going to Nana's to sleep." She takes the coffee, reaches for the milk, but the baby knocks the carton over, and it spills out, making a mess. "Hey, Mallory, don't do that. Sorry, Henry. Mallory, I said—" She turns to Claire. "Here. Do you mind?"

Just like that the baby is in Claire's arms.

The woman hums to herself while she cleans up the spill—No, really, Henry, don't worry, I'll do it—and fixes her coffee. The baby has grown suddenly very still. She studies Claire with serious eyes. Then slowly she reaches out and tugs on Claire's ear.

"Oh, my, Mallory, no!" The woman laughs. "Sorry. She's always doing that. I can't tell you how many pairs of earrings I've lost—"

But Claire is too stunned to answer. Light is streaming through her, from her feet to her belly, through her heart, exiting from the top of her head. No, not light, a feeling, a tremulous feeling she hasn't felt for ages—if she ever truly did—and is so unfamiliar that it takes her a moment to give it a name.

Joy.

The woman fastens the lid to her coffee cup with a snap. "Thanks. I can take her now."

Claire hands the baby back just as a taxi pulls up outside. She's still too shocked to move. There's something she has to say to Roger. She finally knows what it is. She's going back to him with her hands full—no, not just her hands. Her heart. But first she needs to talk to Anna.

"Ma'am?" Henry says. "You called a taxi, right? Ma'am?

It's here."

Claire walks outside, gives the taxi driver Anna's address. How will all the wolves fit into the cab beside her? She looks around to see how they are managing, but the wolves are gone. There's no one but the driver and herself. Hands steady, she pays the fare when they arrive at Anna's house, then walks up the driveway and lets herself in. Cassidy's in the living room, asleep on the couch. She goes upstairs where light burns in a bedroom. Nathan comes out, meets her in the hall. "Claire, is that you? Cassidy said you left. Are you—"

"It doesn't matter. I'm back. Is she—?"

"I'm sorry." His face is tired and grim. "I had to give her more morphine. She was struggling to breathe. She's sleeping now."

"Will she wake up?"

"I don't know."

"I have to talk to her."

"Sure. Go ahead." He smiles. "I've been talking her ear off all night." He steps aside.

"Mom?" Claire says. "It's me, Claire." She steps into the room. "I'm here."

Thirty-Two

ANNA

*C*laire, Is that you?

Anna hears her daughter's voice. She doesn't know what she's saying, but she knows she's there.

Her mind drifts. She's back in Marby, in her bedroom, looking out the window. There's Sasha, alone on the grass. The nanny has left him and come inside; Anna hears her voice on the phone. All at once Hettie runs across the terrace; she must have taken the back stairs. She skips down the steps and races down the hill to the sea wall. Then she climbs up and begins to walk. Sasha runs down the hill after her. He wants to walk on the wall, he always wants to walk with his sisters, but the nanny won't let him, and he's too little to climb up on his own. He walks beside Hettie on the grass, pleading, holding up his arms. She reaches down, pulls him up, and then they are on the wall together, walking back and forth, playing a game of follow the leader. First Sasha leads, then Hettie, then Sasha again. She shouldn't do that, it's too dangerous, he's too little, he might fall. The thought plants a seed in Anna's mind.

She slips down the back stairs and in a moment is on the wall with them. Now Hettie's the leader with Sasha in the middle and Anna following. At the bottom of the wall, rocks rise dark and jagged. Waves hiss at the sand. Tiny tide pools glisten with shiny black snails and silvery fish; fronds of algae wave like welcoming arms. The children walk until they reach the end of the wall, then they turn around. This time Anna's the leader while Sasha follows and Hettie comes in the rear. Beyond them the Sound stretches breathlessly to the horizon, endlessly blue, an invitation to absolution.

When they reach the next turn, Hettie tires of the game, jumps down, and runs back into the house. Now it's just the two of them, Anna and Sasha, walking on the wall, playing their follow-the-leader game. Sasha's in the lead then Anna then Sasha again. The world is made of wind and sun, and water is the summation of it all. All at once the boy stumbles. It happened then, it's happening now, it will always happen, again and again. Anna reaches out to him—she reaches out to touch him—she is always reaching out to touch him. She reaches out and touches him, and then she blinks, and he is gone.

✐Acknowledgements

The author wishes to thank the Alan Mason Chesney Medical Archives of the Johns Hopkins Medical Institutions for permitting her to consult certain Archives collections when conducting background research concerning Adolf Meyer, Leo Kanner, and the Phipps Psychiatric Clinic. As per Archives policy, no individually identifiable health information from Archives material is published in this work of fiction or forms the basis of any event or encounter described in the book.

In particular I am grateful to Andrew Harrison and Phoebe Evans Letocha for their help in accessing the Archives.

I would like to thank Marni Graff, Melissa Westemeier, Mariana Damon, Becky Brown, and Madeleine Mysko for their excellent editorial help. Vicky D'Agostino, Deirdre Johnston, and Lynn Taylor read the novel at key moments in its development. I am grateful to Beth Cole for the beautiful design of this book, and to Mel Berger and David Hinds of William Morris Endeavor for their unwavering confidence.

Special thanks to Maureen David who traveled to Romania with me to find Baruch Zalman.

Thank you to everyone who generously shared personal and family stories with me. Your bravery is inspiring.

Finally, my thanks go to my family, who sustain me, and most of all to my husband, Don, who makes it all possible.